THE
BURIED
HOURS

BOOKS BY R.S. GRANT WRITING AS RACHEL GRANT

Fiona Carver

Dangerous Ground
Crash Site

Flashpoint

Tinderbox
Catalyst
Firestorm
Inferno

Evidence

Concrete Evidence
Body of Evidence
Withholding Evidence
Night Owl
Incriminating Evidence
Covert Evidence
Cold Evidence
Poison Evidence
Silent Evidence
Winter Hawk
Tainted Evidence
Broken Falcon

Evidence: Under Fire

Into the Storm
Trust Me

Romantic Mystery

Grave Danger

Paranormal Romance

Midnight Sun

THE BURIED HOURS

A NOVEL

R.S. GRANT

THOMAS & MERCER

Published by Thomas & Mercer, Seattle

www.apub.com

Amazon, the Amazon logo, and Thomas & Mercer are trademarks of Amazon.com, Inc., or its affiliates.

ISBN-13: 9781662511509 (paperback)
ISBN-13: 9781662511516 (digital)

Cover design by Caroline Teagle Johnson
Cover image: © arigato / Shutterstock; © Cavan Images - Offset / Shutterstock; © Alex Ratson / Getty Images

Printed in the United States of America

This one is for the Plude Girls.
For Lauren for believing in me and making this book possible.
For Sophie for supporting Lauren so she could make this book possible.

PROLOGUE

Los Angeles, California
August

Within moments of the engine being turned off, the car began to bake in the hot afternoon sun. Signe leaned into the headrest, closing her eyes against the painfully bright light of her west-facing parking spot. Her head throbbed, but that was nothing new. She'd been in pain ever since she woke up in a strange hotel room a month ago.

The bruises had faded, the cuts had mended, but she'd learned that headaches like the one she had today would ease only if she took a painkiller that knocked her out. Two hours ago, she'd held the bottle of pills in her hand and imagined taking them all. The headache would go away for good. She'd sleep without nightmares.

She wouldn't hear the screams anymore.

She wouldn't have to face another day of crushing guilt and shame over her words and inaction.

She wouldn't have to face Leo and lie to him.

But taking the pills would be a selfish escape. If she was going to take that route, she might as well confess. Tell the FBI everything. Give them a starting point for their investigation.

Going to the FBI was a death sentence. She knew that. But if she was choosing death anyway, she might as well do the right thing and give law enforcement what they needed first.

The end result was that she hadn't taken even one pill, as that would impair her ability to drive to the FBI's Los Angeles field office. She would have considered using a rideshare app, but she couldn't trust them. Any driver who showed up at her door could be one of them.

Worse, she knew she was being monitored, so she'd had to not only drive the twenty miles that separated the field office from her Redondo Beach home but also conduct a surveillance detection route to be certain she wasn't followed.

Thankfully, she'd learned how to do SDRs as part of her job. But driving an additional ninety minutes in LA traffic while having to be hyperaware of potential tails as she fought a splitting headache and ever-growing panic had been a special torture.

Now her head pounded and heart raced, but she was here. At last. She considered taking a pill before entering the federal building. No. She needed to be lucid for this conversation.

She was doing the right thing.

She'd thought she could keep this secret, but it was too much. Too selfish. So utterly wrong.

Surely, if she removed herself from the equation, everyone she loved would be safe.

Again, her thoughts turned to Leo. Would he ever forgive her? Would he understand she'd done it to protect him?

A tear spilled down her cheek as she considered the magnitude of what she was about to do. This would end her. Even if she somehow survived, her career would be destroyed.

As it should be.

The federal building was to the north and a dog park to the east. Maybe she should go for a walk in the park. Ground herself before she entered the building. Maybe a kind soul would let her pet their dog.

Or she could just sit here with her eyes closed and let the heat of the car take her.

But that would be the same as finishing off the bottle of pills before giving her confession.

Her phone pinged with a message from an unknown number.

Before she even touched the screen, she knew who it was from and why they were messaging her as she sat in the federal building parking lot. They'd managed to track her after all.

Bile rose in her throat as she watched the video and listened to the voice-over, which made it clear her suicide wouldn't protect anyone. In fact, because she'd gone to the FBI, one person would die. Today. Furthermore, if she dared to enter the federal building, someone even closer to her heart would be next.

Chapter 1

Redondo Beach, California
July
Two years later

The first thing Signe unpacked was the bottle of pills. The prescription was long expired, and the number of pills that remained in the brown plastic bottle hadn't changed in two years, but still the bottle traveled with her. Just in case.

Just in case she found the strength or in case she succumbed to the weakness, she didn't know. But international travel always provided a temporary respite from the ongoing fear of being monitored, so the pills traveled with her. At this point, they were more talisman than anything else. A touch point to remind her she was still here. Or, in this case, home again.

Jet lag left her feeling foggy. What day was it? Had it been Friday or Saturday when she left Singapore?

All she knew was she'd been home less than twenty-four hours and couldn't be certain what day it was in California.

She set the bottle on the medicine cabinet shelf and tucked her travel toiletries bag in the drawer, both ready and waiting for the next trip, then returned to the bedroom to grab her cell phone from her nightstand to see what day it was.

An event notification from the calendar app appeared on the lock screen. Black-tie fundraiser at the Wayfinders Museum tonight. No way would she attend that. She could use jet lag as her excuse, but everyone would guess the real reason.

The last person she wanted to see was her ex-husband, who was now producing his own show for the Wayfinders Network, the same streaming app that was home to Signe's docuseries.

She unlocked the phone and swiped away the calendar reminder. The home screen gave her the information she'd wanted: today was Sunday. Her gaze landed on the date, and she frowned. Something nagged at the edge of her fogged brain. The date meant something. What was it?

All at once, it clicked.

Today was an anniversary she'd never expected to face: one year since the divorce. Three hundred and sixty-five days no longer wedded to the man who'd promised to love her until death. She'd thought she was over the ache of it months ago, but the date on the calendar caused the pain to flood back.

A year had passed since the documents were signed and she was a "free" woman again. Free of her marriage to a man who'd believed the worst of her but a prisoner in ways she'd never imagined. The only escape was via pills she would never take.

She gave up on unpacking and headed downstairs, making a beeline for the liquor cabinet in the living room. On the first anniversary of the end of her seven-year marriage, she would have a drink. It didn't matter that it was before noon. She wasn't going anywhere today.

No interviews with informants lined up. No plans with friends—that required actually having friends. She wouldn't see her colleagues either; she'd already planned to skip the fundraiser.

Today was a rare day off, and she'd cope however she damn well wanted, and she wanted alcohol. She opened the massive cabinet, fully stocked with everything imaginable, and realized her first problem. She didn't actually *like* alcohol unless it was mixed with other things. Things she didn't have because she hadn't been to the store since before she left for Singapore two weeks ago.

If the first-year anniversary was paper, celebrated by giving paper gifts, what was the first negative-year anniversary? Negative paper? And how did one celebrate such a thing?

Could photo negatives be considered negative paper? Leo had a fondness for film, and she had stacks of his negatives stored in the editing studio. She could honor the day by purging his negatives. She wouldn't destroy them—she wasn't *that* petty—but she could box them up and tell him to come get them. The act would be symbolic and nudge Leo to collect the rest of his belongings before she got fed up and donated everything to charity.

She'd freelanced for the Wayfinders Institute and the National Geographic Society for years before landing a permanent Wayfinder position with the institute eighteen months ago. She knew at least a dozen world-renowned photographers. She could call one and ask if photo negatives were a good stand-in for negative paper.

She imagined posing the question to one of her colleagues and then explaining, *No, I haven't had a drink yet, but I plan to get blasted as soon as I find some orange juice.* No. She'd be fancy and say tomato juice. Not just fancy, healthy.

She shook her head at the ridiculous imaginary conversation and opened the wine fridge. Inside, she found a bottle of champagne. Expensive and French. The real deal.

This was a reason to be thankful she'd gotten the house in the divorce. Wine had been Leo's thing. He was the one who'd stocked the bar and wine racks for entertaining on their large ocean-view hillside terrace. But she'd gotten the house and the booze in the divorce, and now she would drink his pricey champagne all alone with no one to be impressed by his big bubbly.

It was juvenile, but it made her happy to think how it would irk him if he knew.

She grabbed the bottle and stepped onto the terrace. Above her, the sun was a bright explosion of white inching toward the zenith in a vibrant blue sky, while before her was a panorama of the vast, deep blue ocean, her view limited only by the curvature of the Earth. If this vista didn't make her feel serene, or if the caress of the warm sun and the rhythmic crashing of the waves didn't soothe, nothing would.

Unfortunately, this was a *"nothing would"* sort of day. She popped the cork, and it launched into the air, then dropped on the hillside below. She held up the foaming bottle in salute to the sun and sea. "Happy fucking anniversary."

She took a sip directly from the bottle, then promptly wished she had orange juice to mix with it too.

She dropped onto one of the deck chairs without bothering to remove the protective cover and drank anyway.

Did she even miss Leo anymore?

She hadn't in Singapore. Her new cameraman, Roman, was as good as Leo and getting better with each new episode they filmed. The second season of *Crime Lords with Signe Gates* would be even better than the first, and the first had included some of her best work. And she'd done it all without Leo.

She didn't even resent that he'd recently been named executive producer of a new docuseries for TWN that would be an exploration of the archaeology of the United States.

She took another sip of champagne and remembered the network's press release that had included a photo of Leo, handsome and in charge behind the camera. The photo was one of her favorites, taken during the last year of their collaboration. Of course, she preferred the version in which she hadn't been cropped out.

Okay, maybe she *did* resent him finding success at her network. Just a little. And maybe she hoped he'd screw up and the series would fail. Spectacularly.

You don't need him anymore. Hell, you don't even need Roman.

All she needed was a tripod and a remote and she'd be fine.

Well, most of the time. Roman had been pretty handy in Singapore when a source led them to a back alley that hadn't been cleared by their security team and demanded payment to take her to a meeting with an art forger.

Problem was, Signe didn't pay for interviews. Aside from the fact that it was unethical, there was the simple fact that if she paid once, she'd never conduct a free interview again. Her show was entirely and completely about criminals and the crimes they commit. If word got out that she'd succumbed to extortion, it would be open season on her wallet.

Criminals would crime when given the opportunity, and extortion for interviews was low-hanging fruit. It was just one of the hazards of making global black markets the central focus of her show.

Her specialty was getting the big bosses, the men—it was almost always men—who ran criminal operations, to talk to her, on camera, and tell the world why they trafficked in drugs, sex, art, money, animals, and just about everything else under the sun.

Her body of work was impressive, with a long list of major interviews to her credit. The people she interviewed knew she protected her sources, so they could speak freely. In a world inhabited by cons and thieves, she was trustworthy.

Pain stabbed just behind her eye.

Don't go there. Not today.

She sipped her champagne and focused on her success. She was a prominent rising star in investigative journalism with her own streaming docuseries. She landed important interviews because even murderous cartel leaders wanted to be understood.

In a few rare instances, they'd reached out to her first. Men like the American kingpin who managed marijuana grows in California for a Mexican cartel and who she suspected had a stake in the sex trade. He'd asked for an interview because he wanted attention. Specifically, *her* attention.

She pulled out her phone. She wanted to text a friend and share how great things had gone in Singapore. She'd scored a big interview with a major artifact trafficker. The person she really wanted to tell was Leo, but thankfully, the contacts list on her phone was devoid of all Leos. Roman had done as she'd asked and deleted the entry so she wouldn't give in to temptation and text her ex.

She scrolled through the list, idly wondering who she could share her success with. She was disheartened to realize every name was work-related. She'd been aware since their split that Leo had been her whole social life, but this reminder on the anniversary of their divorce still stung.

Her contact list was mostly coded names of informants. People she wouldn't know if she passed them on the street. This phone was used for initial contacts, before setting up other communication channels.

The Drug Enforcement Administration and Bureau of Alcohol, Tobacco, Firearms and Explosives wanted to know who her informants were, and neither agency was above spying on her phone, so she had an elaborate system of communicating with sources and informants. She rarely knew their names. Just aliases, some they provided, some she assigned them.

As she scrolled through the list, she spotted a message filtered as being from an unknown sender that had been sent when she was on the flight from Singapore to LAX. She thought she'd checked the filter yesterday after landing but must have been too bleary-eyed.

She opened the message. The sender identified themselves as DiscoFever. The name was familiar. From her personal before times. Before everything on her phone had been erased.

No. Don't think about the lost data. Lost life.
Lost marriage.

Had DiscoFever been in drug, gun, or human trafficking? She had no way of checking. Those notes were lost along with everything else.

Labor trafficking? Why did that come to mind? She had few contacts in that area. Traffickers generally weren't willing to speak on camera, and foreign victims who'd managed to escape often had to fear for the safety of their families back home.

Senses prickling, she set the champagne bottle on the still-covered patio table so she could give the text her full, two-handed attention.

She closed her eyes, trying to remember when she'd communicated with DiscoFever. Then it hit her.

Hit was apt. The memory had the power of a gut punch.

Her throat constricted. She couldn't breathe.

She couldn't remember what kind of trafficking DiscoFever was involved in because nearly two years ago, she'd missed their scheduled meeting.

She'd tried to suppress it, but the memory would not be denied. The real reason the divorce stung so much today was because a more awful anniversary loomed on the horizon.

Bastille Day was just a week away.

It was easier to think of it in terms like that. Impersonal. A foreign holiday.

Not her nightmare day.

No. July 14 and the horrific day that followed would always belong to France.

DiscoFever began the message with a shiny disco-ball emoji, just as they'd done two years ago. The text was authentic.

She expected the contents to be cryptic, as these initial communications usually were. She'd probably have to drive out to a meet point to exchange notes at a bus stop or something equally anonymous with lots of strangers passing through.

But no, the message was straightforward and upended her entire world.

DiscoFever: ● Two weeks ago, a man was murdered in Yosemite. He was not a tourist. The death of the climber around the same time was also no accident. The two murders are connected. An informant with evidence waits for you inside the park in the backwoods.

1st meet point is Tuesday. Noon. Coordinates for the 1st meet will be sent when you're in Oakhurst. Be there no later than five p.m. Monday.

2nd set of coordinates will be sent when you're at the 1st meet point inside the park.

The in-person meeting will happen on Thursday.

Minimum day and a half hike to reach the meeting. You and a cameraman. No one else.

It has been two years since your nightmare. You'll find answers in Yosemite. Fail to show up at any of the meet points and the evidence you want will be lost.

She took several shallow breaths as she read the message again and again.

Two years.

Whoever this person was, they *knew*.

Now DiscoFever promised answers waited for Signe in Yosemite National Park, and whatever she'd find there had something to do with two deaths she knew nothing about.

There was no question she'd go.

Dangerous or not, she had to. But she knew nothing about backwoods hiking or camping. Well, except that Yosemite had a robust bear population. She'd need a guide who knew how to navigate a wilderness teeming with wildlife, preferably a person who could also act as cameraman.

Roman, maybe? She didn't know if he knew anything about hiking backwoods, but at least he could operate a camera. He'd want to know why she was jumping on this story, but she had no qualms about lying. She couldn't risk him being targeted as well.

She tapped his name on her cell and hit the "Call" button. He was more of a texting person, but this required a conversation. He was supposed to have two days off to recover from jet lag. She'd offer him a large bonus for returning to work early.

He answered almost immediately. "What's up, Sig?"

"Hey, Roman, I just got a lead on a story, and I'd like you to film it, even though it's not for the show."

"What's it for, then?"

"It's a story I shelved a while back. The problem is, I need to jump on it now. My informant wants to meet in Yosemite this week. I need to enter the park on Tuesday. The meeting is on Thursday."

"Why the delay between entering and meeting?"

"The meeting is going to be somewhere in the backcountry. It could take a day and a half to hike there."

Roman cursed, then let out a heavy sigh. "Damn. I wish I could, but I twisted my ankle yesterday. I never should've tried to go for a run while jet-lagged. The X-ray didn't show a break, but the doc said I need to stay off it. Could take weeks. I'm wearing a big boot, and I still need crutches. No hiking for me."

"I'm so sorry. That sounds awful."

"It'll be fine. Just mad at myself for being clumsy. On the plus side, I'm trying to decide if I can use it as an excuse to skip the fundraiser tonight."

She grimaced. Network executives might not be pleased with her for being a no-show, but she rarely had to see them, and she fulfilled her contract—even the fundraising commitments—to the letter. Roman's situation was different, given that his uncle was the programming director for TWN.

Thanksgiving dinner at the Wiley house could be uncomfortable if Roman didn't go the extra mile. Lucky for him, it was July and not

November, and he'd missed the Fourth of July barbecue as they wrapped filming in Singapore.

"Do what you need to heal up." This was code for: *I've got your back with Uncle Ben.* "I'll be in Yosemite all week. We'll start editing the Singapore footage a week from tomorrow."

"Thanks, Sig. Sorry I can't help you with this one. What's the old story? Why did you shelve it?"

"Timing didn't work out, so I moved on. It still might be nothing." No need to lie at this point, since he didn't need to know details. She said goodbye, then resumed scrolling through her phone contacts. After coming up empty, she went back to the texting app to read the message again.

It was gone.

Poof.

She hadn't imagined it. She knew she hadn't.

She also hadn't screenshotted it. *Dammit.*

It had been real. It said she had to be in Oakhurst tomorrow afternoon to get the first set of coordinates.

She returned to her contact list again, hands shaking now. Or maybe it was an earthquake, because it was more than just her hands—even her chair shook.

A glance at the champagne bottle on the table proved, no, it was just her. She was the earthquake.

Tomorrow, Oakhurst. Tuesday she had to enter the park and go to the first meet point.

Who could she ask to help her?

The list on her phone left her feeling empty. Alone. She really should have cultivated more friendships over the years. Except she was a danger to everyone she loved.

She regretted erasing Leo from her contacts. She wouldn't ask him to accompany her, but he was tight with filmmakers who made nature documentaries. He'd probably be able to give her several names to choose from.

She set her phone on the table next to the champagne bottle and stared at the ocean, not seeing the sun or shades of vibrant blue as she formed a plan. A phone call wouldn't cut it anyway. Leo might reject her call, but he would never say no to her face.

She'd planned to avoid the fundraiser tonight, but it appeared she'd have to face her ex on the first anniversary of their divorce after all.

CHAPTER 2

Signe shut off the engine and gripped the steering wheel, breathing deeply. She'd spotted Leo's Tesla in the parking lot. He was here. This was good. What she wanted. But it was also the thing she dreaded.

Asking Leo for help is the only way to get answers.

If she could find a guide without his help, she would, but she had less than twenty-four hours to get to Oakhurst to receive the first set of coordinates. She'd spent the day at the computer researching recent deaths in Yosemite and coming up with the framework for the cover story she'd need to tell whoever accompanied her into the park.

She'd done everything she could to prepare for the trip. Tomorrow, she would be waiting outside REI as the store opened. She'd called today and asked them to set aside all the gear and food she'd need for two people in the Yosemite backcountry for five days. Once she had the necessary supplies, she'd head north on the five-and-a-half-hour drive to Oakhurst. Tonight, she'd light a candle to the gods of traffic that she'd be able to get out of SoCal with minimal slowdowns.

She'd prepped as much as possible. Now all she needed was someone who knew what they were doing to accompany her.

She mentally reviewed the facts she'd learned today. Two deaths in Yosemite. Both deemed accidents. One man had been identified, the other had not. The only apparent connection was one man was of Filipino descent and the other appeared to also be South Asian.

She had no idea how the two men related to her nightmare, but DiscoFever clearly knew *something*.

The heat inside the vehicle rose, reminding her of another time when she'd sat hesitating too long inside a vehicle in the Southern California summer sun.

Hesitation then had saved the life of a person close to her, but it had cost another.

She opened the door and climbed from the car. The time for hiding and silence was over. It was time to take action. Get answers.

Maybe redemption waited for her in the park too.

She ran her hands down the peacock-patterned gown, checking for wrinkles and glad to see the silk wasn't damp with sweat. Appearance was everything to Leo, and she needed to look her part while she asked her favor. Confident she'd pass muster, she set out for the museum entrance.

Ahead of her, she saw Victoria Lopez, a Hispanic American archaeologist who specialized in Mesoamerica and who filmed travel and history segments for TWN, walking alone toward the museum. Signe squared her shoulders before calling out to the woman. It was time to start making real friends instead of just collecting informants.

Vicki turned and smiled as Signe hurried across the blacktop. "I thought you were still in Singapore."

"Just got back yesterday." It surprised her that Vicki would know her travel schedule, but then, the Wayfinders Network was still a small family and Roman had done some filming with Vicki last month. "Did I miss anything while I was away?" she asked as they approached the arched entryway.

"You know about Leo's show?"

"Yes." The press release had gone out nearly two months ago.

"You okay with facing him? I'm sure he'll be here."

I'm counting on it.

She simply nodded. "Yeah. I figure I need to get used to seeing him at these events. Pull the bandage off quickly."

"Good plan."

Together they passed through the atrium and stepped into the rotunda of the Wayfinders Museum, which was the showplace of the Wayfinders Institute, a nonprofit dedicated to research and learning in science, nature, history, and culture. The museum was small in comparison to other similar institutions, but it was well funded through donations and income earned from the success of the Wayfinders Network, which had launched just a few years ago as a paid streaming service.

TWN was rapidly becoming the go-to network for infotainment, and Signe's show was part of that. She felt a surge of pride at seeing a vertical banner promoting her show just inside the arched entrance.

She focused her gaze on the small articulated dinosaur fossil that filled the center of the rotunda, centering herself so she wouldn't immediately search the room for Leo. She wanted something from him, so she needed to play it cool.

No one knew better than her how to get what she wanted from her ex.

"You've got this," Vicki said.

If only her main concern were looking strong in the presence of her ex-husband. No. She had an agenda, but she could pretend for Vicki. "Drinks?"

"Yes, please."

They made their way to the bar on the right side of the round room and each ordered the theme drink for the night: a cosmos, which was just like a cosmo, or rather cosmopolitan, but with an *s* on the end due to the fact that this event was a fundraiser for a new space docuseries.

"If only I had cranberry juice this morning," she murmured after taking her first sip.

"Why's that?" Vicki asked.

She shook her head. Vicki was not someone she could share her bitter champagne story with. No one knew the reason she and Leo had split, and she was determined to keep it that way.

They stood at the edge of the room, sipped their drinks, and watched all the beautiful people dressed beautifully.

Days ago, she'd been in a back alley in Singapore being threatened by an artifact trafficker's minion; now she shared a room with more than a few A-list actors who'd made the Wayfinders Institute one of their top philanthropic endeavors due to the institute's conservation efforts in California and around the world.

And there was Leo, by the rump of the dinosaur, talking to a stunningly handsome white man with dark hair, lightly tanned skin, and chiseled jawline. He was probably the next Channing Tatum.

Mr. Hollywood's presence meant she wouldn't approach Leo just yet. He needed to bask in the glory of his fame and success with the A-lister. If Signe interrupted that, he'd be disgruntled and less inclined to help her.

She studied him. She'd always thought he looked good in a tux, but he'd never stood next to an actor at the top of his game while wearing one before. She could almost pity him.

A gorgeous, willowy blonde stepped up to Leo's side and linked her arm through his, claiming him for the whole room to see.

Signe turned away. Leo needed to have a few drinks first. She'd time it just right.

A woman who looked vaguely familiar approached almost shyly and proceeded to gush over Signe's show as she explained she played an investigative reporter on TV and watched *Crime Lords* as prep for her role.

Signe smiled. This was just what she needed to buy time.

More fans and several donors chatted up both Signe and Vicki. Vicki got into a deep conversation with another archaeologist about recent finds in the Mayan jungle. Even though Signe presented a relaxed, smiling front, internally she was counting the seconds until the timing would be right to talk to Leo.

She needed a guide, and she needed to get out of here so she could do more internet searches on the dead climber in Yosemite. She slowly sipped her drink, the alcohol mixed with fruit juice doing nothing to loosen the tightness in her chest.

"Signe? Are you okay?" Vicki asked.

She realized she was wobbling on her heels. She wasn't doing as good a job at faking it as she'd thought.

"Just jet-lagged. I'm going to sit for a bit." She spotted chairs set up in conversational circles and made a beeline for the empty seats.

Vicki dropped into the seat beside her, and Signe wished the archaeologist hadn't followed. Maybe Leo would approach her if she were alone. This was the price of attempting to make a friend.

A loud thump in the corridor a dozen feet away drew her attention. She spotted Mr. Hollywood glaring at a taller blond man of similar age. Hollywood spoke in a low, menacing tone. He was clearly angry, but she couldn't make out his words until he shoved the man back and said, "Get the fuck away from me before I shove your ass out the door."

The man's words hardly offended Signe's sensibilities—she'd heard far worse in that alley in Singapore—but in this setting, everything about the argument was jarring. The two men weren't engaged in a black-tie-fundraiser sort of altercation. Hollywood looked ready and able to deliver on his threat. Everything about his body telegraphed violence.

Maybe he played a boxer or street fighter in the movies. She would buy him in that role. This close, she could see his eyes were hard and cold.

"He seems nice," she whispered to Vicki.

"Cole Banner? Or the blond guy?"

"Banner, I guess. Who are they?"

"Not sure about Blondie, but Cole's an archaeologist." She turned and gave Signe an assessing glance. "I thought you'd heard about Leo's show."

Now Signe realized Vicki hadn't been talking about the initial press release as they approached the museum. "What do you mean?"

"Cole is going to be the host of the West Coast episodes. They're starting filming with California."

So Mr. Hollywood wasn't the next Channing Tatum after all. No. He was Leo's next project. His next . . . *Signe*.

She turned to study him, just in time to see the blond man grunt and fall backward.

"Asshole," Banner muttered as he stepped into the rotunda.

Signe caught Banner's gaze and saw a flash of recognition before the blond let out another groan. Anger clouded the archaeologist's face.

After sweeping the room with a glare, Banner nodded to someone behind Signe, then strode past her and out the front door.

Signe glanced back at the blond man. He flashed her a smug grin as he rose from the floor. He brushed off his clothes, then winked at Signe as he made a beeline for Leo.

◆ ◆ ◆

With Leo engaged by Blondie, Signe again had to bide her time before approaching him. When she spotted Roman in his boot and leaning on crutches, she rose from her seat and approached her cameraman where he stood with his uncle, Ben Wiley.

Ben greeted Signe with a kiss on both cheeks. "Glad you returned safely from Singapore. Wish I could say the same for my nephew."

Roman rolled his eyes. "I was fine. I tripped on the sidewalk while running. In *LA*." But he smiled at his uncle's teasing.

"Well, at least you don't need two legs in the editing studio," Ben said.

"True, but I'm giving Roman the week off while I pursue a freelance story up in Yosemite." It was really a personal story, but close enough.

Ben cocked his head. "Do we need to rearrange the editing booth schedule?"

She shook her head. Ben had forgotten that her interviews were never edited on institute equipment. She had strict agreements with her informants about blurring faces and disguising voices, and the assembly and rough cut were always done in her home studio. The rushes—raw video straight from the camera—could not be loaded or stored on TWN servers or any servers that were hooked up to the internet.

"Roman and I had planned to do the paper edit later this week," she said, referring to the time-consuming task of viewing the rushes and transcribing them to create a rough script. "But given the long hours we logged in Singapore and his injury, I figure he's earned a week off."

Roman smiled in thanks. Her wording implied his uncle shouldn't put him to work on another project as she followed her own story.

Over Ben's shoulder, she spotted Leo standing alone. Her moment had arrived.

Now or never, Signe. Follow this path to redemption.

The Cowardly Lion answering the call of the yellow brick road with a fake wizard at the end came to mind. Was she the lion or the witch who'd been flattened by a house?

More importantly, would this wizard be real and have answers that would get her home?

She straightened her shoulders. She'd been through hell and survived. She was no coward. That left the witch, but she'd always figured that particular woman got a raw deal, much as Signe had. Time to rewrite her story.

She excused herself from the conversation and headed straight for her ex.

Leo was handsome. A white man in his midforties, he had crow's-feet around his eyes, and his dark hair was sprinkled with gray. Every line, every speck of gray looked good on him.

His smile as she approached was genuine. And she found her answering smile was just as real. He kissed her cheek, and she caught a whiff of his familiar scent. Not cologne. Just Leo.

"Good to see you, Sig."

She nodded. "Happy anniversary."

He frowned, his brows furrowing. "Anniversary?"

"We're one year divorced today."

"Damn. Has it really been a year?"

"Well, eighteen months since you moved out, but a year since the papers were signed."

He said nothing to that, and she couldn't blame him.

She knew why he'd left her. He thought she'd cheated. The proof had been damning, but still, it had stung that he'd believed it. Would she have if their roles had been reversed?

Probably, but then, she had other reasons for believing he'd strayed.

Bitterness rose. There was no avoiding it. The roles *hadn't* been reversed, and she remained the leftee. She forced a smile and nodded toward Blondie, who was circulating the room like he owned it. "Who's that?"

Leo rolled his eyes. "A guy with grandiose ideas of his brain and charisma. He wants in on my archaeology docuseries."

"You're not interested?"

"No way. He's toxic. But I know how to play nice with potential donors." His mouth quirked up at the corner. "He's a big fan of yours. My advice: give him a wide berth. Don't allow him an opening. Don't even make eye contact."

She'd say, *Too late*, but Leo didn't need to know the man had both smirked and winked at her. Leo often acted as if he didn't trust her ability to deal with creeps and would get weirdly protective. The behavior was irritating given their decade of collaboration filming crime stories.

No one was better than her at putting a crime lord in their place. They loved to test her boundaries before agreeing to the interview.

She held his gaze, not smiling. This was the work face she always used with Leo. "I need to ask a favor. Can we talk in private?"

"Of course. Let me ask if we can use one of the conference rooms."

There was a synchronicity with Leo in his understanding that when she said they needed to talk in private, he got it. After a decade of balancing informants and connections with the criminal underworld, Leo, even more than Roman, understood the stakes.

The museum curator nodded to Leo's request and gave him the passcode for the meeting room next to the administrative offices.

Alone at last, Leo leaned against—half sitting on—the small conference table. His gaze ran down her body. She felt the tug of his charisma and warmth when he smiled again. "You look good, Sig. Really good."

She flushed and wished she didn't feel a rush of pleasure. Lord, how she'd loved this man. Body and soul. But that was in the past. "Thank you." She considered returning the compliment but decided he had a date who could feed his ego. "Still a bit jet-lagged but I should be back on Pacific time by tomorrow."

"I heard Singapore was a success."

"It was. I finally got an interview with the artifact forger." At the knowing look he gave her, she felt a slight jab of disappointment. "You knew that, didn't you?"

His expression turned sheepish as he gave a slight nod. "My informant contacted me. He was surprised to meet Roman and wanted verification he was trustworthy."

She should have expected that. It would be years before she was free of all her tangled informant connections to Leo. But still, it burned that, even now, he played a role in her success.

"I guess I should thank you for that, then."

He chuckled. "And yet you managed to phrase it in a way that gives thanks reluctantly."

She shrugged. "Well, it's not really my fault you weren't in Singapore with me this time."

He arched a brow. "Isn't it, though?"

He hadn't lost his ability to anger and shame her with a single short sentence. Leo knew all her weak spots and cut with precision.

She smiled, showing all her teeth as he'd directed when she'd delivered hard truths to the camera. She spoke in a soft, sweet tone. "Fuck you, Leo."

His smile tightened but didn't otherwise fade. He cleared his throat. "You have a favor to ask?"

She nodded. "I need a guide to take me into Yosemite National Park. I have an informant who's set up a meet in the backwoods. We both know what a mistake it would be for me to go alone."

"What about Roman?"

"Did you see the boot he's wearing? Sprained ankle."

"I didn't see him. Bummer."

"Yeah. Probably better that he can't anyway. He isn't a climber, and I need someone with knowledge of climbing too."

"You'll need to climb? Where are you meeting?"

She shook her head. "As far as I know, it's just a long hike—overnight at minimum—to the meet point. No climbing involved. But I'm looking into the death of a climber who died in the park two weeks ago. I don't know enough about the sport to speak the language, but I *do* know that in Yosemite, climbing is practically a cult among the regulars. It would also help to have a guide who knows their way around a camera."

"That's kind of a tall order."

"You worked the nature end of documentaries before we teamed up, and you're moving back into that field now. I figured you might know a cameraperson who hikes and climbs. Not such a stretch given the circles you work in these days."

He cocked his head. "I can think of a few people, yes. I'll make some calls and get back to you next week."

"I'm heading to Oakhurst tomorrow so I can get the coordinates for the first meet point, which is on Tuesday."

"That's impossible."

She shrugged. "I don't exactly have a choice. I was given this information with no way to contact my informant."

"The demands are unreasonable. Don't go."

"I must."

"If I were your producer, I'd say no."

"I seem to remember you encouraging me to take risks back in the day."

"Not like this, though. This sounds dangerous."

"Of that I have no doubt. But still, I'm going. And I need your help to do it safely."

"It's not like you to give in to impossible demands for an interview. What is this really about, Signe?"

She weighed how much to tell him. He was the only person in the world who knew even part of the truth of Bastille Day, but he hadn't believed her, because she'd waited six months to tell him.

She held his gaze for a long moment, then said, "It's about my lost hours."

CHAPTER 3

After vowing to never set foot in the town again, Signe was back in Oakhurst. It wasn't the town's fault this was where her lost hours began. It wasn't even where the nightmare had ended. But still, the place was hopelessly tainted for her, and she wouldn't have returned if she had any choice in the matter.

How many other promises to herself would she break in the coming days?

She'd made it out of both the camping supply store and LA with only minor delays and made good time to Oakhurst. Once she passed Fresno, she appreciated the winding highway that would take her to the small mountain town a mere sixteen miles from the southern gate of Yosemite National Park.

Needing a break from her usual fare of true-crime podcasts, she listened to music from decades past that reminded her of her mother, who'd died in the first COVID-19 wave.

Signe still ached with the sudden loss that had been shared by a million others in a shockingly short amount of time. Her mother had passed before Signe got the contract for her own show with TWN. She would have been so proud but also terrified that her daughter was sinking even deeper into the criminal underworld by focusing on global black markets.

Her mother's worst fears about Signe's work had come true two years ago, and she found a bit of solace at the thought that her mother didn't know what her only child had suffered. But then, even Signe hadn't known precisely what she'd suffered until she'd seen a video months later. Still, she'd felt the bruises. Had the scars.

Nothing she'd seen—other than her own reaction—in the video had surprised her.

She'd lost forty-eight hours. Her mind did not remember being drugged and raped, but her body did. She still felt the pain of it between her thighs. Phantom pain that pricked along the hairline scars.

At the first Oakhurst traffic light, she drove straight, passing grocery stores and fast-food joints. The dashboard clock showed it was only 4:30. She'd made it with thirty minutes to spare.

The main road cut through the heart of the town. It had been a hundred degrees in Fresno and was only a few degrees cooler after climbing to two thousand feet in elevation.

She quickly checked into her hotel room at the north end of town, on the last developed city block before the road wound up the hillside to the park. The blacktop of the parking lot baked in the sun, and there was a hint of smoke in the air. It was fire season, and she'd received alerts on her drive that firefighters were trying to contain a new blaze that had popped up to the southeast. She'd driven through scorched areas—evidence of last year's fires—and silently offered thanks to the firefighters and pilots who tried to save the forests and towns in her beloved home state.

If she had a different kind of show, she'd do a profile of firefighters. Maybe she would someday when she burned out on criminals.

As she unloaded the backpacking gear, she wondered when that burnout would happen. By all rights, it should have happened two years ago.

What if she'd walked away after her abduction? Would she and Leo still be together as she did stories on firefighters and first responders?

In-depth reporting on water shortages and almond growing was as important as anything she covered. But she had to wonder if she'd have been satisfied, especially knowing she'd been driven out of her chosen field by the very people she worked so hard to explain.

One of them had arranged for her abduction and rape. One of them had made a video of the brutal assault and sent it to her, lest she forget the power they had over her.

The fact that a crime lord had set his men upon her was one of the more galling things about being targeted. She didn't *catch* anyone. Her interviews never led to arrests or prosecutions. She actually gave the monsters a voice. A chance to tell their story. Their reasons.

She approached them with empathy. She listened. She wasn't a threat, and they all knew it. But still, one of them had come after her and done the unthinkable.

Before she was freed, they'd made it clear that if she told anyone what happened, people would die. So she'd lied to her husband, saying words that would eventually break her marriage.

She'd had no choice. They'd proven they'd deliver on their threats in the most horrific way imaginable.

That she'd been betrayed by the very kind of person she gave voice to had been her impetus to stay in the game. Her reasoning was two-fold: she refused to let them believe they'd broken her, and maybe, just maybe, her investigations would lead her to the truth of why she'd been targeted.

And so here she was in Oakhurst again, still in the business of conversing with criminals.

She loaded the camping supplies onto a hotel cart and hauled everything up to her third-floor hotel room with a view of Highway 41. Even with the cart, she needed two trips. In theory, everything would fit in the two shiny-new internal-frame backpacks with detachable day packs. One set was blue, the other green.

The salesperson had been eager to explain how to load the packs and bear canisters, but Signe had been in a hurry to hit the road.

Now she was facing a king-size bed mounded with gear she had no idea how to use. All she could do was hope Leo would come through with a guide who knew the equipment. Last night, he'd promised that if he couldn't find anyone who fit her criteria, he'd send his younger brother.

Steven was a good fallback option. He was a forestry graduate student at Berkeley. At least, she thought he was still in graduate school. She hadn't talked to him since the separation. She and Leo had paid for Steven's education, which would sort of make it hard for the man to say no to Signe's request, even though they'd lost touch. Plus, Signe intended to pay him the same as she would any guide, and what forestry student didn't want an all-expenses-paid excursion into Yosemite?

At this point, given that Leo hadn't indicated he'd found someone else, she assumed Steven would be her guide, and she looked forward to seeing him again. They had always gotten along, often better than the half brothers, who were nearly twenty years apart in age.

Still, the danger that lurked with this expedition nagged at her. Even in a normal interview situation, it was risky to meet an informant in a secluded place. But nothing about this meeting was normal. How much could she tell her former brother-in-law beyond the usual warnings? Was he someone she could trust with a fraction of the truth? How would she impress upon him the danger without telling him about her abduction?

The threats always loomed: *"We'll kill anyone you tell. And then we'll come after people you love."*

Steven was someone she loved. He'd be in extra danger if she told him anything.

They hadn't gone after Leo when she'd been forced to tell him about the rape. She'd told him the bare minimum and begged him to tell no one. She'd had to give him a piece of the truth when he'd seen her medical records. Not to mention he'd been all too aware she'd lost interest in sex six months before they separated.

Leo swore he'd keep the rape a secret between them, but he'd made it clear that was because he thought she was lying. He didn't believe she'd been protecting him with her silence.

Among the supplies strewn across the bed was a locked case containing a gun. Given her name, naturally she had a SIG Sauer.

Never before had she brought a gun when meeting with an informant—a weapon offered an easy way for things to go sideways fast—but this meeting was about what she'd endured two years ago, and she wouldn't take any chances.

She checked her phone for a text from Leo, Steven, or DiscoFever. Nothing.

She sent an email to Leo with her room number to pass on to Steven, all the while wishing Roman hadn't followed her instructions and erased Steven's contact info along with Leo's. It hadn't occurred to her that she could keep him as her little brother after the divorce. She'd gotten the house; Leo got the people.

She paced the room as she waited for a message from the informant with the first location.

Her entire body was tight with fear and anticipation. She was finally on the path to answers. With answers, she could finally break her silence. Make amends for the things she'd revealed while drugged.

The path was made of yellow bricks and she was *not* the lion. Maybe not even the witch. In truth, she was probably the Tin Woodman. She would enter the forest and find her shattered heart.

Her phone buzzed.

She'd set her cell on the nightstand out of fear that she'd somehow manage to squeeze the life out of it or shake it to death if it remained in her hands. Now she lunged for it.

The message was from DiscoFever. GPS coordinates.

She felt light-headed and wobbled on her feet, which was ridiculous. She faced down mafia bosses and cartel leaders and asked them difficult questions.

Get a grip.

She reached for the notepad and pen and wrote down the coordinates. She then grabbed her video camera and recorded a short clip of the text message, just to be certain.

Last, she pressed the buttons to grab a screenshot, and the message flashed away. Gone. Into the ether.

She checked the screen on the video camera to prove to herself it was real. She had, indeed, received the coordinates.

Fear that she'd somehow gone off the edge and this whole quest was something her brain had invented in a moment of grief and weakness had nagged at her since yesterday morning when the text message had vanished.

But no. She wasn't batshit bonkers.

She dropped onto the sofa, gripping the camera as she watched the ten-second clip on repeat. These coordinates would begin her journey to answers.

In the back of her mind, there was a tiny hope she'd get more than that. During her lost hours, she'd committed one of journalism's seven deadly sins and someone else had paid a horrific price. The only path to acquittal on that front was if she could obtain proof she'd been drugged during the exchange.

Could that be the evidence DiscoFever had referred to in yesterday's message?

Or was this nothing more than a snipe hunt set up by the monster who'd drugged her so he could laugh as he watched her chase a freedom she'd never have again?

She held back a sob, not knowing if it was triggered by the pain of hope or the desperation of fear. If she started crying now, she'd never stop. Steven could show up at any minute. He needed to see her as the big sister she'd once been to him. The strong, successful woman who interviewed criminals and asked why they crimed.

Not this pathetic, broken woman who lived in terror of being exposed for a horrific crime she didn't remember committing.

◆ ◆ ◆

The email from Leo hit her inbox at 6:32 p.m. Short and sweet.

He's almost there. I gave him your room number.

Signe bolted to her feet, gripping the phone to her chest, offering thanks to every deity she could think of. She'd known Leo would come through for her, but as the day wore on without word, she'd begun to fear she'd have to enter the park alone tomorrow. She'd have done it, but it was a relief to know that wouldn't be necessary.

A knock sounded on the hotel room door, and she sprinted the short distance. She flung the door wide, ready to greet Steven with a ferocious hug.

But the man framed in the light of the hotel corridor wasn't Steven Higgins or even his older half brother, Leo Starr. No, it was a very angry-looking Mr. Hollywood himself, Cole Banner.

Oh, Leo, what the hell have you done?

CHAPTER 4

Signe Gates in the flesh. She was both everything and nothing like what Cole had expected from watching her show. He knew she'd be petite and pretty in an approachable, girl-next-door sort of way, even though yesterday at the museum she'd been polished and stunning, revealing layers to her beauty that shouldn't have surprised him but managed to anyhow.

Now here she was, no makeup to add color to her pale white cheeks. No eyeliner or mascara to make her eyes look big for the camera, but still strikingly pretty with her shoulder-length dark hair pulled back in a simple ponytail. She wore yoga pants and a V-neck cotton T-shirt that hugged her modest curves. The casual clothes and lack of makeup made her look achingly young—like she was twenty-five, tops—but he knew she was in her late thirties, nearly two years older than him.

Her petite frame appeared almost fragile. How on earth did this pixie of a woman interview drug dealers, gunrunners, and pimps?

But he knew that already. He'd done his homework and watched every episode of her show and many of the segments she'd filmed as a freelance investigative reporter in the years before she landed the eponymous docuseries. He knew part of her guile was her nonthreatening physical presence and those wide, intelligent blue eyes that didn't need makeup to be engaging.

He had a theory her straightforward manner and *I want to understand you* vibe tapped into some kind of universal longing. Even mob bosses wanted to be understood. All the better if it was a pretty woman who came across as steadfast, kind, and smart.

Not that they necessarily *liked* her. She was threatened before or during interviews often. But still, she came through each one unscathed, and he'd bet more than one crime lord held a secret hope they'd won her over.

It was the woman herself—forthright and forceful Signe Gates—who was the person they'd hoped to sway with their explanations, not the nameless viewers.

Now that he faced her in person and really took in how small she was as he towered over her, he added *cunning* to her list of attributes. This woman knew how to wield her looks and size. Not for the first time, he wondered what Leo Starr had forced him into.

He cleared his throat. "Ms. Gates, I'm Cole Banner. Your husband sent me to be your backpacking guide in Yosemite."

"Ex. Leo is my *ex*-husband."

Great job, Banner. Screwed up before you made it through the door.

"Right, sorry. Yes. I meant ex." He rubbed the back of his neck. Would Leo can him from the docuseries if Signe refused him? He might not, but Cole had worked too hard to make it happen to take the risk.

He'd been so damn *close*.

Cole didn't mind going into Yosemite. He didn't even mind having to play guide to a pretty woman. It was the shit about being forced to do it that irked. While he was spinning his wheels playing hiking guide, his shot could slip away.

He never should have let the pseudoscientist prick get under his skin at the fundraiser last night. This scheme wouldn't have crossed Leo's mind without that leverage, and now Cole was snared, tasked with escorting his new boss's cunning ex-wife into the wilderness for a multiday backcountry hike.

"Can I, um, come in?"

She shook her head and dread speared through him. *Shit.* He was screwed ten ways from Sunday if she kicked him to the curb now.

He pushed a foot into the doorframe to prevent her from slamming it in his face. "I need this job."

She shook her head again, then stepped back and waved him inside. "Sorry. I didn't mean *no*. I'm just . . ." Another shake, this one accompanied by a deep breath. "I thought Leo was sending someone else."

He entered the hotel room. The only bed was covered in camping supplies, most items still in the packaging or with attached tags. "Who did you think was coming?"

"Leo's brother, Steven."

"I'm sorry. I didn't know that's what Leo told you."

Was Leo trying to make things difficult from the get-go? He supposed it fit with the two rules the man set down before sending him on this journey, but only the first rule made any kind of logical sense.

She frowned. "I need to call Leo. This . . . I'm just caught off guard."

"Fine."

She picked up her phone and cursed. "Um . . . can you give me Leo's number?"

"You don't have it?"

She gave him a sheepish look. "I sort of deleted it a while ago."

Everything about this felt off, but like a good little employee, he pulled out his phone and recited the number. She dialed, then stepped out onto the balcony and closed the sliding door behind her.

He ran a hand over his face. What the hell was the plan from here?

Leo answered Signe's call on the first ring. "Dammit, Leo. You said you were sending Steven."

"No, I said Steven would probably be able to do it if I couldn't find someone else. But I found someone else."

"Why didn't you tell me?"

"I've had a busy day and was sidetracked after I got Cole to agree. You know, some of us have to work, Signe. I can't just drop everything to accommodate you. The fact that I found someone who could give you a week of their time with less than a day's notice was a frigging miracle. Be thankful."

She huffed out a breath. "I am. I just . . . why should I trust this guy? He got in a fight at a *museum fundraiser* for Christ's sake. Who does that?"

"Odem was faking. Cole didn't hurt him."

It didn't matter that no one was hurt, not when Banner hadn't been faking his anger.

"Is Cole Banner trustworthy?"

"Far as I know. Listen, he knows hiking *and* climbing, just like you wanted. He even knows Yosemite—he worked on digs inside the park as a contractor a while back. He's no cameraman but knows more than Steven would."

Okay, so Leo *had* put thought and effort into this. That, at least, was a relief. "I'm sorry I'm being bitchy. I was just surprised. You're sure about him?"

"Mostly. But, Sig, you can't tell him . . . what you claim happened on Bastille Day. Keep it private. He wouldn't believe you anyway, and I don't need you mucking up my working relationship with my show host."

What are you worried about, Leo? That he will *believe me?*

She took a deep breath. She didn't know Cole Banner at all, but he'd shown up when she needed him. No point in poisoning his relationship with Leo for his good deed. "I know. I won't talk about my missing hours. But he still needs to know this can be . . . risky. I'll stress how dangerous meeting informants can be. If he's watched my show, he'll understand."

"I told him to bring a gun. He knows there's risk involved."

Like her, Leo had rarely—possibly never—brought a gun to a meeting with an informant. That he'd instructed Cole to do so meant he might be coming around to believing Signe's version of events.

Too little, too late.

"Thank you for warning him. And thank you for finding me a guide."

"I care about you, Sig. I want to see you whole again."

She hung up without responding. They both knew he didn't care enough and that she'd never really recover—the woman she'd been two years ago was dead and buried.

She needed to find a way to appreciate this new version of herself and fill her life with others who liked her too. Not people like Leo who demanded she go back to being a woman who didn't exist anymore.

She stood on the balcony for a moment. It was slightly cooler now as the sun lowered, and the warm air felt good on her skin. It would be more like this in the park, especially at the higher elevations. The heat wouldn't be so intense. And hopefully there'd be less smoke.

If only this were just a backpacking trip through Yosemite. She'd enjoy that. A vacation in a beautiful place. Cole Banner was easy on the eyes too. A beautiful place with a beautiful man.

What would it be like to have a life that included hiking for fun?

These wistful thoughts were a waste of time. Nothing about this journey would be fun.

Banner probably didn't even want to be here. As Leo had said, finding someone who could give up a week of their life at the drop of a hat was a monumental task. But Leo had leverage, and her ex was a master at wielding that kind of power. It was one of his greatest skills as a filmmaker.

She straightened her spine and prepared to charm Mr. Hollywood. She had to win him over, because one thing was certain: she needed his help. Desperately.

The cool air inside the room was a shock to the system after being outside. She gave her new partner a wry smile. "I hope you enjoy hiking in hot weather, Mr. Banner."

His gaze swept down her body. Up close as he was, she could see now his eyes were a warm brown. He was every bit as handsome in jeans and a T-shirt as he'd been in a tuxedo. He was also somehow bigger and more imposing as he stood at the foot of the bed, studying her.

Should she be afraid of him? He might not have actually injured that guy yesterday, but he'd radiated violent energy.

She didn't need a hothead for a guide. When dealing with sketchy informants, irrational mood swings were dangerous.

"I'm good with both backcountry hiking and camping in high heat, and Yosemite is one of my favorite places in the world. Also, call me Cole."

"You aren't here willingly, are you, Cole?"

"Depends on how you define *willingly*. I wasn't dragged here, nor was extortion involved."

"But maybe a little coercion?"

He held up his right hand with his index finger and thumb about a quarter inch apart. "Only this much."

She offered a grim smile. "I'm pretty sure it's more than that. That scene at the museum bit you in the ass, didn't it?"

He tipped his head in acknowledgment. "I barely touched the prick."

"I believe you."

"Sadly, you aren't the head of TWN, nor are you the executive producer of the show I'm supposed to host."

"No, but I know both men—one exceedingly well—and can put in a good word for you when we return to LA."

"Which is why I'm at your service with minimal coercion. Now, tell me what this is about."

CHAPTER 5

Cole had picked up takeout Chinese food on his way through town—
Leo had made the order with Signe's favorite dishes—and he retrieved
his duffel bag and the hot food from his car, then stopped at the front
desk to ask for utensils for two before returning to Signe's hotel room.

He laid out the food on the small round table by the balcony and
they each filled a plate, then settled side by side on the love seat to eat
and plan their expedition.

After just a few bites, Signe set her dinner aside and reached for her
laptop. She opened the web browser and angled the screen so he could
see while he ate.

"In the last dozen years or so," she began, "Yosemite has averaged
between thirteen and twenty deaths per year. In the first two years of
the pandemic, the number of deaths dropped well below those averages,
but that was due to a similar drop in the number of park visitors, so isn't
statistically significant for our purposes."

He nodded. He had firsthand experience in that area. He'd been
one of the lucky few who'd gotten a pass to enter the park during the
first year of the pandemic. It had been wild to visit popular landmarks
and have them all to himself.

She pointed to the most recent statistics on the screen. "Deaths
are up by quite a bit this year, especially for being only midway into
the high season, but it's really only these two deaths we're looking at."

She clicked on a short article that included a photo of a man suspended from a rock wall. He had light brown skin; thick, dark hair; and a sharp, square jaw. His mouth was spread in a broad grin and flanked by a pair of dimples. His slightly tattered shirt bore the flag of the Philippines.

In the photo, he was handsome, young, and vibrant.

Except he wasn't anymore.

"Manny Lontoc," Signe said. "Twenty-four. He was eight when his family moved here from the Philippines. His body was found sixteen days ago. No details are given on where or the cause of death, just that he was inside the park. He's described as an active participant in the Yosemite climbing community. He had no ID on him. His remains were identified by other climbers. He has no known address and his family hasn't been located."

She let out a frustrated sigh. "Every call I've made to find out more has been a dead end. No one knows anything about him. The coroner's report hasn't been filed yet—at least not in a place where I can request access to it. I don't even know if there's an ongoing official investigation into his death. I figure our best hope is locating climbers in the park who knew him."

Cole wished Leo had given him this information before he left LA. "I can help with that. I've done my share of climbing and spent time at Camp 4."

Camp 4 was considered the birthplace of rock climbing's modern age—and was even on the National Register of Historic Places for that reason. If Manny Lontoc had been a climber, Camp 4 was the place to start the search for people who knew him.

Signe gave him a thankful smile. "Leo said you know climbing."

"I'm no expert, but I'm familiar with the community." He set aside his empty dinner plate and made a mental note on what he'd say in the texts he needed to send later.

Signe clicked on a new tab. "I'm afraid finding people who know our *other* deceased man is going to be impossible." She paused to eat a few more bites, then returned her focus to the computer. "His body was found three days after Manny Lontoc's. As you can see, this article doesn't include a photo, as no one could provide an image of him in life. I contacted the medical examiner and told them I'm working on a story that could help with identification of the remains. The office got back to me this morning. They sent me an autopsy photo along with an artist's rendering of what John Doe might have looked like when he was alive."

Cole studied both images. The face was battered and bloated, but the artist was skilled and he guessed had a good eye for the underlying bone structure, which, like Manny Lontoc, appeared to be South Asian.

"The park and medical examiner have been unable to identify the man," Signe continued. "No one fitting his description has been reported missing, and they have no idea when he entered the park. They estimate he was in his late fifties. He appeared to be undernourished, so it's really hard to say. He has South Asian facial features, but that's based on bone structure statistical data and really not reliable. His DNA has been sent for testing. There's no rush on what appears to be an accidental death, so it'll probably be a while before results come in."

"That's all we know about him?" he asked.

"Sadly, yes."

"Yet this death is supposedly connected to the climber—Manny Lontoc."

"According to my informant, yes."

"The informant whose message you no longer have." He knew he sounded skeptical, but there was no point in hiding it.

"Vanishing messages are not all that odd in my line of work. I have informants who use special message apps that delete the message as soon as it's been read. I just didn't expect it this time or I'd have taken a photo like I did with the coordinates."

The coordinates. That reminded him. It was time they found out where they were headed.

He rose from the love seat and plucked the brand-new handheld GPS—still in the package—from the bed. The device was top-of-the-line. He'd never used one of these in the field for archaeology but was no stranger to the technology. "We need to set this up. Charge the batteries."

"Shit. I meant to do that as soon as I got here. But I only got as far as my phone, computer, and cameras."

It took a few minutes to free the unit from the packaging and plug it in. While he did that, Signe finished her dinner. He was glad to see her eat without him having to nag her. She hadn't shown much interest in the food even though she'd admitted the dishes were her favorites. If the text she'd received was accurate, she was going to need a lot of fuel for the coming hike.

The GPS unit powered on and he went through the setup menu. Once the Yosemite area maps loaded, he found the menu for wayfinding using coordinates and punched in the numbers Signe had copied on the hotel-provided notepad.

He stared at the screen in surprise. She hardly needed a special guide for this. Or a fancy GPS. She could have looked this up on her laptop, which made him wonder why she hadn't the moment she received the text. "The meet place for tomorrow is Glacier Point."

"The overlook with views across the valley?"

"Yep."

"Well, that makes sense. If I remember correctly, there's cellular service at Glacier, so I'll be able to receive texts."

"Your informant won't be there in person?"

"Actually, I'm pretty sure whoever it is *will* be there, which is why we'll take videos of the crowd."

"That might not help much. Glacier Point is one of the most popular places outside the valley floor. It was busy even when the park severely limited visitors after the initial COVID closure. I know because I was able to get a pass that July. Glacier was the only place I visited that was anywhere near capacity."

On his second day in the park, he'd enjoyed the majesty of the giant sequoias in Mariposa Grove all by himself. It was an experience he'd never have again in this lifetime. But now wasn't the time to brag about that to Signe.

She shrugged. "It's a long shot, but maybe we'll get lucky and catch a face I'll recognize."

"Won't your mystery informant wear a mask?" People were still selectively masking. Especially those who didn't want to be recognized.

"Probably. But if it's someone I've met in person before, then I know what they look like masked too."

"Okay then. We'll get to Glacier early and walk through, filming. After you get your text, we'll head to the valley and Camp 4." He studied the pile of gear. "We should get this stuff packed except for the items that need to charge overnight. We'll need to get up early to hit the grocery store for perishable items to consume tomorrow. We'll save backpacking food for Wednesday."

He showed her how to pack the bear canisters most efficiently and inventoried the food she'd purchased. She'd gotten enough to feed two people for a week, more than enough, even if they ran a day or two long.

"Are we going to be obvious about filming in the park, or will we try to look like tourists?" he asked.

"A little of both." She cinched the top of the canister she'd carry in her pack and set it aside. "At Glacier, when we film the crowd, we're tourists. But in Camp 4, it will be easier to get people to talk if they know I'm looking into Manny Lontoc's death."

"If they're camping and not heading out of the park after climbing. There are limits placed on climbers now." He'd never been a true member of the Camp 4 climbing community, but he'd climbed enough in Yosemite to be aware of how they rotated camping permits to skirt park rules. There was a summer in which he'd managed to eke out an extra week in the park without the rangers catching on.

He'd had to change his lawless ways when he got a job on a dig in the park and got to know several of the law-enforcement rangers. After that, he'd been friends with The Man. In Yosemite, climbers and rangers often found themselves on opposing sides of a war.

His life since those days had seen him on both sides of the law. That experience had taught him a lot and he had no doubt he could get reluctant climbers to open up to Signe.

They had a plan for tomorrow. They were packed. It was late and he was tired. But he was uneasy about leaving her alone for the night.

He had zero doubt the first thing she'd do after he left the room was google him. While it was unlikely she'd find anything, he still wanted to avoid that. As an investigative reporter, she had access to information that hid behind paywalls and firewalls.

She could be lethal with a search. He knew that better than anyone.

"I wasn't able to get a room for the night. Last minute and after a major holiday . . ." He let his voice trail off.

It was true this hotel was booked if the No Vacancy sign was to be believed, but he hadn't bothered to look elsewhere. He hoped she wouldn't suggest he grab the tent and sleeping bag she'd bought for him. He had his own in his SUV and even knew exactly where he could camp for the night, but that would leave Signe free to dig deep into his background.

This would be a lot easier once they entered the park and Wi-Fi was nonexistent and cellular service spotty.

She frowned at him. "You suggesting we share a bed?"

He grunted. "Hardly. I'm not eager for your ex-husband to fire me before we even start filming."

She rolled her eyes. "Leo has no say in what I do."

"Doesn't mean he wouldn't fire me." Hell, the man had said as much, but he had a feeling telling Signe that wouldn't exactly endear him to her, and he needed to make this assignment work.

"That's ridiculous. Leo hardly cares what I do."

She seemed to believe that, which didn't fit with what he knew of Leo at all. But Signe might be the key to understanding his new boss. "For what it's worth, I think he's still in love with you."

She snorted. "Strange. Leo said you were smart and he's usually a good judge of people."

He smiled at that. "Bullshit. Leo never compliments anyone but himself."

That earned a smirk. "Not completely true, but close." She let out a heavy sigh. "Believe it or not, the back of the love seat folds down. It's a small bed, but I'm a small person. You can have the king."

He refrained from showing his absolute relief. He'd be safe from her mad internet skills until morning.

He set up her bed and cleared the camping supplies and empty packaging from the king-size mattress while she called the front desk to request extra bedding. Cole finished off the rest of the takeout while they waited for her sheets and blankets to arrive.

It was only ten p.m. when they settled in their separate beds. He was usually up until midnight or one, but they needed to get an early start tomorrow and he had no doubt it would be a long day. If things went well, tomorrow night they'd be sleeping four miles deep in the backcountry.

The room was dark, with only the intermittent white noise of the air conditioner to mute footsteps and voices in the hallway. He was just drifting off to sleep when Signe said, "You're wrong, you know."

"About what?"

"Leo isn't in love with me. If he were, he'd be here instead of you."

Chapter 6

Signe slept fitfully but at the same time was surprised she'd been able to sleep at all. She gave credit to Cole. It was strange his presence could make her feel safe, considering she didn't know him at all and didn't have much reason to trust him. But this was Oakhurst, where her nightmare had begun, and having a big, strong man in the room as she slept had been comforting.

Dawn was just lighting the sky when they took turns in the shower, then loaded Signe's vehicle. Cole made arrangements with the hotel staff to leave his car in the parking lot for several days.

As planned, they went to the grocery store for one day's worth of fresh food before setting out. Cole bought twice as much food as she would have expected, but then given his size, he probably put away three times the amount of food she did. She hoped she'd gotten enough for him for the hike. It was hard to estimate without knowing their final destination.

The drive to Glacier Point would take a little over an hour at this peak time in the tourist season. Before they reached the end of town, Signe turned into a shopping center with a western facade and a mural of a bigfoot strolling through the woods.

"What's going on?" Cole asked. "Did you forget something?"

She studied her hands on the steering wheel, seeing the ever-so-slight tremble. In all her years as an investigative journalist, she'd never trembled like this on the way to meeting an informant. And she'd met with—literally—dozens of murderers and rapists.

But this story was different. Personal. And if they knew she was delving into her lost hours, they'd kill her.

She hoped Cole didn't see the trembling. She needed to get her emotions under control. "Do you mind driving?"

"Not at all. Why?"

"I want to write some notes," she lied.

They traded places, and she settled into the passenger seat and buckled in.

"Huh." The sound escaped without her realizing it.

"What's that?"

"I've never ridden in the passenger seat of this car before." She'd bought the hatchback because she'd been convinced her old car had a tracker hidden in the undercarriage, even though repeated searches found nothing. That had been a few months after her abduction. She rarely drove with passengers. Cole might even be the first one.

It was oddly comfortable, though, letting this stranger drive her vehicle. Same as she'd felt with him sleeping in her room. Her nerves settled almost immediately.

"I thought you were going to take notes."

"Oh. Yeah. Right." She let out a nervous laugh. He must think she was a twit.

She pulled her notepad from her day pack and looked at the script she'd written for an intro she planned to record when they were on the valley floor. It was in good shape. She added a few lines she probably wouldn't use, then tucked the pad away again.

When they reached the gate, Signe handed Cole her National Park annual pass to cover the entry fee. As he showed the person in the kiosk the pass, he said, "I need to pick up a wilderness camping permit for Mirror Lake to Snow Creek. Can I do that at the Wawona Visitor Center, or do I need to get it in the valley?"

Signe was so startled by his words that she didn't hear the woman's answer as she handed Cole the park map.

Signe hadn't mentioned their lack of campsite or wilderness permit last night because she didn't want him to use it as an excuse to back out. As the car pulled away from the gate, she stared at him, slack-jawed.

He wore a smug grin on his handsome face as he navigated the roundabout to Wawona Road with just one hand on the steering wheel.

"You got us a backcountry camping permit? How on earth did you manage that?" She'd spent hours Sunday trying to get a reservation to no avail. The rule was steadfast: the park required seventy-two hours' notice for wilderness permits. All the organized campgrounds were booked. Her last hope was Camp 4, which sometimes had last-minute cancellations, but she'd had no luck when she tried again yesterday. There were no same-day first-come, first-serve campsites in Yosemite.

"Were you planning on finding a parking space somewhere and hoping not to get ticketed or towed?"

She shrugged. "I figured I'd go to a ranger station and flash my TWN credentials, bat my eyelashes, and beg. The network has filmed a fair number of segments in the park, so I hoped they might be sympathetic. And yeah, if that didn't work, I'd have parked illegally and paid whatever fine they threw at me."

"Were you going to tell them you're investigating the two recent deaths as potential homicides?"

"Not if I was begging for parking. I doubt they'd appreciate my meddling in their investigation—if there even is one. So how'd you manage to get a permit?"

"A while back, I worked with a few people in the culture and history department. I made some calls and one of them was able to snag us a permit, even though it was just twenty-four hours from park entry."

"It's good to have friends." She realized she'd always left it to Leo to be charming and convince others to adjust their rules to accommodate them. She was good at getting subjects to talk to her, while he was the one who knew how to schmooze.

"Yeah," Cole said. "But we're screwed if the trailhead I got is far from our end point. I got a trail that starts in the valley, so hopefully we'll be okay. Tonight, we're required to camp in a certain area, but after that, we're free to roam—well, except for around Half Dome, which requires a different permit—as long as we return to the same trailhead at the end."

"Much as I appreciate this surprise, why didn't you tell me last night you got a permit?"

He turned the question back on her. "Why didn't you mention you *didn't* have a permit?"

There wasn't any point in holding back the truth now. They were in the park. "I didn't want you to use it as an excuse to back out."

He flashed a smile, then returned his attention to the road. "I don't scare easily. And for what it's worth, if I hadn't been able to snag a permit, this wouldn't have been my first illegal night in Yosemite."

She remembered the anger and violence he'd exhibited at the museum and her idle thought that he might have made his name in Hollywood playing street fighters. He'd seemed dangerous in his tux as he cursed at the blond man. But overstaying in a national park was hardly the type of crime she'd imagined.

For the first time, she asked herself the question she should have asked *him* last night: Who was Cole Banner?

CHAPTER 7

Signe Gates was a puzzle. She'd done a decent job of hiding her emotions, but he'd seen her hands shake as she gripped the steering wheel. The woman was deeply afraid of something.

Hardly what he'd expected from the calm, cool, nerves-of-steel Signe Gates he'd seen on TV.

It occurred to him that there was a difference between the person she'd been on TV when she worked with Leo Starr and the woman who took cues from Roman Wiley. It appeared Leo had done a better job of capturing who she really was.

The Signe Gates who narrated and appeared in every scene of *Crime Lords* was colder with icy control. Harder. More closed off. She fit the role perfectly, considering the subject matter, but he had to wonder at the difference between personas. Was it the change in cameraman and producer, or was it that she was a different person post-divorce?

All he knew for certain was this story mattered to Signe. So much that she wasn't following her usual narrative format. He wanted to know why.

They were just a few miles from Glacier Point when Signe broke the long silence. "What was the argument about?"

"Sunday night, at the museum?"

"Yes."

His answer would be evasive but still true and accurate. "It was a classic battle between good and evil. Science and antiscience."

"I'm going to guess you're team science?"

He pressed a hand to his heart. "It cuts deep that you even pose the question."

She let out a soft laugh. "I'm a reporter. It's my job to ask questions, even when I know the answer. I like to have everything on the record."

He gave her a side-eye. "Are our conversations on the record?"

"No. You're a colleague, not the subject of the interview."

"But if you were to do a story on artifact trafficking, and decided to interview me, there'd be clear boundaries about what happens to be conversation between colleagues and what is on the record?" He needed to establish this point now, as it was certain to come up later.

"Of course." She paused, then added, "Speaking of, I *am* doing a story on artifact trafficking. I planned to ask you and Victoria Lopez for interviews. Well, I was going to ask just Vicki, but seeing as how you're helping me, I'd like to return the favor."

"I'm not sure that's a good idea."

"Why not? I'd think it would be good crossover between your show and mine. Prerelease promo for you if mine is aired first. Not sure what your timeline is with Leo."

"I meant the part about interviewing Vicki."

Signe straightened in her seat, dropping her feet—bare, as she'd slipped off her sport sandals not long into the drive—to the floor.

"Well, now, this *is* interesting."

"And off the record."

"Of course. What's the problem with Vicki?"

"She's the one who invited that prick Grayson Odem to the party on Sunday."

"Is he the guy you argued with?"

He nodded. "I found out later—from Leo, who checked with the curator—that Odem was listed as her date."

"That's . . . bizarre. Leo made it sound like he was a donor, but also, I entered the party with her, and she never spoke to Odem as far as I saw. When I asked her who both of you were, she said she didn't know who he was, but she named you."

"Yeah, well, she got him inside the building. His only purpose for being there was to harangue me." To rile him up. Get him to throw a punch. A test? Did Leo suspect?

"Explain, please, exactly who Grayson Odem is. I take it he wasn't a donor."

"I doubt he's any sort of philanthropist, but he does have money. He's a racist pseudoarchaeologist pushing theories about aliens building pyramids, white people populating the US and building things like Cahokia Mounds before—according to Odem and his crackpot buddies—Asians invaded and seized the land. It's tried, true, and vile white supremacy, making up fake history to justify their racism and try to strip rights from Indigenous people."

Cole knew Odem was involved in other businesses that would align quite well with Signe's interests, but he wasn't here to introduce her to another element of the criminal underworld. He was playing hiking guide and nothing more. She could find her own damn monsters to give a platform.

"Odem is a Nazi who wants to use TWN to recruit followers. I kind of wish I had punched him."

He said *"kind of,"* but really there was no equivocation in his mind. He absolutely itched to deck the guy. The satisfaction of breaking the prick's nose had been denied him. His fist longed for contact like lungs demanded air.

What would've happened if he'd punched Odem at the museum in front of all the executives and donors? Would he have been fired on the spot?

He guessed Signe would've been appalled. He'd bet she was a pacifist, given all the crap she witnessed. A devout turn-the-other-cheeker. How else could she talk to murderers and thieves and their victims on a daily basis and not crack?

There was no satisfaction in turning the other cheek. Throwing a punch was infinitely better.

"So Odem figured he could convince you to put him and his gross theories in a science-based archaeology docuseries?" Signe asked.

"That's always their goal. If they can get true scientists to debate them and appear to consider their bullshit 'evidence,' then it's a win for them. It puts their beliefs on par with theories backed by scientific models and implies credibility. It's like saying Holocaust deniers should have space on library history shelves, which would lend credence to the idea the Holocaust didn't happen and the lies deserve to be part of any World War II history curriculum.

"But there is no 'both sides' when it comes to the Holocaust." He noticed his knuckles were white on the steering wheel and loosened his grip. "And no 'both sides' when it comes to racist prehistoric alien pseudoarchaeology. It's all, every bit of it, bunk spread to justify hate crimes."

He'd spent a lot of time the last few years studying these hate groups, learning the ways they acted as a front for criminal activity. It was one reason seeing Grayson Odem at the museum had come as such a shock. And a dangerous one.

"I'm trying to wrap my brain around why Vicki would invite some-one like Odem to a science museum."

He shrugged but didn't point out that she hadn't invited someone *like* Odem. She'd invited the white supremacist himself.

"Maybe someone else invited him, and they used Vicki's name to discredit her?" Her voice sounded hopeful. He guessed she and Vicki were close friends.

"It's possible. There's a fair amount of rivalry in archaeology, and Vicki has made a name for herself in popular media. Academia sneers at her because she's not tenured or known for answering any major research questions or innovations in field methodology. Jealousy is ugly."

"I hate to say it, but there's a lot of rivalry and jealousy at Wayfinders—both the network and institute."

"That's no surprise," he said. "We're competing for resources within the org and also competing with commercial networks that dump money into pseudoscience shows about looking for Atlantis and crackpot secret alien history theories because they make money—but those shows are recruiting tools for white supremacists. It's an ugly cycle." He knew enough on this subject to talk in depth. It was a relief to not have to work to pretend knowledge he didn't have.

"And how did you end up with Leo and your own show? Are you some fancy-pants scholar or something?"

His relief disappeared like water vapor in the hot California sun.

He wasn't a fraud, but he wasn't who Leo thought he was either. He knew this game. He was good at it, but Signe was a damn good investigative reporter.

It was one thing to pass Leo's test, but Signe was next-level. *This* was why he'd resisted this assignment. Three days in Yosemite with the *it girl* of investigative journalism without giving away his true agenda.

He could be totally screwed before he even got the job rolling. "I'm surprised you didn't research me," he lied.

"I would have if I'd known Leo was sending you."

"Right. I forgot." He wasn't certain why Leo hadn't told her, but it had worked for Cole. "I'm not a fancy-pants anything. I have a bachelor's degree, but I've never worked in or been interested in academic archaeology. I dig bummed for a few years. Worked for some CRM—cultural resource management—firms on projects all over the West Coast."

He cleared his throat. "Mine is the typical story of boy lands in LA working on a dig and a news crew comes out to report on the excavation. I was, . . . uh . . . water screening shirtless, and the news clip went viral for all the wrong reasons." This was actually true, but it was years ago. "I guess the internet liked my face."

She snorted. "Suurre it was your *face*."

He gave her a faint smile. "You don't think I'm pretty?"

"Ha. Your face is exceptional, to be sure. When I first saw you chatting with Leo, I assumed you were the next Channing Tatum. I just have a feeling your *face* wasn't the reason it went viral, because you mentioned shirtless water screening. I'm guessing there was a nice sheen coating perfect abs?"

He grinned. "Ah, so you *have* seen the video."

"No. But I'll be sure to look for it next chance I get."

He'd try to keep that from happening, but if she did manage to find it before they were out of cell range, it would only confirm his story. Time to redirect. "Sadly, I don't have Tatum's dance moves."

"That *is* a shame. But there really can only be one Channing Tatum."

"The world couldn't handle the awesome if there were two."

She laughed lightly—but it was still more laugh than he'd seen from her to this point, and he felt a surprising rush. He reminded himself she was a means to an end. Nothing more.

"So what happened after the internet discovered your pretty face?"

"Well, living in LA, I decided to capitalize and look for work in front of cameras, talking about archaeology and history. It's not like Josh Gates—the host of *Expedition Unknown*—has a graduate degree either." He put a little defensiveness in his tone. He was a struggling wannabe TV star who'd finally gotten his big break.

"I approached several producers, including Leo. When he was offered the contract with TWN, he remembered me and gave me a call."

"And here we are."

He let out a strangled laugh. "Yeah, we'll pretend it was that simple."

"When do you start filming?"

He glanced sideways, taking his eyes off the road ever so briefly. "Uh, well, we were going to start yesterday."

She jolted. "What? No. No way. Leo wouldn't have changed the filming schedule. Not for me."

"You see why I said he's still in love with you?"

He wished he could see her face as she digested *that* information, but they'd reached the final turns before the parking lot, and he needed to focus on the road.

She said nothing, not even when Half Dome came into view in all its majestic glory, then disappeared as the car rounded another curve.

He drove slowly through the parking lot, where pedestrians milled about. As expected, it was packed and he was lucky to find a space after circling only once.

He shut off the engine and offered her the key. She remained stiff in her seat, staring out the window. "Signe?"

She shook her head. "Sorry. I'm just . . . stunned." She took the key. "And I'm so sorry I interrupted the start of filming for you. I know what a big deal that is."

He shrugged. "It's not your fault. It's not like you requested *me*. That was Leo's decision." The truth was, it was a big-ass deal. Cole had been pissed. So fucking close to the end zone and the ball had been yanked from his grasp by his own teammate.

"Yes, but I'm still sorry. You should know . . . I have a lot of mixed feelings about Leo, but rest assured, he *is* a good producer. No one knows that better than I do. Working for him was never more difficult than it had to be, and I learned so much from him."

She was trying to ease potential jitters he might have, which was nice but unnecessary. He wanted to return the focus to Leo. "Pardon me for being cynical, but you were sleeping with him. That's going to change the dynamic."

"Yeah, but when we were filming, I wasn't his wife. I was the talent, same as you. He was very good at separating the two. Remember, I wasn't the only talent he was producing during the years of our collaboration. I saw how he treated everyone. He was fair."

Cole figured Signe was as in love with her ex as the man was with her, which raised a lot of questions. "We should get to work filming the crowd. We've got a little over two hours before the meet time."

She nodded and slipped on her rugged sport sandals, then reached into the back seat for the day pack with her cameras. Outside the vehicle, they both lathered up with sunblock. Signe donned a wide-brimmed sun hat and crammed a mask into her pocket. Masks weren't required outside but Signe told him she preferred masking indoors when possible and had asked him to do the same. "I want to film a short intro segment here."

He nodded. "With the tripod?"

"No. It's too busy here. We'll use that when we film the full intro on the valley floor."

He nodded. She was the director for this entire gig. His job was to work the camera, navigate using a compass or GPS, and ensure they didn't burn through their food too quickly. Oh, and make sure that if they attracted attention from a bear, he extracted her from the situation without harming either wildlife or woman.

Given that they'd entered the park to meet an informant with intel on two potential murders, he figured they had more to fear from humans than bears. Even in this busy, populated place, he itched with foreboding and wanted to grab his gun from his pack, but there was no place to conceal it under his hiking pants or shirt and this wasn't an open-carry state.

He filmed Signe walking down the long path that led to the over-look, capturing the moment Half Dome came into view.

She turned and smiled at the camera and said, "Much as we aren't in Yosemite to take in the sights, I wouldn't be human if the view we're about to see didn't stop me in my tracks with the sheer beauty of it. I've traveled all over the world as both a tourist and a journalist, and few places take my breath away as much as this one."

She stood still for a moment, then continued the final steps with him following until the vast valley was captured by the camera lens. Cole zoomed over her shoulder as they walked slowly toward the railing that lined the overlook. Once there, he angled the camera to capture the Merced River as it flowed through Yosemite Valley, panning from El Capitan to Half Dome and beyond. Between the two massive rock formations, a tall curtain of water sparkled in the morning sun as the flow plummeted more than two thousand feet to the lower falls, which then dropped another three-hundred-plus feet to the river.

He felt the same awe that Signe had described. Even though most of his visits to Yosemite had focused on climbing or fieldwork, neither of which had been near Glacier Point, he'd still visited this place at least a dozen times, and he had to catch his breath at the sheer beauty with every viewing.

Signe gave his shoulder a bump and whispered, "Time to start filming the crowd."

"Do I have to?"

"Eat your vegetables, Cole, and then you'll get dessert."

He laughed and did as instructed, turning away from the majestic view and panning the crowd.

From there, they followed the path to explore the rest of the overlook, and he took the opportunity to climb on top of boulders and film the milling tourists from above.

They walked the full length of the overlook, then returned to the middle section, where Signe snagged an open spot at the railing with a perfect view of Upper and Lower Yosemite Falls. The falls were a thin stream now that they were more than a week into July—a month in which the valley would likely get only a scant half inch of rain—but still breathtaking due to the sheer height of the drop nonetheless. He filmed Signe as she shared Yosemite fun facts that probably wouldn't make it into the story, given they had nothing to do with two men whose bodies had been found just days apart in the park.

After she gave a hand signal to cut, a tall woman wearing big sunglasses, a broad sun hat over long dark hair, and a disposable N95 mask stepped forward. "Excuse me, are you Signe Gates?"

Signe turned a bright smile on the woman. Cole flicked the "Record" button just in case this was the contact they were expecting.

"I am."

"Oh my goodness! I am *such* a fan of your show!"

Signe's smile tightened, showing just a hint of strain, and Cole realized she'd expected the same thing he had—this was the informant or someone acting as their proxy.

Her expression relaxed just enough to appear natural. "Thank you! I appreciate hearing that."

"I just can't believe the people you interview!"

Cole figured she was in her twenties, but it was hard to tell with the sunglasses and mask. Her head shifted left to right and back again, as if looking for something.

"Are you here to . . . ?" She trailed off as she seemed to realize the need for discretion.

Signe smiled. "No. Just here on vacation."

"It looked like you were filming. I'm sorry, I shouldn't have—"

"Really, it's fine. Cole isn't my cameraman."

He stepped forward and draped an arm around Signe's shoulder. "Just taking a video of the most beautiful woman in the world with the most gorgeous backdrop in the world." He pressed a quick kiss to her temple.

"Oh! You *are* on vacation. Well then, you must let me get video of you both together with the falls!"

Before he could stop her, the woman snatched the extremely expensive camera from his hands. She twisted it around and frowned at the screen on the back, then shifted to focus the lens on Signe and him. "Closer together now! Oh, perfect. I've got the falls on one side and Half Dome on the other. Oooh. You look adorable together!"

Cole glanced down at Signe. She had a slender build and stood nearly a foot shorter than him. With his thick shoulders, he imagined he looked like a beast in comparison.

She glanced up at him and gave him a rueful smile and, well, he had to do something about that lest this woman not buy their unplanned couple charade.

He placed his palm at the back of her head, leaned down, and brushed his lips over hers, pausing to draw out the kiss for the video. His mouth remained closed, but still, it was a solid lip-smacking that had their camerawoman squealing with delight.

He released Signe's mouth but kept his arm around her.

"Oh my goodness!" the woman said as she handed the camera back to Cole. She waved her hand as if she needed to cool herself. "And I thought it was hot outside already. I'm so excited to get to meet you. I'm such a huge fan. I hope you enjoy your time in Yosemite." Fast as she'd appeared, the woman took off, swept into the crowd on the path.

"That was . . . *interesting*," Signe said.

"We didn't have a plan for what to do if you were recognized. Since we don't want her raising alarms about you doing a story on Yosemite, I improvised."

"I'm not talking about that. The interesting part is I've never been recognized by a random stranger before."

"Always a first time."

"Sure. It's possible. But I think it's more likely she wasn't random."

CHAPTER 8

Unease slid through Signe as she scanned the overlook. No one was paying undue attention to her and Cole. She'd be delighted by the fan interaction, except that it happened at this particular time and place. And it had felt . . . *off.*

Her journalist instincts were on high alert.

"If she's not random, who is she? Connected to your informant?" Cole asked.

"She took the camera."

"And she gave it back."

"Let's take a look at the video." She nodded toward an easily climbable granite boulder, then scrambled to the top and settled in a spot with her back to the valley. From this vantage point, she had a better view of the tourists who milled about the overlook. The only drawback was she was highly visible to anyone watching. She shrugged it off. She wasn't trying to hide. DiscoFever knew she was here.

Cole dropped down beside her and handed her the camera.

Should she be irked he'd given it up so easily? Neither Leo nor Roman would have made that mistake, but for them, the camera was their business. For Cole, it was more or less a prop.

She examined it closely, studying all angles before finally turning her attention to the playback screen that was the size of a credit card.

She rolled her shoulders and went over her conversation with the woman. Was it normal for fans to fail to introduce themselves? As someone who wasn't famous enough to experience random recognition, she had no clue what was normal there.

The woman hadn't even tried to shake Signe's hand, but that could be respect for COVID protocols. She was wearing a mask outside, after all.

"I began recording the moment she started talking to you," Cole said.

A point in his favor. She would let go of her pique if he got a close-up of the woman's face.

She hit "Play." Cole leaned over to shade the glare on the small screen as she held the camera between them.

White. Tall. Long dark hair. Features hidden by hat, sunglasses, and mask. She was far from the only woman in hat and sunglasses—Signe included—and there were also enough people in masks to not stand out in the crowd of tourists.

There was an odd movement and angle as the woman studied the camera before she turned the lens toward Cole and Signe. Then the image settled and there she was, tiny next to giant Cole. Side by side as they were, he looked larger than life.

No wonder Leo had hired him for the docuseries. The camera loved Cole Banner. The magnificent backdrop of vast, glacier-carved granite walls and cascading waterfall had to compete for the viewer's attention.

In a smooth motion—no hesitation or any hint this wasn't something they did all the time—Cole's lips pressed to hers. He was a good actor and the kiss looked romantic on camera. On par with the eye-popping backdrop.

She skipped back to the beginning and played the recording again at slower speed.

"I know the kiss was good, but shouldn't you wait until later to watch it in slow-mo?"

She gently elbowed him in the ribs. "It's not the kiss that interests me."

"Tell me what I did wrong, then." His voice was husky with a hint of laughter.

She smiled but rolled her eyes and watched the exchange play out again.

The scene shifted as the camera was seized. Then there was the pause as the woman stepped back. The camera was aimed away from Signe and Cole, capturing a snippet of people milling on the path near the gift shop.

It hung there for a beat too long. She let out a gasp and hit "Pause."

"What's wrong?"

She zoomed in on one face among the dozen or so people.

This camera was the best quality for its size that money could buy. The zoom was excellent and had been set to autofocus while Cole panned over the ever-shifting crowd of tourists.

The slight pause had given the camera a chance to focus and get an HD image. She zoomed in until Roman Wiley's face filled the small screen.

What was Roman doing here?

She pressed the button so the paused image panned down to show Roman's legs. He was behind several people, obscuring the line of sight, but it didn't look like he wore a boot.

He definitely didn't have crutches.

Speedy recovery or faked injury?

Why would he do that, and why would he show up here now? If he wanted to help her after all, he'd have called. And how on earth did he know she'd be at Glacier Point, when *she* hadn't even known until yesterday evening?

Had DiscoFever texted him too?

Impossible. Signe hadn't even known Roman two years ago. There was no reason for DiscoFever to have his number, especially not in connection with her. It was much more likely they'd have messaged

Leo, but she didn't think Leo had known about DiscoFever. At least, not their name or which black market they were associated with.

She wished she had her phone data from before Bastille Day so she could refresh her memory on her communications with the disco-loving informant.

She stiffened as another thought occurred to her. Had *Cole* told Roman where they were meeting today?

But how would the two men even know each other? They'd both been at the museum on Sunday, but as far as she knew, Cole had left before Roman arrived.

Who could she trust?

She'd been working with Roman for eighteen months, while Cole was a complete stranger.

There was the tiniest of possibilities Roman had decided to take a spontaneous trip once his sprain turned out to be no big deal. She'd told him he had the week off, and maybe her mention of Yosemite had piqued his interest.

Still, it didn't make sense that he hadn't called her to give her the heads-up. And then there was the fact that the woman had clearly wanted Signe to know her cameraman was here.

Who was the woman, and how did she know about the connection between Signe and Roman? Roman *never* appeared on camera. They'd agreed to that from the start.

She rubbed her temples and stared at the screen. None of this made sense, but if Roman was involved in this meetup and didn't tell her, then he was fired.

It didn't matter that his uncle was the head of programming at TWN. Hell, if the Wayfinders Institute was involved in any way, then her show was dead.

Her throat clogged. She could barely breathe.

No. No way.

"Who is it?" Cole asked.

She'd forgotten Cole wouldn't recognize Roman's face.

"That's my cameraman, Roman Wiley. Nephew to TWN's head of programming."

"Whoa. Um. Shit. What do you want to do?"

"Call my attorney," she muttered.

"I mean right now. Want to look for him?"

"I have a feeling he's long gone, but yes, we should try to find him. And later, I want to look at all the crowd footage on the laptop and see if you caught him on film as well."

They spent the next hour searching for Roman. He wasn't in the gift shop, parking lot, restrooms, or among the crowd exploring the overlook.

It was a waste of time, but it kept Signe occupied as she waited and waited and waited for the coordinates for Thursday's meeting.

They grabbed sandwiches from the cooler in the car and ate lunch as they searched. Cole ate two large fully loaded subs while she could barely stomach half of a Thai chicken wrap. But then she'd lost her appetite the moment she spotted Roman.

She tried to give Cole the second half of her wrap, but he frowned and refused. "You need to eat. We've got a big hike ahead of us."

"Yes, Dad," she muttered. "I'm going to put it back in the cooler for now and grab a soda." She could use a sugar hit as her adrenaline waned. "Want anything?"

"I'm good. I'll check out the restrooms again, then loop through the gift shop."

She followed the path to the upper parking lot and pressed the fob to unlock the hatchback. After trading her wrap for a Coke in the cooler, she closed the back and leaned against the bumper. She pressed the icy can to her forehead, then ran it along her neck. It was *hot*.

Glacier Point sat at an elevation of just over 7,200 feet. She supposed some of her nausea could be from the 5,000-foot elevation rise from Oakhurst to the overlook, but it was more likely stress and heat.

She wanted to watch the video again and study Roman's face, but as she powered on the camera that hung from a strap around her neck, she noticed her hands shook.

Low blood sugar or anxiety?

Both? *Both.*

She held the remedy for the former in her hand. She popped the top of the soda and took a long drink.

Prior to Bastille Day, she'd been an adrenaline junkie, but not the kind who enjoyed BASE jumping or skydiving. No. She thrived on the danger of meeting monsters and asking them uncomfortable questions. The interview process delivered an endorphin kick no drug could reproduce.

Now here she was, on the trail of the ultimate interview—uncovering the identity of the crime lord who'd ordered her abduction—and instead of feeling a thrill, all she wanted to do was puke.

It would be different if Leo were with her. If he hadn't abandoned her when she needed him most. Here, now, he'd have been her strength. Instead, she was with a man she'd known less than sixteen hours and his presence, while helpful, didn't lessen her anxiety.

The last time she'd been proactive toward taking action against her abductors was when she'd gone to the LA field office of the FBI, with horrific results. Days later, she'd received a package with proof they'd followed through on their threat to kill one of her informants.

It had been the second death due to disclosures she'd made while drugged. The first had died before her lost hours had even ended.

Any thought that someday she'd be able to come clean had died with her sources. She couldn't even speak to a counselor or psychotherapist to process her trauma. If she did, their blood would be on her hands too. They would *always* follow through.

Six months after Bastille Day, Leo had confronted her with evidence she'd cheated on him, forcing her to tell him about the rape. But it was too late. Six months of silence and lies had undermined his trust.

He didn't believe her. She'd kept the worst thing that had ever happened to her a secret to protect him, but in so doing, she'd irreparably broken her marriage.

She'd never have told Leo a thing if he hadn't seen her medical records and accused her of cheating. She'd told him the truth: she'd gotten the sexually transmitted disease—which had been knocked out with antibiotics and was no threat to him even if they'd had sex in the months since the rape—when she was abducted, drugged, and raped after he'd stood her up in Oakhurst on Bastille Day.

He'd fired back that if that were true, she'd have told him in July, not waited six months. She'd told him the bare minimum: there had been threats to him and she'd lost forty-eight hours.

Two full days remained a blank void in her mind.

She didn't know exactly what had been done to her, but the bruises and other injuries indicated she'd been raped and beaten. She'd explained that was why she hadn't been interested in sex since early summer.

His accusation that she hadn't been interested in sex with *him* because she was getting it elsewhere had stung more than any argument they'd ever had—and there had been plenty as they lived and worked together.

At that point, she'd shown him the scars. He hadn't seen her naked since Bastille Day. And even after seeing what had been done to her, he'd left.

Within an hour, her marriage was over.

She'd cried for days and even then feared she'd told him too much. That there would be a lethal price for attempting to defend herself against accusations of infidelity.

And there had been a price, but it wasn't one Leo paid. It had been all her.

They had to make the news of their separation public because she'd been in talks with TWN for *Crime Lords* and they were down to final contract negotiations when she found herself without a producer or cameraman. The day after the press release announcing their separation went out, she received a message with a video link from an anonymous source.

In her line of work, she always clicked the link.

What she saw had her vomiting as if she'd gulped ipecac.

A sex video. Her with three men, proving what her body had known all along: she'd been raped repeatedly during the forty-eight hours she couldn't remember. Only, in the video, it didn't look like rape. She'd been drugged and appeared to be an active—even enthusiastic—participant.

The message was clear: *No one will believe it was rape, especially not your husband.*

Still, Signe knew the truth. She'd been raped and brutalized, no matter how it looked on film. Watching video of herself being violated repeatedly by multiple partners had been traumatizing, no matter how much she'd looked like she was enjoying what they did to her.

The video disappeared after one viewing. The shock of seeing herself violated had scrambled her focus. Her memories—both real and imagined—were foggy and sickening.

Forty-eight missing hours boiled down to fifteen minutes of video that made her lose the contents of her stomach when it was done. But she'd seen enough to remember skin color, build, and the scars and tattoos of the three men who raped her. Only faces had been blurred.

When she was able, she'd written down what she could remember before the memories could become distorted by time and uncertainty. Two white men, one light brown. All had dark hair. The white men were large with thick muscles. Linebacker build. One had a jagged scar on his hip, the other a tattoo of the sun on his chest. The brown man was lean and wiry and covered in tattoos.

No way would that man ever sneak up on her. Too many distinctive tattoos.

After that day, the video had become part of her nightmares, and now she didn't know if her dreams were expanded memories or an embellishment of the horror she'd been subjected to. Violations to her drugged body that hadn't been in the fifteen minutes of spliced video.

Ever since she received the first message on Sunday, she'd wondered if the informant she was on her way to meet was someone who wanted to help her bring the men who'd hurt her to justice or if she'd meet a man who had a tattoo or scar that would identify him as one of her rapists.

Sure, it had said she'd get answers and evidence, but it wasn't like she'd respond to an invitation to meet her rapist deep in the Yosemite backcountry. They *had* to entice her with a shot at justice.

But really, there could be no redemption for her. She'd burned sources while drugged. Two had died because of it. And she'd never told law enforcement what she'd done.

CHAPTER 9

After finishing the soda, Signe crossed the parking lot to deposit the can in a bear-proof recycle bin, then slipped into the shade of the forest that abutted the lot. She leaned against a thick tree trunk and took a deep breath. The sugar had helped, but she still felt like she could toss what little she'd managed to eat without much provocation.

Get it together, Gates.

Where is Roman? Why was he here?

It was simply too much to believe it had been a coincidence he was here and that some stranger caught him on video. The first she could maybe believe if she closed one eye and squinted the other.

But the second?

It was just too bizarre.

She took a deep breath to keep bile down as her brain processed the ramifications.

There would be no Season Two of *Crime Lords*. The Singapore story would go unfinished. If she couldn't trust Roman, she couldn't trust anyone. Especially not when she considered the interviews he'd played a hand in organizing.

Hell, was Season One tainted now too?

Of course it is.

But then, everything she did was tainted. And that wasn't Roman's fault. It was all hers. At this point, she should be less focused on getting justice and more focused on staying out of prison.

Her phone vibrated and she pulled it from her pocket to check the screen. Did she even want the coordinates for the next meeting at this point?

Her answer came when she felt a ripple of disappointment at seeing the text wasn't from DiscoFever. Yeah. She was going to the meeting and she'd be prepared for anything.

Even vengeance.

Her phone vibrated with another message and she swiped on the screen to open the conversation. A message from a five-digit number she'd never seen before.

56920: Nice kiss. Does your new boy toy have a cock as big as mine?

56920: Does he make you scream like I did?

Her stomach dropped as the meaning sank in. Another message arrived before she could catch her balance.

56920: I miss fucking you. The way your pussy squeezed my huge dick as I pounded you. My hand on the back of your head pressing your face into the pillow. You writhed until you passed out. I marked you as mine.

She bolted from her hidden spot in the shade and ran to the middle of the hot parking lot. She needed to be in the open. Visible.

The sun emoji. The sun tattoo on her rapist's chest. White skin, dark body hair. Large. Muscular. Built like a linebacker.

I didn't receive a text until I was alone.

He was here. Watching her.

How close was he? Did he hope to grab her, or was his goal merely to terrify?

Her wild, panicked gaze could hardly make sense of what she saw as she scanned the lot, forcing herself to hold back a scream. She didn't want the man to see her panic, but the idea of him grabbing her when she'd been hiding in the shade was too terrifying to contemplate.

She needed Cole. Or her gun.

Her phone vibrated again.

56920: Tell your new boyfriend about me and he's a dead man.

She fumbled with her pack to dig out the weapon when a car horn honked. She glanced up and saw she was blocking the road and the line of cars waiting to drive down the row was growing.

In that moment, she saw Cole. It appeared he'd been using his cell phone when the horn got his attention. This was Yosemite, not a city street. People didn't honk here.

He tucked his phone in his back pocket and headed in her direction.

She got a grip on her panic enough to know she needed to get out of the road so the cars could drive down the row. She moved to the sidewalk.

Cole reached her side. "What's wrong?"

She couldn't tell him. He didn't know about her missing hours or why they were here. And it had to stay that way.

The words were right there on her phone: Tell your new boyfriend about me and he's a dead man.

She glanced at the screen, intending to close the conversation. She shouldn't have been surprised to see all four texts were gone. Poof. As if they'd never existed.

This can't be happening. He's not here. Anyone could have sent those texts.

She looked at Cole, trying to figure out what to say, when she spotted his cell phone in the mesh pocket on the side of his day pack.

It was a different phone from the one she'd seen him shove into his back pocket.

She didn't see the bulge of a phone when she finally got a chance to look. But he could have moved it when she sprinted to the sidewalk. Or really any moment as he was walking toward her because she hadn't been focused on him. She'd been looking for the person who texted her.

Had that person been Cole?

But how? And why?

Maybe he'd moved it to the mesh pocket when she was in the middle of the whirlwind of pummeling thoughts.

Cole was safe. He had to be. Leo had sent him.

And Leo was still in love with her.

No. No, he wasn't. If he were, they'd still be together. He'd be the man in the park with her. Not a nondancing Channing Tatum wannabe.

Signe sat on a boulder, sipping from her water bottle while facing an incredible view, but she saw none of it as her brain traveled well-worn paths that led nowhere.

Her memories of Bastille Day and the day that followed remained blank. Forty-eight hours gone. She could not see Sun Chest's face. Scar Belly remained a mystery. Tattoo Body would always be headless.

Cole had given her space as she collected herself. She'd offered no reason for her obvious panic. She'd simply claimed the heat was getting to her and she needed water. So here she was, drinking like a good girl while he prowled the crowd, looking for Roman.

One thing Signe did know was Roman Wiley was definitely *not* one of her rapists. Not only was he the wrong build, she'd seen him shirtless. No scar. No tattoos.

The water bottle was empty by the time Cole settled beside her on the boulder. He didn't say a word, and she appreciated that about him.

Her phone pinged and she checked the screen to make sure it wasn't another blister from the sun before tilting the phone so Cole could see too.

DiscoFever: ● Change in plans. Meeting is Friday, 11 AM.

Shit. She'd be fully unhinged by Friday.

Did she have a choice? No. All her choices had been stolen from her two years ago. Her fingers shook as she typed her reply.

Signe: Where?

DiscoFever: Will send coordinates tomorrow AM. Do not leave the park. If you do, the meeting is canceled.

She let out a pained growl.

"We'll be out of cell range tomorrow," Cole said. "We have to camp on the trail in a certain area tonight."

She huffed out a breath and replied.

Signe: Need coordinates now. Will not have cell coverage where we must camp tonight if we can't leave the park.

DiscoFever: Backpacker campground in the valley. You get one night coming and going.

Did DiscoFever know they had a wilderness permit, or had they guessed?

Please, please, please don't be Cole, both luring and leading me into the wilderness.

Signe: Why the schedule change?

She waited for a reply. Minutes went by. Nothing.

Finally, Cole said, "Is this guy . . . DiscoFever . . . is he—or she—just jerking your chain?"

"Honestly, I don't know. But what they said about two deaths in Yosemite in the original message was accurate."

"But the info was also a matter of public record."

She shrugged.

Was DiscoFever trying to help her or was this a trap? As far as lures went, this was a damn good one. A cryptic message she couldn't resist followed by changing the date once she was committed and inside the park.

She met Cole's concerned gaze. Was she endangering him? Was she the worst person in the world for not warning him about who might be waiting for them in the forest?

Or was *he* the real danger?

Regardless, they were stuck together until Friday. Longer, really, considering there would be a return hike.

"There's nothing more we can do here," she said as she climbed to her feet and dusted off her pants. "Let's go to Camp 4."

Again, she asked Cole to drive. She didn't have the focus and she was used to letting her cameraman do the driving in his big SUV full of equipment.

My cameraman.

And now her brain circled back to the problem of Roman. It had never once crossed her mind that Roman could have anything to do with what happened on Bastille Day. But now?

She pulled out her phone, curious to know if he'd lie when she asked where he was enjoying his unplanned vacation. But of course, there was no cellular coverage as they descended into the valley.

They drove in silence, her tension building as she considered Roman's possible role here. At last, they reached the road that paralleled the Merced River. It was nearly two o'clock on a Tuesday in July, so naturally, the road was bumper to bumper with cars.

"I've always avoided this place in summer," she said.

"Back in my climbing days, summer was the only time I could get here. I'm used to this."

They were slowly making their way to the heart of the village so they could cross the river to get to Camp 4 when a car pulled out of a parallel parking spot on the right in front of them. Cole slipped into the open spot and put the car in park but left the engine running.

"Why are we stopping here?"

"Because we can. We need to talk." His voice had an edge.

Her spirits sank. It appeared she wasn't the only one who was suspicious now.

His next words confirmed her fears. "You're holding out on me, Sig."

They'd made a quick progression from Ms. Gates to Sig, but then, they'd spent nearly every minute together for the last twenty hours. Except for the brief break when maybe he'd sent her some horrible texts.

No.

She wouldn't believe that. She couldn't.

"What makes you think that?"

He gave her a pointed look. "This isn't your kind of story. Since when do you investigate random, potentially accidental deaths? Where's the organized-crime connection?"

"That's what we're here to find out."

"And you've just dropped everything to spend a week in Yosemite on the basis of a flimsy text from a person you don't know?"

Dammit, why did he have to be so astute? She met and held his gaze. "Yes."

"And your usual cameraman just so happened to be at Glacier Point at the same time you were there to get the coordinates for the meet."

"I can't explain that part because I don't understand it myself."

"This isn't a Signe Gates story."

Oh, Cole, on that point you are so very wrong. This is the ultimate Signe Gates story in that it is all about me. My own personal crime story.

"Why are we here? Why aren't you balking at the change in date for the meeting?"

She gave him the serious look she gave the camera when she found herself in a dangerous situation on the way to an interview. "I can't exactly force them to meet me early."

"But you can leave. Bet they'd text real fast if you stopped jumping to their commands."

She couldn't take that chance. Not this time.

"You trust this guy?" he asked.

"Hell no."

"But we're still doing this."

"Yes."

"Am I risking my life here, Sig?"

If she told him yes, he'd turn the car around and drive back to Oakhurst. She itched to grab the keys and take control. If he wanted to leave, he could get out and take the bus. Her car. Her rules.

She glanced at the gear in the back seat. The hatchback's rear seats had been folded down to make extra room for cargo. Everything was packed and ready to go. Cole had helped her with the most efficient method of packing the bear canister. She knew how to use the Sierra stove and he'd shown her how to operate the GPS unit.

The idea of facing whoever was behind her nightmare alone was . . . beyond terrifying. But she'd do it. She had a gun, and she knew how to use it.

"Since the wilderness permit is in your name, after we check in at the trailhead, you can leave. Take the bus back to Oakhurst and pick up your car. Hitchhike. Whatever you need to do."

"You think I'll bail because of a little danger?"

It wasn't exactly a *little*.

Tell your new boyfriend about me and he's a dead man.

He *should* take the bus. She needed to send him home. "That's why you're asking, isn't it?"

"No. But warning would be nice."

"Did you bring a gun like Leo instructed?"

"Yes."

"That was your warning."

"Jesus. It would serve you right if I did leave."

"Then why don't you?"

"I'm considering it."

Even though it was the right thing to do, she balked. "You won't because Leo will replace you in the show if you do."

His face tightened and his words came out tinged with bitterness. "Yeah, because like you, I only care about the show."

Well, that told her Leo had shared some of their more intimate arguments with this total stranger. *Thanks, Leo.*

"Yes, well, the sooner you accept that about me, the better." She nodded toward the scorched trees that flanked the open field that ran along the river. On the other side of the Merced were El Capitan and other granite walls that lined the valley. Upper and Lower Yosemite Falls were lightly flowing. Tourists milled on the sidewalk and field near a footbridge that crossed the river, but there was a lot of open space too. They could film a short segment with the falls as the backdrop and position it so there'd be no need for tourists to sign releases or blur faces.

"Let's film our opening segment near the bridge."

Cole gave a cold nod. "Yes, ma'am."

His body radiated with the same tension he'd shown in the hallway when he argued with the pseudoarchaeologist Grayson Odem. But now the pent-up violence he exhibited with every movement was directed at her.

Chapter 10

Signe was holding out on him, and it seriously pissed Cole off. She intended for him to walk into danger without giving him a clue as to what he was stepping into.

He wanted to like her. Hell, if he were being honest, he'd be happy to fuck her. But his dick was less picky than it should be, and in this instance, the only reason he'd attempt to get into her pants was if he thought it would get him what he was really after.

Leo had given him no choice but to follow Signe down the rabbit hole, which wouldn't be so bad if it were actually cute little bunnies at the end and not a nest of venomous Komodo dragons.

Here be dragons, indeed.

He took several calming breaths as he set up the tripod and reminded himself he was in one of the most magnificent places in the contiguous United States. He could hear the flow of the Upper and Lower Yosemite Falls as the water cascaded more than two thousand feet into the Merced River.

Breathe. Get your shit together. And play nice with the pretty, secretive journalist who might be the key to what you need.

Think of Jasper. Stay in character.

He raised his gaze from the camera and faced the glacier-carved granite walls and journalist. He shifted the camera so she was centered with the falls on her left.

He hit the button and gave her the hand signal to start. She wore a wireless mic so her voice would override the falls and nearby tourists. He listened with headphones.

Her voice was slightly husky and deadly serious. This was her on-camera voice, delivered straight to his ears. "Deaths in Yosemite National Park are nothing new. In fact, more than fifteen hundred deaths have been recorded in the park since 1851. Park deaths aren't unique to Yosemite either. On average, more than three hundred people die in US national parks every year. The cause is frequently accidental, but heart attacks and other natural causes are also factors. In some parks—like Yosemite—people just . . . disappear. Many of those are presumed to be suicides, which is another leading cause of death in national parks. But hidden among these accidents and suicides is the very real possibility of a well-disguised murder.

"Regular viewers of *Crime Lords* know that my investigations give a global view of a type of crime, followed by a deep dive into the inner workings of the system that makes that crime profitable for those who commit it. I interview the perpetrators, their victims, law enforcement, and prosecutors. I've spent many hours with drug traffickers, gunrunners, animal traffickers, counterfeiters of all trades, along with pimps and sex workers. I don't investigate to *solve* a mystery. The *who* is obvious even though faces might be blurred and voices distorted. What my show has always sought to do is explore the *why* and *how* of criminal behavior and to shine a light on the root causes for different types of crime."

She paused for drama, tilting her head slightly. Cole zoomed in as instructed with that signal. Switching the focus from the distracting backdrop to Signe and only Signe.

"This episode, however, is different. In this investigation, I will examine the recent spike in deaths at Yosemite National Park, and for the first time in my career, I'm looking for a killer."

She held the pose for a beat, then signaled for Cole to stop recording.

Through the headphones, he could hear her clearly. "I think I was a bit stiff. I want to get a few takes so we can splice as needed. Not sure I like the abrupt ending, but it will work for the cold open or at a cut to commercial."

She cleared her throat and squared her shoulders, then signaled for another take.

In the end, they recorded her speech a half dozen times with slight variations in the script as well as her cadence and pitch before she was satisfied they had something she could use.

She unclipped her microphone and approached him. "Most of the show is unscripted," she said. "It's not often we have the luxury of multiple takes like that, so it was good practice for you to get familiar with the camera if nothing else."

There was a chill in her voice, and he knew his anger had rattled her. Or maybe she was still freaked out by what had happened when she was alone up at Glacier Point.

His phone buzzed and he pulled it from the mesh pocket on his pack to check the screen.

He kept his face blank as he read the text, then tucked the phone away without responding; he couldn't reply while she stood beside him.

He folded the tripod while she filmed random bits of scenery with the camera. She slowly drifted away from him, eyes on the screen more than the magnificent setting.

Should he respond to the text while she was distracted?

No. That would be a rookie mistake and he was no rookie in this. He shut off the phone and swapped it with his personal cell, which was tucked into an interior pocket.

Signe returned to his side just as the screen lit up with a new text. He smiled when he saw the message. Here was his ticket back into Signe's good graces. They might even learn something about the two dead men.

He sent a thumbs-up emoji before slipping the phone into the mesh pocket again. To Signe, he said, "We need to go, our table is waiting and I'm hungry again."

"We have a table waiting? Where?"

He flashed a grin. "The Ahwahnee Bar. Outside on the patio."

"How did we get a table at the bar? Do they even take reservations?"

"A park ranger—interpretive, not law enforcement—friend of mine got off work at two. She grabbed a table and is waiting for us."

Signe gave him a curious look. "You got any other surprises for me?"

He shrugged. "Let's go meet Wanda and find out."

Now that it was past two p.m., traffic was beginning to thin in the valley and the drive to the historic hotel went quickly. Naturally, the parking lot was full, so they backtracked and parked next to the Church Bowl Picnic Area and walked down the road alongside the sweeping Ahwahnee Meadow toward the historic lodge with the same name.

Cole pointed across the grassland. "The backpackers' campground where we'll sleep tonight is on the other side of the hotel. We'll have to drive around and cross the river because the only car access is by the North Pines Campground. The campground is actually close to our trailhead, which will make it easier to set off once we get the coordinates in the morning. There's an unloading zone for vehicles, but that's it, so we'll have to park either in the trailhead lot or in Curry Village and hike in after we nab our spot."

He wasn't sure if she was paying attention as she stared off in the direction he'd pointed. Was she worried about camping tonight? Whoever was pulling her chain *knew* her only option would be the backpackers' campground. Had they delayed the meet to force her to camp in the valley?

The instruction not to leave the park sure made it look like that was the goal.

He would sleep with his gun handy. That was nothing new but still not something he'd done in Yosemite.

"We need to head there and reserve our spot for the night after we talk to Wanda."

Finally she faced him, and her eyes were focused—not the dazed expression she'd had when they first left her vehicle. "You knew about the backpackers' campground and rules. You planned to stay there tonight already, didn't you?"

He nodded. "If the coordinates you received weren't too far, then yes. I figured we'd be better off gathering information tonight and setting out first thing in the morning."

She stopped, planting her feet in a way that said she wasn't going to budge unless she got answers. "So why did you tell me to text DiscoFever that we need the coordinates today because we'd be out of range tomorrow?"

"Why not push back? Why let them jerk your chain? Besides, we learned they know about the wilderness permit. That feels important."

"It might just be a guess on their part. If I'd read the first text on the day it was received, I'd have had the full seventy-two hours to get a permit."

Cole shook his head. What was it with the faith she had in an anonymous mirrored ball? "They *know*, Signe. Maybe they've hacked your phone and are using it as a microphone. They could be listening to us right now."

"That's not possible."

"Sweetheart, that's been possible since 2008."

She huffed out an exaggerated sigh. "I *know* that. Listen, given my line of work, the DEA and ATF want nothing more than my informants' contact information and to listen in on my conversations. But if a drug trafficker is arrested because they agreed to an interview with me, I'm dead, and I don't mean that metaphorically. So I spent a small fortune on the most secure phone money can buy. It's made by a cybersecurity company and it has a manual kill switch to turn off the camera and microphone so no one can hack my phone and use it to spy on me.

I know what I'm doing, Cole. If anyone's phone is being used to spy on us, it's one of yours."

The fog that had clouded her gaze was long gone as she glared at him, and he was glad to again be with the tough-as-nails reporter who'd vanished once she spotted Roman Wiley at Glacier Point.

He tilted his head in acknowledgment of his error. "I'm sorry. I should have known you'd be far more aware of the dangers of tech surveillance than I. And you're right. It's more likely my phone is the culprit."

Too late, her words sank in. *One of yours.*

She knew about his second phone.

How? Did she search his bag when he was sleeping?

Not possible. He was a light sleeper and hadn't heard her get up at all. Besides, why would she do that?

All he could do was ignore her words for now. His second phone was encrypted and currently turned off. It wasn't the culprit.

She held out her hand. "Your phone?"

He pulled it from the mesh pocket and handed it to her. She raised a brow when she was met with the locked screen.

"I'll tell you mine if you tell me yours."

She shook her head, but her smile showed amusement. Yeah. Signe was back.

Good.

He took his cell from her and unlocked it before pressing it into her palm again. "Are you divining whether or not it's been hacked? I'm pretty sure you can't tell by looking at it."

"No. But I can read your texts. Who is Wanda, anyway?"

"A friend." He paused, then added, "We dated for a few months. Never got serious, we just found we fit better as friends."

"How very adult of you."

He shrugged. "I'm friends with most of my exes."

She let out a snort of disbelief.

"It's true. You aren't friends with yours?"

"Nope. Not a single one."

"What about Leo?"

Her mouth pinched with irritation as she handed him back the phone with only a cursory glance. "Definitely not Leo." She resumed walking. "So, what did you tell Wanda about why we're here?"

"I said I'm here with one of my new TWN colleagues doing background research for a show. I didn't say who you are or clarify that it is for your show, not the episodes I'm filming with Leo."

"Why Wanda and not someone else? Eager to see an old flame?"

"Fishing for information on my love life, Ms. Gates?"

"I lost interest when you told me you can't dance like Channing Tatum. I mean, knowing that, what's the point?"

He couldn't help but laugh. "That's just an excuse. It was the kiss, wasn't it? I can do better, I swear."

Now it was her turn to laugh. "We'll save that challenge for another day. So why Wanda? I'm asking because it's always good to know what her biases toward you—and me—might be. It can affect what she's willing to share, even unconsciously."

"I worked with her on a dig years ago, before she got the ranger position. We've kept in touch. She's the one who helped me get the wilderness permit and suggested we meet if there's time."

"Given that our shows for TWN are vastly different, is she going to wonder why we're together?"

"She'll be curious but won't pry. She might assume we're a couple if we don't say otherwise."

"If she assumes we're dating, will that be a problem?"

"Nah. We were always more friends than anything else. I'm sure she was disappointed about my lack of dance skills too."

Signe snorted. "Your honesty about your lack of prowess is refreshing."

"Hey, we're talking about *dancing*. Only dancing."

"Mm-hmm."

They reached the parking lot and made their way to the hotel's front entrance. "I'd like to be as vague as possible. I don't want to bring up the details about meeting a source deep in the backwoods and needing a guide. My sources are nearly always criminals and as a park ranger, she could want to raise alarm bells."

"She's not law enforcement," he repeated. "She's an interpretive ranger. The kind who gives tours and talks. Her focus is the history and prehistory of Yosemite."

"Still, she likely knows rangers who *are* law enforcement, and we really don't want to be followed into the forest by a ranger looking to make an arrest."

"Gotcha. No mention of meeting criminals in the backwoods. Just going for a hike to show you some of my favorite places from back in the day as long as we're here."

With that, Wanda would definitely assume they were a couple, but that could be distracting enough to work in his favor. She only knew the surface about what he'd been up to since they met as dig bums a lifetime ago, but she'd met Jasper when she visited LA several years back. He had to hope she wouldn't ask about his roommate in front of Signe.

◆ ◆ ◆

Cole hadn't denied having a second phone, but she had no doubt he'd caught her mention of it. His anger earlier had rattled her, but they were back on even ground. Still, she wouldn't be surprised to learn he was prone to violence and she wished she'd had a chance to google him before they'd entered the park.

Was she being paranoid? Too used to looking for threats everywhere? Or was she not paranoid enough? After all, just hours ago, she'd lost her faith in Roman, the first man she'd trusted since Leo.

Nothing made sense anymore. Her finely tuned skills at reading people—reading criminals, no less—had been shattered.

Cole led her to the outside patio, where a pretty woman with light brown skin and long dark hair pulled back in a ponytail sat alone at a table for four.

The woman smiled and rose to her feet, and Signe realized Wanda was as tall as Cole—at least an inch over six feet.

Cole hugged Wanda and kissed her cheek, and the tall woman held his gaze for a moment, wearing a fond expression. "Good to see you, Cole."

He turned to Signe. "Wanda Montano, this is Signe Gates."

She shook Wanda's hand, feeling like a sapling among giant sequoias. "Thank you for meeting us on such short notice." She glanced around the busy patio bar in a hotel that was one of the most popular tourist spots in the valley. "And getting us a prime table to boot."

They all took their seats as Wanda said, "It's my pleasure. I didn't have plans after I finished my early-afternoon history walk, so the timing was good."

A waiter came by and they ordered drinks and appetizers—more than enough to appease Cole's massive appetite. Task complete, Wanda leaned forward and placed her chin on her hands. "What brings you to Yosemite? Cole said you work for TWN? Are you an archaeologist too?"

"No. I'm an investigative journalist." She told Wanda about receiving a tip on the two recent deaths being connected and deciding to follow up with a trip to the park.

Wanda turned to Cole. "Are you just along for the ride? If there was an archaeology connection, I'd have heard about it. But as far as I know, we're looking at a dirtbag and a John Doe."

Signe frowned. "Dirtbag?" That seemed rather judgmental, which surprised her. She'd read about the tension between climbers and law enforcement but had never heard of issues with interpretive or wilderness rangers.

Cole let out a soft laugh. "It's a badge of honor, not an insult. People who devote their lives to an outdoor sport—climbing, kayaking, hiking. Anything that keeps them outside. No job. No home. Just a sleeping bag they toss in the dirt. Dirtbagging." He cleared his throat. "I attempted a summer of dirtbagging myself right after I graduated college."

"Oh." Signe leaned back, smiling at Cole's confession. "So . . . if the dead climber was a dirtbag—it's going to take some effort to get used to calling him that—I've interviewed my share of the other kind of dirtbag, after all." She shook her head. "Anyway, if he was a dirtbag, that's why I couldn't find an address for him?"

Wanda nodded. "That would be my guess."

She pulled out her notebook and next to the address question for Manny Lontoc wrote: *Dirtbag*. She faced Wanda again. "Does that mean he lived in the park illegally? Staying past the seven nights allowed during high season?"

"I'm not sure," Wanda said. "But . . . do you mind if I invite a law-enforcement ranger to join us? He spends a lot of time dealing with climbers who push park rules to the limit. He probably knew the climber."

"Please do," Signe said, barely containing a rush of excitement. This was better than going to the ranger station and probing for information. It would be casual and friendly, not adversarial.

Wanda shot off a message and a few minutes later her phone vibrated. "We're in luck. He's off duty today. He'll be right over."

Signe met Cole's gaze and gave him a grateful smile. She would have to send Leo flowers as thanks for strong-arming the archaeologist.

Cole flashed a confident grin and leaned back in his chair. Smug looked rather good on him.

He hadn't shaved before they set out this morning, and between the scruff on his face, his linebacker's build showcased in a lightweight hiking top, and the rustic lodge backdrop, he looked so very much in his element.

It was clear why Leo had cast him. The outdoors looked good on him. She'd bet his charisma was magnified by the camera lens, and she had no doubt his appeal was exponentially higher when he focused on the viewer and shared information about archaeology and history.

Knowledgeable, charismatic men were catnip for documentary viewers.

Signe sipped her soda while Cole and Wanda chatted as they waited for Wanda's ranger friend to join them. The fondness between the two was genuine. It made her wonder about Cole's life—both his work and his romantic history. That he'd worked with and dated Wanda was pretty much the most he'd told her about himself.

She assumed he lived in LA as he tried to break into the infotainment business, but even that was just an assumption. Was there any chance he had a sun tattoo or scar on his hip?

The thought was chilling. She forced herself to brush it away. Impossible.

The arrival of law-enforcement ranger August—"call me Gus"—Tyler freed her from her dark thoughts. Gus was dressed like any other tourist as he settled into the seat across from Signe at their table, but it was easy to imagine him in the broad-brimmed ranger cap that was an iconic part of the uniform for National Park Service rangers.

More drinks and food were ordered, and Signe made it clear this was her treat. She didn't pay for interviews—no self-respecting investigative reporter would—but that didn't mean she couldn't grease the skids with booze. Alcohol was an excellent tool for opening roads of access with her seedier informants, but even an NPS park ranger appreciated a free beer.

After quickly bringing Gus up to date, Signe settled back in her seat, nibbling on a thick Bavarian pretzel dipped in beer cheese as she studied the ranger's face to determine his general attitude toward both journalists and dirtbags.

Gus met her gaze. "I can answer questions but only off the record."

She nodded. This was all background and unless he had some kind of bombshell reveal, anything he said she'd likely be able to confirm once official reports were filed. "Off the record. If something comes up and you do want to go on the record—even be interviewed—I can obscure your face and voice to protect your identity. Although, to give weight and authority to anything you share, I'd want to be able to identify you as a law-enforcement ranger."

"I don't know anything that would warrant being filmed, but I can say I did have a few interactions with Manny Lontoc."

She straightened in her seat as a light jolt rippled through her. She would send Cole flowers too. "When was this?"

Gus shrugged. "Last summer. This summer. As recently as a week or so before his body was found. Manny Lontoc was twenty-four years old, Filipino American, and a true and proud dirtbag. Climbing was his world. He wanted to be the next Alex Honnold or Tommy Caldwell. Create new routes, set a record with speed climbing, or be the first to free solo something exceptional."

"Honnold's the climber in the *Free Solo* documentary?" Signe asked. She hadn't had time to watch any of the climbing documentaries on Sunday, but the name had popped up everywhere in her searches on Yosemite and climbing.

Cole nodded. "Yes. Plus, Caldwell was in *The Dawn Wall*." He turned to Gus. "Was Lontoc that good?"

"Not sure. I wasn't part of his death investigation. Just telling you what I know from other interactions with him."

"Did Lontoc have any sponsors?" Signe asked.

"None that I know of, but he had enough money for a car and gas, so he had income from somewhere."

"Could have family money," she murmured, but given that his family hadn't been located, there was no way of knowing.

Yet.

That he had a car was new information. If she had internet, she'd be digging deep into every scrap of information Manny Lontoc's car could provide. She made a note on her pad and looked up to address the ranger again. "So you had run-ins with him because he was basically living in the park?"

Gus shook his head. "He didn't live here, but he rode the edge of what's legal. Climbing in Yosemite has changed and crackdowns by rangers have pretty much made it impossible for dirtbags to live among the rocks near Camp 4. For a while, they shifted to the bear caves around here." He waved to the rocks and forest just beyond the patio. "But we patrol this area, too, now. Anyone living in the park illegally would avoid Camp 4 at all costs. But we do see groups of young climbers nostalgic for the ages of climbing they missed out on, when Camp 4 was the summer home to the Stonemasters and later Stone Monkeys, before there were strict limits on the number of nights that can be spent in the park.

"The nostalgic ones play by the rules even if they ride the edge. They get a reservation and spend a few nights at Camp 4, spread out over the summer. They trade off with others in their circle—so a few camp spots are always filled with climbers. I think there's a house in Oakhurst where they either squat or the owner lets them stay for free for long periods. They climb all day, then gather at the campfire of whoever is legally in Camp 4. But they can't sleep in the camp if they aren't named on the permit and they can't sleep in their car no matter where it's parked. In the past, we've had rules about day-use entry ending at eleven p.m., but now there are no nighttime restrictions beyond not sleeping in cars."

"And you've caught Manny Lontoc sleeping in his car or a campsite that wasn't his?"

Gus shook his head. "No. In general, we give a nudge to people like Lontoc if it looks like they're going to break the rule and share a camp that's not theirs or sleep in a vehicle. We encourage them to leave before it's a problem. Then there's no law broken and they can return the next day and climb to their heart's content. I write down names of people who walk the line in my logbook, but I try to get them out before midnight so there's no need for any real kind of legal action. Climbers will deny it, but we law-enforcement rangers *do* try to keep things amicable. We don't want to arrest them, but we need to uphold park rules."

"What triggers you to check campsites for too many campers? Do you patrol Camp 4 every night?"

Again, he shook his head. "To start with, we look for cars without a proper overnight permit—either for a hotel, campground, or wilderness trail. But we also get called if there's a campfire getting rowdy. The last time I caught Lontoc staying late—a week, maybe ten days before his body was found—it was because another guy in his group was making a lot of noise. The camper with the permit was drunk and decided everyone wanted to hear him sing. Lontoc seemed fine but I Breathalyzed him to be sure before I sent him on the road. His blood-alcohol level was zero."

Gus paused, then let out a heartfelt sigh. "That reminds me . . . he mentioned that night that he never drank alcohol or did drugs. He was doing everything he could to be like Honnold. He'd even gone vegetarian. He was lean and strong, like the best climbers." The ranger stared down at his beer, frowning. "He was a good kid even when he pushed park rules. It's a shame he's gone."

"You liked him," Signe said.

He gave an ever-so-slight nod. "He wasn't the kind of climber who makes trouble. He didn't BASE jump or do any of the other stupid shit that's illegal and likely to get him killed."

"And yet he died in the park."

"But not from climbing or BASE jumping. Drowning of all things."

"What?" Signe asked. "Every headline read, *Yosemite Climber Found Dead in Apparent Accident.* I took that to mean it was a *climbing* accident."

The ranger shrugged. "No. He might've fallen, but not from a wall. He was found in Tenaya Lake early one morning."

"That's the big lake up near Tuolumne Meadows?"

Gus nodded. "A fall into the lake can be deadly. Tenaya Lake is *cold*—the elevation is over eight thousand feet—and he was out there alone as far as anyone knows."

"You're sure he wasn't swimming?"

"Not sure of anything. He was naked, so he could've been skinny-dipping."

"But you didn't find his clothes?" she asked.

"Which can simply mean they haven't turned up yet. It's a wilderness."

"When was he last seen?"

"Officially, a few days before his body was found. He was caught on camera at the Mountain Shop at Curry Village. I don't know when his climbing friends last saw him."

If they'd been looking for him on security cameras, then there had been an investigation into his death. She made a note on her pad. "What did he buy?"

Gus shrugged. "I wasn't part of the investigation. I just remember hearing one of the others mention it. I'm sure they got a list of what he bought."

"What does the Mountain Shop sell?"

"Aside from climbing gear—which easily explains why Lontoc might have been there—the store sells outdoor gear for the camper who forgot stuff. Clothing. Backpacks. Dishes. Sleeping bags. You name it."

She could only imagine how much those items would cost inside the park. What Lontoc purchased could tell her a lot. Unless he bought climbing gear, which would tell her exactly nothing.

"So we can place him at the Mountain Shop, then a few days later, he's found in Tenaya Lake. Think he was camping illegally in that area?" She paused and checked her notes for the date his body had been found. "Wait, was Tioga Road even open yet?"

"It opened a week before his body was found. As far as camping illegally, yeah, it's a possibility. He might have figured we weren't patrolling that area yet."

"His car was found nearby?"

"No."

A naked body miles from the valley and no vehicle or clothes to be found. Signe figured it was a stretch to *not* call it a suspicious death.

Her face must've shown her thoughts because Cole said, "He was a dirtbag, Signe. It's possible his clothes and sleeping bag are tucked away in the forest and he made a habit of camping away from the valley. He could've left his car in Oakhurst and had a friend in the park who picked him up near Tenaya Lake to bring him to the walls."

Damn. He had a point. She didn't know enough about dirtbags to assume anything. Cole was the expert there.

Gus nodded in agreement. "If his car had been found inside the park, I'd know about it, but I can't speak for the towns outside the gates. Lee Vining, Merced, Oakhurst."

"You said he might have a place in Oakhurst, though."

"A climber mentioned a place in Oakhurst at some point. I don't know if Lontoc was staying there, too, but it rings a bell. Maybe he mentioned it one of the nights I sent him home. I can't be sure. It's not the kind of thing I'd keep a record of."

"Thank you for sharing what you do know," Signe said. He'd given her a lot, even if she couldn't follow up until she was back in Oakhurst. Was the Oakhurst squatters' house the reason the initial text had specified Oakhurst as her starting point?

Or was the connection that it was where she'd been when she was abducted two years ago?

Gus studied Lontoc's photo, which Signe had placed on the table at the start of the conversation with Wanda. He smiled as he tapped the flag on the young man's tank top. "He told me once that he wore this shirt often because when Filipino tourists saw it, they'd get excited and strike up a conversation. He loved it. He was fluent in Tagalog and liked helping visitors who weren't fluent in English. He was a self-appointed ambassador for Yosemite to visitors from his home country. I think he helped out a few times with translation when none of our Tagalog-speaking rangers were available."

Signe's heart ached a bit more as she looked at the smiling man in the photo. She cleared her throat. "It sounds like his death was a great loss to the park and climbing community."

Gus nodded. He picked up the printout of the sketch of John Doe and placed it over Manny's smile, almost as if it hurt to see it.

She flipped the page on her notebook to her scant notes on the unnamed man. "So, what can you tell me about our John Doe, whose body was found three days after Lontoc's?"

"Not much there. No name. No tattoos. No friends or family stepping forward to identify him. No unaccounted-for vehicles in the park that could have been his. He was in the backcountry. Thin—potentially emaciated—which led to speculation he'd been camping in the backcountry for a while, but no one ever reported seeing an apparently homeless man around the dumpsters or any of the other places dirtbags go to find food."

"Do you know how he died?"

"It appears he slipped as he was climbing over loose rocks. They rolled under his feet and triggered a small rockfall. He was hit in the head by a large granite cobble, fell, and likely hit his head again. Body was found by hikers two or three days after his death."

Which could mean he died the same day as Manny or they died up to two days apart.

"Was his body anywhere near Tenaya Lake?"

"He was in the backwoods near Yosemite Creek. About six miles as the crow flies, but twice that by road."

"He might be South Asian. Like Lontoc."

Gus shrugged. "Hard to be sure given his battered features. But I hear they're running a DNA test."

It was clear Gus didn't have anything new to add to the information she'd already collected on the John Doe.

Gus cocked his head. "So why are you so interested in both men? I've watched your show. This isn't your usual kind of story. Are you doing an exposé on Yosemite or something? If so, I will not go on record. I like my job and want to keep it."

"Not an exposé. This is a more personal story for me. Possibly related to a previous investigation. Or it could be a wild-goose chase. But if you've gotta chase geese, might as well be in Yosemite, amirite?"

Wanda laughed. She'd been quiet the entire time, her gaze bouncing between Gus and Signe. Curious, but not particularly invested.

"We're heading to Camp 4 next," Cole said. "Anyone we should look for who might know Lontoc?"

The ranger sat back and ran his hand over his jaw. Finally, he said, "You can usually find the hardcore climbers in the sites closest to the Columbia Boulder—that's the biggest boulder at Camp 4."

Cole nodded. "I know it. I've failed at Midnight Lightning and most other bouldering problems."

Signe had no idea what that meant, but clearly Gus did. "You climb?" He gave a quizzical look. "I'd imagine it's hard given your build."

"Yeah. I'm terrible at bouldering because I can't really free climb. My fingertips can't hold my weight and even if I lost every ounce of fat, I'd still be too heavy. I need assist from ropes, but I enjoy it just the same when I get a chance."

It hadn't occurred to Signe that Cole wasn't the right build for climbing, but that just proved she knew nothing of the sport.

Wanda leaned forward and said in a stage whisper to Gus, "Before you got here, he admitted to a summer of dirtbagging."

Cole raised his hands. "Statute of limitations. Also, I didn't last long as a dirtbagger. Went legit when I did fieldwork in the park."

Gus chuckled. "How long are you going to be in the park this trip?"

"Through Friday at least," Signe said.

"You camping or have a room?"

"Completely legal backcountry camping permit," Cole said. "We're staying in the backpackers' camp tonight. Then heading out in the morning."

"You better grab your spot now if you haven't already."

Crap. Signe hadn't thought of that.

"What trail are you hiking?"

"Snow Creek," Cole said.

Gus let out a low whistle. "That's a tough one, especially in this heat. Bring lots of water. And when you think you have enough, bring another gallon."

Signe hadn't let herself think about the difficulties of the hike itself. She'd been far more concerned with what she'd find at the rendezvous point.

"Is it a busy trail?" she asked.

Gus shook his head. "Not compared to the other ones that start in the valley because it's such a strenuous hike without a lot of shade while you do the switchbacks. But the views are incredible. The lack of people makes it even better."

The difficulty of the hike had to be why Cole was able to get a permit at the last minute. She wouldn't complain. She would do absolutely anything to get the answers she needed.

CHAPTER 11

They picked up their backcountry permit from the wilderness center and managed to snag a campsite by the creek. They set up a single tent and clipped the receipt showing they'd paid the eight-dollars-per-person fee for the campsite to the front as instructed by the camp host, but they didn't offload any gear. If things went well at Camp 4, they'd be away from their campsite for a few hours.

From there, they went to the grocery store and purchased a half rack of cold beer, the better to woo climbers returning from a long, hot day on the rocks.

"The more serious climbers don't drink so they can keep their weight down—the summer party days of Camp 4 are long gone—but I bet we'll find a few takers," Cole said as he hefted a cooler loaded with icy brew from the trunk after parking in the Camp 4 lot.

They headed for a boulder so large it had its own Wikipedia page. Signe spotted a bright white lightning bolt on the giant granite rock. "I was confused by your conversation with Gus. I know this is Columbia Boulder, so what exactly is Midnight Lightning?"

"Midnight Lightning is the name of one of the world's most famous bouldering problems."

"Bouldering problem?"

"Yeah. It's like a puzzle or a math problem, but the way you solve is to free solo—no ropes—over the lip." Cole pointed to the lightning bolt. "Thousands of people have climbed all over this boulder, but only a handful have made it to the top using the route marked by the lightning bolt."

Even a nonclimber like her could see the problem. There was deep overhang. "No ropes? You'd have to be a spider to do that. You've tried it?"

"Only as a joke. I can't even free solo easy routes."

Yet he enjoyed climbing anyway. From what he'd said earlier, his body type meant he would never improve as a climber, or at least, not by much. What did it say about a person who pursued hobbies they knew they'd never excel at?

She guessed it said he was comfortable in his skin and knew how to enjoy life.

She wondered if she'd ever been like that or if she always put herself in competition with herself and others. She had to strive to be the best or it wasn't worth doing.

She studied the lightning bolt, thinking it must be significant to the history of climbing or what looked like graffiti wouldn't remain painted on the natural wonder. "Is Columbia Boulder a glacial erratic?"

"No. The boulders you find in the valley are the result of rockfalls."

She smiled. She hadn't expected him to speak with authority on this, but of course he knew the answer. He was an archaeologist and had worked in the park. He'd know the geologic history too.

There were lots of boulders and talus slopes closer to the wall, but Columbia Boulder couldn't help but command attention, massive as it was. A group of tourists was gathered under the lightning bolt for a photo op, but when they were done, they moved on, leaving Signe and Cole alone at the foot of the famous rock.

Cole sat at the picnic table and popped open a beer. "Climbers returning from the rock faces might join us, and if no one does, we can wander through the campground looking for people with climbing gear."

"You've spent a lot of time at Camp 4?" She really should have asked Cole more about himself before they set out.

She pulled a cold can from the cooler and rolled the sweating aluminum over her forehead and neck. They'd been shaded behind the Ahwahnee, but now they were in direct sunlight and the sweltering air caught up with her. She'd had sodas at the bar with Wanda and Gus, and a beer sounded really good now. Plus, it would make her more relatable to climbers who drank.

"We'll take it slow tomorrow," Cole said. "In case you're worried about the heat on the switchbacks."

She nodded. "Slow will definitely be my speed. I'm in decent shape but I don't know how prepared I am for uphill with a heavy pack."

"That's why you've got me. I won't let you overdo it."

She popped open the beer and took a long sip. The cold liquid slid down her throat and she didn't even care that she wasn't a fan of IPAs. It was cold and wet on her dry throat. She raised the can to him in a toast. "Thank you. For getting the backcountry permit. Reaching out to Wanda, who recruited Gus. I-I'm not usually this disorganized when it comes to prep for a story."

"Why *are* you so unprepared?"

She licked her lips, feeling the hot sun on the top of her head. She should have put her sunhat back on, but she'd forgotten it in the car. Another sign of her lack of organization. "This . . . *story* . . . is more personal than most. I wasn't lying when I told Gus it's connected to an investigation I did in the past."

"Which one? I've watched all the episodes of your show."

"It wasn't a piece for *Crime Lords* and it's not one I finished for another news org. This is . . . the fish that got away."

In a sense, it was brutally taken from her. But close enough. "Tell me about you, Cole. You've seen my shows. I'm not the unknown here. But who are *you*?"

"I'm just a guy, sitting in front of one of the world's greatest bouldering problems, asking a girl to trust him."

She smiled. "A guy who quotes *Notting Hill*. Interesting, but not an answer."

"Damn. My best bud promised me quoting that line was foolproof for getting into a woman's pants."

She rolled her eyes. "Since when do you want in my pants?"

"Probably since Leo told me I'm not allowed to fuck you. Things like that make me rebellious."

She practically choked on her sip of beer. "He didn't really say that."

"Oh, he certainly did."

"Did you agree to his edict?"

"Of course I did. I'm trying to get back in his good graces after screwing up at the museum."

"And now that we're far from Leo and he has no way of knowing what we're up to, do you want to keep that promise?"

"I want things from Leo that you can't give me, so yeah. I do."

His wording was interesting. And for the first time, she knew he was being 100 percent truthful.

"I appreciate your honesty. And never fear, your virtue is safe with me. I'm not here to get laid."

He raised his beer in a toast. "Here's to not getting laid."

Cole smiled as he waited for Signe to tap her can against his. Her eyes lit with humor as she did, but her focus wasn't on him, it was on something over his shoulder.

"Dude, that is the . . . worst. Toast. Ever." The voice came from behind him, and now he knew where her smile had been directed.

He turned and faced the quintessential dirtbagger. The man was in his early twenties. He was shirtless with wiry muscles on a lean, lanky body. His hair was pulled back in a man bun and he looked like he hadn't seen a shower in days. Possibly weeks.

Seeing an opportunity, Cole plucked a beer from the cooler and offered it to the younger man. "What can I do? She doesn't want me."

The guy took the beer and threw one leg over the picnic bench, straddling it. "Always important to respect a woman's boundaries, but before you turn to celibacy, I suggest you look for other trees in the forest."

He smiled. "I might do that."

"Good. And when your ladylove here sees you with other women, she will change her song. See you as desirable. And then you get that greatest of all things . . . a ménage."

At that, Signe spewed her last sip and the man winked at them both, then flashed her a grin. "I'm Reef. Thanks for the beer. And if you aren't with this guy, I've got a campfire with a spot just for you."

Two men and a woman joined them as Reef finished his introduction. Cole scooted to the end of the bench to make room on his side. The woman rolled her eyes as she sat between Reef and Cole. "He's a player. And frankly, a lousy one at that."

"Hey now!"

She bumped his shoulder with hers and Reef kissed her. Were they a couple or just casual lovers? Whatever their relationship, the young woman was staking a claim in front of Signe, but not in an antagonistic way.

Perhaps this was Reef's "other trees" advice taking root. There was something to be said for knowing someone else was interested. Or having your boss tell you a person was off-limits.

Would he be attracted to Signe if Leo hadn't gotten territorial?

Well, she was Signe Gates. So probably.

She offered the three newcomers beers and said, "You're all climbers? You hang out at Camp 4 a lot?"

"Much as we can," the man who'd circled the table to sit on Signe's side said.

"Did you know Manny Lontoc?"

The jocular mood shattered with the question and Cole knew they'd hit the jackpot.

"Yeah. Manny was one of the best," the woman said. "I just can't believe . . ." She cupped the cold beer between her palms, not opening it, staring with an unfocused gaze.

Reef stiffened, the arm that had been around the woman's shoulders dropping to the bench behind her. Interesting that he removed the comforting arm instead of pulling her closer. Had there been a romantic rivalry between the two men?

"Why do you ask?" the guy on Reef's other side said.

Signe slipped a business card across the table toward the group. "I'm an investigative reporter looking into Lontoc's life and the accident that killed him."

The man next to Signe let out a snort of disgust. "*Accident.* Right."

"You don't believe it was an accident?"

He shook his head. "Doesn't make sense that Manny would be anywhere near that lake."

"It wasn't a place he normally went?" Cole asked.

"No." The woman's voice was sharp. "It's gotta be a coverup. It took them days to even tell us he'd drowned. And now they won't tell us exactly where he was found. Said it would be a problem if we put bouquets on the lakeshore—they can't allow a shrine by the water because flowers aren't part of the ecosystem."

"Gotta admit, you would make it a shrine, though, Carmen."

"Well, Manny fucking deserves it. They won't let us bury him. They won't let us honor him." The young woman popped open her beer and tilted her head back, taking a long, angry drink.

Signe's voice was soft as she probed. "I understand there's a search going on for his next of kin. Have you been able to help with that?"

"No one knows where his family is," the man next to Signe said.

She pulled out her phone and set it on the table. "Do you mind if I record this? I'd like to get all your names and a little background. Ask a few questions on the record?"

The four people glanced at each other before Carmen gave a slight nod, then the others mumbled agreement.

Signe hit "Record" on her phone, and they all took turns consenting to be recorded and introducing themselves, starting with the man to Signe's left and going clockwise. Oscar was white, twenty-two years old, and from Sacramento. Carmen, Hispanic, twenty-one. She grew up in the Bay Area, most recently from Hayward, where she graduated from high school and attended community college. This was both Oscar's and Carmen's first season of dirtbagging. Tyson was Black, twenty-four, from Reno, Nevada. He'd spent the last four summers dirtbagging in the High Sierras. Last came Reef, white, twenty-four, and from Billings, Montana. This was his second year of dirtbagging in Yosemite.

None of them had a campsite for the night. They were just stopping by Camp 4 to see if a friend, who had a site for the next three days, was back from his climb yet.

As they spoke, they took turns writing down their full names and contact information in Signe's notebook.

"How long did you know Manny?" Signe asked.

Tyson had met him three years before, Reef last year. Carmen and Oscar had known him only since May.

"I hear there's a house in Oakhurst where you all stay?"

Tyson bristled. "Where'd you hear that?"

Signe's mouth curved at one corner ever so slightly. Friendly. Not at all put off by the shift in attitude. "One thing you need to know about me up front. I *never* give up a source."

"There's no house," Oscar said softly. Obviously lying.

Signe shrugged. "Moving along, then. Do you know where Manny stayed when he wasn't sleeping in the park?"

"His car, mostly," Carmen said.

"And do you know where he parked it?"

All four shrugged.

Yeah. There was a house in Oakhurst and they were probably squatting. Was Manny's missing car parked there now?

"What kind of car did Manny have?" Cole asked, jumping into the questioning for the first time. The car was a tangible thing connected to the dead man and could provide answers.

"A piece-of-shit Plymouth," Oscar said.

"Model?" Signe asked.

"Wind? Storm? Something like that," Carmen said.

"Breeze?" Cole suggested.

"Yeah. That's it."

"Color and year?" Signe asked.

"Green," Reef said. "Course, that could be all the lichen growing on it."

The guys all chuckled at that.

"I think it was a '98 or '99," Tyson said. "Damn, we joke about it, but it was a good car."

"How are you getting back to Oakhurst tonight?"

"If we can't get a ride from other climbers, there's a bus that departs the visitors' center at 7:35."

"I bet that gets pricey," Cole said.

"Fourteen bucks one-way," Reef said. "Per person."

Cole did the math in his head. "Four people that would be . . . a hundred and twelve a day, round trip." A hell of a lot of money for people without a home or income.

Dirtbagging was a hard way to live.

"Soon as my next payday comes, I'm getting a car," Reef said.

Cole had a feeling he knew what Reef was selling and wondered if the house where they squatted was where he grew the weed.

Ironically, Signe Gates was probably the safest reporter in the world for Reef to go on the record with. If the dirtbag knew anything about her, he'd know she'd hung out with more growers and seen more weed—at all stages in the process—than he and his friends could smoke in ten lifetimes.

But if drugs fueled the Oakhurst climbing crew, how did Manny Lontoc fit in? According to Ranger Gus, Lontoc didn't smoke or drink. Of course, selling weed and smoking it were two entirely different things.

"What can you tell us about the last week of Manny's life?" Signe asked.

"We didn't see him much," Carmen said. "At least not during the day. He was here one or two evenings."

"His car broke down," Tyson said. "He did odd jobs in Oakhurst for money to fix it."

"Is his car still in Oakhurst? At a mechanic's?" Cole asked.

Tyson shook his head. "Manny always got parts from junkyards and did his own repairs. I'm pretty sure he got it running again. The last time we saw him, he drove in late in the afternoon and came to Camp 4 just for the campfire."

"How long was this before his body was found?" Signe asked.

"Two days," Carmen said.

"Did he stay late?" Cole asked. Gus had said the singing and Breathalyzer incident had been more than a week before Manny's death.

Reef frowned. "No. He was only with us for about an hour, then he left and didn't come back."

"Did he say where he was going?"

"No," Oscar said. "He didn't say anything. I thought he was just going to the bathroom."

"Was this unusual behavior for him?" Signe asked.

Tyson shrugged. "Sometimes he'd take off if the group was drinking heavily or someone lit up weed. Manny didn't like to rock the boat with rangers and we'd been flagged a week before."

"Do you know where Manny's car is?" Signe asked.

"Probably stolen by whoever killed him," Oscar said.

Signe paused a beat. "Did you tell the rangers investigating his death that you think he was murdered?"

Oscar shrugged. "What investigation? The only question we were asked was, *'Where is his family?'* The minute we said we didn't know, he thanked us for our time and went on his merry way."

"Do you know the name of the ranger you spoke with?"

"Older white dude. Thinks he's our buddy." The others snickered, and Oscar added, "Always insists we call him Ranger Gus."

CHAPTER 12

"I don't get it," Cole said once they were back in the car. "Why would Gus lie to us about investigating when he knew we were going to Camp 4 next?"

Signe had wondered the same thing but had come to a different conclusion, knowing climbers tended to be biased against law enforcement. "I'm not sure he lied. He said he wasn't on the Lontoc investigation, and according to our new friends, he didn't ask any investigative questions. Maybe he assumed they'd all been questioned already."

"Since when do cops only ask about next of kin after a suspicious death?"

"I'm not certain Gus thought it was suspicious. Even you pointed out it might not be. If Gus had been concerned, he probably wouldn't have answered my questions at all, no matter how fond he was of Manny Lontoc."

"And he was just humoring you by answering your questions?"

"Never underestimate the power of free beer and appetizers." She leaned back in the passenger seat, marveling at the fact that it hadn't even registered in the moment that once again she'd gone straight for the passenger side of her car, allowing him to drive to Curry Village. "You were good back there. Keeping the conversation going. Don't be surprised if Oscar shows up at your doorstep looking for a job in the fall."

The guy had been psyched to learn Cole was an archaeologist. Oscar had taken archaeology classes at his community college, hoping to get work as a dig bum, which, like dirtbag, Signe had learned wasn't a pejorative.

Cole proudly had both dirtbag and dig bum on his curriculum vitae.

"He's not really qualified. He doesn't have a degree or field school or other practical experience."

"But you didn't shoot him down."

He flashed her a grin as he pulled into the village parking lot. "I figured you'd have better luck with follow-up questions if he thought I could help him break into the dig-bum network."

"That was considerate of you."

"I aim to please."

He said it without innuendo, but after their conversation in front of Midnight Lightning, she mentally added it.

Did he mean it when he said he wanted in her pants? She shook off the thought. It had been a joke. Nothing more.

She climbed from the car and circled to the hatchback. "We can drive to the loading zone for our campsite to offload."

"Tomorrow morning, everything at the site needs to go with us on our backs. Might as well start now."

She grimaced. She'd been dreading this part. She wasn't concerned about the hiking part—she was in good shape and jogged regularly up and down the hillside from her Redondo Beach house. It was the heavy pack that worried her. She'd never carried this much weight on her back for a lengthy—and uphill—hike. Plus, there would be no comfy bed and shower at the other end.

People did this kind of thing by choice? For *fun*?

Signe had been on some grueling hikes to get to meth labs in California forests, grow sites in Colombia, or narco-trafficker hideouts deep in Central American jungles, but in those instances, the expedition was always for work. Plus, narcos had quads or other vehicles so they could transport their product, so it was rarely a foot-only journey, at least not in both directions. And while she'd made more than a few of those site visits in the middle of the night, she'd never slept in the jungle or spent multiple days there.

The only camping she'd ever done was car camping at campgrounds, usually with bathrooms, showers, firepits, and sometimes even mini-mart grocery stores for last-minute marshmallow shopping. This hike would push her beyond her comfort level.

But then, she'd been living far beyond her comfort level for two years.

"We forgot to pack marshmallows," she murmured as she cinched her sleeping pad to the outside of her large-frame backpack.

Cole said, "Be right back."

She glanced up to see him heading toward the grocery store. It took her a moment to realize he'd heard her mumbled words. "We also need graham crackers. And chocolate."

He nodded without looking back. "Of course."

"And vodka." Surely they'd sell the little bottles they used on airplanes? "And juice boxes!"

He stopped and turned to face her, sporting a slight smile. "Juice boxes?"

"To go with the vodka. I don't care what kind."

"Got it. Anything else?"

Condoms.

The thought caught her off guard. She hadn't even *considered* sex in two years. Why now? She studied Cole and amended the question. *Why him?*

She shook her head. "That should do it. Unless you need more food. I've noticed you eat a *lot*."

He grinned. "I might get a few things if the marshmallows don't take up too much room in the bear canisters."

"Thankfully, squashed marshmallows taste fine in s'mores."

He nodded and disappeared into the store.

She resumed assembling her pack. Her phone buzzed and she pulled it out. A text message from a five-digit number. Different from the last one.

28907: You going to fuck him tonight?

28907: He won't give it to you like I did.

A ten-second audio recording came next. She stared at her screen, her chest heaving as she tried to take in air that was suddenly thick and probably lacked oxygen. Her finger shook as she hit the right-pointing triangle to play the MP3 file.

A scream of what sounded like pleasure emitted from her phone. The sound pitched higher, transforming into a scream of terror and a cry for help.

The voice was unmistakably her own.

CHAPTER 13

She set the phone in the back of the car and continued assembling her pack as if her hands weren't shaking and her heart wasn't pounding. She had no doubt the bastard was watching. She couldn't let him see how he'd affected her, no matter how much she wanted to fall apart.

She controlled her breathing, inhaling deep through the nose and expelling with her mouth. This kept panicked tears at bay as she grappled for control of a body that wanted to choose flight over fight.

There was no place she could flee.

She'd answered DiscoFever's call to meet with someone who knew what had happened to her, and clearly, her attackers knew it.

The sun emoji included in the texts she'd received at Glacier Point couldn't be random, and only one of her rapists—or someone who'd seen the video—would know to use it. But it was the audio clip of her scream that truly sent her into flight mode.

They had the video.

Was this a threat to use it? Publish it to a porn site?

She'd monitored porn sites regularly, making sure no one was monetizing her rape. She couldn't search all the corners of the dark web, though, and there was always the chance people who had nothing to do with her abduction had copies.

Still, none of those people would have motive to stalk her in the park. These texts came from someone involved in her lost hours. But they weren't trying to stop her from entering the forest.

If they didn't want her to meet the informant—if they even knew that was her end goal—they would simply threaten another informant she'd revealed. Or Leo. Or Steven.

Strangely, these thoughts calmed her.

They aren't trying to stop me. Just scare me.

Again, her thoughts turned to her partner in this venture. Cole hadn't been with her either time the creep had messaged her.

He was built like a linebacker, but surely he wasn't one of the men on the video. Odds were she'd see him shirtless at some point in the coming days, exposing a damning scar or tattoo if he had one or the other.

Plus, she couldn't even begin to imagine how an archaeologist with dreams of being the next Josh Gates would be involved in what happened to her. Still, ruling him out could be a mammoth mistake. After all, she'd trusted Roman without question and now she didn't know what to believe.

She got herself under control and by the time Cole returned, she was sitting on her rear bumper in the shade of the open hatchback, drinking the last soda from the cooler as if her world hadn't been totally upended in his short absence.

She studied his face as he approached.

She could read criminals. Knew them better than anyone. But what did she know about the men who populated her professional world? She'd had faith in Roman. But really, now she had to wonder if he was less forthcoming than the criminals she interviewed.

When a kingpin tells you he considered stealing your equipment and leaving you for dead in the desert, he was being scary but honest. Did she get more truth from her criminal interview subjects than she did from the men she worked with every day?

Gear loaded on their backs, Signe followed Cole down the path to the campsite they'd claimed earlier. He came to an abrupt stop. Momentum combined with the unaccustomed weight on her back caused her to crash into his jutting pack. She rebounded, but her center of balance was thrown off and she windmilled her arms, trying to stay upright as the pack pulled her down.

Cole twisted and grabbed, dragging her to his chest, halting her fall.

His big hands gripped the padded shoulder straps, holding her in place. His large body blocked her view of whatever had caused him to stop short to begin with.

He closed his eyes and took a deep breath. When he opened them again, his warm brown eyes probed her face, his expression showing anger and concern. "I have a feeling whoever did this—Roman?—is watching. Hoping to get a thrill from your reaction."

"What's wrong?"

"Our tent has been slashed to pieces."

Maybe they are *trying to stop me from entering the backwoods.*

But no. This was just another scare tactic, and an obvious one at that. "Should we head back to the Mountain Shop and see if they sell tents?"

He shook his head. "Once we're out of the valley, I wasn't planning to use a tent anyway."

"And tonight? I don't think I'd be comfortable sleeping out in the open in the campground. Not when someone already slashed one tent."

"You get the tent. I'll sleep outside the door to protect my fair lady."

She couldn't help but smile at the image. She *would* sleep better knowing he was on guard duty. "My dirtbag knight."

"Shh. Don't tell Gus." He paused. "Well, unless you want to report the vandalism?"

She frowned, considering. "No. We won't get answers, and all it will mean is questions on exactly why we're here."

He nodded. "All right then. Let's set up our camp and have dinner. I'm feeling peckish and I think we both could use a drink."

CHAPTER 14

Signe plopped down on the inflatable sleeping pad that clipped together on the sides to make a chair and let out a sigh as Cole set a match to the fire he'd carefully constructed while she assembled their remaining tent.

The kindling lit and Cole added larger pieces of wood with practiced skill. In minutes, they had a respectable campfire in the protected ring.

He settled in his own seat and they stared at the flames in silence. In all likelihood, this would be their only campfire, as they could have fires in the backcountry only in established rings, and staying on well-traveled paths didn't feel safe given that someone was already stalking them in the valley.

"What am I going to do about Roman?" she said, breaking the silence.

"Wiley's nephew?"

She nodded. "Yes, the big boss's nephew."

"How much of Season Two have you filmed?"

"We've got most of two episodes in the bag. We're about half-done with the artifact-trafficking one—Singapore is only about a third of it—I have all the rushes. I don't need him to edit but I'd need *someone* skilled in that area. The other five episodes we've started to one degree or another but they involve travel that we haven't even scheduled yet."

"Can you use what you've filmed with him even if he's no longer part of the show? Who owns the intellectual property on the work that's complete?"

"He's work for hire for me. I'm the executive producer with final cut. However, the work he's edited already . . . my attorney will have to look at his contract. We'll also have to go over my TWN contract. It could get ugly with Uncle Ben."

"He might be innocent, you know. Could be a coincidence."

"Explain the woman who filmed him. Or why he didn't reach out. He knew I was going to be in the park. He was the first person I asked to join me."

"I'm crushed I wasn't your first choice."

"I didn't even know you existed when I called Roman."

"Weak excuse. You should be clairvoyant. But back to your initial question, it's possible his ankle wasn't as bad as he'd feared and so he decided to take a last-minute vacay, but he knows his boss will be in the area. Last thing he wants to do is call and get roped into working."

"'Kay. Now explain the woman who grabbed the camera and filmed him."

"Someone is setting you up? Maybe they're setting him up too."

She considered the possibility and hoped it was true, but Cole didn't know about Bastille Day. Nor did he know about the texts she'd received today.

Unless, of course, he was the one who'd sent them.

How many men would betray her before this was all done?

She yanked her thoughts back to Roman. She'd been in final negotiations with TWN when Leo left her, and the TWN head of programming, Ben Wiley, had suggested his nephew. She'd viewed Roman's body of work before meeting with him, and they'd clicked immediately.

Working with him had been easy from the start, and she'd felt so damn lucky to have replaced Leo so quickly.

117

Now she had to wonder if Roman—and even Ben—was involved in what happened to her. But why and how? Nothing made sense.

She stared into the orange flames that licked at the firewood Cole had purchased in Curry Village. Her brain was on overload and she hadn't even begun to process the purpose of the horrific texts she'd received. "I think we should start with s'mores. Then move on to vodka. Then dinner."

Cole snickered. "Now who needs to be told to eat her vegetables?"

"If you got tomato juice, we can start with the vodka. There. Vegetables."

"Technically, tomatoes are fruit."

"That leaves no choice but to start with chocolate. Cacao is a bean."

"I can't argue with that."

She pumped her fist in victory. "Finally."

Cole raided the bear box where they'd stored the food and came back with graham crackers, marshmallows, and squares of dark chocolate. It pleased her that he had gone for the costlier, higher-quality chocolate. If she was going to indulge in a messy, sticky, melty treat, might as well have the best.

She scrounged a stick from beneath a nearby tree and plucked her pocketknife from her backpack, then quickly whittled a point at the end.

"Ah. So you have camped before," Cole said approvingly when she presented her stick for its marshmallow sacrifice.

"I have camped," she confirmed. "But it's always been car camping, with the big, green two-burner propane stove; a selection of metal enameled dishes; cutting boards and dishwashing tubs. My mom always said if she had to cook in the forest, at least she'd have proper tools and the ability to clean up so no one would get sick."

"Where did you camp?"

"Usually on a lake or a river. Sometimes the lake or river was deep in a mountain forest, other times near the coast. Our days were spent playing in the water or tag and four square or whatever games were part of the campground's entertainment for kids."

"You have siblings?"

"No. I always played with the other kids at the campground." She turned her focus to him. She still didn't know much of anything about him. "How about you? Any siblings?"

He shook his head.

For a guy who wanted to be on TV, he was strangely reluctant to talk about himself. If he hadn't introduced her to Wanda, she'd know nothing except his current work for Leo—which she'd rudely interrupted. "Okay then. Tell me about your friend with the *Notting Hill* advice."

He startled. "Ja-hhax . . . ?" His voice trailed off, then he added, "Why do you ask?"

"I don't know. Making conversation. Is Jax an archaeologist? Does he have other pearls of wisdom to offer men who want to score?"

Cole let out an almost bitter-sounding laugh. "No, not an archaeologist. And no. That was his only advice. He wasn't much of a player."

"You slipped into past tense. Is he married now?"

"Dead." The word was flat and cold. He set down his knife and inspected the point of his stick, then planted a marshmallow on the end.

"I'm sorry."

He nodded and extended the stick until the soft white cylinder was close to but not touching the embers that glowed bright orange on the underside of the largest log. His gaze fixed on the stick and task at hand as he murmured, "He would have enjoyed this. He loved the outdoors. Hiking, rafting, climbing."

She wondered if Jax had been a dirtbagger with Cole. "What happened?"

He shook his head. "I don't want to talk about him."

She had to respect his boundary even though the reporter in her had been awakened and now was practically bouncing with the desire to ask follow-up questions. She wanted to *know* Cole. And pondering his pain would be so much better than analyzing the mess she was in, and the danger she could be leading him into.

◆ ◆ ◆

Sleep didn't come easily for Cole, even though he was armed and more dangerous than Signe or anyone involved in this mess suspected.

Her question about Jasper had rattled him. For the first time, he wondered if she somehow knew. He'd screwed up royally when he almost said his name.

He mulled all that had happened. The slashed tent was a deterrent. Someone wanted Signe to back out of going to the rendezvous, but they were stopping short of physically preventing her. Was it because she wasn't alone?

His first guess would be Leo, because using logic had failed to sway his ex-wife to stay home.

Cole mulled Leo's second edict. Why *that* of all things?

In the last twenty-four hours, Cole had made one important mental shift. He was no longer pissed at Leo for sending him on this assignment, even though it had messed with the schedule. In fact, he was now certain this was where he needed to be. The answers he needed were here, with Signe.

His boss would have to let him back in the fold if he delivered Signe Gates.

Once he did that, there would be no more threat and he could get back to his life of dealing in trafficked artifacts and drugs.

CHAPTER 15

Even before the morning sun reached the valley floor, the tent grew hot. Signe groaned as she squeezed her eyes tight against the bright morning light. Her back ached from sleeping on a thin pad, sweat drenched her body, and she had a headache.

On the plus side, this is probably the best I'll feel all day . . .

She groaned again at the cynical but absolutely true prediction.

See, Cole, I can be clairvoyant.

Outside the tent, an upbeat voice said, "Sounds like someone isn't excited to greet the day." His peppy tone made the morning worse.

"What's there to be excited about?"

The tent unzipped and a muscled arm extended through the small opening with a travel mug clutched in his big hand. The aroma of hot coffee filled the tent. "This."

She rubbed her sleepy eyes just to make sure she wasn't having a visual and olfactory hallucination. Okay, she could tolerate his chipper attitude if it meant hot coffee delivered to her in bed. Or, rather, sleeping bag.

She plucked the warm mug from the extended hand and breathed deeply to take in the scent before enjoying her first sip. "How did you make coffee without waking me?"

"I walked to the Curry Village store."

She unzipped the side of her sleeping bag and scooted toward the door, then poked her head through the opening. "Clever. And thank you."

Cole was fully dressed and sitting in his camp chair, drinking his own mug of coffee. "You're welcome." He handed her a paper bag. "I also got breakfast."

She peeked inside to find a hot breakfast burrito. Knowing they'd be eating dehydrated everything for the next few days, this was a major treat. "Hiring you to be my guide was brilliant on my part. I'm quite pleased with myself."

He grinned and sipped his coffee.

She sat in the tent opening with her legs stretched out before her and set her coffee on the ground in front of the tent as she dug into the burrito, relishing it like a condemned person might savor their last meal.

She knew why he'd gone to the store for a hot breakfast. He'd lectured her on how important it would be to eat so she'd have calories to burn while they hiked. "What is our elevation gain going to be today?"

"Two thousand seven hundred feet, give or take." He paused, then added, almost reluctantly, "We'll climb that in two point six miles."

"Is that steep?"

"Very. It's probably the most grueling trail in Yosemite. There's a reason passes were still available in the middle of high season."

She let out a soft whimper. "Probably good you didn't tell me that yesterday."

He shrugged. "It's not like you'd have balked."

He was right about that. She'd do whatever it took to reach the rendezvous in time. "I'm pretty sure I'm going to be happier after it's done than actually doing it."

"The hike has stunning views of Tenaya Canyon and Half Dome. You might be surprised by how much you enjoy it."

It was hard to imagine enjoying anything about this. But she reminded herself that Glacier Point was majestic. Now she'd get the view from the opposite side of the canyon.

Her phone chimed, causing her to jolt.

She let out a breath and said, "Here we go."

She checked the screen and confirmed the text was from DiscoFever, complete with the disco-ball emoji. The coordinates for their meeting and a repeat of the time. Eleven a.m. on Friday.

Cole took a photo of her screen and wrote down the numbers. He then punched the coordinates into the GPS. After a moment, he let out a low whistle. "Good thing we've already got breakfast. Given that we have to start with Snow Creek Trail, we'll be too tired to cover a lot of ground once we reach the top. Which means we'll have to make up the distance tomorrow. Today we go up. Tomorrow across. We can save the last three miles or so for Friday morning."

He paused, staring at the screen. "Honestly, I bet that's why the meet time was changed. It would be impossible to get to the meet point tomorrow morning on foot, even if we'd started yesterday afternoon. If we were camping in one of the grounds off Tioga Road, it would be easy, but those don't open until next week."

"But it's doable from here, taking Snow Creek Trail?"

He nodded. "It won't be easy, but we can do it."

Somewhere past nine a.m., Signe found herself wondering at what point today she'd reach peak misery. They were still in the shade, but that would change soon. The trail was uneven, littered with rocks and roots that meant every foot had to be placed carefully. She'd left the sport sandals she'd worn yesterday in the car and was now wearing rugged leather hiking boots that prevented her from twisting an ankle more than once as they climbed.

The path ahead consisted of dozens of switchbacks to navigate before they reached the top of the ridge.

Dozens. *Plural.*

Still, this wide, forested section of trail was a slice of heaven compared to what they'd face in the next twenty minutes or so.

"You're doing great, Sig," Cole said from behind her.

She grunted a response. He was being encouraging and positive and she hated that it was so clear she needed bolstering.

It had taken less than twenty minutes for them to realize Signe needed to take the lead on their hike, because the pace Cole set naturally was too fast for her short legs. Two steps for him was four for her.

She reached the corner of the wide switchback and took a small sip of water, just enough to see her through the next stretch. When they reached the Snow Creek footbridge at the zenith, they could refill their water bottles. Until then, she needed to ration.

"Do people really do this for fun?" she asked, causing a group of hikers who took the opportunity to pass the slowpoke short woman on the inside curve to laugh.

A tall man who probably could make it up the mountain in only a hundred strides said, "Wait until you see the view. It'll be worth it."

"I still have my View-Master from when I was ten. I've seen it."

The man laughed again and said, "See you at the top, where you will change your tune."

He and his buddies continued up the slope like they were on Jet Skis.

Cole's face was lit with humor. "He's right. The view will blow your mind."

"My mind is fine without being blown, thank you."

"You'll feel different when you see it."

He was right, dammit, and it didn't even take reaching the top to come to that conclusion. They were probably halfway up when they were able to pause in an area with spectacular views of the canyon.

There was Half Dome from a different angle. Even better than when they'd viewed it this morning from below at Mirror Lake, near the Snow Creek trailhead.

They were almost eye to eye with Half Dome now, and from the top, it would be similar to the view from Glacier Point, except closer and across a different valley.

She drank her water and looked across Tenaya Canyon and reminded herself to take in this moment. She might join the hundreds of others who'd died in this park. This could be one of her last days on Earth.

The least she could do was enjoy the damn view.

Not surprisingly, the thought wasn't comforting. What had her informant, Muriel Klein, done in her last days? Or Jasper Evans? Had he kissed anyone goodbye the morning he'd been taken?

She huffed out a breath. She'd committed a deadly sin of journalism: *Thou shalt not burn a source.* It didn't matter that she'd been drugged out of her mind. The guilt still pressed on her.

They would always follow through.

"You need to eat," Cole said, holding out apple and cheese slices.

She took his offering with a murmured thanks and ate without conscious thought. The crunch of the apple and sharpness of the cheese barely registering as she once again pondered which crime lord she'd interviewed had ordered her abduction. Counterfeiter? Meth manufacturer? Pimp?

Some diversified and had a stake in multiple black markets.

She needed to identify the crime lord so she could figure out how to expose him. She had no doubt it was a man. Men used rape as a weapon.

And only a man would send texts taunting her with the violation of her body.

If this expedition failed to give answers, what would she do? All she knew was she couldn't live in this state of waiting, wondering when the knife would be twisted for the last time. Unable to make friends or find a new lover for fear they'd become a target.

How many informants had she compromised? Five? A dozen? All of them?

She only knew about two for certain: Jasper and Muriel.

She shook her head. If she didn't get her bleak thoughts under control by the time she finished this little hiking break, she'd be planning what to wear in her casket.

Except, really, she'd prefer to be cremated, so what to wear to the funeral pyre was the more pressing issue.

Leo had always said she looked good in blue. Ocean blue, navy blue, periwinkle, or sky . . . it didn't matter. Maybe she'd wear the peacock dress. Yes. She'd have that detail added to her will.

"What in the world are you thinking about?" Cole asked.

She startled at the question, like she'd come up for air. Good lord. It was like she'd forgotten where she was and who she was with. Unable to think of a proper reply, she went with the truth. "I was planning my funeral."

"That's . . . pretty dark for a snack break in the midst of a glacially carved wonder."

"Well, technically, it wasn't my funeral, it was my funeral pyre, and which dress I'd like to be burned in."

"That changes nothing about my assessment."

She felt her eyes burn with tears and wondered where the hell they came from. What was wrong with her?

But she knew. It had been nagging at her subconscious since Sunday morning.

The horrible truth she didn't want to face: she'd never be able to clear her name.

No one will ever believe me.

There was no way DiscoFever or whoever was at the end of this journey could have proof that exonerated her. The videos would be released and the truth of what she'd done would come out.

One thing she hadn't delved into was *why* DiscoFever had chosen Yosemite. Of all the places in the world for a meet spot, why here?

The hoops required were impressive—backcountry permits and rules for where to camp the first night. Vehicles could only go so far. There was logic to it all, but the climber's death . . . was it just a red herring?

What did a dirtbag have to do with her lost hours?

She'd accepted the final destination without questioning it. She'd believed Manny Lontoc's and John Doe's role would make sense once she had more pieces to the puzzle.

She'd embarked on this journey without hesitation, illogically hoping she'd find something here that would set her free. Worse, she'd forced Cole Banner to accompany her as she willingly walked into what could well be a trap.

And that was the truth that settled into her gut now. This was a trap, but nothing would stop her from going full steam ahead into the open jaws. It was one thing for her to make that choice, and quite another to demand it of Cole.

"I'm sending you home," she said softly. "I'm going the rest of the way on my own. Next time I'm in range, I'll text Leo and make sure he knows it's not you, it's me."

"Seriously? *Now* you're done with me? Halfway up the mountain? You know, you're really starting to piss me off."

"Good. It'll be easy for you to leave, then. You can take the bus in the valley with the climbers we met last night."

"It would serve you right if I did abandon you here. What will you do if the GPS cuts out? You know how to navigate by compass? You got a quad map?"

"Why would the GPS cut out?"

"Cloudy day, insufficient power, gets dropped in the water. You name it. *Never* rely on technology alone to save you. Always have old-school backup."

"Then give me your compass and map."

"You know how to wayfind? Triangulate?"

It was true that while she worked for the Wayfinders Institute, she had little clue how to navigate herself. She always relied on guides, security personnel, and informants to set her path and get her to the next meet on time.

"I learned how to use a compass at sleep-away camp in fourth grade just like all the other kids."

"Yeah. That makes you totally ready for the Yosemite backwoods."

"Why are you fighting me on this? I thought you'd be relieved. You can go back and start filming with Leo."

"Relieved to abandon you after one of our tents was slashed last night? After you've been jerked around by the informant with different dates, meeting times, and locations? What kind of asshole do you think I am? Jesus, Signe, do you really believe someone is going to be at the meet point and it won't be a note nailed to a tree that sends you deeper into nowhere?"

"Why do you think I'm sending you home? Because only one of us needs to plan their funeral. You have nothing to do with this. Go home."

"You think this guy might kill you, and you're going anyway?"

She closed her eyes, and the tears that had pooled spilled over her lashes. All she could do was nod as she tried to will the tears away.

Signe Gates does not cry.

She cleared her throat and gave him the only answer she could. "My life is over either way."

"What is this about, Signe?" His voice was a low whisper.

She wanted to tell him. Lord, how she wanted to tell *someone.* Anyone. But the punishment for telling was death.

Signe had gotten only as far as the FBI parking lot when Muriel paid that price.

She swiped her eyes and scooped up her pack. In seconds, she had it settled on her aching shoulders and clipped the straps together. "You'll still be paid the full amount we agreed on and when I get back, I'll call Leo and tell him you were great. Five stars. Would hire again."

She turned toward the next switchback. She'd follow the trail to the footbridge, refill her water bottles, then break out the GPS and plan her route.

From here on out, she'd be on her own. She'd put no one else in danger. Trust no one.

If she came face-to-face with one of the men who'd drugged and raped her, she'd kill him and there'd be no witnesses.

If she'd learned anything in her quick dive into deaths in national parks, it was that Yosemite had lots of options for hiding a body.

The bears could take care of the rest.

CHAPTER 16

Cole couldn't believe she'd ditched him after they'd barely begun the hike. Anger and frustration threatened to boil over. He flexed his fingers, telling himself it would do no good and a lot of damage if he punched a tree.

He didn't know why he was gobsmacked by her decision. He knew something had frightened her yesterday—hours before the tent was slashed, which was alarming in and of itself. But once they'd left the valley, he'd thought it would be smooth sailing. He'd said as much when he texted his report this morning.

He didn't care what Leo thought. It was his other boss he had to consider now.

In the last twenty-four hours, he'd realized Signe—not Leo—might be his ticket back into the fold.

He scanned the trail where she'd disappeared into the woods and debated his options. She didn't want him with her. In general, he didn't believe in forcing himself on women who didn't want his company. But there were exceptions.

He watched the path with the steady trickle of hikers ascending and descending.

His best bet was to wait. Let her think he'd given up, then follow. He had the coordinates and had picked up a GPS unit at the Mountain Shop last night. Same make and model as hers.

He could follow her from a distance. She'd never even know he was there.

Movement down the trail caught his eye. A lone woman came into view as she hiked the steep incline toward him. He frowned, studying her. She looked a lot like Carmen, the climber they'd spoken with last night.

He pulled out his binoculars for a better look. Sure enough, it was the young climber. She spotted him and waved, then broke into a jog.

She came to a halt in front of him. "Oh, thank god I caught you!" She bent over, hands on knees as she wheezed in shallow breaths.

The woman was in good shape—climbing every day did that for a person—but she'd clearly been hiking the steep path at a rapid rate and had jogged uphill the last fifty yards.

Once her breathing was under control, she grabbed the water bottle from her hip holster and took a long drink. "I heard this hike was hard. They weren't kidding."

"We're not even halfway to the top."

"Think I'm gonna pass on that. Planning to climb today."

That made her trek even more curious. "What's up?"

"Where's Signe?"

He nodded toward the switchbacks above them. "Ahead on the trail."

"I need to talk to her."

"About?"

"Last night after I got home . . . I googled her. And saw a photo that made me remember something."

"What?"

"I was . . ." She paused, took a deep breath that had nothing to do with exertion. "I had a thing for Manny. Nothing ever happened between us. There's no reason to tell Reef now that Manny's gone. But I liked him, and so a few times I would . . . follow him when he went off for walks at the end of the day. Look for excuses to have a moment alone with him. One time, I followed him to the restroom and overheard him talking to another guy in his other language. The Filipino one— Tagalog? They were inside the men's room, but I recognized Manny's voice even if I didn't know what he was saying. Anyway, I'm thinking it's possible Manny was talking to the other dead guy Signe asked about."

"You never saw his face?"

"No. Reef walked up and asked why I was skulking by the men's room. I said I had a rock in my shoe and had just paused to get rid of it, then went back to Midnight Lightning."

"How long before his death was this?"

"I'm not sure. Four, five days? It was when his car was broken down because I remember we didn't see him again until we were on the bus to Oakhurst a few hours later."

"And you didn't tell us this last night in front of Reef because you didn't want him to know you were stalking Manny?"

She flinched. "No. I didn't think of it until after I googled Signe and saw a photo of her cameraman. That's when I remembered the last time I followed Manny and saw him talking to Signe's cameraman."

Carmen had his full attention now. "You saw Signe's cameraman in the park a few weeks ago?"

She nodded.

How long had Signe and Roman been in Singapore?

"You're certain?"

"Yeah. It was a few days after I overheard Manny speaking Filipino—er . . . Tagalog?—it was the night he drove into the park in the afternoon and left the campfire without a word. I followed him. I think he was walking to the store, but he was stopped by a guy. I had to keep walking or Manny would know I was following him, so I passed by them on the path."

"Did you hear what they were talking about?"

"No. The man went silent as I walked by. I waved to Manny and pretended I was going to the store myself. Anyway, I was surprised Signe didn't mention her cameraman knew Manny, but seeing his face made me remember both times I followed him. Signe had specifically asked if there was a chance Manny knew the John Doe, so I wanted to find her and tell her what I remembered. I'm glad she's looking into Manny's death. Someone needs to."

"Thanks, Carmen. Appreciate you hiking to find us. You've literally gone more than the extra mile. Uphill."

She shrugged. "I would have called, but Reef had Signe's business card, and when I searched his stuff, I couldn't find it. So I tried to get to the park early enough this morning to tell you before you set off, but . . . I needed to ditch Reef first. Please don't tell him. It was just a stupid crush."

That she worked so hard to convince Cole yet wasn't willing to give Reef even a hint of her mental infidelity made him think it had been much more than a crush. Had she been involved with Manny? Was there more she wasn't telling?

He didn't think he'd get answers if he pushed now, so he chose to stick with his most immediate concern. "I honestly don't care if you were sleeping with him."

Cole considered his options. He needed confirmation of who Carmen had seen on the sidewalk, but he didn't have a photo of Roman on his phone. Plus, Roman might have been in Singapore. But before Roman, Signe had a different cameraman.

"Really, all I care about is knowing who you saw talking to Manny. Was it Roman Wiley or Leo Starr?"

"I don't know. It was the same guy I saw in a photo on Signe's website. He was behind a camera and Signe in front of it."

Cole pulled out his phone. No bars, but he had photos of Leo saved in his research on the documentary producer.

He opened Files and scrolled until he found the press release from TWN that included a photo of Leo behind the camera; it was the same photo that was on Signe's website but with a different crop. "Is this the guy?"

Carmen took the phone in both hands, then met his gaze and slowly nodded.

CHAPTER 17

Every step on the trail sharpened Signe's focus. She would figure out the game plan and turn the tables on the bastards who'd targeted her. It wasn't like she was going to walk out of this forest with a career anyway.

Once she'd settled on the idea of killing whoever was waiting for her in the backcountry, breathing had come easier. Her steps were lighter. It was like the pack she carried weighed nothing at all. And it didn't—not when compared to the nightmare that had weighed her down for two years.

She'd be free in two days.

Forty-eight hours. The same amount of time she'd lost.

She wished she'd changed her will before setting out. Right now, everything would revert to Leo because she had no one else. But if she could choose today, she'd give it all to Cole.

He made just as much sense as any random person, and more sense than Leo. After all, he didn't even want to be here, but he'd shown up while Leo stayed home in his safe little condo.

Maybe she could record a last will and testament on her phone.

She stopped in her tracks.

Would a cell phone will be valid in a court of law? Her phone was the most secure phone on the planet with the microphone and camera kill switch and thumb and face recognition. She could make a video will here and now.

She could change her lock-screen image to the combination of the safe in the Redondo Beach house that held all her passwords so if something happened to her, all her accounts would be accessible.

Still, she shouldn't plan to die. If she killed whoever was waiting for her at the end of the trail, she needed to make the death look like an accident. Accidents happened all the time in Yosemite.

That would give her time to return to her life, sell the house, and then disappear.

She'd have to hope the cartel behind her abduction didn't figure out she'd killed one of their own, or she'd spend the rest of her days dodging assassins.

Murder for hire was another crime she hadn't managed to do a report on. Like human trafficking, it wasn't something people were willing to discuss in front of a camera.

She imagined having an assassin show up at the Redondo Beach house and then asking them if they'd be willing to do a quick interview before offing her. It would be a hell of an exit from her career.

She might even get a posthumous Peabody.

She let out a grim laugh and resumed walking. One foot in front of the other.

Tears leaked from the corners of her eyes. Subconsciously, that was probably why she'd sent Cole away. She knew this breakdown was coming and wanted no witnesses.

She'd dreamed of being an investigative reporter since she was a teen. Everything she'd done was in service to her career. To share the knowledge she learned about how crime worked. To shine a light on the systemic causes. To give voice to victims. To show the cracks in society that spawned criminal behavior.

It was never her job to do the work of law enforcement, so she'd protected her informants. Protected all her sources. She conducted her interviews with empathy, giving criminals their say without judgment.

And then one of those bastards had trapped her. Scooped her up when she was unprotected and forced her to violate the first rule of investigative reporting: protect your sources.

She was good at her job and Leo had been a big part of that. He'd financed her long-form documentaries when she couldn't get a news channel to fund the multiyear investigations. The story she'd done on fake charities to line the pockets of wealthy grifters had been nominated for all the big awards. It had been Leo's first major documentary as executive producer. He'd had minimal outside financing. The seventy-five-minute show had boosted both his and Signe's visibility.

They'd been a team. But it was his financing that had put them on the map, she couldn't deny that. Had she overlooked the power he held over her career because she wanted his financing? Would she have fallen in love with him without his money?

It was rather late in the game to be asking that question.

Why had it even occurred to her now? What did Leo have to do with anything? He'd dumped her after she told him about the worst thing that had ever happened to her. He'd made it about him and said she'd cheated.

Her tears dried up as the rage, shock, and horror surged. She'd been violated and brutalized. Had shown him the scars she'd kept hidden, and he'd called her a whore.

Signe knew and respected sex workers, who faced danger every day. Leo using the word *whore* as a slur was a deliberate jab at everything she believed in.

He'd asked her if she'd done it because she wanted to better understand sex traffickers and their victims. If she'd gotten too close to the story and decided to insert herself into the narrative.

Like a vice cop who became a junkie.

She'd slapped him and didn't even regret it. She'd never in a million years thought she could be reduced to violence against the man she loved, but she'd never imagined him saying something so terrible.

After seven years of marriage and a decade of working together, he'd known her body and soul, yet he took one look at the scars she'd kept hidden for six months and still hadn't believed her story.

Powered by anger, she climbed one steep switchback after another, moving faster now.

She didn't see the rocks or trees or even smell the wildfire smoke that tainted the air. No. In her mind, she was standing in an entryway, trying to decide if she should step into the room.

Don't do it. Leave Oakhurst. Go home.

But Past Signe couldn't hear the warnings from the woman she would become.

CHAPTER 18

Oakhurst, California
Two years ago

At three o'clock on a weekday, the hotel bar was quiet. A couple sat in a booth in the darkest back corner. A lone man at the bar. The bartender's gaze fixed on a TV showing footage from the Tour de France.

Signe stood in the entryway, trying to decide if she wanted a drink or if she should just head up to her room to sulk. She huffed out a breath and checked her phone again, rereading the message.

Leo: Sorry. Big find. We'll continue filming through the weekend. Won't be able to make it to Oakhurst until next week.

On the surface, his excuse for missing their planned romantic getaway was reasonable. They'd had to switch up the schedule when there'd been a wildfire that had delayed the fieldwork for the archaeology of Mount Shasta documentary. But . . . Leo wasn't the cameraman, he was the executive producer. He didn't *have* to be on-site every day when most of the time the documentary crew was just filming raw footage of digging square holes.

They'd planned this getaway because they'd had almost zero time together for the last six months, as he worked on other projects and Signe freelanced for Nat Geo while she waited to hear from TWN about the pilot for *Crime Lords*.

When a source requested a meet in Oakhurst a few days after a break in Leo's filming schedule, it had felt like kismet. She and Leo would have a few days together before they'd meet with the new informant. Then Leo would return to Mount Shasta.

She'd mortgaged her left kidney to secure a last-minute reservation at the Wawona Hotel inside Yosemite National Park for three days, starting tomorrow, and had arrived in Oakhurst a day early because she'd been filming a news segment in Fresno about a Mexican weed grow operation and it made more sense to drive an hour north than it did to go home to Redondo Beach for a day before returning for a rendezvous with her absentee husband.

She'd been so looking forward to having a few days off with Leo. That their hotel room was in a historic hotel in a beautiful park was merely a perk. It was Leo who'd requested the Wawona. She'd have been happy with a crappy roadside motel as long as she could be with him.

She was having a hard time remembering the last time they'd had sex. She missed sex. But more than that, she missed Leo. His laugh. His smile. Their late-night conversations.

Leo stimulated her brain like no one else ever had, and the last six months of them working separately had been harder than she'd imagined it could be. Worse, even, because she suspected he was sleeping with someone working on the archaeology documentary.

She didn't for a minute believe he needed to stick around for filming these next three days. No find was so big that it couldn't be filmed without Leo's constant input.

Her executive producer husband had found a new woman to feature in his documentaries and was replacing Signe with someone younger and more exciting. She didn't know if she should fight for her marriage or walk away.

Their nearly ten-year collaboration and professional association was only part of it. There was also the simple fact that she loved Leo.

But dammit. He was probably fucking another woman, saying to her the things he'd said to Signe all those years ago when their relationship was new and sparkled like glitter on a Christmas ornament.

She'd forgotten that glitter was also insidious evil that clung to anything it touched and refused to go away even long after the ornaments were packed up for next year.

Was Signe glitter in Leo's life, clinging long after the celebration was over?

No, dammit.

They'd made *vows*. And Leo was breaking them.

She crossed the threshold and entered the bar, reminding herself with each step that she *could* be wrong. She had no proof. Just gut instinct.

Instinct and enough knowledge of his work to know that he didn't need to be on-site right now. He was making a choice in standing her up.

She sat on the barstool.

The last time he'd canceled on her and extended a work trip, when he got home he hadn't loaded any files onto their server. He *always* backed up his files to the home drives. They had massive storage and a quadruple backup system that was fully enclosed and unhackable.

In her line of work, this was vital, and there was no reason for him to avoid backing up his files at home. Unless there was something he didn't want her to see.

Or, more likely, he hadn't been filming at all.

The bartender approached and she considered her options. She ended up choosing a margarita because it was happy hour and she'd get two. She had a room in the hotel, no need to drive until tomorrow morning, when she'd go to the Wawona for a decidedly lonely romantic getaway.

Tequila usually gave her a headache, but she didn't care. She could get plowed tonight and it wouldn't matter.

She glanced across the bar and met the gaze of the lone drinker. He was big. Broad-shouldered. Handsome.

He smiled at her and cocked his head in question.

She shifted her gaze to the bartender as he placed the icy green salt-rimmed glasses before her. Both drinks were huge.

Gigantic, even. Like the attractive man at the far end of the bar.

Her headache tomorrow would be massive.

She raised the drink and took a salty sip. The flavor brought with it memories of a honeymoon with lazy days on the beach and cocktails delivered by men in tuxedos to their private cabana.

It wasn't her preferred type of vacation, but Leo had wanted it and she'd ended up enjoying the quiet laziness more than she'd imagined.

Leo had shocked her by insisting on sex in the cabana, and she'd surprised herself by enjoying the risk of being observed.

She hadn't even been marginally famous then, so sex in a public place hadn't been nearly as risky as it would be now. Not that she was famous now, but she was known in circles. She had a fan base. She received her share of rape and death threats. The life of an outspoken woman in the era of social media.

These thoughts flooded her with the taste of lime, salt, and tequila.

She took a second sip, hoping more would quash the memories and replace them with today.

Did she want to forget her honeymoon?

If Leo was fucking another woman right this moment . . . well, yeah.

The lone man picked up his drink and walked the length of the bar until he was by her side. He raised a brow and asked, "Seat taken?"

She debated but then raised her left hand, flashing her plain wedding band—she didn't wear diamonds when meeting with informants—and said, "If you're looking for a hookup, it's not going to happen."

His smile deepened as he lowered his huge frame onto the barstool next to her. "Just looking for conversation."

She snorted. He'd been checking her out rather blatantly. "Right."

He shrugged. "I wouldn't say no if you changed your mind, but I can be content with conversation."

"Fine. We can talk until someone open to your attention shows up."

He smiled and signaled for the bartender to bring him another drink.

Signe's head hurt. It might even be the worst headache of her life. Was this a migraine? She'd never suffered one before but could easily believe this was the kind of pain she'd heard about.

The room—when she managed to open her eyes the tiniest bit—was dark, but light seeped around the drawn shades.

Was she in her hotel room?

How did she get here?

Her brain throbbed in agony as she searched her memory. Was this the Wawona? If so, how—and when—did she get here?

She'd been planning a getaway with Leo. Before the meet with the informant. Disco . . . something. They were a trafficking victim. Sex . . . or maybe labor? Or they weren't a victim at all but someone who worked at the lowest level of the crime pyramid.

She shook her head, trying to force the memory. She groaned as the slight movement sent daggers of pain along her occipital nerve.

How much did she have to drink last night?

She tried to move her hand so she could cradle her head and met resistance. Her brain couldn't process. Why couldn't she move?

And then she realized her wrists were tied to something. Separate corners of the bed?

Legs too.

All at once, the truth flooded her. She was tied spread-eagle to a bed.

She twisted to test the bonds. Pain that had been masked by the nightmare going on in her head reared up, making it known that her entire body hurt.

Fire seared along her inner thighs.

She was bruised. Beaten. Sore.

She tilted her pelvis as much as her bindings would allow and felt the soreness in her hips and butt. Burning pain in and around her vagina.

No. No. No. NO. NO. NO NO NONO . . .

Vague memories assaulted her. Men—plural—between her legs. And elsewhere. Forcing their penises inside her. Everywhere.

She groaned and the sound came out hoarse. Her throat ached. From screaming.

A sob escaped. She was still tied up. They'd be back. They'd repeat what they'd done.

How did she get here?

Again, she searched her memory.

The bar. Leo canceled on her. Probably cheating.

Two margaritas and a handsome man named . . . Stone? Rocky? Something like that.

Had he roofied her? Was he one of the men who raped her?

Probably yes to both.

Her breathing came in shallow as she struggled against the bonds and tried to remember.

How long had she been here?

Worse, what came next? Were they going to kill her? Drug her again? Rape her again?

Sticky fluid between her legs could be semen or blood. Probably both.

Nausea surged. She twisted to the side in case she puked. Tied as she was, she could aspirate her own vomit if she wasn't careful.

She forced herself to take slow, deep breaths. She needed to get her panic under control if she was going to find a way out of this.

What did she know about her situation? She was in a hotel room. It was dark, but there was light around the edges of the blinds. It was daytime.

She'd entered the bar midafternoon on a weekday. Hours had to have passed for the drugs to have worn off, so it must be at least the next day, but more days might have passed.

The room smelled of sweat, sex, and blood.

Her stomach roiled again and this time she couldn't stop herself. She heaved. Bile surged and splattered the pillow, the putrid fluid dribbled down her cheek.

At least it masked the scent of semen.

She heaved again and more bile ejected from her esophagus. She had nothing substantial in her stomach to heave. When was the last time she'd eaten or drunk?

Had it been days?

She let out a small sob.

A circle of green light flashed at the foot of the bed. She heard a long tone followed by a distorted voice. "Hello, Signe."

She studied the light and tried to decipher what was happening. And then she recognized it for what it was. One of those assistive devices that played music and turned on lights. It was on the dresser. Someone was using it as an intercom.

Should she answer?

"We know you're awake. You just vomited."

Oh god. There were cameras in the room. Probably everything that had happened to her on this bed had been recorded.

Again, she retched. There was no bile left to spew, so it was a dry heave.

The voice said the wake word for the device through which it was speaking and turned on a small projector she hadn't realized was mounted to a tripod to the right of the bed. The projector went through its power-up routine, then landed on the home screen with a list of apps for viewing streaming content. With more commands from the distorted voice, an app that played MP4 files opened. The voice named a file to play.

The image was projected on the bare wall above the small TV that sat on the dresser opposite the bed.

Signe guessed cheap motel art had been removed to make room for the projected image. The camera was off-center, projecting at an angle. The distorted image was shorter on the left than the right. The lines of the bland, beige-striped wallpaper gave an eerie texture to the scene.

But she didn't need perfect perspective and a clean backdrop to understand what she was seeing.

There she was, sitting at a table in another room, her eyes a bit glazed—but it was hard to tell with the distorted view—talking to someone who was just off camera.

There was no sound, but her mouth moved. There was a cadence to it, her responding to the person who was visible only when they lifted a cocktail glass to take a drink.

The hand was large and masculine.

All of a sudden, the sound came on, and Signe heard her own voice clearly say, "That's Jasper Evans. He's an undercover agent for the FBI."

The pain in her head exploded.

No. No. No. She hadn't burned Jasper.

Hadn't revealed his real name to a crime lord.

NO.

But clearly, she had. There she was, on-screen, doing exactly that.

She'd been drugged, but it was hard to know if it would be clear to other viewers. Her voice wasn't slurred or hesitant, just a little flat. She didn't look like she was in any sort of trance, but the distortion could hide that.

Regardless, there were those who would never believe her. Not when stacks of hundred-dollar bills were slid across the table and she reached out and stroked the nearest pile, thumbing the edge to fan it like it was a familiar act.

She had, in fact, done that when she filmed a segment on counterfeiting and the man she interviewed invited her to touch the merchandise and tell him if she could tell the difference between the real and fake stacks before her.

In her drugged state, had she mentally returned to that touch test and repeated it?

Regardless of what had been going on in her mind at the time, this video made it look like she'd been paid several thousand dollars for the name of an undercover FBI agent.

CHAPTER 19

Signe reached the top of the last switchback. She'd been so lost in her miserable thoughts, she'd finished the relentless climb in something of a daze. Rendering the sense of accomplishment of reaching the summit totally wasted on her.

Yesterday, she'd stood at Glacier Point and spoken to the camera about not being human if she didn't pause to take in the magnificent view. Now, she trudged toward the overlook that would give her a glimpse of the valley from the other side, where she could wave to tourists at Glacier Point, and the sense of wonder she should feel had been crushed by the weight of fear and sorrow.

Jasper Evans had been a good man. Risking his life every day in an effort to remove drugs and guns from the streets and put the men she interviewed out of business.

As a general rule, people who worked for the FBI weren't friendly with her. They wanted the intel she had, but as a journalist, she was ethically bound to protect her sources.

She'd made her name in the business because she'd refused to give up a source when a judge ordered her jailed to intimidate her into backing off investigating the sexual harassment allegations against him.

Nine years later and she was still that reporter who'd go to jail before compromising a source.

Except that wasn't true. Two years ago, she'd watched a video in which she was drugged out of her mind and revealed the name of a deeply embedded undercover FBI agent and appeared to accept money for it.

Now she sat on a rock that overlooked the magnificent display of glacially carved granite and didn't see the beauty of it. In her mind, she was back in that hotel room as a distorted voice told her she'd revealed more than the FBI agent's identity. Other sources had been compromised too.

The message was clear: *I own you now. You will do what I say.*

And the first order of business was to tell her that she couldn't reveal anything that had happened over the past forty-eight hours to anyone. Not even to her husband.

One word and the named informants would die.

Her husband would die.

She would be exposed for selling information to a crime lord. She would lose her career and reputation.

She'd go to prison.

And lest she not believe they were serious, she needed to see another video.

Strapped to the bed in that hotel room, she witnessed a new horror: Jasper Evans tied to a chair, a heavy chain wielded like a whip lashing repeatedly at his head and torso. He screamed until he lost consciousness.

Stripes of red opened on his face, neck, and arms.

She'd dry heaved again and again, her body producing nothing to foul the sheets she was strapped to.

Next, they showed her video of Leo entering the Wawona Hotel.

He'd shown up for their romantic getaway after all. But she hadn't been there.

Tears poured down her cheeks as the distorted voice said, "We know where he is at all times. You tell him anything and he's a dead man, just like the FBI agent."

Then the voice gave her instructions on how to untie herself. She had one hour to vacate the hotel room or one of the other informants she'd named would be beaten with chains.

She'd managed to free herself and then went straight into the shower—there was no way she could walk through the lobby beaten, bloody, and covered with bile. When she emerged from the shower, the assistive device, the projector, and the storage drive with the videos were all gone. Her car keys rested on the dresser where the assistive device had been.

She left the hotel with fifteen minutes to spare and found her car under the entranceway awning. Her purse, suitcase, and laptop bag were in the trunk. Nothing had been taken from her wallet, but her phone and laptop had been erased.

She drove away, her fogged brain vaguely registering she was in Modesto, about two hours from Oakhurst. She drove forty minutes north to Stockton, where she bought enough meals to last two days from a fast-food drive-through, then found a motel room.

In her drab room, she ate what was likely her first meal since she'd been drugged in the bar. Her head throbbed and she was bleeding from cuts she hadn't been able to bandage in the Modesto hotel room, but food was her first priority.

Second priority was reconfiguring her blank phone so she could check messages. Anything received after the wipe should still be delivered.

She logged into her cellular account and reset all her passwords. Once it was linked to service again, the phone pinged with messages. The first message from Leo had been sent the previous morning, asking why she wasn't at the Wawona. His messages grew more urgent as she failed to respond.

She tapped out a reply explaining that she'd been so upset when he canceled on her that she'd gone to the coast to think. She'd dropped her phone in saltwater and was only now getting it to work again.

The phone rang immediately, and Leo launched into a tirade about how she'd worried him and should have called.

Now, sitting on a rock in Yosemite, she remembered the jab of pleasure and pain she'd felt at hearing his voice. He was safe. Alive.

It didn't matter that he was angry with her, not when, unlike Jasper Evans, he was still breathing.

She'd told him she hadn't meant to worry him. She'd just needed time to figure things out and didn't think he'd notice she wasn't at the Wawona as planned. Then she added she'd woken up feeling crappy that morning and had taken a COVID test. It was positive. Her throat was raw from coughing, which was why her voice was so hoarse.

She figured her voice was raspy from screaming, but Leo would never know about that.

Instead of going home, she'd explained, she planned to get a vacation rental for two weeks. She'd recuperate and quarantine with a full kitchen and have food delivered.

Leo offered to drive north—he'd returned to the Redondo Beach house when she didn't show up at the Wawona—and take care of her. She insisted she could take care of herself. No need to get him sick too.

And then she did exactly as she'd said and moved to a vacation rental in San Jose. She saw no one for two weeks. When she returned to Redondo Beach, Leo was back up at Mount Shasta, and she realized she no longer cared if he was sleeping with the archaeologist.

Someday, she might care again, but in the weeks after her abduction, her emotions were erratic.

She'd made the decision to go to the LA field office of the FBI days before Leo was set to return from filming. He was safe up at Mount Shasta. She'd figured after she gave the FBI a starting point to find Jasper's murderers, she'd kill herself before they had a chance to go after Leo.

But then she'd received the message that changed everything. It was a video. With shaking fingers, she'd tapped the "Play" button and there was Muriel, sitting in a coffee shop. The time stamp showed she'd been recorded a few days before. They'd been tracking the young widow, an informant whose name Signe hadn't even known she'd revealed.

A distorted voice narrated the video. *"Say goodbye to Muriel."*

The voice went on to threaten Leo and everyone else she loved, then, a few days later, she'd received a package that contained a necklace she recognized as Muriel's and four links of a heavy chain. Both were streaked with blood.

After she'd opened the package, her phone had buzzed. Another video. She clicked the link to see Leo with the dig crew on the site near Mount Shasta. Handsome and in control as usual.

The voiceover made the message clear: *"He's next if you say a word. This is your last warning."*

She'd believed the voice then. She believed it now.

They would always follow through.

◆ ◆ ◆

Signe swiped away the tears that poured down her cheeks as she relived the horror of those days.

Who else had she given up during those buried hours?

"I know it's a spectacular view, but I have a feeling that's not what brought you to tears."

She wiped her eyes on her sleeve before facing Cole. "I thought I told you to go home."

He dropped his pack on the ground next to hers, then settled onto the boulder by her side and faced the intersection of Tenaya Canyon and Yosemite Valley. "And miss this view? No way."

"Great. You've seen it. Now go away."

"Why were you crying?"

She glared at him. "What makes you think I was crying?"

"Talk to me, Sig."

"No."

"What have you gotten yourself into?"

"I told you. I'm following a story. A lead from an informant."

"Have you ever . . . considered going to the feds? Tell them what you know?"

She reared back. "What the hell does that mean?" Was Cole probing to find out if she'd break and reveal what had happened to her? Was he working for the man who'd orchestrated her abduction?

He ran a hand over his face. "It doesn't mean anything other than what it sounds like. You're hiding something. My guess is you're in over your head. Maybe you should tell someone."

"Tell *you*, you mean."

"That would be a solid start."

"Pass, thanks."

He draped an arm around her. She couldn't stop herself from leaning into him. Dammit.

"I'm not going to let you push me away. I'm with you until we meet with your informant."

She rested her temple against his shoulder. "Why?"

"Because I like you."

"Why?" she repeated.

"Well, it's not your honesty and candor, that's for sure."

She let out a soft grunt of amusement. He wasn't wrong.

"C'mon, Sig. Throw me a bone. Say something nice about me so I don't feel alone in my affection confession."

"You have a nice body."

He laughed. "That's it? It's all physical with you?"

"Not usually, but I haven't had sex in more than two years, so . . ." Her voice trailed off. It wasn't a lie. Rape wasn't sex. Even if she'd orgasmed, it wasn't sex.

God, how she hated her body right then.

"Over two years? I thought you and Leo split eighteen months ago."

She nodded, not even caring that Leo had obviously shared the timeline of their separation and divorce. What did it matter?

"Yes, but we were apart—filming different projects—for a lot of months, and then things . . . *changed*."

"He was having an affair?"

She honestly didn't know anymore. She'd never confirmed it. But it was the easiest answer to give, plus it was true. "I thought so at the time."

"No one would blame you for not sleeping with him, then. At the very least, you could have gotten an STD."

She stiffened. He couldn't know about that, too, could he? Had Leo told him everything and now he was pretending ignorance?

She pushed away from him and rose to her feet.

"I don't want to talk about Leo anymore."

He stood and brushed off his pants. "Neither do I." He slipped an arm around her waist and pulled her to him. They were chest to chest. "I'd be content to pretend Leo never existed."

"Neither of us would be here without him."

He gave her the slightest of smiles and said, "Shh. We aren't talking about Leo." His lips brushed over hers. A soft caress that made all her suppressed emotions well up until tears spilled from her eyes.

Guilt made it impossible to enjoy even a simple kiss with a backdrop of awe-inspiring rock formations.

She reminded herself she was a victim too. She didn't deserve what had happened to her any more than Jasper and Muriel had deserved to die.

Still, another tear spilled as she rose to her toes and pressed her lips to his. His mouth opened and she slid her tongue inside, crying even as she shared a soft, sweet kiss with the first man she'd desired since Leo.

Ending the kiss, he shook his head and gave her a wry smile as he swiped away her tears. "I'm doing something wrong in the kissing department."

She let out a laughing sort of sob. "It's not you, it's me."

He snorted. "Sweetheart, that you can even *think* about something that makes you cry while I kiss you means it is definitely me."

She cleared her throat. "I don't want to want you."

"Why not?"

"Aside from the fact that I don't trust you?"

"Yeah, aside from that."

He didn't even sound insulted, and she liked that about him.

"I don't deserve anything good. Not anymore."

"Explain."

She shook her head and stepped back. "No. That's all I'm going to say."

"For now. We need to hit the trail if we're going to be able to reach the rendezvous point on time."

She lifted her heavy pack from the boulder and balanced it on one knee so she could hoist it to her back. Once she had it in place, she buckled the hip and chest straps, then cocked her head at Cole, who'd managed the whole maneuver much faster than she did, probably thanks to his pretty muscles.

"Why did you come and find me?"

His gaze met hers, his brown eyes probing as he seemed to weigh his answer. Finally, he said, "I wasn't going to let you get far. I figured you just needed time to cool off."

Did she believe him?

Worse, were his words true? Had she simply been in a moment of hotheaded irrationality?

What had happened to the nerves-of-steel investigative reporter she used to be?

That woman died in a hotel room in Modesto.

Chapter 20

They filled their water bottles at the creek, then continued a mile down the trail before finally breaking away from the marked route and entering the undefined backwoods.

The air was hot and fresh as they hiked in and out of the cover of forest. Signe almost enjoyed traversing the bare granite as Cole told her stories of the archaeological survey he'd worked on for the park years ago, fully embracing his "guide" role as he pointed out landmarks and features or simply explained what to look for to identify an archaeological site in this setting.

He was competent and knowledgeable and, most important, a distraction from her dark thoughts. Slowly, the vise on her chest loosened.

Thoughts of Jasper's brutal murder didn't magically fade away, but continuous reminders she'd been drugged worked to keep the oppressive guilt at bay.

They took a break in the shade near a stream and had a salty snack and refilled their water bottles after again drinking them dry.

It was getting toward late afternoon and they'd hiked more than seven miles since leaving the backpackers' campground this morning. It was the limit of what Cole had believed she could do, but she wanted to push forward, another mile or two if possible.

But first she needed to catch her breath.

She leaned back and poured crisp, cold stream water over her head.

"You should soak your sunhat in the stream. It'll dry quickly in this heat, but it will help for a little while."

"Was it this hot when you did fieldwork here?"

He nodded. "It was August and a bad wildfire year. Brutal. Made me question the wisdom of my chosen profession."

"And that's why you decided to go Hollywood?"

He shrugged. "Probably? It was a gradual thing. Without a master's degree, there's only so far I can go in the field and I didn't want the debt of going back to school. It's not like archaeologists make the big bucks even with a higher degree."

"I have a sad truth to tell you about documentary work. Unless you're willing to be a pseudoscientist sellout and work for a commercial network . . ." Her voice trailed off.

He let out a bark of laughter. "Point taken. But at least I don't need a graduate degree to host a docuseries. Lord knows the pseudoscientist pricks don't have degrees in anything real."

"Where did you go to school?"

He paused a beat, then said, "UC Davis."

"Good archaeology program?"

"Anthropology—only a few schools separate archaeology out of the anthropology program. And yeah."

"Leo has made several archaeology documentaries over the years. After we split, he decided to move away from crime and focus on the natural and cultural history stuff he specialized in before we teamed up."

"I thought we weren't going to talk about Leo?"

"Sorry. But don't you actually want to know about him, since you'll be working for him when we get back?"

"I can find out about him on my own. I don't want *you* thinking about Leo."

"Why not?"

He cocked his head. "Gee. I wonder. Maybe because the guy is still making you cry. Even while kissing *me*."

She couldn't help but snicker at the clear affront to his ego. Still, she could throw him a bone. "I'm an emotional wreck. I cry easily and often." That was true enough.

"Why, Sig? Your split with Leo is old news. You're at the top of your profession. Why the waterworks now?"

"I'm hormonal."

"Bullshit. I don't know a single woman who would ever use that excuse except to deflect."

He was right on that point. She'd inwardly cringed even as she said it. "This story is personal. I told you that."

"But you haven't told me why or how."

"I can't."

"What do I need to do to get you to trust me?"

"Show me your burner phone."

His face remained blank. "What?"

"Don't bullshit me, Cole. Show me your second phone."

His nostrils flared as he held her gaze, then he reached for his pack. She expected him to make a show of searching and coming up empty, but he surprised her by pulling out every item and laying them in a line. Included in the collection were a GPS unit, a box of condoms, and two cell phones.

"I got the GPS unit last night from the Mountain Shop after I picked up marshmallows and booze from the grocery store."

"And the condoms?"

"I thought you'd be more interested in the phones, but yeah, I got those last night too."

She picked up both phones. The second phone was no burner. It was a smartphone. Expensive. She realized the cell he'd let her see up until now was the burner. Why use a burner to communicate with old friends like Wanda?

"Why two phones?"

"My boss insisted on it."

"Your boss?"

"Leo. The guy we aren't talking about."

She studied his face. Looking for deception. "That's not the phone you got his number from in the hotel on Monday night."

"No. I have his number on both phones. But he didn't want you to see my other phone. I blew it Monday. Forgot to make the switch before going into your room."

"Why didn't Leo want me to see your real phone?"

He shrugged and took the phone from her, powering it on. He punched in his password and handed it back to her. "He was probably afraid you'd see this."

She looked down at the screen to see the text conversation with Leo Starr. More texts from Leo than from Cole as he demanded updates—and coordinates.

"He wanted the coordinates for the meet?"

Cole nodded. "Time, place, and . . . scroll up."

She did as instructed, going back in time to Monday, when Cole must've been on the road to Oakhurst.

Cole: Thirty minutes out. Send me the name of the hotel and her room number.

Leo had replied with the information requested.

Cole: I should pick up dinner on my way through Oakhurst. What does Signe like?

Leo: I'll place an order for Chinese.

The next text gave the address of the restaurant and the total of the bill—with the note that the balance was due. She rolled her eyes. Leo was wealthy to the tune of millions in the bank, but he hadn't bought dinner for the man he'd coerced into helping her?

She glanced up at Cole. "I'll pay for dinner."

"That's *not* what I wanted you to see." He pointed to a message below the one about dinner.

Leo: Don't fuck this up. Do NOT get her to the meet point on time. You do and you're fired.

She jolted. "What the hell? He told you to prevent me from being on time?"

Cole nodded, his expression a cold mask.

"Why?"

"You tell me. What's his deal? What's *your* deal?"

She said nothing, just continued scrolling, reading Leo's messages. And there it was, black text in a gray bubble.

Leo: Fuck her and you're fired.

Cole had told her about this, but somehow seeing the words directly from Leo triggered a burn of outrage she'd brushed off before. She met Cole's gaze and then looked again at the box of condoms, bought well after Leo's threat. Purchased, in fact, just an hour after he'd told her about said threat.

"Leo is such an asshole," she muttered.

"Pretty much."

"It would serve him right if I jumped you right now."

Without missing a beat, Cole jerked his shirt over his head, revealing a plethora of muscles. More important, he had no scars and no tattoos. He was just a big, gorgeous man who'd spent hours in the gym to sculpt his body for his big break in infotainment streaming television. "Okay, let's go, then. Because I totally want to be used for sex because you're pissed at your ex."

She realized he was angry. Not at Leo. At her. "I'm sorry. I—"

He shrugged and pulled his shirt back on. "You want to see this, go to YouTube and search *water screening Adonis*."

"It is *not* called that."

"It is. Worth noting that I'm using a shaker screen, which means my hands are holding on to the screen at hip height and I'm vigorously rocking my hips just so, leaning into the screen to shake that dirt." He mimicked the action as he said the words, and she understood why he'd gone viral.

She glanced at his phone and confirmed there was no cellular service. "Damn."

He plucked the cell from her hand and began returning the items he'd removed from his pack, his movements still jerky and angry. "My point is, Signe, if you want more than a video, it's got to matter that it's *me* and not just a random desire to get back at Leo."

He released the pack and rose to his feet. He hooked a finger into one of her belt loops and pulled her toward him. He leaned over her— so very large and imposing—his mouth just inches from hers. "If anything happens between us, it will have absolutely *nothing* to do with your ex."

They were inches apart, chest to chest, and her heart pounded as she waited for him to kiss her. She would *not* cry this time. No. She was absolutely thinking about Cole and only Cole as he stared down at her.

Then he smiled, released her, and stepped back.

"No kiss?" Her voice came out as a high squeak.

He shook his head. "You'll have to be satisfied with being flashed by the water-screening Adonis."

He finished reloading his pack and they set out again. Cole led the way using the satellite GPS unit to find a good camping spot in the middle of nowhere for the night.

Signe broke a long stretch of silence by asking the question she'd wondered from the moment she saw Leo's text. "Were you going to do it? Make me late to the rendezvous?"

"No."

"What do you plan to tell Leo?"

"It depends on how everything goes down. But personally, the way I see it, once I walked into your hotel room, I was working for you, not Leo. You call the shots. Not him."

"Are you prepared to lose your job over it?"

"If that happens, I can point to my signed contract, although I'm sure he has a good lawyer."

"You'd think, but our divorce settlement was strangely in my favor."

"Why strangely? California is a no-fault state."

"It is, but Leo could have pushed for me to be penalized in the proceedings. Instead, he was generous."

Cole stopped and faced her. "What are you saying, Signe?"

She took a deep breath. Could she really tell him?

She held his gaze. His eyes probed hers with concern.

She sucked in a breath and blurted the truth before she could change her mind. "Leo had copies of medical records that showed I had an STD. He believed I cheated on him."

"But you didn't."

"No. I was raped. But I didn't tell Leo when it happened, so when he found out about the STD, he didn't believe me."

CHAPTER 21

The feeling that rushed through her—was it relief or terror? Was she signing Cole's death warrant? Or did it not matter anymore now that they were deep in the middle of nowhere without any chance of the crime lord who'd kept tabs on her the last two years learning what she'd just revealed?

She didn't feel safe, exactly, so much as *safer.*

"You were raped and Leo didn't believe you?"

She nodded.

"That motherfucker. Does he even *know* you?"

"Well, we were together for ten years, married for seven, so I thought so." Still, it was gratifying that this man she'd known only forty-eight hours could accept her word when Leo hadn't. "What makes you so certain I didn't cheat and lie about being raped to cover it up?"

"You wouldn't lie about something like that. I saw the episode of your show where you interviewed sex workers who shared stories of being raped."

The interviews had been excruciating to film, especially when the women talked about how police wouldn't even let them file a complaint because no one would convict a man for raping a prostitute.

"That's why you didn't have sex with Leo during the last months of your marriage, isn't it? And why you're so angry but still love him."

"Whoa. Hold up. Yes on the *no sex at the end of our marriage* thing, but I'm *not* in love with Leo. He *abandoned* me when I needed him most. He can go fuck himself."

She resumed walking. She needed to move as she gave him the rest of the story. "My love for Leo died in the months between separation and divorce, when he had a chance to look into my story. He's investigated with me for years. He knows how and where to look to verify details. But he didn't even try. He didn't love me enough to do the merest fact check. And even before I was raped, I was pretty sure he was cheating on me."

"I'm sorry that happened to you, and I'd happily deck Leo on your behalf."

"I've accepted that Leo will never understand the depth of his cruelty."

"You shouldn't have to accept that."

"Who ever said life was fair?" She huffed out a breath. "I need you to understand something, and it's a thing I remind myself of regularly. A horrible thing happened to me, but I survived. I'm healthy—the STD was cured with antibiotics and it's not the recurring kind. I have a house, money, food, and a career. I interview people on a regular basis who've been through worse than I have. These same people also have so much less. Women who've been maimed by their pimp for trying to escape. Victims of cons who ended up homeless. Hungry. And these are the people who are *alive*. For me to pity myself would be horrific in the face of the mother of three whose thirteen-year-old daughter was raped and killed by a rival cartel that wanted the guns she was moving over the border. Or the drug mules swallowing balloons that break. I put the horrors of my life into this context every damn day and count myself lucky to have survived."

Cole stood frozen, taking in her words, which were so similar to what he told himself on a daily basis as he navigated the underworld of artifact and drug trafficking and did what he had to to survive.

He'd made some awful choices that would haunt him for the rest of his days. But then, days were often numbered in his line of work. He had to get out if he expected to have much of a future, but it was a vicious cycle and currently, he was trapped in limbo.

He knew too much to leave cleanly, but not enough to end things for good.

But Signe . . . she had the intel he needed. She was his ticket to freedom.

Just when he'd been making good progress, his decision to seduce her to get her to confide in him felt wrong now. And he'd been so damn close with that little game with the water-screening motion.

He should have made his move then, *before* she'd confided in him. Because he was ten kinds of asshole, but manipulating a rape victim with sex was harsh, even for him.

Still, he was running out of options and running out of time.

CHAPTER 22

According to the GPS, they'd hiked nearly nine miles by the time they dropped their packs in a small clearing not far from a lightly flowing stream. They were deep in nowhereland and about eight miles as the crow flies from the rendezvous location. The foot distance would be much longer, as more elevation gain and other obstacles prevented a straight route.

After the long day, Signe had just enough energy to remove key items from her pack to make dinner—Sierra stove, food canister, pan and utensils.

Cole was off taking care of private business. She'd wait for him to return to do the same. They had to pack in and pack out everything except bodily waste and she had a separate plastic pouch just for used tissue paper.

Given that there were no bear boxes in the backcountry, Cole had explained that they'd have to tuck their canisters between logs a fair distance from where they slept. It was dangerous to store their food in camp, and bears were known for pushing the canisters down hills in an attempt to break them open if they weren't sufficiently secured.

She forced herself to her feet and picked up the bag with the tent. After clearing obvious rocks from the spot where they'd decided to pitch it, she set to work, using loose cobbles to pound the stakes into the dry earth.

Tomorrow, they'd cross Tioga Road, which cut across the north end of the park and had a few primitive campgrounds accessible from the road. When she'd grumbled that they could have camped much closer to their eventual end point, Cole reminded her that a) he hadn't been able to get a permit for any of those backcountry trails, b) he'd had no idea the final meet point would be so far from the valley, and c) none of the nearby campgrounds were open yet.

All his points were entirely valid, but damn, her back and feet would have loved to skip the climb out of Tenaya Canyon, no matter how gorgeous the view.

As it was, she couldn't wait to pull off the thick hiking boots, but first she had business to attend, which she set off to do once Cole returned. She kept an eye out for poison oak and other cruel plants as she picked her way through the thickening woods. It wasn't long before their chosen campsite was lost from view and the woods closed in.

A rustling in the underbrush got her attention and she rang her bear bell as she searched for movement to identify what kind of critter had made the noise.

She wobbled on unsteady legs. She was so damn tired. She closed her eyes and leaned against a tree, urging her legs to move forward, but she should probably make certain no bears were nearby before dropping trou and squatting.

More branches rustled, and her eyes popped open as she looked for the source. She stepped forward, ringing her bell. The tinkling sound and twittering of birds were the only noises to be heard. There wasn't even a slight breeze.

She heard a cough behind her, but it was distant. Cole, back at the campsite.

He was close enough that he'd hear a shout for help, which was comforting.

She felt a tingling sensation along her neck. Was the fear psychosomatic? The thought of yelling for help the trigger that made her afraid?

Or was someone watching her?

She heard a noise. It wasn't close. The sound was faint. A whisper on the nonexistent breeze. Had she imagined it?

She felt a ringing in her ears, the kind that sometimes came with headaches or altitude, and their elevation was more than seven thousand feet now.

That's all this was. Altitude. Exhaustion.

The low buzz in her ears changed, like the screeching of microphone feedback. A few jarring notes her brain wanted to make into a word. Similar to gibberish run through a voice distorter.

Voice distorters were used regularly for her interviews. She knew all their tones and resonances.

A voice distorter alone didn't scare her. But the man who'd whispered instructions to her in a hotel room using a distorter did.

A sharp pain lanced down her neck—triggered by the memory of the headache she'd had two years ago? She turned and ran back to the campsite and safety of Cole.

◆ ◆ ◆

Signe sat in their camp with her gun in her hand while Cole searched for signs that others shared this section of backcountry with them. He'd drawn his gun and walked with a practiced posture as he left her alone.

He returned thirty minutes later, shaking his head. "Didn't see a thing. No footprints, no broken branches that looked like they'd been stepped on by a human."

He didn't say it had all been her imagination, and she was glad for that.

Truth was, she wasn't certain she hadn't imagined it. Her brain was ripe for creating horrors where there were none.

But still, she felt uneasy. If she wasn't so utterly exhausted, she'd have insisted they move camp a half mile away. But she didn't have another half mile in her. Not if she was going to be able to walk at all tomorrow.

She simply nodded and rose to relieve her bladder. This time, she just tucked herself behind the nearest wide tree for privacy. She had no intention of straying far from him again.

"Even if it was a person, it could just be other backpackers who heard your bell and gave us a wide berth. Backcountry campers like their privacy."

She nodded. The tones could just have been ringing in her ears. Altitude sickness.

By all rights, she *should* have altitude sickness after the hike from the valley floor, then the steady rise of another thousand feet from there. Tomorrow, they'd climb another thousand until they leveled off at just over eight thousand feet.

It had to be altitude sickness.

It was a shame she couldn't quite convince herself of that.

Cole handed Signe a one-pot meal that consisted of mashed potatoes, chicken, corn, and gravy. It was like a fast-food meal but made by adding hot water to rehydrate the potatoes, then adding the other ingredients and baking them all together in a metal pot the size of a dinner bowl.

Famished after getting more exercise in twelve hours than she'd ever attempted in her life, she enjoyed the meal as much as any she'd ever had in a gourmet restaurant, even though the food was extra salty. The salt wouldn't be good for the ringing in her ears, but that was abating as she drank water.

After dinner, they washed their dishes in the stream and repacked the bear canister with the empty food packaging to ensure no food scent

escaped. As they stood by the stream, Signe looked longingly at the cold trickle of water. "Do you mind if I do a quick wash? I'll sleep better."

He agreed, and they took turns with quick pack-towel baths, then placed all scented items in the bear canisters for the night and tucked them between logs.

Fires weren't allowed in the park outside a fire ring, so they sat in their sleeping-pad chairs and looked up at the darkening sky. As she'd been promised in every Yosemite guidebook, the stars were spectacular.

They must've sat for a half hour before either of them spoke. Signe didn't know if it was exhaustion or simply that there was nothing to say, but she suspected Cole's mind wasn't much calmer than hers, and hers was tracing paths outward from every question that had been raised in the last few days.

"I still don't understand what this trek through the backwoods has to do with Manny Lontoc or John Doe," she said, breaking the long silence.

"I've been thinking about that. Ranger Gus said Manny wore the flag of the Philippines tank top because it caught the attention of Filipino visitors, and sometimes he helped with translation for tourists who speak Tagalog."

"You're thinking John Doe was one of those tourists?"

"I am. But it's hard to believe an emaciated man would be a tourist."

"A lot of trafficking victims come from the Philippines," she said. "It would make much more sense if he was a labor trafficking victim, given his physical state."

"You said this is connected to a story you worked on before. Did it involve labor trafficking?"

Her throat was dry. She hadn't been able to remember that part and figured the blank spots in her memory had something to do with the drugs she'd been given. Or maybe DiscoFever had simply been vague, but she remembered that moment when she received the first text and her senses had prickled at the thought of human trafficking.

"I'm pretty sure there was some kind of human trafficking—sex, labor, or both—involved."

"Have you ever done a story on labor trafficking?"

"Nothing in depth like I do on *Crime Lords*. It's extremely hard to get informants to go on the record, people who escape need to stay in hiding. The people who enslaved them don't leave witnesses who can testify. But it's big business in California. Mostly farm or domestic workers."

"Not a lot of farming in Yosemite," Cole said.

"No. But not everyone who works in the park works for the park service. Concessionaires run the hotels and stores. You worked here. Were you a park employee?"

"No. I worked for an archaeological consulting firm that got a contract for a survey. Only our field supervisors worked for the park's culture and history department."

"Another area where we find labor trafficking is custodial work—unskilled maintenance for golf courses, beaches, and"—she paused for just a moment—"parks."

"Damn."

She nodded. "I wish I'd asked Gus and Wanda when we had the chance, but I imagine a good number of the custodial workers are employed by concessionaires. Probably even subcontractors to the contractor."

"It's been a long time, but I seem to remember the summer I worked here seeing busloads of workers brought in. Maybe once a week to do a deeper cleaning? They sometimes worked at night to minimize the impact on tourists."

Her heart began to thud as she considered that possibility. "Late at night, these workers wouldn't have much contact with visitors."

She sat up straight as their theorized connection between Manny and John Doe ticked the logic box. "It's a tactic employed by human traffickers to use the language barrier to keep laborers trapped. Bring in people who know very little English and they can't ask for help. In California, that limits traffickers' ability to exploit Spanish-speaking workers—of course they find other ways to trap them—but that's not what we're looking at here. The result is some traffickers have chosen to cast a wider net to find people to exploit.

"The Philippines has a huge human-trafficking problem. Within the country, children are enslaved for sex work, while adults are shipped outside the country. Foreign-worker trafficking follows the same pattern no matter what country the victims come from. They sign contracts that use their family's home as collateral to pay the ten- or fifteen-thousand-dollar fee to bring them to the US. Often they even have to put a few thousand down in cash. Then, when they get here, they're forced to work long hours on farms and their paycheck is withheld to pay back the amount they 'borrowed' to get here. Paying off the loan is never possible, while attempts to escape put their family in their home country at risk."

She wished she had more information on DiscoFever. That was the true starting point. But her contact with DiscoFever had all happened in the days prior to her abduction and she hadn't been home in Redondo Beach, where she'd have stored notes offline. No. Everything she had on DiscoFever had been on her phone, laptop, or in her hotel room when she was abducted.

When she woke in Modesto, she had a blank phone, blank computer, and no handwritten notes.

She'd lost only two weeks of data from the computer—she had backups in the Redondo Beach house—but the phone was a complete loss.

She stared up at the canopy of stars and wondered what she'd missed. What she'd forgotten, her memory as blank as her phone.

Cole broke the silence. "So you think Manny came across a laborer from the Philippines—our John Doe—who was being forced to work for one of the custodial contractors."

She imagined the scene in her mind. The flag shirt. Manny's outgoing personality, especially to his countrymen. "I wish we'd found someone who saw Manny talking to John Doe. It might be something to follow up on when we get back to the valley."

"Good idea."

In the meantime, she wished she had cell service so she could start looking into the park's custodial contracts and maintenance schedules for park facilities.

She'd been forced to enter the park with minimal information and scant time to research before setting out for the backcountry. But that had been the plan, hadn't it?

Separate her from the ability to dig deep. Cut her off from the world.

Again it made her think the meeting was a trap. "What are we going to find at the end of this yellow brick road?" she murmured.

"Manny's car?"

"Improbable, given that the meeting is deep in the forest, far from any road or trail, but I like the idea of it."

"Same. It bothers me no one knows where it is."

"You sound like an investigator."

"I guess you're rubbing off on me." He shrugged. "Besides, archaeology is all about forensics and investigation. We just don't have living witnesses to corroborate our theories—unless you count DNA evidence."

"Interesting framework. You should use that in your show."

"At this point, I really don't see the show with Leo happening."

"I'm sorry. I didn't mean to ruin things with you and Leo."

"Don't be. This is where I need to be."

The entire time they spoke, she'd been looking up at the stars, her vision lost in the cosmos while her brain traveled the backcountry. Now she turned to him. He, too, looked upward. Slowly, he faced her. There was enough starlight to see his features, but it was hard to read his eyes.

One corner of his mouth quirked up and he reached out and offered her his hand. She took it and threaded her fingers between his. They lapsed back into silence and gazed up at the stars.

◆ ◆ ◆

They laid out their sleeping pads and bags side by side out in the open with just a foot separating them. The tent could hold their gear. The stars were too pretty and the night too quiet not to enjoy the serenity of the isolated backcountry without barriers.

She wasn't without concerns, however, so she placed her gun inside her sleeping bag. It offered a different kind of comfort than a stuffed animal.

She noticed Cole kept his gun close too.

As she stared up at the stars, her brain traveled the path it had gone over and over in the last hour.

Had Manny Lontoc met a trafficking victim? Had he tried to help him, resulting in both their deaths? Manny died in a drowning accident in a part of the park he didn't usually visit. John Doe died miles away, emaciated and weak.

Enslaved?

The puzzle pieces almost fit together, except for the several-mile gap between bodies.

Eventually, exhaustion won over and she drifted off. Still, she never slept deeply. Even tonight, her body utterly beat, she wavered between states of consciousness, with thoughts turning into dreams that included Leo, Cole, Jasper, Muriel, and Manny.

People morphed into one another in the way that made sense only in dreams. Voices shifted. Sex with Leo became sex with Cole. Then the inevitable images from the video took over and she woke with a start.

She was drenched in sweat. Cole was snug in his sleeping bag beside her, his breathing barely audible in the still night.

She stared up at the stars. They'd shifted enough to let her know hours had passed. Her body ached from hiking and sleeping on hard ground. She would never make it as a dirtbag.

She breathed slowly and deeply, catching a whiff of smoke on the air, but it was the same distant scent from the fires to the south. Everything was as it should be.

She closed her eyes and drifted off again, this time waking as she heard the crunch of footsteps on twigs and realized Cole had slipped from his bag, probably to answer a call of nature.

His footsteps faded in the distance. She closed her eyes, drifting back into sleep. She was so damn tired and the only thing that was keeping her from really sinking into oblivion was the anxiety that dogged her. She again heard the crunch of footsteps, this time to her right. Cole must have circled around.

She turned to her side, the sleeping pad beneath her squeaking as it shifted beneath her weight.

A low tone sounded, and then there was a voice. Distorted. Not saying any real words as far as she could tell. Just . . . sounds. Metal jangled, and she sat bolt upright.

It wasn't just metal. It was the sound of chain links clattering as they hit something.

Human flesh?

CHAPTER 23

Signe screamed, loud and shrill, in the way she couldn't when she'd been in the hotel room and forced to watch a video of Jasper's murder.

She screamed so loud as she groped for the gun that she didn't notice the distorted voice had gone silent, nor did she hear Cole's returning footsteps. Didn't know he was there until his arms were around her, removing the gun from her grasp as he held her and demanded to know what had happened.

She screamed one more time because the sound in her throat needed to get out, then she collapsed against him, sobbing.

"Sig, what happened?"

"The voice. It was back. And there were chains, like the Ghost of Christmas Past."

His body stiffened against hers, then he leaned back and cupped her face between his hands. "Sounds like you were having a nightmare."

"No. I was awake. It was here." She waved in the direction where the sounds had emanated from. "It was . . . it was just like before."

"Like before? Like when?"

She took a deep breath. She couldn't tell him now. Not when she was hysterical. It wouldn't make sense.

She swiped at her tears. So many damn tears these last few days.

She hadn't cried this much since the days following Leo's exit from her life.

"If you really think someone is out there, I should go search."

She grabbed his shirt and pulled him back to her side. "Don't you dare leave me alone again."

When he remained stiff against her, she said, "Please? I—I just can't be alone right now."

He unzipped her sleeping bag and lay down beside her, taking her into his arms. He stroked her cheek, then touched her hairline with gentle fingertips. "Tell me, Signe. Maybe I can help you."

"You are helping me. You're taking me to the meet point. That's all I need."

"What are you holding back? Are you protecting one of your crime lords?"

She stiffened at the question. "What? No. I don't—that's not my job. I just interview them."

"Then what aren't you telling me? Why are we going to this meeting? What can you possibly learn that's worth the danger you're putting us both in?"

"I think—" She hesitated. They weren't alone in the forest. If anyone heard, Cole was dead.

They might even kill Leo too. Just because they could.

"I can't say." She then leaned close and spoke into his ear, her words so faint she didn't know if he'd hear more than her expelled breath. "They might be listening. I don't want them to kill you too." She paused a moment, then added, "It's all connected. My rape. Manny's and the other man's murder. DiscoFever promised me answers."

◆ ◆ ◆

Sleeping outside and on top of the world as they were, they had no choice but to wake with the dawn. It wasn't like Signe had gotten much sleep after her brief whispered confession.

Cole had followed up with questions she refused to answer and they both lay in the dark with the ever-shifting star scape as the only indicator time passed.

Cole had pulled his sleeping pad, bag, and pillow closer and eventually dozed while holding her. She'd drifted in and out of consciousness, but only for the briefest of intervals.

She was glad he managed to get some sleep. She was counting on him to navigate today. Between her sore legs, back, and poor sleep, she was likely to be nothing more than a zombie with a heavy backpack today. How in the world was she going to be able to make the hike back to the valley when this was over?

Of course, that presumed the meet went off without complications and then they could just hike out of the park, easy peasy.

Nothing about this would be easy.

The cynical thought was proven true when they went to collect their bear canisters . . . and one was missing.

Cole searched all the hollows between logs. "Maybe I'm wrong about where we put the second one."

"You aren't wrong. It was taken. I *told* you someone was here last night."

"But why only take one? Maybe a bear got the one and didn't find the other."

"Show me the bear claw marks." She didn't understand why he resisted this . . . until she realized that both times she'd heard the voice, Cole hadn't been with her. He had, in fact, claimed not to hear it.

Both times.

Was it possible Cole had scared the hell out of her, then comforted and gaslighted her?

She could understand that more than she could understand him removing half their food supply—because, given his appetite, that would hurt him even more than her.

No. Cole wouldn't have tucked their food away in a place she wouldn't find it, but would he terrorize her? She didn't want to think so, but what did she know about anything anymore?

"Exactly how did you meet Leo?" she asked.

"We met a few times when he was filming archaeology segments around the state."

"Including the one at Mount Shasta two years ago?" Did Cole know the woman Leo had been screwing while she was in a bar getting roofied?

"Mount Shasta? Is that the project Vicki worked on?"

"Victoria Lopez? I thought she was a Mesoamerican archaeologist."

"Sure, but she went to school in California—Chico, I think—and knows the archaeology of the region. I think Leo brought her in to film some knowledgeable sound bites because the principal investigator was too busy and he wasn't as photogenic as Vicki."

"He?"

Cole cocked his head. "Yeah. Small consulting firm based in the Bay Area. The guy running the dig had a brand-new master's degree but not a lot of experience running projects. Tended to stutter. I heard about the filming and went north to help, but Leo had already brought Vicki on board. I'm surprised you didn't know that."

Signe had been AWOL from life for several weeks after the rape. Then, later, every time the Mount Shasta documentary came up, her stomach had turned. So she didn't ask about it. Didn't watch it. It was inextricably linked to her nightmare and she'd avoided knowing anything about it.

"I had no idea Vicki ever worked with Leo." She frowned. "If she worked with him and has expertise in California, why did Leo pick you for the West Coast episodes of the show? Doesn't she have a PhD?"

He shrugged. "I guess he wanted Channing Tatum."

That was entirely possible. It had probably pissed Vicki off to no end.

Signe dropped onto a rock and let out a deep breath. "It's not here, Cole. We've lost half our food." If they were lucky, the canister they'd lost would be the one that contained the pouch of used toilet paper.

He nodded. "We need to ration. We've got at least two more nights in the forest before we make it all the way back to the valley."

Last night's extra-large meal seemed extravagant now, but at the same time, at least they'd eaten large when they had the chance.

"We overpacked, so we should be fine, but no meal splurges from here on out."

She nodded.

They quickly warmed water and mixed it with instant oatmeal for a pasty, gooey breakfast that checked the carb box until they'd have a small snack in two hours.

Thankfully, they'd cleaned their pots and utensils last night instead of storing them dirty in the bear canister, or they'd be without a pot to cook in and eating with their fingers.

She was hungry enough that the pasty breakfast was satisfying, but she didn't really notice the taste. Her brain was too busy buzzing over questions about Cole.

And Manny, John Doe, and DiscoFever.

She felt Cole's gaze on her and looked up. He stared with an intensity that surprised her. "What?" she asked, feeling a strange flutter—not the good kind—low in her belly.

"Let me help you, Signe. You only told me part of it last night."

She frowned as her gaze darted from left to right—as if she would see her tormentor listening. "I told you what I can. I'm trying to keep you safe."

"Bullshit. You're protecting yourself."

She reared back. "What? Are you fucking kidding me? *Everything* I've done for the past two years is to protect others. I've never given a damn about my own safety. If I did, I wouldn't be here right now."

"Why *are* you here right now, then?"

"I want the threat to those I love to be lifted. I want to be able to breathe again without fearing for everyone I've endangered."

"You've endangered people?"

She held his gaze. A tear spilled down her cheek as she remembered Jasper's last scream before he slipped into unconsciousness. At least, she told herself it was just unconsciousness. But whether he died then or later, she didn't doubt it was the last sound he ever made. The chain had struck him in the head. The blood had sprayed both the wall and camera.

"Yes," she whispered.

She didn't say that the people she'd endangered—the ones who'd *died*—were sources she'd vowed to protect.

CHAPTER 24

Signe grumbled under her breath when they crossed Tioga Road in the early afternoon. "We could have *driven* all the way here and *then* set out." She knew the reasons that hadn't been possible, but still, her legs, feet, and back ached for all the miles and elevation gain they'd traversed on foot that could have been covered by car.

"If you stop grumbling, I'll take you someplace nice for dinner."

"A Michelin-starred restaurant?"

"Aim lower."

"In-N-Out Burger?"

"Aim . . . different."

"Cup Noodles in Yosemite high country?"

"It's almost uncanny how you nailed it."

"You said I should be clairvoyant. So what great plans do you have for dinner, considering we've lost half our food supply?"

"It's not about the food. It's the ambiance. Late this afternoon, we'll be passing a small lake. How about a swim followed by an early dinner?"

"A swim in a frigid-cold alpine lake?" She wasn't sure if that sounded good or not. But they had to eat sometime, and maybe the setting would help her forget they were rationing.

They continued on, everything aching as she set one foot in front of the other. Her feet were downright angry at being in the boots again. Her back wanted nothing to do with the heavy pack. Her hips chafed from the padded belt. And her thighs burned from the steady uphill climb.

As her aches and pains added up, she started to think a cold swim might numb her complaining muscles. Plus she'd probably appreciate the weightlessness of water after carrying thirty pounds on her back. Not just uphill, but *relentlessly* uphill.

Her mind wandered between sore muscles and what lay at the end of the journey, then circled back to Cole's suggestion she'd dreamed the chains and distorted voice. In the warm light of day, the idea had merit. It would even be logical for her to have dreamed of Jasper's murder now. He was connected to this as much as her rape was. It was all intertwined.

It was with great relief that Signe finally dropped her pack on the ground by the small lake. The pool was surrounded by tall grasses, the water a flat sheen of clear crystal that reflected the deep blue of the sky. No other hikers were in the area as far as she could tell.

They hadn't seen a single person since late yesterday afternoon. Not even when they crossed Tioga Road.

"Is the water deep?" she asked as she began unlacing her boots.

"No clue how deep it is, but it's large enough that I imagine it's well over our heads in the center." He pulled off his boots and socks, then rose to his feet and pulled off his shirt. His hands went to the waistline of his hiking pants and he stopped when he caught her stare. "If you're going to ogle, I get to do the same."

She shrugged as she pulled off her boots. "That's fair." She had no intention of looking away. Cole's body was quite impressive. He'd clearly worked on his muscles in anticipation of going Hollywood. An excellent move on his part. She almost had to wonder why Leo was the first to give him a real shot at the big-time, given the eye candy on display.

She rose to her feet and pulled off her top, hesitating only a moment before reaching for the tight elastic band at the bottom of her sports bra. Her intention to strip quickly was thwarted when the damp band twisted and got stuck around her shoulders.

A hazard of sweaty sports bras.

Cole stepped forward and said in a low voice, "Can I help?"

Her breasts were already bare. Her arms were crossed over her face as she gripped the twisted elastic. She let go of the band and raised her arms until they pointed straight up, narrowing the width of her shoulders, where the bra was stuck. "Please."

He eased the elastic upward until it was past the widest part of her shoulders, freeing her.

"Not exactly how I imagined undressing you for the first time, but it'll do."

"You've imagined undressing me?"

"I plead the fifth."

"That's not how it works. You've already admitted it."

"Then why did you ask?"

"I'm a reporter. I ask questions to get answers on the record."

"Am I on the record here, Ms. Gates?"

"That's entirely up to you." She reached for the clip at her waist and hesitated. Even if she kept her underwear on, the scars would be visible. Outside of a medical professional, only Leo had seen them. And that had been only once, on the day he left her.

She could swim in her pants. They would dry quickly.

Cole doffed his pants and underwear in one motion, and she was presented with her first in-the-flesh naked man who wasn't Leo in ten years.

Her gaze swept down his body, not bothering to hide her curiosity as she admired *all* of him.

She nodded toward his penis, which was responding to her blatant stare. "The cold lake will take care of that."

He rolled his eyes. "Your turn."

Could she? Should she?

She took a deep, calming breath, then dropped her pants and panties. Naked, she turned and ran for the lake before he could get much of a glimpse.

"Hey, no fair!"

She might have laughed at his protest, but she'd entered the icy water and all she could do was shriek. It was colder than she'd imagined it could be on such a hot day. But then, the elevation was just over eight thousand feet. Not much different from the lake where Manny died.

She needed to wade deeper if she wanted to keep her scars hidden, so she bent her knees and pushed off, taking a shallow dive and swimming just beneath the surface of the frigid water.

After several strokes, she emerged to find she was chest deep in water so cold it burned. But even with the aching chill, it felt strangely good.

She was free. Light. In her skin.

Phantom pain couldn't penetrate this kind of cold.

Beside her, Cole floated on his back, eyes closed against the bright sunlight. He looked so damn perfect, a topography of muscular peaks and valleys that glistened in the lake water.

"You are a beautiful man," she murmured.

His eyes opened and he dropped his hips, shifting from floating to standing. "What was that? My ears were underwater."

"You heard me."

"But I want it on the record."

She took a step toward him, shocked she felt this kind of desire for the first time in forever. "I said you're beautiful."

He closed the distance between them until they faced each other just inches apart. She placed a hand on his chest and thumbed his peaked nipple.

"What are you doing, Signe?" His voice was soft and deep.

"I think it's obvious." But even as she answered, she asked herself the same question. Did she really want to do this?

With him?

Now?

His arm slipped around her waist, but he didn't pull her closer. Her heart stuttered as she realized he was leaving every step to her.

That scared her. She didn't know if she had it in her to seize this moment. Seize him. Ask for what she wanted. Take what she needed.

She'd never feared sex prior to being raped. She'd been comfortable in her body with Leo and the handful of partners she'd had before him.

But she was a different woman now, who'd been betrayed by her body when she was assaulted. Could she orgasm without feeling guilt? Would the memory of the video intrude?

There was only one way to find out. And *that* terrified her.

She held Cole's gaze. His warm brown eyes held nothing but desire. She cleared her throat. "Kiss me? I promise not to cry this time."

He let out a soft laugh, cupped her cheek, and pressed his mouth to hers. He slipped his tongue between her lips and woke her cold body with a kiss that was somehow gentle and incredibly arousing.

She could do this. Reclaim her body.

He raised his head. "We can stop here."

"I don't want to stop." She slid her hand upward until it was behind his neck. She pulled him down for another kiss. She wasn't gentle or sweet like he'd been. She was anxious. After two years of wondering if she'd ever be able to enjoy sex again, she wanted to get this done.

He pulled back.

Shit. She was screwing this up. "I'm sorry. I'm just—I don't know how to do this."

He brushed a thumb over her lips. Cold lake water dripped into her mouth. "It's the most natural thing in the world, but only if you truly want it. Want me."

"I do."

"Then show me by kissing me—for real this time."

She closed her eyes and relaxed her body against his. She did want him. It was the first time she'd wanted anyone in years. And wonder of wonders, she could have him.

She kissed him, and this time, it was neither soft and sweet nor hard and harsh. It was sexy and carnal and perfect as he responded with his own heat and desire.

His large body wrapped around her like a bear, but she wasn't afraid. His big palm found her ass underwater, then explored higher and lower. His erection returned, an impressive feat in the frigid lake.

She wrapped her legs around his hips and enjoyed the sensation of being weightless. She could do this. More important, she *wanted* this. Him.

"Take me to shore," she whispered.

His hands cupped her ass as he carried her from the lake. He set her to her feet in the tall grass, then pulled a thin ground cloth from his pack and spread an open sleeping bag on top. He waved toward the bag, inviting her to lie down.

She took a deep breath, then stretched out on the makeshift bed. "You're determined to make me a dirtbagger, aren't you?"

He laughed. "I put down a ground cloth. This is dirtbagging lite."

She turned to her side and kept her thighs together. She was tempted to enclose herself in the bag, but it wasn't large enough for two. She'd have been much happier if they could do this without her body being exposed, but there was no light switch for the sun and the lake was too cold. "We need a condom."

He held up the box but said, "I want to go down on you first."

She stiffened.

He settled beside her and pulled her to him. He brushed her wet hair from her cheek. "Or we can stop here."

"No!" The word was almost panicked. She'd never imagined getting this far. She couldn't stop now. If she did, she'd probably never have sex again.

He held her gaze. "I won't do anything you don't want."

She threaded her fingers through his thick, damp hair. "I want you. I want this."

"That's a solid starting point."

"I just—I—it might take me a bit to relax."

He nuzzled her neck. Between kisses, he said, "Stop me if I make a move you aren't ready for."

Desire pooled again as his hand cupped her breast and his mouth explored her neck. She let out a soft mew, encouraging him to continue.

"That's more like it." His mouth covered hers again.

This kiss was deeper and better than the one in the lake. She placed a hand on his muscled chest and leaned into the pleasure of his mouth, hands, and body. By slow degrees, she relaxed to the point that she was no longer thinking about anything but how he made her feel.

His lips trailed down her body. It wasn't until he nudged her thighs open with his chin that she remembered her scars and stiffened, her body coiling like she'd received a jolt of electricity.

"Stay with me, Sig," he whispered. He kissed her belly and hips as his fingers slipped between her thighs and stroked her clitoris.

She let out a breath and closed her eyes, letting herself feel what he was doing to her. Relaxing into the pleasure of his touch. His exploration of her with his tongue was a natural progression and she was all in, no longer worried about scars. No longer thinking about anything other than Cole Banner and how he woke something she thought she'd lost.

His mouth on her as she felt the warm sun caress her face, breasts, and belly was exquisite, but she needed more to finish this reclaiming of her body.

She pulled at his hair and demanded he put on a condom. She needed the feel of him inside her to close this circle.

He held her gaze as his sheathed cock pressed against her opening. "Tell me if you want me to stop. If it hurts and I need to change something. Don't worry about me. This is for *you*."

She gripped his hips and raised her head so her mouth was close to his. "This is for *us*." She tugged at his hips and he thrust inside her, and she let out a whimpering groan as he filled her.

She hadn't even known she'd missed sex until this moment. But she had. She'd missed the connection. The skin-to-skin contact. And the orgasms.

She was in the moment. In her body. Enjoying the intimacy of him moving inside her. So much so, it didn't take long for her to come. She'd been 90 percent there before he'd rolled on the condom.

Her cries echoed across the lake, making her laugh. There was nothing discreet about this.

Cole's orgasm followed soon after hers, and his groan of pleasure was equally loud. Spent, he rolled to his back, pulling her with him so he remained inside her. He kissed her neck and she lay on top of him, limp like a rag doll and oh so very happy for the first time in forever.

"Thank you," she whispered.

His lips found her temple. "Thank *you*."

"Can we just stay here forever?"

"Sure," he said, and she liked that he gave her a ridiculous answer to an impossible question.

After a few moments, he took care of the condom, then settled beside her, pulling her snug against him. He kissed her neck as one hand touched her damp hair while the other cupped her butt.

He took a breath, the kind that preceded words.

She stiffened. *Don't say it, Cole. Please.*

"Are the scars from . . . what happened to you?"

She didn't know what was worse, that he'd asked the question or that he couldn't say the word *rape*.

"You mean when I was raped."

"Yes. Are they letters? Or numbers?"

She shrugged. "Your guess is as good as mine. Zero-six, or O-G. Old guard? Original gangster? The word *GO*?" As she spoke, she scooted away from him.

She was no longer relaxed. No longer languid or happy.

Of course he'd asked. She'd known he would.

Anyone would, really. It might have been better if she'd warned him beforehand. But she hadn't wanted to dwell on it then either.

She rose to her feet and made a beeline for the lake. She needed to get clean.

"Signe—"

She whirled to face him and saw he was following her. She held up a hand. "No."

He stopped.

She ran into the water until she was knee-deep, then dived under. The shock of cold as she submerged was comparable to how she'd felt at being relaxed in Cole's arms, then having him ask the one question that had the power to destroy the oasis his touch had created.

Her first sex in more than two years followed up with questions about the symbols that had been carved on the insides of her thighs.

It would always be this way. She would never have sex without her partner asking questions about the brutal violation that had changed her forever. Even if they didn't ask, they would wonder, just as Cole had. Every sexual encounter would force her to relive the horror in one way or another.

CHAPTER 25

Signe watched Cole swim laps across the small lake, his body a sleek missile. She couldn't read him, had no clue if he was angry, sad, or indifferent. The only thing she knew for certain was that he wasn't happy with the way their interlude had ended.

That made two of them.

Did she regret having sex with him? She didn't think so. There had to be a first time—unless she wanted a life of celibacy, which now she knew she did not—and it might as well have been him.

The sex itself had been very good, when she could get out of her head and just let herself feel. But she'd realized something when she took her post-sex swim. Letting Cole inside her body hadn't completed the circle of reclaiming her sexuality. It had merely been the first step.

Now she knew she needed to set ground rules prior to intercourse. First and foremost: no questions about scars before or after.

Yeah, sex moving forward was sure to be a carnival of fun. Her best bet would be to invest in a good vibrator. Vibrators couldn't ask questions.

He emerged from the lake, the clear water dripping down his beautiful body. She had a pang knowing they'd probably never be intimate again. It wasn't like she'd been a stellar lay, and she came with enough baggage to fill an airplane.

She assembled their dinner—cold beans, cheese, and taco sauce wrapped in a tortilla—while he dried off and dressed. The meal would be far too small for a man of his size, but they needed to ration.

She'd berate him for swimming and burning more calories, but it was her rejection that had sent him into the lake to begin with, so she refrained.

She handed him his cold burrito and asked, "Is the rendezvous spot in the woods or a clearing?" It was time to use their dinner break for something productive.

"According to the GPS, it's treeless. Looks like it's the top of a rock outcrop. Steep enough that we might have to climb on all fours."

"So there's no way to approach it without being seen."

"Bingo," Cole said.

"Think that's why it was chosen?"

"Probably. It's absolutely nowhere. No lake. No stream. Nothing remarkable about the spot except that it's on top of a steep hill. In archaeology, it would be the worst place to look for any kind of habitation. No resources nearby. Too steep to climb for more than a lookout. Exposed, bare rock that bakes in the sun."

"Interesting. Whoever gets there first literally has the upper hand." The thought gave her a chill, and she made a mental note to arrive early. Hours early, if possible.

"Kind of makes you wonder why Leo wanted you to be late," Cole murmured.

"What does that mean?"

"Exactly what it sounds like."

His tone made her want to defend Leo, which was ridiculous. Why would she defend him? He saw the same scars Cole had, and instead of asking questions that made her want to run away, he'd been the one to run.

"Let me see the GPS," she said. He'd been carrying it in an effort to lighten her pack as much as possible.

He powered it on and handed it to her.

"How do you drop a pin? To mark a location."

He scooted close to her so he could see the screen while she held the device. He smelled of lake water and taco sauce. He showed her the menu option for marking locations, and she dropped a pin in the middle of the lake.

"Why there?"

She shrugged, not wanting to give the real answer. *This is the first time I've enjoyed my body in two years.* She gave a partial truth. "If I end up needing to return here to film more segments as follow-up for the story, I'll need to know our exact route. And this lake makes a pretty backdrop."

His expression said he didn't believe her, and there was a small spark of heat in his eyes, but he didn't argue the point.

"So where is the meeting going to take place?"

He zoomed out and showed her the route that had already been plotted. She noticed the lake's lonely pin wasn't entirely on their planned path, but was close enough to not be considered a detour. "I can see what you mean by it being nowhere. Even if they drive to one of the trailheads on Tioga Road, it's still a haul."

He nodded.

"Getting there isn't just a chore for us—it's a chore for them," she said. "Why here? Because it's so remote, random tourists aren't likely to interrupt?"

He shook his head. "Yosemite is vast. There are plenty of places to find privacy closer to the valley or Glacier Point or Wawona. My guess is they chose the high country for a reason."

"Manny died in the high country."

"Yeah. I've been thinking about that. Miles from where we're headed but still a part of the park he wasn't known to visit."

"Why was he up here?" she murmured, staring at the small screen. She faced Cole. "I'm paraphrasing because I don't have a copy of the first text from DiscoFever, but they said something like, 'the two murders—meaning Manny Lontoc and John Doe—are connected, and the informant will have evidence about the murders.' The meet point is closer to where both men died than it is to the valley." She paused. "Again, why was Manny here? And what did he buy at the Mountain Shop before he died?"

"One would expect climbing gear—but I'm guessing you're thinking camping supplies."

She nodded. "If you were going to camp anywhere near the rendezvous point, where would it be?"

His face lit up and he rose to go to his pack. A moment later, he was beside her with a stack of paper USGS quadrangle maps.

"Why are we going analog?"

"These aren't just any quad maps. These are maps I used when I worked in the park all those years ago. I marked all historic and prehistoric archaeological sites previously recorded in the park on these maps."

"And why does that matter to us now?"

"Because prehistoric sites are a good indicator of where good campsites would be today. Then and now, people have the same needs: access to water, food, shelter."

"You mean like caves next to a river?"

"Sure, but vegetation that can be used to build a shelter in the absence of a tent also works. This time of year, the lack of rain means less need for shelter than shade anyway."

Cole pointed to the rendezvous location. There were no notations for archaeological sites anywhere in the vicinity. "I definitely wouldn't camp anywhere around there."

He drummed his fingers on his knee. "We received the coordinates yesterday, but odds are, this spot was chosen days—maybe even weeks—ago. Which means the informant was here. Dropped a pin in their GPS because it was ideal for this kind of meet."

"But no one would hike this far just to pick a random place," Signe said.

"Exactly. They'd scout it out. Maybe set up a base camp. If you're going to be up here for any length of time, you need to know where the water is. Water brings game. Fishing and fowl. Which you need if you're living off the land."

Signe sucked in a breath as another detail clicked. "John Doe was emaciated."

Cole's finger traced Tioga Road on the paper map. "Why way out here, on the north side of Tioga Road, a part of the park that only opened a few weeks ago? A place where several campgrounds *still* aren't open?"

"How far in advance do workers come in and clean up the campgrounds to prep them for opening? I'd imagine there's a fair amount of work, what with cleaning pit toilets, clearing winter debris from the sites, and making sure the bear boxes are in working order."

"Holy shit," Cole said. "Subcontracted labor would probably be tapped for those jobs. Easy to bus in. They can work during the day because no tourists are around. Monitor the team in a remote area with no one else around."

They'd circled back to the theory they'd developed last night. Labor subcontracts for unskilled workers—the kinds of jobs labor-trafficking victims were forced to work in California and elsewhere in the United States, but now they also had a theory for why a group of laborers would be in the high country just days after the road opened.

"I wonder how many laborers would be needed to prep a primitive campground?" She paused, then added, "And how many might have escaped."

"You think more than John Doe might have escaped?"

"It's possible."

"You sound certain of this scenario."

She shook her head. "I'm not. Just mulling. But it fits what we know so far. A group of workers could have been prepping White Wolf or Porcupine Flat. A few escape, and they send one to hike to the valley for help, which he finds in the form of Manny, who goes to the Mountain Shop and gets supplies."

"We know Manny's car was broken down," Cole added, "at least for a few days. Without a car, he can't simply drive John Doe back to Tioga Road and pick up the other workers. He needs to repair his car first, hence the need for supplies."

Signe nodded. "And given what we know about trafficking, John Doe wouldn't want to reach out to law enforcement, because he knows the traffickers are searching the woods and were likely monitoring ranger activity."

"It fits. Manny gets his car fixed and returns to the park. Two days later, his body is found in Tenaya Lake."

"Manny and John Doe were found, but what if others weren't and they're still hiding in the high country? They're stranded in Yosemite, unable to speak the language, with no one to trust."

There was a lot of supposition—including the idea Manny was buying anything other than climbing gear at the Mountain Shop—but still, this fit everything she knew about human trafficking. Escape was difficult because where they worked was remote. Isolated. Easy to guard.

"That would mean DiscoFever could be leading us to them," Cole said. "We're the rescue squad."

"Maybe," Signe said.

"But why doesn't DiscoFever rescue them if they know where they are?"

"Maybe they can't. Maybe they're a trafficking victim too. Or they work for the traffickers but were facilitating the escape."

Signe mentally poked holes at the theory. It would make sense that someone who worked for the trafficking boss couldn't get themselves out. They'd be killed faster than Lontoc and Doe had been.

But if that were the case, how had DiscoFever known where the escapees were without others in the organization finding out? And how had they known what happened to her two years ago?

"So what comes next?" she asked.

"If the rendezvous point is anywhere near where escaped trafficking victims are hiding, we need to look for them. But it will be dark by the time we reach that area tonight. We'll have time tomorrow if we start at first light."

"And how will we find a campsite in the vast Yosemite high country?"

Cole tapped his temple. "We're going to use my mad archaeology skills."

She smiled. Who knew having an archaeologist as guide would come in handy? On impulse, she kissed him, a quick smack on the lips before jumping to her feet.

She gathered the packaging from dinner and secured it in the bear canister. "Let's get going, then. The sooner we go to sleep tonight, the sooner we can wake up and start searching."

"We're actually limited by when the sun rises, but close enough."

Chapter 26

It was full dark when they reached the area Cole had selected for their campsite. A cursory check revealed no bear dens or other hazards and, with relief, Signe removed the heavy pack once again.

"Everything hurts," she moaned.

"For not being a regular hiker, you're doing amazing."

"That feels like it might be a backhanded compliment."

He laughed. "Correction: you're doing amazing for any level of hiking experience. This is a difficult hike even for avid outdoorswomen."

"Better. If only Leo could see me now."

Cole frowned. "What does he have to do with anything?"

"Sorry. He just . . . didn't think much of my athleticism."

"Then he's a gaslighting, negging prick."

"True." She paused. She never should have brought him up, but now that she had, she couldn't help but ask, "What are you going to tell him?"

"You think I'm going to announce I fucked you?"

She winced and shook her head. "No, about the meeting tomorrow. The journey to get here. He'll demand to know everything."

"He can demand all he wants." He shook his head. "Honestly, I'm insulted you'd even think I'd report *anything* to Leo at this point. I won't work for him. I might beat the shit out of him for treating you as he did."

She flinched at his casual reference to violence, even if it was in her defense. Cole was a little too comfortable in that area for her tastes.

For the first time since Tuesday, she remembered the angry energy he'd exhibited at the museum on Sunday and the flashes she'd seen of his temper since then.

Was he the kind of guy who always followed through on threats?

◆ ◆ ◆

Since they'd already had dinner, they limited themselves to a dessert of dried fruit. Signe grumbled over the loss of their s'mores makings, as they'd been in the missing bear canister. After eating, Cole chose the spot for their remaining canister with care, including placing a bear bell on top and covering it with leaves. "It'll be hard to move it without us hearing the bell."

"Good plan."

They readied for sleep as they had the night before, then she settled on her sleeping pad mere feet from his, clothed in her lightweight long underwear that was comfortable to sleep in but not exactly pajamas.

He lay stretched out on his sleeping pad. A glance to the side confirmed he was wide awake, staring up at the stars, of which they could see only a handful through a small window in the forest canopy.

"Do you trust me, Cole?"

He turned to face her. "Honestly? I want to, but no."

"Why do you want to?"

His mouth quirked to one side. "I don't know. Because you're a good lay?"

She snorted. "So flattering."

"Sorry. I don't do sonnets."

"And you can't dance."

"Yet somehow, I get by."

"What are you going to do after this is over? You know I'll tell Leo you were a great guide, and I won't tell him we fooled around. That door isn't closed if you still want it."

"Don't worry about me. I'll be fine." Again, his voice had an edge.

"You didn't answer my question. What are you going to do after this? I mean . . . how do you even make a living? You never told me. You just said you aren't doing fieldwork anymore."

Wait, had he said that? She didn't even know. How in the world had she spent every hour with this man since Monday evening and she hadn't even asked him what he did for a living?

"I have work here and there. I'm not a dirtbag, if that's what you're wondering. I've got money. And no, I don't want to work with Leo. I've already made that clear."

"Where does your money come from?"

"The usual places. Banks. Cash back when I pay with my debit card."

"You know what I mean. Why are you being evasive?"

"I'll tell you, but you need to tell me where your money comes from first."

"I . . . have a job? I'm even rather successful?"

"You live alone in a five-million-dollar home in Redondo Beach. Your show is popular, yes, but it—and much of your reporting—is done for a network that's an environmental nonprofit exploration institute. You aren't Diane Sawyer, Norah O'Donnell, or Rachel Maddow, who are all big-name anchors working for for-profit news organizations and make big bucks. I'm guessing your salary covers your property taxes and not much else."

"I got the house in the divorce. And I can live off my salary just fine."

"Because your house is paid for."

"Yes."

"How did Leo pay for it?"

"He inherited and made good investments. He got into crypto early and got out before it got ugly."

Cole snorted. "Right. And he just gave you a five-million-dollar house even though he believed you cheated on him."

"How do you know so much about my house?"

"I know a lot about you, Signe Gates. I do my homework and eat my vegetables. Now, explain why he was so generous in the divorce settlement, which you yourself said was strangely in your favor."

"Given my specialty, I need my own editing studio and massive digital storage for all my raw footage. Many of my sources require anonymity, which means I can't upload files to TWN servers without faces blurred and voices distorted."

"I still don't see why Leo would give you the house."

"I needed the studio. Leo doesn't because he's not working the crime beat anymore. He's moved on to nature and archaeology documentaries, as you well know."

"And you expect me to believe Leo just walked away from several years' worth of work. Let you keep the only archive of everything he's filmed for the last ten years?"

"He has another studio and took backup drives with his files."

"He had to buy another studio, yet he gave you the expensive house?"

"No. He already had the other studio in a cabin he and his brother inherited."

"Where is this cabin?"

"I don't know. Near Tahoe, I think? An uncle he didn't like was living there up until a year before we separated. The uncle died and Leo and Steven inherited. Leo installed the studio in the basement not long after the title transfer."

"Sounds like Leo planned to leave you a year before he moved out."

"*What?* No. Never. That's ridiculous."

"You've never visited this mysterious cabin?"

"I was busy when he inherited. Never had time. But we talked about spending a few weeks there at the end of the summer. Then

I was raped and didn't exactly want a romantic getaway, so it never happened."

"One last time, why would a man give a woman he believes cheated on him a house free and clear? I get that you didn't have a claim on the cabin he inherited with his brother. But still, it's hardly equal distribution of joint assets."

"I think Leo was cheating on me. If the divorce got nasty, I would have found proof of it. I'm an investigative reporter who knows how to cross-check and validate information."

"Listen to yourself, Signe. Really *listen*. Even if you did fire back with evidence he'd been unfaithful, at best you'd have split the house. It would have been sold and the money divided equally. But he *gave* it to you. You really should be asking yourself why."

Her stomach knotted as she considered the implication of his words.

What was Leo's motive? At the time, he'd presented himself as magnanimous—and she'd believed him, clinging to the idea that it meant deep down, he didn't believe the worst in her. He gave her the house out of guilt over not standing by her when she told him she was raped. Guilt over his own cheating.

She'd made many excuses and hadn't ever asked questions. She'd been too afraid Leo would ask difficult questions in return.

And now that she considered it, he probably had done it out of guilt, but now she wondered what else he was guilty of.

CHAPTER 27

It was a testament to her exhaustion that Signe was able to sleep at all.
But her body needed to recover from the unaccustomed workout and
when she slipped into sleep, it was the deep, dreamless kind she seldom
experienced.

She woke with a start in the predawn hours, surfacing abruptly.
Something must've woken her. Her brain was sleep-fogged and it took
her a moment to remember where she was, who she was with, and why
she was here.

She reached toward Cole to ground herself but didn't feel him
beside her. She turned to her side. Light from the stars filtered through
the trees. The forest at night was all shades of gray, and she could see in
the gray darkness that Cole's sleeping bag was empty.

She slid a hand inside his unzipped bag. The soft nylon was cool to
the touch. No residual body heat.

She didn't think his getting up to empty his bladder was what woke
her, not with his bag already being cold.

Yesterday, she'd briefly wondered if he'd moved the missing bear
canister. Now she considered the possibility he was doing it again. Or
maybe he was off finding chains so he could haunt her. Was Cole the
person behind the horrific texts?

She'd discarded all those suspicions yesterday, but they were back
now and couldn't be ignored.

She checked her watch. It was almost five a.m. Where had he gone this time of morning?

She sat up and grabbed her flashlight, then searched the contents of his backpack. She didn't even feel slightly guilty about the invasion of privacy. She'd bought this pack and most of the items in it. Besides, she highly doubted he'd leave anything behind he didn't want her to see.

She noted what was missing: wallet, phones, GPS, gun.

What remained: toilet paper.

If he wanted her to believe he'd left for a normal and valid reason, he'd failed to make it plausible.

Dammit. She'd *liked* him. In spite of his bouts of anger. Or his ease with expressing violent ideation. And even though he'd avoided every personal question she'd asked him.

Shit.

Last night, he'd done it again and turned her questions about how he earned a living back on her.

Why? What was he hiding?

How was he involved in all this?

A cold chill settled in her heart as she asked the most important question of all: Who was he *really* working for?

He'd make a good investigative reporter. He knew how to direct an interview so he gave nothing away. She wasn't usually easy to trap with that technique, but given that this story they were supposedly investigating was about her, his questions had merit. Not for him to figure out, but for her.

Why *did* Leo give her the house?

Why hadn't she ever questioned it?

The sound of a stick snapping caught her attention. She raised the flashlight in the direction of the sound and caught Cole in the bright beam.

He raised a hand to cover his eyes. "Was that really necessary?" he snapped.

She lowered the light as he approached. "Yes. Where were you?"

"Bathroom break."

"Bullshit." She threw the toilet paper pouch at him. It bounced off his chest and landed on his empty sleeping bag.

"I'm a guy. I piss standing up and shake it off."

"You always need a gun, GPS, and a half hour to pee in the woods?"

"Something woke me and I wanted to check it out. I took the GPS in case I walked far—which I *did*."

"And why didn't you give that excuse first?"

His expression was cold. "I didn't want to scare you after what happened last night."

"I don't believe you."

He shrugged. "I don't really give a fuck." His gaze scanned the contents of his backpack strewn about on his sleeping bag. "Searching my stuff? Nice."

"Technically, this is all *my* stuff. You took every item *you* own out of the pack."

He cocked his head. "Huh. Okay, fair point."

He pushed aside a coil of paracord and a camera and sat down with his back to her and began unlacing his boots. "Now, if you can pack it back up so I can get another hour of sleep, that would be appreciated."

She wanted to make him do it, but it was indeed her mess. She quickly tucked everything away, then watched as he put his wallet and phones in the front pocket. The gun, he kept with him.

But then, so did she with hers. "See any bogeymen in the woods?"

"Don't ask questions if you aren't prepared for the answer."

"You'd make an excellent investigative journalist."

"I know." He lay down and closed his eyes, pulling the sleeping bag only partially over him. "Now, let me sleep."

"I'm not the person who stopped you to begin with."

"Sweetheart, you have no idea."

She could ask what he meant, but he'd never answer, so she flopped down and punched at her pillow to make it just so, then pressed her cheek to it and closed her eyes.

Several minutes passed. The night sounds of the forest no longer acted as a soothing lullaby. Next to her, Cole's breathing evened out. He wasn't bothered by any forest bogeymen.

She imagined how things could have gone if he hadn't asked questions by the lake. Then she wondered when she'd learn there was no point in wishing to change the past.

What would have happened if Signe hadn't entered that bar? If instead, she'd read Leo's text message and turned around, got into her car, and drove north to Mount Shasta to confront him?

The thought hadn't even crossed her mind at the time, but now it haunted her like Jasper's ghost.

She lay stiff on the hard ground and waited for sunlight to touch her eyelids, so she could get up and search for men who probably didn't exist anywhere but in her fantasies.

She knew deep down that she'd attached herself to the idea that she might be able to rescue human-trafficking victims, because if she did, it would be a small redemption for two years of complicit silence.

CHAPTER 28

"Explain how your mad archaeologist skills are going to help us today."
Signe posed the question as they neared the area Cole had selected for
them to begin searching for a squatters' camp.

"The first rule of archaeology is work smarter, not harder."

"I'm pretty sure that's not limited to archaeology."

"Yes, but given that our work goes back millennia, we probably
applied it first."

"I'm calling bull. You *study* cultures that go back millennia. That's
different."

"Fine. We didn't originate it, but I'm sure we perfected it."

She rolled her eyes.

He nodded toward a low rock and said, "Sit. We need to look at
the map for this and make a plan."

Any excuse to drop her pack worked for her. She took a sip from
her water bottle as he again pulled out the quad map for the area they
were traversing.

"So, in archaeology, we conduct pedestrian transects in survey areas
to look for sites. It's exactly how it sounds. A surveyor walks straight
lines across a survey area at a specific interval. Usually ten meters, but
closer or farther in areas of high or low probability."

"And what does *high or low probability* mean?"

He smiled. "That's the key to working smarter, not harder. See, walking a full ten-meter transect of all of Yosemite—or anywhere— would be ridiculous. Working way too hard for little chance of return. You don't need to look *everywhere*. But you do need to look in the right places. Places with medium to high probability. We determine probability for historic and/or prehistoric occupation based on what we know about human behavior and basic survival needs. Access to water, plenty of resources, etcetera, just like I mentioned before."

He pointed to penciled markings on the map. "This is an archaeological site. Note the proximity to a stream. In six or eight weeks, that stream will be low and might even be dry, but right now, it should be flowing. Which means fresh water and plenty of game coming to drink. There might even be some trout, but it's not big enough to be reliable for that."

"So you think if there are people hiding in these woods, they'd be somewhere in this area."

"If they have a camp anywhere near the meet point, yes, that area has the highest probability. If they aren't near the meet point, then there's no way in hell we'll find them."

"Okay, so how do we do this, search the area?"

"We're going to conduct ten-meter pedestrian transects—that is, you and I will space ourselves ten meters apart and walk parallel lines that are as straight as possible given the terrain, looking down at the ground for signs of human activity. We're each responsible to look five meters on each side. That is, five meters to your left and to your right, so technically the entire ten meters between us is scanned."

Cole laid out the boundaries of their survey area. The western boundary was defined by the proximity to White Wolf Campground. No need to explore close to the campground because even though White Wolf wouldn't open until next week, squatters would be in danger of being spotted by park rangers or hikers who might explore the area that offered easy road access.

There was a section of a good-size creek that was far enough away from the established trails to look promising, so they set the creek as their northern boundary for north-south transects. Upon completing each transect, they would shift over ten meters from the previous transect—twenty meters total, given that there were two of them—and walk south. If they found nothing on the south side of the creek, they'd do transects on the north side.

Cole determined they'd walk 150 meters—about a tenth of a mile—south from the creek, figuring the people they were searching for wouldn't want to be farther than that from the water source. Still, when they reached the survey area, Signe could see it was a good thing they'd gotten an early start if they were to have a shot at finishing the survey before they needed to head to the meet point that had been their destination from the start.

Worse, it was also a lot of extra walking while wearing heavy packs.

Five transects in, Signe grumbled, "If we don't find anything, I'm going to hold this against you. We've already added a half mile to our hike today. Feels a lot like working harder."

"You'd make a terrible archaeologist."

"The worst," she admitted.

Three transects later, something shiny caught her attention. She studied the ground to see what it was but didn't see anything except rocks and roots and plants she couldn't begin to identify. She'd also make a terrible botanist.

She backed up and repeated her previous step. The flash returned. Sunlight filtering through the trees had caught an object just so when viewed from the right angle.

She dropped to her knees and pushed aside leaves and twigs.

"What is it?" Cole asked.

"Something metal. Partially buried. I think it's a piece of silverware."

He dropped down beside her and pulled off his pack. "Wait. I've got a trowel."

He held up the diamond-shaped tool with a wooden handle that had clearly seen lots of use. She imagined he never went hiking without it. Always an archaeologist, but also a handy tool, as it was sharp on two edges and pointed.

He scraped around the object until a spoon popped free.

"Dirt was pretty compact around it. My guess is it's been buried here for a while. Not our guys."

Disappointment filtered through her.

"Still, good eye. This is exactly the kind of thing we're looking for."

She frowned at the metal utensil. "What do we do with it? Leave it here?"

Cole paused to study the object like he was the Little Mermaid adding an item to her collection. "If it were a prehistoric artifact, yes—we don't have a permit and aren't doing an official survey, so collecting it would be looting. But given the style, my guess is this is less than twenty years old, so we'll bag it as litter. I'll mark it on my map, though."

It took him only a moment to make the notation on his quadrangle map, then they resumed their survey.

Several transects and twenty minutes later, Signe paused at spotting something that couldn't be decades old.

"Cole?" It was almost hard to get the name out, as her throat had constricted with excitement.

"Whatcha got?"

"A footprint."

◆ ◆ ◆

They trod carefully, slowly, making sure not to disturb other evidence of human occupation as they continued searching. Seven meters from the first footprint, Cole found another. He measured by pacing the distance between each—a technique archaeologists used for mapping, he explained—and began a sketch map. Using graph paper and his compass, he plotted the location of the two footprints before continuing to search.

By the stream, they found more footprints—one half washed away by the flowing water, proving they were *very* recent, given the decreasing water level as summer dried out the high country—and several in an area where rocks had been stacked in the stream, creating a deeper pool.

"That's no natural beaver dam," Cole said. "That was made to collect water from a shallow stream."

She stared at the well that had been created at the side of the trickling stream. It was about three feet in diameter and a foot deep. The rocks were carefully stacked. They fit like puzzle pieces.

"Someone really has been living here." She almost couldn't believe it. What had started as wild supposition could be true?

"More than one person from the different sizes of the footprints. Three, maybe four people?"

He took photos of the well and added it to his map, while Signe filmed the flow of water into and around the human-made well.

Evidence documented, they continued their search.

"Where are they now?" she asked.

"They could be hiding from us. Or they left."

She wanted to call out, in case they were nearby, but they didn't know who else was in these woods. For example, if her chained ghost the other night hadn't been a dream. It wouldn't be safe to alert anyone to where Signe and Cole were or what they'd found here so far.

Next, they found more utensils—modern bamboo ones, lightweight for hiking. Just like the ones Signe had purchased on Monday.

Cole then spotted a mat of shrubs and brush that looked like it had been woven together. He photographed it, then lifted the meter-diameter sheet of vegetation. Beneath the mat was a small circle of rocks with charred sticks in the center. The dirt and ash were damp, as if water had been poured on it to douse embers before it was covered by the camouflage matting. The cover would have trapped moisture and delayed drying, but only by hours in this weather, not days.

CHAPTER 29

Signe filmed Cole as he knelt by the fire ring. If this did become part of a story, she wanted the raw footage, but either way, it was evidence. Sure, it was all speculation on their part, but she believed they really had found a refuge for human-trafficking victims.

"What did they eat?" she asked as the camera rolled. "We haven't found any wrappers for packaged hiking food."

He set aside the matting and pulled his trowel from his back pocket, then scraped across the wet ash and charcoal at the center. "Each fire creates a new layer of ash. Materials burn differently and you get different shades of gray ash and black charcoal."

He cut into the ground next to the damp area—where the ash and charcoal hadn't been compressed by water—and pulled out a slice like it was a wedge of cake. The greasy black and gray ash was stacked on top of his trowel, an inch high. And, sure enough, she could see very thin layers. Like cake tiers, but most only an eighth of an inch thick. And there were white items that looked like sticks poking out in a few places.

Cole pointed to the sticks. "That's calcined mammal bone. Squirrel, rabbit, if they were lucky maybe they got something big a few times like a porcupine. My guess is they were snaring game however they could and eating it to survive."

"Where are they now?" she asked. "How long ago did they douse this fire?"

"They could have doused it last night and the matting kept the ash from drying overnight. The temperature dropped to fifty-two degrees last night. It wouldn't have dried much until the sun hit the matting this morning, and, as you can see, this area only gets dappled sunlight. But it's also possible the fire was put out not long before we entered this area."

She studied the forest where they'd been searching for the last forty-five minutes.

She'd guess people hiding here were always prepared to bolt. Douse the fire, hide the hearth, grab anything within arm's reach, and run.

She used the camera to film the woods, panning in a circle, looking for the most logical exit route.

Go deeper into the woods or head to the road?

If one of their members was injured or ill, the road could mean rescue. But the road could also mean capture, which had to be their biggest fear.

If they'd been hiding out in the same area for weeks, they were *waiting* for something. In that situation, if they feared discovery, they'd go deeper into the woods. Across the stream.

She turned the camera toward the water, which was only fifty yards away and just visible through a gap in the trees. This was a good location for the hearth, close as it was to their water source but also far enough back with a small window in that direction, so they could see if anyone was following the stream to a small lake that showed up on the USGS quadrangle map. A lake so small, it didn't even have a name.

If they followed the creek in the other direction a few miles, they'd reach a rustic NPS campground that would open in a few days. As long as the creek was in sight, no one would get lost, even without a compass and a map.

"We should walk along the stream. Toward the lake."

Cole had replaced his dirt cake in the hearth. He took the matting and placed it over the rock ring again, just like they'd found it.

She now realized that even though they'd found footprints in multiple sizes, they hadn't found many of them, which meant whoever had been living here had been careful—maybe until this morning. They also hadn't created trails in the woods, which meant they must've varied their route among the trees. That took incredible discipline.

The degree of care they'd used was admirable, but then, if they were trafficking victims, who knew what horrors they'd escaped and feared being returned to?

Of course, the fear wasn't being recaptured. John Doe had suffered the penalty for escape: death.

A shiver went down her spine.

The camp didn't feel abandoned so much as *empty*.

Cole rose to his feet to join her as she explored along the creek. She tucked the camera into her pack, her excitement over the footage they'd gotten dimmed as she considered the fate of the men who appeared to have hidden here.

"Why aren't you filming?"

She should record this. It was her *job*. She'd even stated at the beginning that this wasn't her usual kind of story. She needed to be a damn investigative reporter and see it through.

When places were abandoned, people moved on. But empty? That was a void. Like when Jasper stopped screaming. Stopped breathing. His body had been empty.

So many deaths. She couldn't count them all, simply because she didn't know the extent. She'd lost several informants in the divorce, but always the question nagged: How many hadn't been lost at all but instead were killed?

She passed the camera to Cole. "You film. If we find something, I'll go on camera."

The creek was just wide enough to provide a break in the trees and the morning sun hit the shallow water, making it sparkle. Wildflowers grew in colorful swaths along the opposite bank, which got more sunlight.

"It's so pretty here."

She wondered at the lives of the men who'd hidden in these woods. If they were from the Philippines but didn't speak much English, they were probably from a remote village, just as wild and beautiful as Yosemite. They'd probably signed on to be foreign workers with plans to send money back to their families, only to find themselves enslaved.

What had they seen of California beyond brutality? Forced to clean up after tourists, bussed in by a concessionaire to clean pit toilets and waste stations. Brought in in the night so as not to disturb the tourists, but also to limit their access to people who could help them.

Sunlight hit a patch of blue flowers on the far side of the stream, but one flower was a different shade of blue. "Film me," Signe said as she darted across the stream.

She made herself pause and take a photograph with her phone before reaching down and spreading the flowers to see what she'd found. Her breath caught.

She'd wondered what they'd used to collect water from the pool.

"What is it?" Cole asked.

With trembling fingers, she brushed at the dirt on the side of the container, and her heart squeezed.

She took another photo. She didn't think this had been hidden among the flowers. It had been dropped here. She lifted the blue Nalgene one-liter water bottle and held it up so Cole could film from across the stream. "It's not just any water bottle—we know who it belonged to."

She turned the container so the name painted in all caps on the side was clearly legible for the camera: LONTOC.

◆　◆　◆

More searching on the far bank turned up a tote bag with a cache of items: camping dishes including a pan, a flint-and-steel fire-starter kit on a paracord lanyard, a wind-up flashlight, a drained portable charger with micro-USB cable, and finally, a cheap two-way satellite messenger with a dead battery.

Had Manny bought the messenger device at the Mountain Shop? It would explain how DiscoFever got the coordinates even if they never entered the park.

The tote bag had the CAMP CURRY WELCOME sign on the side. "I saw bags just like it in the grocery store and Mountain Shop on Tuesday," Cole said.

"It's weird that it's just dropped here, given how careful they were to hide their presence in their camp."

"Same with Manny's water bottle. My guess is they were fleeing."

She could see it in her mind. If she had to run for her life, the first thing she'd do is drop her pack. Of course, this bag wasn't nearly as heavy, but it also wasn't wearable like a pack and they might have had important items to hold on to, like a sleeping bag or weapons.

Signe held it together for the camera while Cole filmed her examining each item.

When they were done, Cole handed her the camera. "There's something in the tree behind you I want to check out."

Signe filmed him as he made a beeline for what looked like a piece of white cloth. He pulled it from the branch, studied it, then dropped his head. His shoulders hunched. Then he stood straight and faced her, holding the object up for the camera. A tank top. Printed on the front was a flag: red, blue, and a golden yellow sun.

The flag of the Philippines.

She pulled out her photo of Manny and noted the tear on the collar matched the tear in the shirt Cole now held.

Manny had given these men the shirt off his back.

The only difference from the photo was the blood that streaked a gash on the left side was fresh.

CHAPTER 30

Signe's heart ached at having to leave the camp behind, but they were running out of time to get to the meeting set up by DiscoFever, which was the purpose of this whole journey. Part of her held on to the hope that they'd find the men from the camp at the meet point, but the blood on Manny's shirt hinted at something far more sinister.

Now they approached the clearing. They were only thirty minutes early, but it was better than nothing.

Her hands trembled and breathing grew labored to the point of only being able to take shallow breaths. This was it. It was time to find out who DiscoFever had sent her to meet.

She'd had a dozen ideas and a thousand fears about what this meeting would bring, but now she was utterly blank. She had no clue who awaited them on top of the granite outcrop that jutted thirty feet from the rocky, treeless ground.

"You okay, Sig?" Cole's whispered words let her know that she wasn't doing a great job of hiding her distress.

Was this a panic attack? She'd never had one before.

Well, except for in the days after being raped, but that was likely one long panic attack that lasted several weeks.

Now her heart pounded and stomach twisted.

You are Signe Gates. You have tea with mob bosses and beer with Colombian cartel leaders. This is nothing.

But it wasn't nothing and her body knew it. Fight or flight was kicking in and flight was fighting dirty, throwing up images of a skewed video playing on a hotel-room wall. Bland striped wallpaper became spattered with blood.

Hands cupped her upper arms. "Breathe, Sig. Deep, slow breaths. Do it with me."

She focused on Cole's eyes and inhaled slowly as instructed.

"You got this."

She closed her eyes and took another breath, then whispered, "I got this."

Lips brushed her forehead. "And I've got your back."

Once her breathing was less labored, she opened her eyes. "Let's do this."

His lips pressed to hers—soft and brief—then he released her shoulders and stepped back. "You want to go first or me?"

"Side by side."

He nodded and they entered the clearing together and crossed to the granite outcrop.

There was just enough slope for an all-fours climb. Hands and feet seeking purchase, but not the kind of steep that required ropes. Just agility.

Sweat gathered between her backpack and skin, soaking her sports bra and moisture-wicking top. The good thing about the exertion required was it made her forget to be afraid of what they'd find at the top. Instead, she focused on her hands and feet and pulling her body and pack ever upward. At last, she reached the lip and climbed over, congratulating herself as if she'd just solved Midnight Lightning.

She let herself breathe for a few seconds with her head hanging down, giving her vision a moment to clear. The altitude was messing with her again.

Finally, she pushed off the ground with her hands to give her the boost she needed with the pack weighing her down. She raised her head to take in the treeless, uneven granite slab littered with small boulders and cracks in the pale surface.

A boulder a dozen yards away looked odd and she shook her head, realizing her vision wasn't yet clear. She focused again. Her eyesight wasn't the problem. It wasn't a boulder.

It was . . . a body?

She took a step forward but tripped on a rock and teetered, once again windmilling under the weight of her pack. Cole caught her, preventing her from face-planting on granite, but she was too transfixed by the shape on the ground to care.

It was definitely a body.

A man.

A . . . oh *no*. No. No no no nonono.

The nos in her head erupted into a shrill scream that echoed across the high country.

She screamed and screamed until she finally dropped to her knees and cupped Leo's cold, dead face.

CHAPTER 31

Signe felt the tug of Cole's hands as he pulled her to her feet and away from Leo's body. She jabbed an elbow backward, catching him in the chest or ribs. "Don't touch me!" she shrieked.

He released her and she dropped to her knees again next to her husband. A man she'd known since she was in her early twenties. She'd worked with him for more than ten years, had lived with him for eight, and they'd been married for seven. She'd wanted to have his children. She'd expected to grow old with him.

He'd broken her heart, but there were pieces left that loved him still. "Leo. Oh my god, Leo." His sightless eyes stared up from under a neat bullet hole in the forehead.

His cold skin meant he'd been dead for some time. A few hours, at least.

Yesterday, she'd told Cole about her rape. Now Leo was dead.

"He's next if you say a word. This is your last warning."

They always followed through.

Tears poured down her cheeks as she pressed her lips to his. "I'm so sorry. So sorry. I tried. I tried so hard to keep the secret. For you." She swiped at the tears that dropped from her face to his. "I love you."

"He doesn't deserve it."

She whipped around to face Cole. "Doesn't deserve to be killed? Yeah. I *know*. This is *my* fault."

A horrific truth settled in. For her tormentor to know she'd told Cole, they'd either have to have bugged her sleeping bag or Cole had found a way to tell someone. And she highly doubted anyone could have bugged her bag.

"You did this, didn't you? Either you told the crime lord or . . ." Her voice trailed off as his absence last night registered.

He'd had his gun and GPS unit. Something had woken her a full thirty minutes before he returned. Had she heard a shot? Had he killed Leo, then calmly returned to her side and claimed it was a piss break?

She reached for her gun, which she'd placed in the side mesh pocket for easy access today, and racked the slide. "You did this."

"No, Signe. I meant he doesn't deserve your *love*. He's the guy behind everything. He's been looking for the escaped trafficking victims. He was here, in the park, three weeks ago. He was seen talking to Lontoc."

"Bullshit. How could you possibly know that?"

"Because Carmen told me. Two days ago, on the path after you insisted on going alone. First she heard Manny talking to a man who could be John Doe. They were both speaking Tagalog—"

"Impossible. If that were true, you'd have told me when we talked about the possibility Manny met John Doe in the valley."

"It's true. And a few days later, Carmen saw Leo talking to Manny. I think he was looking for John Doe—and I highly doubt it was part of a story. He doesn't work the crime beat anymore, as you well know."

He was lying. What he was saying about Leo made no sense. "Again, I'm calling bullshit."

"I'm sorry but Leo is in deep." He glanced behind her and amended, "*Was* in deep."

Rage surged through her. "Right. And you're just conveniently saying this *now*?"

"I couldn't trust you weren't still working for Leo. I was hoping you'd spill what you know about his operation."

She pointed the gun at his chest. "Shut up. I'm so sick of being manipulated. Lied to."

"I'm telling the truth. Signe, I'm here to find answers, just like you. I've been suspicious of both you and Leo. I was just—"

She couldn't listen to his crap. Not when she'd just lost everything.

She squeezed the trigger, firing several feet to his right. Stone flecks ricocheted, skipping over the rocky surface as the bark of sound echoed across the granite clearing, reverberating through the high country. "I said shut up."

"You won't shoot me."

"Yeah, well, I never thought you would shoot Leo, but here we are."

"I didn't shoot him. I'm on *your* side."

"Bullshit. You were the one rattling the chains the other night, weren't you?" She broke out into a cold sweat as pieces came together. "There's only one way you'd know they beat Jasper with a chain or about the distorted voice. You're one of them."

She squeezed the handle of the gun. The metal had warmed in her hand. Rage blurred her vision. "Then, when I told you, you followed through with their threats and killed Leo."

"I don't know what you're talking about. Who's Jasper?"

His tone was completely off. He was lying. "You know exactly who Jasper Evans is."

And there it was, a flicker in his eye.

Yes, Cole Banner was lying.

He held her gaze. He was trying to figure out how to salvage this. Searching for the best lie to bring her back into the fold. In the end, he settled on the most ridiculous lie of all: "Listen, I know people who can help you. If you report what you know, they can protect you."

As if it wasn't bad enough that he'd fucked her and then killed her husband, now he was trying to get her to confess by claiming to be able to connect her with law enforcement?

"Really, Cole, you've fucked up. Played your hand too soon when you killed Leo. Go tell your crime-lord boss to leave me the fuck alone. I've got no one left to lose."

"You can still cut a deal with law enforcement. You know what happened to Jasper."

Wow. He must think she was a total chump. Still, she'd tell him exactly what she knew. Then he could tell his boss he had nothing to fear from her. The only thing she could give the FBI was her own confession. "No, I don't. Not his body. I just saw video of him being beaten to death with a chain. And the only person that video implicates is *me*."

"You were the one with the chain?"

She recoiled. "No! I'm the one who revealed he was an undercover FBI agent. It's my fault they beat him to death."

◆ ◆ ◆

And there it was. The confession he'd wanted, but not the person he'd expected to hear it from.

But then, Leo was dead, so he could hardly confess now.

Signe's allegiance to Leo was disturbing. He had a hard time believing a woman who made crime lords the focus of her reporting failed to recognize the criminal she was married to, which meant she was complicit as hell, and now she'd just confessed to signing Jasper's death warrant. Cole would be a fool to trust her with his own life.

"Dammit. I wanted to like you, Sig. But you're just another fraud."

She flinched. The hands holding the gun that was currently pointed at his chest shook. He didn't believe she had it in her to intentionally shoot him, but she might by accident.

"Put the gun down, Sig."

She shook her head. "You aren't calling the shots." She gave a faint smile as her gaze dipped to the gun and added, "No pun intended."

She straightened her stance until she stood at her full five feet three inches. She looked almost calm. "This is what we're going to do. You're going to use one hand to unclip your pack, and then slowly, one shoulder at a time, you're going to lower it to the ground. I'll do the same with mine, and then you're going to transfer the food canister from your pack to mine."

She took a step toward him. "But before we do any of that, you're going to raise both your hands and clasp them together above your head, and I'm going to take your gun. You so much as flinch and I will shoot you between the eyes."

He had no choice and did as she instructed. When she was close enough to touch, he clenched his hands together to resist the urge to grab her. Shake her. Demand she see reason.

He needed to get through the next ten minutes. Then he'd figure out how to deal with Signe Gates, whose words had triggered the brutal murder of his best friend.

Chapter 32

A cold calm settled in and Signe's hands no longer shook as she kept the gun pointed at Cole while he made the transfer of their food supplies. At least she wouldn't accidentally shoot him. The only reason she didn't *want* to pull the trigger again was that she didn't believe in being judge and jury, not when she knew Cole wasn't her rapist and didn't have proof he'd killed Leo. No, instead of shooting him, she'd get the hell out of this forest and get the evidence she needed for an actual trial.

"Give me your phones. Both of them."

"You're going to leave me out here without food or communication."

"Consider yourself lucky that I'm not taking your water bottle."

"Yay?"

She'd had sex with this man, and he'd killed Leo. Either by action or words, he'd killed her husband.

Ex-husband. But still, the love of her life. At least he had been. For a time.

Why had Leo insisted Cole be her guide?

She had to get away so she could think. Put the pieces together. Create a picture that made sense.

Once she had what she needed to make the journey back to the valley without him, she instructed Cole to lie flat on his stomach. She grabbed the paracord coil from his pack and tied his hands together at the small of his back.

He'd be able to get loose eventually, but this would buy her time. She needed at least a mile head start. Two would be better. For the trek back, she'd stick to the road and trails. She'd be easy to find, but there'd be people around.

At least this hike would be mostly downhill. Four thousand feet down, and if she did her math correctly, once she reached the Porcupine Creek trailhead, she had five miles to go before she'd reach Snow Creek Trail. From there, it was five or so miles down to the valley, including the dozens of switchbacks that had been so grueling on the hike up.

If she didn't have to hike the miles from here to the road and then along the road to the trailhead, she'd be able to do it in one day, but she had at least eight miles from here to the trailhead. Even hyped on adrenaline and fear, there was no way she could do eighteen miles in a single day. She wasn't superhuman.

But Cole wasn't, either, and he wouldn't have food to power him for the journey.

Once he was bound, she dumped out the contents of his pack and hid the items like Easter eggs among the rocks. Anything to slow him down.

"Don't do this, Signe. We can hike out together. Report finding Leo to the rangers. It'll be easier if we stick together."

"Right. You're just going to walk up to the ranger station with me and say, *Hey, I shot this guy. Here's where you can find the body.*"

"I didn't shoot Leo. That's why you shouldn't go off alone. Whoever shot him could still be here. Watching. Waiting for *you.*"

That gave her a moment's pause, but she shook it off. She was safer without Cole than with him.

He lay on his belly with his left cheek pressed to the ground, facing her. She picked up her pack and moved out of his line of sight, then tucked her gun in the outer mesh pocket and hoisted the pack to her back. It was heavier again with the weight of the canister full of food, a second gun, two more phones, and the tote bag with Manny's gear strapped to the outside. The pack was now at the upper limit of her strength. Eighteen miles she'd haul this thing.

Five days ago, she'd received a text that set her on this journey. She never once hesitated or considered not going, even though she knew it would be beyond her ability. It was the same today.

She would do it. She'd take every excruciating step—even when she had no energy left inside her to power forward, she'd find a way.

She'd get out of this park, and then she'd get justice for Leo. And Jasper. And Manny.

Without a word or a second glance, she left her bound lover and climbed down the steep rocky hillside.

CHAPTER 33

Cole started working at the knot that tied his hands together the moment she slipped below the rim of the outcrop. He moved to a rock where he could watch the clearing. It wasn't long before she disappeared among the trees. From her trajectory, he guessed she was headed straight for Tioga Pass. Probably she'd head to Porcupine Creek Trail, unless she managed to get a ride from a passing tourist.

But given that she had to worry Leo's murderer—allowing for the possibility it hadn't been Cole—would still be in the area, she might decide to avoid flagging down a vehicle. At least she would if she were smart.

And he knew for a fact that she was very, very smart.

She'd been clever to tie him up and scatter his things. He had yet to find the knife that would make quick work of the paracord, so he worked at the binding in an attempt to loosen it. She hadn't tied any kind of traditional knot as far as he could tell, but there were six or seven tangled knots and she'd bound his wrists in a figure eight with several—but not all—the knots being in the center.

He wouldn't be able to undo or loosen them. He couldn't get his fingers on the main mass between his wrists.

As he fiddled with the knots, he moved to stand above Leo's body. The dead man might have a knife in a pocket. Signe hadn't searched the body. She'd only touched him in the first moments as she'd cried over him.

Her grief had been deep and real and had cut a small slice out of Cole's heart. It bothered him that she still cared for the bastard, which was illogical. Of course she cared. They'd been married.

Every awful thing she'd done was to protect Leo. She'd said as much several times. She was as guilty as her ex.

He hadn't wanted to believe it. Still struggled with the idea of her guilt. But she'd admitted it, straight up. She'd sold out Jasper.

It had probably happened when she was raped, but she hadn't offered that excuse. Worse, she hadn't reported what had happened once she was free. If she had, the search for Jasper would have started sooner. They'd have had a lead on who'd abducted him.

But no. She didn't tell a soul. To protect Leo.

Now Leo was dead anyway and Cole didn't have an ounce of remorse.

He probed at the body with the toe of his boot, tapping pockets to determine if they could hold a knife or other weapon.

He gave up and scanned the ground for a rock with a sharp edge. Time to put his archaeologist skills to use. Who knew his past career would come in handy yet again?

He found a wedge of granite that was the right size for him to manipulate the edge to saw on the cord. It took several minutes and more than a few nicks on his wrists, but at last, he severed the first strand. When he cut through the second, the figure eight loosened, and by the time he was through the fourth layer, it was loose enough for him to slip out his right hand.

Once his hands were in front of him, he could see which knot to loosen to free his left. He rubbed his wrists as he searched for his gear among the rocks. Relief swept through him when he spotted the GPS hidden in a crevice. He wasn't worried about getting lost—he had his compass and map and a solid idea of where he'd intersect with the road the fastest.

No, the GPS was key for another purpose.

He'd wanted Signe to believe he'd gotten it Tuesday evening at the Mountain Shop because that would mean he didn't have a chance to set up the texting feature on his computer, but that had already been configured when he picked it up.

Now he sent the text that would give him a huge lead in the race between him and Signe to get back to Oakhurst. Or rather, Redondo Beach, because he had a feeling the answers he needed waited in Signe's magnificent cliffside home.

He finished gathering his belongings from their hiding places— making sure not to leave anything behind both because this was a leave- no-trace wilderness area and because he didn't want to leave anything that could implicate him in the vicinity of Leo's corpse.

He hadn't touched the body beyond probing with his foot, while Signe had touched his face and likely shed some hair as she cried. If animals didn't take care of Leo's remains before law enforcement got here, and she'd left DNA, that would be her problem to deal with.

He couldn't alibi her any more than she could alibi him for the time of Leo's death, and he could paint an ugly picture that directed suspicion away from him and right back to her.

His pack was lighter without the food canister, but it didn't matter much. He wouldn't be hiking for long.

He set out for the road, not bothering to follow Signe's route. She'd go east on the road, while he was heading west for his meet point.

It took him two hours to reach the coordinates he'd sent earlier. Minutes before arriving, he texted again.

Not thirty seconds after he stepped out into the road, a car drove up, then slowed as it reached him.

Cole ducked his head to see inside and confirm this was his ride. He was surprised to see the passenger seat was occupied. Even more surprised to see the woman's familiar face.

He opened the rear passenger door and tossed his pack in before climbing inside.

"Jesus, you reek," the driver said.

"I've had a rough morning after a rough week with hardly any sleep. Did you have to do the chain-rattling thing? It scared the crap out of her."

"Quit your bitching. I haven't gotten much sleep, either, and at least you got laid."

Okay, so he wasn't sleeping with the woman in the front seat. Who was she, and how had he gotten her to pretend to be a fan of Signe's at Glacier Point that first morning?

He was about to introduce himself when the driver turned and faced him. The scars on the right side of his face still prominent after all this time. "So? Did you get what we need from her?"

Slowly, Cole nodded. "I think so. She confessed. It wasn't Leo—it was Signe who blew your cover, Jasper."

CHAPTER 34

One foot in front of the other. Don't think about Leo. Don't think about Cole. Just keep moving forward. Get to the valley. Get the car.

Go home.

Why did Leo give her the house?

Cole's questions echoed in her mind.

Don't think of him. Don't think at all.

"Sounds like Leo planned to leave you for a year."

No. Leo loved her. He had the studio installed in the cabin because he wanted a retreat. A place in the woods that would be all his own.

Well, his and Steven's, but according to Leo, Steven had been fine with the upgrades. The cabin had a full basement that had never been finished. Leo had paid for everything, including a rec room with a pool table and bar and a laundry room and extra bathroom.

Steven had benefited from the renovation as much as Leo.

Leo hadn't been planning to leave her. He'd just wanted a better man cave to share with his baby brother.

Steven.

She'd have to tell him Leo was dead.

Don't think about Steven.

Walk.

She heard an approaching car engine and slipped into the woods at the edge of the road. She couldn't trust anyone. Not anymore.

Her legs ached and she longed to take a break, but feared that if she sat for any length of time, she wouldn't be able to get up, so as soon as the car passed, she resumed walking on the shoulder.

One step after another. She was in a daze when she reached the trailhead.

She used the pit toilet, then headed down the trail. Cole had probably been free for at least two hours. If he wasn't shy about hitching a ride, he could show up at any moment.

She'd been on the trail for at least an hour when she found she didn't have the energy to take another step. She needed to eat.

She tucked herself into the woods, hidden from view of the trail but close enough to hear voices as people passed her hiding place. She leaned against a thick tree trunk and ate the last apple in the canister followed by three protein bars.

Done eating, she tilted her head back and closed her eyes. Exhaustion weighed down on her, but she needed to keep going. Cole could find her if she sat here too long.

But she couldn't move.

She thought she might cry again but found her tears had dried up. Exhaustion had numbed her. Or maybe it was shock.

She didn't make a decision to rest, it just happened. She slipped into oblivion without even realizing it.

The next time she opened her eyes, it was dark. A glance at her watch showed she'd slept for hours. Sitting up against a tree.

She slowly rose to her feet and stretched. Her body ached after holding one position for so long, but not horribly so.

Her feet hurt. Her legs were sore. Her shoulders protested when she considered strapping on the pack again. But the nap had helped and she knew her body could take it.

She donned her headlamp and walked into the wee hours, enjoying the quiet loneliness of the trail at night.

Again, she stopped to eat at the base of a tree, but this time she knew she would sleep if she could. It felt safer somehow to have a tree at her back and the pack with two guns at her hip so she could lean on it in her sleep. It wasn't safe for her to sleep using the bear canister as a pillow, but at this point, it wasn't bears she was worried about.

She woke with the dawn and had another protein bar for breakfast before setting out once again. This would be the last stretch. According to the GPS, in one mile she'd be at the top of the switchbacks that would take her into the valley.

Her steps were small and slow, but her legs worked and her feet had pretty much melded with the boots at this point. She considered the possibility of having them surgically removed when this was over and smiled grimly at the prospect.

Twenty-four hours after leaving Cole on the granite mound, she was halfway down the switchbacks. Downhill was so much easier than uphill, but her knees were now complaining about the strain.

Somewhere on the endless journey, she'd managed to quiet the whispers of Cole and Leo and betrayal. She truly wasn't thinking about anything except her feet, her knees, her back, her legs. Every body part that was doing the work to get her down the trail.

She would have sobbed when she reached Mirror Lake and gazed up at Half Dome, except there were far too many people around and she didn't want anyone to notice her.

When she finally reached her car, she was torn between driving off immediately and entering the store to buy a cold drink and a sandwich.

Thirst and hunger won the war and when she finally sat behind the wheel and took her first bite, she was fairly certain it was the most delicious turkey sandwich ever made. Likewise, an ice-cold Coke had never tasted so good.

She debated her route home and decided Oakhurst was the way to go. She'd stop at the hotel and take a photo of Cole's license plate on her way through town. She'd drive to Fresno and get a hotel room, because there was no way she had the energy to drive all the way to Redondo Beach, but she also wouldn't stay in tiny Oakhurst longer than it took to get Cole's license plate.

If she had her way, she'd never pass through Oakhurst again.

◆ ◆ ◆

Cole's car wasn't in the hotel parking lot. A shiver went down Signe's spine as she considered the possibilities. He might have passed her on the path when she was sleeping. He could have taken a shorter, more direct route through the forest. But in either of those scenarios, he'd have to catch the bus to Oakhurst, which didn't leave until the evening. No way could he have hiked that far and caught the bus yesterday.

The most logical option was he'd gotten a ride. Had he hitchhiked or did he have an accomplice in the park all along?

She'd taken his phones. How in the world had he contacted anyone?

She dug through her pack, pulling out phones. One of hers. Two of his.

And next to it, her GPS unit. The kind that had texting capabilities but she'd failed to set it up when she had the chance.

Cole had the same one.

He'd somehow managed to set up texting.

She didn't know how or why, or even how it all connected to DiscoFever, but Cole must have been playing her from the start. She had to marvel at his planning.

How had he convinced Leo to send him to be her guide?

And why was Leo in the park at the meet point? Had he realized his mistake in sending Cole and gone to warn her?

Was that why he demanded the coordinates? Insisted Cole delay her? Threatened to fire him if they had sex?

She'd *slept* with the prick.

She put the car in drive and pulled out onto the highway. An hour to Fresno, then she could take a shower.

She scrubbed her skin until it was raw, then crawled into the king-size bed and slept for sixteen hours.

She wasn't sure what day it was when she woke, but her phone informed her it was late Sunday. The last time she'd checked her phone for the day of the week, she'd discovered it was the one-year anniversary of her divorce.

Her legs were wobbly. There was no way she'd be able to drive four-plus hours to Redondo Beach. Thankfully, she'd booked the room for two nights, knowing she'd probably sleep past the noon checkout time.

She filled the deep tub and soaked for more than an hour, draining and refilling as needed when the water cooled, but mostly she just soaked, trying not to think. Trying not to remember what it had been like the last time she fled to a hotel room and soaked her body to ease both emotional and physical aches.

Then, she'd been taken against her will. This time, she'd willingly shared her body. She'd thought it was the first step to taking back her life. Reclaiming her body. Empowering.

But instead, she'd handed herself over to another monster.

She didn't know how Cole fit into the tangle of crimes, but he was part of the web. Part of the underground. And now he knew her secret.

Early Monday afternoon, Jasper paced the hovel he'd been living in since his "death" two years ago. Twenty-four months, biding his time, recovering from a beating that should have killed him and researching everything he could find on Leo Starr. Not a day had gone by that he didn't wonder if Signe Gates was in league with her husband.

He was certain of it, in fact.

Cole's take on Signe was suspect. Jasper had spent too many hours hating the journalistic duo to see any reason to change his opinion now.

Signe Gates had burned him after assuring him she'd protect his identity with her life.

It was a miracle he'd survived. Or maybe not a miracle so much as luck that days before he was taken, he'd identified a potential processing point where containers filled with humans who'd made the long journey across the Pacific were being sorted into different labor groups, and he'd texted Cole photos along with the coordinates.

The lowlife who'd been tasked with disposing of Jasper's body in the ocean had instead tossed him in a dumpster by the warehouse. At least that's what he believed happened. He'd slipped in and out of consciousness while orders were being delivered and only had vague memories of surfacing from the fog while he waited to die in the fetid trash bin.

Next thing he knew, he was in the back of Cole's car, en route to a hospital. The pain of waking had almost made him pass out again, but he had to stop Cole. No way could he go to a hospital.

The kingpin knew he was FBI but believed he was dead. No one would expect his body to turn up, not when he'd been dumped in the ocean. With off-the-books medical care, Jasper could stay dead while he healed. He'd have a much better chance of identifying who was behind his beating and murder if no one knew he'd survived.

No hospital. No FBI. No one but Cole.

Cole had rented this place, cheap and anonymous. Jasper's alias had thousands in cash to maintain his cover as a dealer and pay confidential informants. Once Jasper died, there was no way for the FBI to locate and claim the money. It became Jasper's medical nest egg.

Cole found doctors who made house calls for criminals. They knew to keep their mouths shut. Jasper was missing teeth and had broken ribs, a broken arm, broken cheek and jawbones, a concussion, multiple contusions, but shockingly, no internal bleeding.

Black-market surgery had set his jaw. He'd spent months with it wired shut. There was nothing to be done about the ribs or cheek. His arm had healed faster than the rest of him.

All in all, it had been months before Jasper had been well enough to work his own case, and during that time, Cole had been his only contact with the outside world as he ate dinner through a straw.

Jasper spent those endless hours retracing everything that had happened in the months before he'd been taken. He kept circling back to the investigative reporter who'd made him during an interview with the kingpin of a group Jasper had infiltrated.

But even more interesting to Jasper had been witnessing an exchange between Leo Starr and one of the other men in the organization.

It was possible the man had been Leo's informant, but Jasper hadn't thought so. Not then. Not now.

When Signe tracked Jasper down in a seedy dive bar several weeks later, he hadn't known what to expect. Were she and her husband in league with the organization that trafficked in drugs, guns, and humans?

She knew he was a mole. Even knew he was FBI. He *still* didn't know how she'd made him. Just that she had. He'd left the bar with the tentative hope he could trust her not to blow his cover, but it nagged at him that Starr was probably in deep with the kingpin. If he was, how was it possible Gates remained ignorant of her husband's side deals?

She was supposed to be some kind of expert in criminals.

None of it added up. And eventually, he'd nearly died because he'd trusted Gates to keep his secret. The minute she approached him in that bar, he should have pulled out of the cartel. He'd been compromised. That was the protocol.

But he'd been so damn close, on the verge of the biggest bust of his career.

Then Signe Gates sold him out. How much had they paid her for his name? How many people had been trafficked in the intervening years?

What did she spend her blood money on? Was his life worth a car? A boat? A trip to Disneyland?

Jasper's phone buzzed, pulling him from his bitter thoughts. He braced himself to hear Cole make excuses for her. "Where is she?"

"She just filled up her tank an hour north of LA."

"On her way home at last. Thought she'd chicken out." Jasper had figured a woman like Signe Gates would have a backup plan and a bug-out bag ready to go.

"And I told you she wouldn't," Cole said in a smug tone.

He ignored the statement. "What's up with her house?"

"As expected, it was ransacked."

"Think they found the information?"

"I doubt it. The safe is intact. Bolted down. It's a vault. Leo was beyond careful."

"If they couldn't find it in the house, they'll go after her."

"From what she told me, she doesn't even know where it is."

"You're assuming she's innocent."

Cole was silent. Finally he said, "Hoping. Not assuming."

That was the best Jasper could hope for. "Innocent or guilty, at this point, Signe is the key. Even if she doesn't know where it is, she's the only one who can find it."

"Yeah. Without Leo, it all falls to Signe. Shouldn't have killed him."

"It was a massive miscalculation. You know they'll be watching her house," Jasper said. "Waiting for her to get home."

"Yeah," Cole murmured. "That's what I would do."

"It's what *we* need to do." He paused. This was the part where Cole would balk. "She won't willingly help us. We need to convince her we're on her side. You're going to have to lie to her. Again."

Chapter 35

One week after she'd set out for Oakhurst, Signe was finally home again. She sat in her driveway and stared at the large two-story house built into the hillside. Three stories if you counted the daylight basement with that oh-so-important home studio.

She loved this house. It was the palace of her childhood fantasies, just slightly smaller and with fewer Barbie dolls. She'd been in awe when Leo first showed her the place. They'd been working together for more than a year, but had only been dating for a few months, when he brought her here and said he'd made an offer—and hoped she'd consider moving in with him if he got it.

In the end, they'd bought it together, with Leo covering the lion's share of the down payment. A few years later, he'd paid it off with proceeds from his Bitcoin investment.

Cole's questions had taken root and now she wondered about Leo's gift of the house he'd mostly paid for. And the Bitcoin profits.

Crypto was the currency of the underworld. She'd done a show on cryptocurrencies in the first season. Unregulated banking was the ultimate money laundry, and the spike in Bitcoin value a few years before had Leo in a happy tizzy as he watched his early investment go up and up.

He got out before the drop and paid off this house. She had no idea how he'd spent his other crypto gains but guessed renovations on the cabin he shared with his brother were one investment.

She didn't question it because she'd always considered the crypto his money. He could play with what he was willing to lose. Her money went into a local credit union.

When they'd divorced, his crypto balance hadn't been on the list of assets and she didn't fight him on that point. It was his money.

When he offered to give her the house, she'd told herself it was guilt and the knowledge that she wasn't even trying to go after the millions he had in crypto that triggered his generosity.

Now she wondered. *Did* he have millions in crypto? If he did, how would Steven—his presumptive heir—get it? Did Steven have the crypto key passwords? Could he access the thumb drives that held digital millions? Where had Leo stored that information?

She hit the button on the garage door remote and held her breath. Had her home been violated in her absence?

The door lifted and the garage was neat as a pin as usual. Leo had taken his tools and workbench when he left, and she had only the basics when it came to wrenches and hammers and saws. Home repair wasn't something she'd made a point to learn once she could afford to hire someone to do it right.

She pulled into the garage and shut off the engine. Her hands shook as she pulled the key from the ignition. Dammit. This was her home. And she was scared to step inside.

Was Cole Banner said bogeyman?

She climbed from the car and stretched. Her body ached from the long drive and days of unaccustomed exercise. At least she'd managed to wash away the stench of Cole's touch.

If only she could wash him from her mind. Send him to the ether along with memories of her rape.

Cole hadn't raped her, and she hated herself for that fact.

Sex with Cole wasn't her body betraying her, it was her betraying her body.

She reached into the car and grabbed her gun from the center con-sole. She'd unload the rest of the car later. First she'd do a walk-through.

Then she'd do what she should have done days ago and report Leo's murder and the location of his body. There would be massive blowback for her delay, but she'd been too desperate to get out of the park and far too tired to be detained.

Now she'd be the prime suspect. Hell, she'd even touched the body.

She should probably call her attorney before she called Ranger Gus.

At least she wouldn't be alone under the interrogation lights, but Cole was just as likely to point the finger at her as she was at him.

She'd even made it easy by taking his gun. If he'd used it to kill Leo, the bullet would match. She didn't know if it had been fired—she hadn't thought to check and wouldn't really know what to look for beyond a missing bullet. Plus she'd fired her own gun, then stored the two next to each other. The scent of spent gun powder probably permeated both.

She'd royally fucked herself.

Slowly, she climbed the stairs, leaving the basement-level garage for the main floor of the house. She stopped short at seeing the interior door ajar.

It should be locked and fully alarmed.

Her phone was on. If her alarm had been tripped, she'd have received a notice. But then, these weren't the kind of people who let alarm systems—even the best of the best like she had—get in their way.

She could name a half dozen people who had the code, starting with her dead ex-husband. Then there was Roman and the weekly housecleaner, who also watered the plants twice a week when Signe was out of town.

But this wasn't the housekeeper's doing.

Signe should turn and run now. Anyone could be inside. Instead, she straightened her spine. She'd lived in fear of this moment for two years. Had just spent a week braced for it only to find the one person she'd never had reason to fear dead at the hands of her tormentors.

She wouldn't run. She raised her gun and racked the slide, chambering a bullet.

No more running. No more fear. She was done being a victim and would fight with everything she had.

CHAPTER 36

Every door and drawer in the kitchen was wide open—including the refrigerator. Joke was on the vandals, because she still hadn't gone shopping since returning from Singapore and the only things in there were salad dressing and various condiments.

The freezer was another story but from the state of her frozen meats, she'd guess the door had been open for only a few hours. Most items would be salvageable.

She used the barrel of her pistol to shut doors and nudge drawers closed, then moved on to the living room. Things were in disarray but not vandalized.

It was a message. A childish display to make sure she didn't miss that they'd *been here*.

The study next to the library was a different story. This was her home office and her files had been dumped and spread everywhere. These were her financial files—car purchase and repair, insurance, bills. Nothing related to her work because that was locked tight in the safe in the editing studio in the basement.

It was doubtful anyone but a next-level bank robber could crack the safe. It was massive and bolted to the floor. More vault than safe, really, and it had to be what Cole and his cronies were after. Not that she had a clue what he expected to find other than names of more informants.

She finished inspecting the ground floor, then went upstairs to check the bedrooms. The primary suite had been tossed and the french doors to the balcony had been left wide open to the afternoon sun.

She went straight to the bathroom and opened the medicine chest. There was the bottle of pills. The ones she'd refused to take after that August day, because she'd deserved the headaches. Deserved to live in pain. Eventually the physical pain had faded, but the mental pain had only increased. The pills could have fixed that too.

But she'd denied herself that escape because her suicide wouldn't protect Leo.

She no longer wanted to escape. Not into pills. Not into death. No, she wanted to fight.

She pushed down on the plastic cap and twisted to open the bottle, then lifted the toilet seat lid and dumped the remaining pills in the bowl. After flushing, she threw the empty bottle in the trash and returned to the bedroom, where the open french doors beckoned her.

She stepped onto the balcony and looked out over the ocean. The top floor was set back from the main floor, and the balcony barely overhung the large veranda below.

She thought of all the evenings she and Leo had watched the sunset from this spot, their private paradise. She raised her face to the warm Southern California sun and thought of his laugh. His smile.

Leo hadn't just left her this time. He was *gone*.

She went back inside and crossed to her nightstand. The drawer hung open, and there was the wedding photo she'd tucked away after the divorce but had never had it in her to pack up and put in the storage room next to the basement studio.

Cole—or whoever had ransacked her home—had found it. The glass protecting the image was cracked.

She dumped the broken pieces into the drawer, hoping the shards hadn't gouged the print. Then she touched Leo's forehead where the bullet had pierced his cranium.

He's really and truly gone.

A tear spilled down her cheek.

What do you know, she wasn't done crying after all.

"He's not worth your tears, Sig."

She jolted, dropping the picture. She reached for the gun she'd set on the nightstand, but Cole was too fast for her and knocked it aside before she could raise it.

If her finger had been on the trigger, it might have gone off. Instead, it dropped to the floor. Cole kicked it and the weapon slid across the polished wood surface, landing under the plush love seat in her reading nook.

With a feral scream, Signe aimed for Cole's eyes. Her nails were short but she could still blind him.

He caught her hands and raised them over her head and pushed her backward so she landed on the bed.

"Stop! I'm not going to hurt you."

She responded by shifting her knee to aim for his groin. He dropped all his weight on her, crushing the momentum from her maneuver. He grunted, letting her know she'd hurt him, but it wasn't nearly enough.

Her body went into full panic mode as he lay on top of her on the mattress. She yanked a hand free and raked it down his cheek.

"Dammit, Signe! We need to talk! I didn't kill Leo!"

"Right. You just invaded my house and broke my things for kicks."

"I didn't do that either. We got here after whoever tossed the place left."

She wanted to ask who *"we"* referred to, but then he'd start thinking she believed his lies.

She struggled against him but his weight was making it hard for her to breathe, which ratcheted up her panic. She headbutted his chin and he jerked back, allowing her to take a shallow breath.

"Fuck, that hurts."

"You're smothering me. If you want to rape me without a fight, you'll have to drug me. Again."

He reared back. "I didn't—"

"Jesus, Cole. You had your chance to talk her down and blew it. Now we'll do it my way."

The male voice was deep and raspy. Familiar. She turned and Cole shifted so she could see the man who stood to the side of the bed, facing away from her as he gazed out toward the Pacific.

He was tall and lean. Dark hair. The right side of his face was scarred, a large divot where his cheekbone had been smashed and what she suspected were surgical scars along his jawline.

He turned and faced her, letting her see the unscarred left side.

Her whole body rocked with a jolt. Like she'd been hit by lightning.

Jasper Evans flashed a vicious smile and raised a length of chain that was at least five feet long. "Hello, Signe. Did you miss me?"

CHAPTER 37

"What the fuck, Jasper!"

Signe heard Cole's shout as if through a tunnel. The sound stretching and pulsing. Bouncing off the sides of her skull as she battled her body's physical reaction to Jasper's presence and words.

And the threat of the chain.

She might be hyperventilating. Or going into shock.

Strange, with all the interviews she'd done over the years, all the threats she received from crime lords on camera and off, nothing rattled her. Nerves of steel. But a smile from a dead FBI agent and she was in full panic.

Perhaps even having an actual heart attack.

It should be wonderful news that Jasper was alive, but with the shake of the chain, he made sure she regretted his life as much as she'd regretted his death.

He wasn't dead, which meant she had to question everything. Had she been wrong about him being FBI? Her brain twisted in circles as she tried to figure out what was real.

"Breathe, Signe."

She somehow found herself on the love seat—the one her gun was taking a nap beneath—with Cole kneeling in front of her, his face a picture of concern.

Like she would believe his act now.

His hands pressed down on her knees, holding her in place. "Breathe. Slow and deep."

She did, but only because it was the right thing to do to survive the next few minutes.

She focused on Cole's brown eyes and the red stripe on his cheek where she'd scratched him. It was beginning to welt.

She'd shared her body with this man. Laughed and cried with him. Told him about her worst nightmare and confessed her worst sin.

"You—you knew Jasper was alive? The whole time?"

He nodded.

"You knew he rattled the chains that night? Played the distorted voice?"

He nodded again.

She raised her hand and slapped him as hard as she could across his scratched cheek. His head jerked back, but his hold on her thighs never wavered.

His gaze held hers. "I didn't know he was going to do that. Just that he was the one who did it."

She raised her gaze to Jasper. "You sent the texts? Taunting me about being raped? Or was that Cole?"

"What texts?" Cole and Jasper asked at the same time.

"Right. You spent days tormenting me but you're not guilty of *that*. So who are you *really* working for, Jasper? Are you the kingpin for the human-trafficking ring?"

"Right now, I'm not working for anyone. Hard to use your social security number when you're dead."

"Well, human traffickers don't tend to worry too much about legal work papers and paying taxes, so I would imagine you've had no trouble finding a job in the organization."

"I'm not with them, Signe. I'm working my own murder."

"Uh-huh. And trying to drive me insane in the forest was totally going to do that for you. Also calling bullshit because the FBI would never let you near a case when you've been compromised."

"I figured tormenting you might get you to finally talk, with Cole ready to be your shoulder to cry on."

She held Cole's gaze as Jasper spoke. His nostrils flared and she figured he wanted to throw out some denial of the manipulation, but he said nothing.

She wanted to slap him again.

"As for the FBI, that's exactly why they believe I'm dead. I wasn't sure who else had been compromised or if we had a mole. So I stayed dead while searching for a break to get close to Leo. Then, like magic, Leo called Cole."

"You aren't making sense. Why Leo? And what does a Channing Tatum wannabe turned con man have to do with any of this?"

"Sometimes the best cover is your own personal history," Cole said softly. "In spite of Jasper's behavior, we're not here to hurt you."

Jasper made a sound that said he begged to differ.

"Cut it out, Jasper. You've terrified her enough. Yes, she blew your cover, but it was when she was raped. I'm guessing they tortured her."

"Right. And yet she kept silent about being tortured by criminals. Because that's totally what a crime reporter would do."

Her gaze snapped from Jasper's angry glare to Cole's stern concern. He took a deep breath. "Jasper's got issues. He'll see a therapist as soon as he's alive again. But he can't be alive until we expose the people responsible for his death."

"One of whom is me." With her foot, she probed beneath the love seat. The toe of her shoe tapped the gun.

"You didn't wield the chain. You were under duress. I think we can find proof of that. In Leo's recordings."

"Why do you think Leo would have proof that exonerates my actions?" She nudged the gun forward a tiny bit, the motion so small, her leg muscles under Cole's hand didn't even flex.

"Because I think Leo is the reason you were raped."

She shoved at his shoulders. He was a solid wall, but he moved back, releasing her legs. "That's impossible."

"And denial is a river in Egypt."

She needed to get out of here. Both men were psychotic. And Cole was a master manipulator. With one swift move, she scooped up the gun and pointed it at Cole. "You killed him, and now you want to pin all your crimes on him."

Jasper swore but he didn't make a move. He probably guessed she'd chambered a bullet before entering the house.

Cole raised his hands and stepped back. "No, Signe, we didn't kill him. We're the good guys." He nodded to her hands. "You think I didn't know you were going to go for the gun? I let you have it."

"Dipshit move," Jasper said.

He ignored Jasper and kept his focus on her. "I wanted you to have a small sense of control so you would hear us out."

He tilted his head back slightly. "Check my back pocket. I'd reach for it, but I don't want to get shot."

"Try getting beaten with a chain," Jasper said.

"Shut up, Jasper. You aren't helping." To Signe he said, "Please. Back right pocket."

Given that she didn't think she could pull the trigger at this point—she had way too many questions and she'd hate to have to kill Jasper again—she decided to take a chance and do as he said.

She kept the gun pointed at him—mere inches from his heart—as she slowly reached around and slid her hand into the pocket. Her fingers wrapped around something metal. She pulled it out and ran her thumb over the surface as she read the embossed letters.

F. B. I. Cole Banner was an agent for the Federal Bureau of Investigation.

CHAPTER 38

Cole watched as Signe poured very fine forty-year-old scotch into two cut-crystal rocks glasses. After handing the drinks to Jasper and him, she took the bottle and raised it to her lips, taking a deep swallow.

She made a face and glared at the bottle. "I hate this stuff. Wish I had some damn orange juice to go with vodka."

Cole turned to Jasper. "The other bear canister still in the car?"

He nodded. "Yeah, why?"

Signe gave a faint smile and said, "Juice boxes."

Cole sent Jasper to the car to get the canister, giving him time alone with her.

"Why did Jasper steal our food?"

"He figured you might try to send me away again. Only one canister would make that harder. Also, he wanted to scare you."

"He hates me for what I did. I mean, I get it, I've spent two years hating me."

"He'll get over it when we get the dirt on Leo."

He could see she wanted to argue Leo's innocence once again but didn't. She was beginning to open her mind to the possibility. It bothered him to realize how much it would gut her as the full truth sank in. Leo's betrayal would cut deeper than anything she'd faced so far, and Cole was the last person she'd want to have by her side as she processed that pain.

"So explain to me how an undercover FBI agent was going to record several episodes of an archaeology show for the Wayfinders Network? You'd have to be vetted."

"I *was* an archaeologist. Remember Wanda? She really is an old friend from my dig bum days." He was well aware that meeting Wanda was one reason it had never crossed her mind he could be lying.

"Does Wanda know you're FBI?"

He shook his head. "My friends in that world all think I inherited a bunch of money and am looking to go Hollywood after that old screening video went viral."

"So that was true?"

"You didn't look it up? I'm crushed."

"The only thing I've done since I got out of the park is bathe, sleep, eat food delivered by room service, and drive."

He imagined the trek she'd made to get to the valley by Saturday afternoon. Guilt trickled through him, but she was the one who'd tied him up and left him without food, which tempered his feelings a tad.

"It was true, and it wasn't long after that when my background check and vetting was complete and I'd been accepted into a training class at Quantico. I told my friends I was going to dig bum on the East Coast for a few years.

"About five years ago, the bureau got a tip on an artifact-trafficking ring that's an exchange for drugs with a Colombian cartel. The bureau sent me in undercover because they wanted a line on the artifacts specifically. When it comes to art and artifacts, the agency has a different approach. It's more about recovery than it is about arrests and justice. Because an artifact or a painting by an old master, by definition, can't be replaced. If it's destroyed or lost to the black market, the world has lost a piece of human history and culture. In that instance, we recovered the artifacts and my cover remained intact. The bureau decided to move me back to California permanently to work the artifacts and drugs beat— mostly under deep cover. I'm a wannabe Hollywood archaeologist with one viral video to my credit. My name isn't attached to the video, so if it's found, it doesn't hurt me. I generally keep a low profile and work a very specific section of the market."

"So how is taking the job with Leo 'low profile'? Your face would be all over the network."

"I sorta didn't tell the bureau when the offer came in from Leo, because I knew they'd say no for exactly that reason."

"So what do they think you're doing this week?"

He flashed a grin. "Two weeks' paid vacation, hiking Yosemite National Park. They were even kind enough to get me a backcountry permit, since I changed my plans at the last minute."

"I thought Wanda got us the permit."

He'd forgotten he told her that, which wasn't like him. "Well, I could hardly tell you I got it from the FBI."

"So you took two weeks' paid vacation because you were supposed to start filming on Monday, but then Leo made you take me into the park."

"Bingo."

"So the FBI has no idea what you and Jasper are doing or that Jasper is even still alive?"

"It's complicated."

"No more lies, Cole. I'm still considering shooting you."

"Shooting a federal agent is even worse than blowing one's cover. Just sayin'."

"In for a penny, in for a pound."

"I promise I'll tell you everything, but Jasper needs to be here for it."

"Then tell me how you got hooked up with Leo. It can't be a coincidence."

"It's not. I met Jasper when I moved back to LA. He was working deep undercover, too—had been for a year at that point—and he got me in the door with a few of his confidential informants. I needed a place to live, and he was barely living in his apartment because his cover had a seedy dive where he spent nights when he couldn't return home. I moved in and got my own shithole backup apartment. As far as roommate situations go, it was great. House to myself a lot of the time when I was home, but also, when Jasper was home, he was someone I could really talk to about the cases I was working. There's so much secrecy with undercover work. It's good to have someone you can mull things with."

"You're saying you and Jasper were living a real-life version of *Graceland.*"

Cole snorted. "Hardly. Our apartment is a lot smaller, for starters. I enjoyed the show, but it's not exactly realistic when it comes to undercover work."

"We'll critique the plotlines later. So you and Jasper were roommates. Working the same cases?"

"No except in drug cases that overlapped. Otherwise our circles were very different. But we could talk about the job and work the problems. As roommates, we were a good fit even if we were just griping about the lowlifes we had to deal with on a daily basis." He couldn't help himself and added, "I know you do your best to paint a pretty picture of your criminals, but a lot of them are cold bastards who aren't worth shit."

She bristled. "I don't paint anything. I show who they are."

She had to know that most people in law enforcement weren't fans of her work. Not only did she jeopardize investigations, she also made the pricks look *sympathetic.* She walked a fine line, and of course, with Leo there was a chance she'd crossed it and covered for his crimes. He didn't really think that—not anymore—but to Jasper he had to admit there was still some doubt.

"Right."

"Get to the part about Leo."

"Fine. So Jasper'd been working a source for access to a guy who was the top dog in the US for a Mexican cartel. They're into everything—including human trafficking—and Jasper finally gets his break and is supposed to cut a deal with the guy. He goes to the meet, but what does he find, you and Leo setting up for an interview with the mystery man, and Leo films Jasper before he can duck out.

"Jasper's face on a crime reporter's camera—that just can't happen. Leo refuses to erase the shot and one of the flunkies touts the agreement about how no worries, if you put anyone on screen without the boss man's approval, you, Leo, and your whole crew are dead."

She gave a slight nod, clearly remembering the exchange.

"At the same time, Jasper saw something pass between Leo and the flunky, and his radar went up."

"The flunky was probably Leo's informant."

"Maybe. Jasper considered it too. But it wasn't that. He wondered if Leo had made him. But Leo wasn't the one who tracked him down in a bar several weeks later. He still wants to know what tipped you."

"A few years ago, I was working a story on fentanyl. Had a meet set up. My source was a no-show. Everyone fled when I arrived and I figure I'd been set up to make it look like a raid. My security had broken down. There was a moment when I had a gun pulled on me by a drugged-out guy. I thought I was toast, but then another guy intervened and dragged the guy threatening me away. It all happened so fast and I was scared. It was chaotic. I didn't even see my rescuer's face. But I heard his voice as he talked the junkie down. Raspy.

"I don't know. The voice stayed with me. I was almost certain he defused the situation because he . . . wasn't one of them. Another junkie wouldn't care if a stupid reporter with bad security got killed. Anyway, fast-forward a year or so and I heard that voice again. This time he's trying to talk my husband down from recording his face. Two plus two equals undercover cop.

"When I learned about the bust of people who were associated with the kingpin I'd interviewed that day, I scoured all the filings for information. Flagged a few names of persons of interest I thought might be his cover—one of which was Bobby Jenkins."

Cole nodded. That was Jasper's alias.

"Then I went further back, to the fentanyl story and earlier. Looked into some closed cases and got access to an audio recording of an interrogation from about eight years ago."

"Before Jasper was undercover."

She nodded. "I recognized his voice, and now I had a name. I did a deep dive and eventually found Jasper's high school yearbook. Nearly twenty years older, but still pretty like Bobby Jenkins."

An irrational twinge of jealousy made him say, "He's no Channing Tatum, though."

Signe rolled her eyes.

Behind Cole, Jasper said, "At least not anymore. Still think I'm pretty, Signe?"

Cole had to hand it to her, she didn't even flinch as she cocked her head. "If there's a juice box in that canister for me, I'll say you're even prettier than the water-screening Adonis."

Jasper's smile was lopsided thanks to the surgery around his mouth and dead nerve endings. It was a dark smile. Dangerous.

"You're growing on me, kid," Jasper said as he twisted open the canister.

She glared at him. "I may be five foot three, but I'm not a child."

"Sure thing, kiddo. Here's your juice box." He winked at her, closing the eye that drooped at the corner.

Signe let out a choked laugh and took the cran-apple juice or whatever it was Cole had bought days ago.

She crossed to the bar and mixed a drink that had to be more than half vodka based on how long she poured, then drank the entire tall glass in one long pull.

"Damn," Jasper said, voicing Cole's thoughts.

"Gentlemen, I'm a lightweight and will be utterly smashed in about"—she glanced at her watch—"fifteen minutes. So if you want me to open the safe, I'd better do it while I can still remember the combination."

◆ ◆ ◆

It was stupid to get plowed with these two men she didn't trust, but dammit, her ex-husband had been murdered, her house broken into, her most recent lover was an undercover FBI agent who'd screwed her for information, and the man she'd thought she killed was standing in her living room returning a juice box he'd stolen while tormenting her in the woods.

Cole believed her safe contained proof Leo was a crime lord, and the dread that settled low in her belly told her to believe him. There were so many small things that had happened in the last years they were together. Long work trips that resulted in no film being uploaded on the home server. She'd written it off as a sign Leo was cheating, but added to times when he'd initiated meetings with informants that didn't include her and his actions took a more sinister bend.

But what she really, really wasn't prepared for was the thing Cole had said that had nagged at her from the moment the words hit her cochlear nerve.

"I think Leo is the reason you were raped."

She'd never once considered it but she'd also never understood how he could see her scars and not believe she'd been assaulted. There had been a moment that day, when she first told him, that it flashed through her mind that he already knew. He was faking outrage. Faking ignorance. But she was so devastated by his leaving that the doubt had been buried in a deluge of tears.

Leo had known. Probably from the start.

They didn't see each other until five weeks after her rape. Leo made sure of it, staying far longer at the dig near Mount Shasta than he needed to. And when he got back, he gave her a wide berth, never questioning her obvious depression and lack of interest in sex.

He *knew*.

And when she showed him the symbols that had been carved into her skin, he called her a liar and a whore.

She popped to her feet and ran to the bathroom, where she knelt in front of the toilet and vomited pink liquid until there was nothing left. Drained and shaking, she leaned her head against the wall as a cold sweat coated her skin.

She looked up to see Cole in the doorway. "I guess you won't be getting drunk after all?"

"Apparently, my stomach wants me sober for this."

"I'm sorry," he said softly, and she wondered exactly which offense he was apologizing for. There were far too many at this point.

She climbed to her feet, flushed the toilet, then went to the sink and drank from the tap, swishing and spitting, glad the juice flavor hadn't had time to turn to bile. She ducked her head under the faucet and let cool water run over the back of her neck.

When she raised her head, Cole was there with a fluffy towel, which she took and patted her neck and hair, catching the drips that streamed down her skin and slid under the collar of her top.

"We're on your side, Signe. We're going to figure this out. Get justice for Jasper."

"And Leo?" The question was reflexive. Out of her mouth before she had a chance to think.

"He was murdered, so yes, we'll find his killer, but he was no innocent. I meant it when I said he doesn't deserve your tears."

Deep down, she finally believed his words could be true.

CHAPTER 39

Signe was holding up amazingly well all things considered. Cole figured even Jasper was impressed and he was working extra hard to dislike her.

Back in the living room, they finished the story of how Cole had come to meet Leo, with Jasper giving his side of the story. "Leo was on my radar even before you met with me in the bar and assured me only you knew I was FBI. He seemed a little too familiar with some of the lowlifes and far too easy with his camera. He filmed more than he was supposed to, that was for sure. He was good, mind you, very good. But Leo was a master with the camera and I knew what to look for. I worried he knew I was undercover. It was implausible you wouldn't tell him."

Signe flinched at Leo being referenced in past tense, then bristled at Jasper's last sentence. "I didn't tell him," she insisted. "It wasn't part of the story we were working on and it was my choice to look into your background. I wanted to know if you were the guy who saved me."

"And you thanked me by digging deep in an area that put me at risk."

Another flinch. She swallowed and wisely didn't say anything. Cole doubted Jasper had it in him to be kind even in the face of a heartfelt apology.

She cleared her throat. "When I do deep dives like that, I never tell anyone. It's just part of my process. If it had been nothing, it would have been a waste of time. When it did turn into something, well, I know how important a secret like that is. Leo had no need to know."

"Maybe you didn't tell him, but he had access to your notes, your computer."

She shrugged. "Sure, but why would he—"

"Because he was a criminal and you were doing his homework for him."

She held Jasper's gaze, then nodded.

He resumed his tale. "At the same time, I was hearing whispers that someone had dirt on several major players in different trafficking areas, and I started to wonder about Leo and his fast and loose filming. Was he planting cameras and microphones while you held crime bosses enthralled with your pretty smile?"

"I'm a journalist." Signe's jaw was tight and tone clipped.

Jasper nodded. "And a very, very pretty one, interviewing men who lack moral compass, consider themselves virile gods, and who very much want the attention and empathy you give them."

"Fuck you. I'm a journalist."

"And I'm just saying what I saw."

"I do *not* flirt with my interview subjects. I rarely even smile at them."

"That doesn't change what they want from you. It only means you don't give it to them."

"Get to the point."

Jasper huffed out a sigh. "Listen, I've spent the last two years wondering how deep you're in with your ex. I'm not entirely convinced you aren't and we both know your 'deep dive' into researching me led to you blowing my cover, leading to a beating that would have killed me if Cole didn't find me in time. So I'm not exactly thrilled to be reading you in on this and not inclined to listen to your protests about what a kick-ass reporter you are. If you want to hear this, I suggest you shut up and listen."

"Jasper—" Cole began.

"You shut it too. Just because you're half in love with her doesn't change how *I* feel. Yesterday you were Team Jasper, but the minute she walked into the room, you started thinking with your dick."

Arguing the first point about having feelings for Signe would be futile given Jasper's mood, and the second point . . . much as he wanted to deny it, part of him had to admit he could be letting his stupid head do his thinking when it came to Signe.

She saved Cole from having to respond by saying, "And here I thought you were angling for a threesome, Evans."

Jasper let out a bark of surprised laughter.

She rose and crossed to him, then ran a finger down his chest. "I'm going to have to pass, I've got enough pricks in my life."

Jasper's arm slid around her waist and his voice dropped to a husky whisper. "Aw, but babe, you haven't had *quality* prick."

Cole bristled the moment Jasper touched her but relaxed when he realized the jab was aimed at him. Physically, Jasper wouldn't hurt her, and any jealousy the man stirred was Cole's own damn problem.

For her part, Signe traced the divot in Jasper's cheek, where the chain had shattered his zygomatic arch, then she cast a sideways glance at Cole and said, "True. But I suppose Cole did the best he could with what he has."

Jasper laughed again, harder and longer. A rare sound coming from his best friend. Cole didn't even mind being the butt of the joke if it meant Jasper could still laugh.

If he could laugh again, then maybe more of Jasper had survived that beating than he'd thought.

Jasper's arm fell from Signe's waist and she stepped back, her gaze still on the scar she'd just touched. Cole feared she was about to say something that would spike Jasper's anger—like that apology she'd avoided earlier—so he stepped forward and placed an arm around her shoulders and whispered, "I'm game to prove you a liar about my prowess whenever you are."

She shifted her gaze from Jasper to him and, for a brief moment, he saw desire in her eyes.

Things weren't done between them. They should be, but they weren't.

She stepped back and crossed her arms over her chest. Closed-off and defensive. As an interviewer, she had to know how she presented herself. She was nearing the end of her endurance for this conversation.

It was time for the CliffsNotes version. "After your conversation with Jasper in the bar, and given the whispers Jasper was hearing, he started to look into Leo, suspecting he'd used your connections in the crime world to set himself up in the business, be it through blackmail or worming his way into the supply chain. Jasper figured Leo was able to glean the ins and outs of how to become a key player in black markets from your work."

"I'm always careful in my reporting to not give the methods employed. My stories aren't how-to manuals."

"No, but Leo wasn't limited to the final product. He recorded the raw footage. He was privy to your research. You were his master-class teacher in how to become a crime lord."

She closed her eyes and gave a slight nod.

"I was having a hard time getting a read on Leo," Jasper said. "So when I heard he was filming an archaeological dig up near Mount Shasta, I asked Cole to use his credentials to try to worm his way into Leo's production."

"Jasper wasn't with you?" she asked Cole.

He shook his head. "Too risky if he knew Jasper was a fed. I couldn't be a known associate. I called some friends from back in the day, found out who was working the project, and finagled an intro. I showed up at the site knowing Vicki was filming—which was good, since the last thing I wanted was to be on camera under my own name—and schmoozed with Leo, gave him my contact info, and hoped he'd reach out to me at some point. If he was trafficking drugs and guns after you showed him how, there was always a chance he'd get into artifact trafficking too. Jasper and I would both keep eyes on him—and you.

"When I got back from Mount Shasta, however, Jasper had gone AWOL. It didn't sit right because we always checked in with each other, and I knew he was working a human-trafficking case and had been contacted by someone who had info about a boat that was due to arrive any day with 'cargo' from South Asia."

Jasper joined the story again. "My informant said they specifically wanted to speak to *you*, Signe. So I gave them your cell number."

"Me? Are we talking about DiscoFever?"

He shrugged. "That's not the name they used with me, but probably."

"Why me?"

"That's what I wondered too. I figured either they were someone on Leo's team and testing you or it was someone who knew what Leo was and they wanted to tell you so you could help them escape from your husband."

"Leo was going to attend that meeting, though."

Jasper shook his head. "I told them to keep me in the loop on the meet time and place. I said I'd make sure Leo sat that one out. I'd figured I could convince you to ditch Leo and your usual security if you had a fed with you."

"But the meeting never happened," Signe said. "Because I was abducted on Bastille Day, drugged and questioned until I revealed your identity, and then you were also abducted and killed. Except for the actually dying part."

"Bastille Day?" Jasper said.

She shrugged. "I try not to think of it in terms of my personal trauma. If I think of it as Bastille Day, then it's not connected to me. It's not the second anniversary of my abduction, it's French Independence Day."

"You're certain it was Bastille Day, July fourteenth?"

"Didn't I just go over that part? No matter how much I try, it's not a date I can forget."

"Signe, I was abducted on July tenth. Four days before Bastille Day."

Chapter 40

For the second—or was it third?—time that day, Signe couldn't breathe. But this was for an entirely different reason.

Jasper's words had literally made her dizzy, and she gripped the back of the couch in an effort to stay on her feet as her mind swam with the implications.

"I—I—" She couldn't voice the words. Afraid if she spoke them aloud, she'd wake or lightning would strike or somehow the truth of them would dissolve into bitter ash and the weight of guilt would crash in again.

"You weren't the one who blew Jasper's cover," Cole said, recklessly tempting fate by speaking the possibly cursed words.

Her gaze locked with Jasper's and he looked as stunned as she felt.

He turned a greenish color. "Motherfucker. If that's true, then . . . *fuck!*"

"What?" she asked in a low rasp.

"It might be my fault they took you. They told me to smile for the camera. Said they were filming a present for the person who sold my name. I was sure it was you, and after the first lash of the chain, I cursed you for burning me."

So there really was a curse. She just hadn't been the one to invoke it. It was almost too much on top of everything else. Because this could mean only one thing. "If it wasn't me who burned you . . ." Her voice trailed off as yet another betrayal sank in.

"It must've been Leo," Cole said.

◆　◆　◆

The two undercover FBI agents flanked Signe on the stairs as they descended to the basement. The men had assured her at the start that they'd searched the house, and while the editing studio had been breached, the safe was intact. The plan now was for Signe to gather what she needed to find the location of Leo's cabin. It was unlikely he'd left incriminating evidence in Signe's studio safe. Cole and Jasper believed Leo's cabin studio was where the mother lode was hidden.

It stunned her to learn no one knew where Leo's cabin was. The reason Cole had been eager to take the docuseries job in the first place was Leo had promised Cole he'd be actively involved in the editing process. Cole had planned to make sure it was Leo's studio and not TWN, by sabotage if necessary. That was why he'd been so frustrated at the delay in filming. Leo had said they'd begin editing at the end of the first week of filming.

Her mind reeled with this new information.

Leo had begun work on the studio at least a year before their separation. As Cole had first suggested, it *did* appear that he'd been planning to leave, he just needed a new base of operations before he could make the split.

Leo had burned Jasper, but she wasn't exonerated by not being the first to utter his name. She'd been the one to inadvertently expose him to Leo, and she was the one who went to the FBI and triggered Muriel's murder. But for now, she'd focus on the fact that Jasper had been beaten days before she'd sat down at that bar and ordered a drink as balm against her cheating husband.

Turned out, cheating was the very least of Leo's sins.

She entered the studio and made a beeline for the safe. As she'd been warned, the studio was a mess—in the same disarray as the rest of her house—but the massive vault was just fine.

She remembered the day Leo told her he was having it installed. She'd thought he was nuts to go to such extremes, but then they were obligated to be extra careful with her raw interview footage. Still, the safe was overkill by far.

She cleared her throat. "Five years."

"What?" Cole asked.

"It was five years ago—I remember because it was summer and I'd just finished a one-hour stand-alone documentary on cryptocurrencies and the black market—when Leo told me he wanted to upgrade our security. We got this safe and the alarm system that was an epic fail today."

"Leo probably gave them the passcode."

"*Them*" being the people who'd killed him.

"I changed the combination to the safe after the divorce. Leo couldn't give anyone that." She met Cole's gaze. "At one point last week, I considered recording a new will on my phone, so if I died in Yosemite, Leo wouldn't inherit everything. I figured if I left the combination to this safe as my lock screen, all my accounts would be accessible."

"Who were you going to name as heir?"

"I couldn't think of anyone, so it probably would've been you."

His eyes widened and then burned with something she couldn't quite read. Or maybe she just didn't believe it.

"It's not your house that I want."

Okay, so maybe she could read him. Still, she had to be suspicious of his motives. He'd screwed her once as a manipulation. "Well, that's good, then, because I'm not dead."

"Getting closer to what I want."

"Yeah, well, I want to get out of here," Jasper said. "So hurry the hell up."

"Don't mind him," Cole said in a stage whisper. "He's just feeling guilty for hating you for two years and finding out that *I* was right all along when I said my money was on Leo." He turned to Jasper. "What's worse, me being right or you being wrong?"

"Getting beaten with a fucking chain and being left to die."

Signe held her breath against a bitter laugh and then did the thing she hadn't dared to do from the first moment she saw Jasper. She turned and wrapped her arms around his waist and pressed her face to his chest. "I'm so glad you aren't dead. I know there's nothing I can say that will make anything better. Just know I grieved for you every day."

He was stiff in her embrace, and then, all at once, his arms came around her and he relaxed ever so slightly. He was easier to hug than Cole. He wasn't built like a tree trunk.

"I'm glad you aren't dead, too, Signe. And . . . I'm sorry if . . . I was the cause of what you endured."

She raised her head so she could meet his gaze. "I'm almost convinced the ultimate blame belongs to Leo."

"Almost?"

"I'm there. I know it fits . . . but I need to see hard evidence before it will be real. But regardless, I can't blame you for cursing me. None of this is your fault."

Jasper cupped her cheek. "You are an appealing woman." He winked, leaned down, and whispered, "Counting down until Cole intervenes. Five, four . . ."

"Enough of that."

"False start," Jasper said.

She shook her head. "He's playing defense, which makes it a neutral zone infraction."

Jasper grinned. "I might even like you, Signe Gates. But only if you promise to keep Cole on his toes."

She glanced at the scowling linebacker. "I promise nothing when it comes to the fake archaeologist."

"Hey. I'm the real deal. Once an archaeologist, always an archaeologist. Like the marines."

She released Jasper and turned back to the safe. She punched in the code, making sure her body prevented Jasper or Cole from seeing the combination. They might all be on the same side right now, but she wasn't entirely convinced that would last. Especially if they didn't find the hard evidence they insisted existed.

She still wondered how much she could trust either man, and she was fairly certain neither was entirely convinced she hadn't been in league with Leo.

She stared at the shelves in the metal box and decided to grab the storage drives that contained the raw footage from the last months of their marriage. The Mount Shasta documentary should be on the drives in addition to a dozen other projects. Leo was always working on multiple things at once, while Signe approached her stories with a single-minded focus whenever possible.

She filled a tote bag with hard drives and project files for stories she'd worked on with Leo, then closed and relocked the safe. The plan now was to head to an anonymous rental house to review the digital and paper files. "I need to pack a bag. If you make me wear my hiking clothes for one more day, I will scream."

"What do you think, Cole?"

"It's no fun when she screams."

"Then you aren't doing it right."

She rolled her eyes and pushed past them to the hallway that separated the editing studio from the game and laundry rooms.

Jasper stepped in front of her. "Always let one of us go first." He jogged up the stairs in front of her. She followed at a slower pace. She was never going to get used to this—Jasper and Cole acting as if they were her personal security guards, even as they sniped and bickered and flirted and complained.

Her life no longer made sense.

But Jasper Evans was alive. No matter what happened, she would always be grateful for that.

CHAPTER 41

"Why aren't we going to the FBI?" Signe asked from the back seat of Cole's car as he drove a surveillance detection route to a house he had rented with an alias using an app. "For that matter, why haven't you reported Leo's murder?"

"Why haven't *you*?" Cole asked.

"Because I didn't want to be detained by law enforcement in the park or in Fresno."

"Same for us."

"But you're FBI. They'd listen to you."

"Before or after they freaked out about the fact that Jasper is alive and I hid it for two years? We knew they'd target your house. I didn't want to leave you vulnerable, and I doubt the bureau would have moved fast to get protection for you in place. Instead, they'd have focused on getting a warrant for those storage drives you're clutching in that bag."

Oh. Lord. Her recordings. If the FBI got a warrant, they'd seize the rushes. All the raw footage of every interview. With the exception of the ones who'd been masked and used a voice distorter even in person, everyone she'd interviewed would be identifiable. Compromised.

Of course the FBI would want her storage drives. Probably even more than they'd want to catch Leo's murderer.

Before they went to the FBI, she should talk to her attorney about what she'd have to surrender to them. Maybe it could be limited to Leo's rushes and leave her files safe.

Except, for the years of their collaboration, the overlap between her work and his was almost a total eclipse. Leo did projects without her, but she rarely did stories without him.

Another headache to sort out. They needed to locate Leo's studio and go there before they notified the FBI so Signe would have a chance to recover any storage drives that belonged to her. Because while a search warrant of her house could be limited to Leo's files, everything in Leo's editing studio would be fair game.

They picked up takeout on their way to the house. It was early evening and they faced a long night of tedious work. She needed to go through Leo's papers and scan the videos for clues to the depth of Leo's corruption. Hours and hours and hours of video.

The rental was a two-bedroom bungalow on a quiet street. It was shabbier than the online photos had indicated, but she hardly cared about chipped paint, warped countertops, or broken appliances.

It was cheap, available, and had high-speed internet.

Signe set her laptop and the bag with the storage drives on a chrome and mint green Formica kitchen table set that had begun life in the '50s as ultramodern, passed through at least two decades of being yard-sale rejects, but was now a trendy classic. Or it would be if the seat cushions on the matching chairs were reupholstered, which was probably why it was still in the rental and not in some fancy kitchen with retro decor.

Tonight it would be her workstation and she just hoped the torn seats wouldn't have springs poking through. She set to work plugging in her laptop while Cole and Jasper unloaded the SUV.

She'd left that job to the men because she didn't care about her suitcase nearly so much as the storage drives, which wouldn't leave her sight if she could help it.

She had a new motto: trust no one ever again.

Jasper stood in the intersection between kitchen, dining nook, and living room and nodded to the short hallway. "I'm taking one bedroom. You and Cole can fight over the other one."

"I'll take the couch," Cole said, then he continued down the hall and dropped her bag in what she presumed would be her room. She didn't care. Doubted she'd even sleep tonight, but if Cole wanted points for giving her the bed and taking the couch, he could have them.

Before booting up her computer, she lowered the blinds on all the windows in the living and dining areas. They needed privacy for this and thankfully the cheap blinds were solid vinyl rolls that covered the entire window.

She'd eaten half her massive chicken burrito on the long drive, and now she pulled out the clamshell with a basic salad and poured the blue cheese dressing on top so she could eat while she worked. She was constantly hungry since leaving Yosemite. Her body was probably still angry with her for hiking a ridiculous number of miles while carrying a heavy pack in an extremely short period of time.

She stuffed her mouth with lettuce and cheese, then asked, mouth still full, "What's the Wi-Fi password?" She'd left her manners in Yosemite, it seemed, but she didn't give a damn that her mom would be horrified.

Cole dropped into the seat next to her. "I thought you didn't want your computer to be online while we watch the videos on the hard drives?"

"Not for the computer. For my phone. I turned off cellular so I don't ping towers and turned off locational data so it's safe for me to use Wi-Fi to see if DiscoFever has tried to contact me."

"What makes you think DiscoFever is still alive?" he asked.

"What makes you think they're dead?"

Jasper sat in the chair on her other side. "We need to figure out who DiscoFever is."

"Agreed."

Cole found the card with the password and she punched it into her phone. She checked messages. Nothing from DiscoFever.

She turned off the phone. It might be the most secure phone in the world, but she still didn't take chances.

She stacked the storage drives—each one was slightly larger than a deck of cards and held at least four terabytes of data—by date, with the one on top containing the oldest files.

She turned to Jasper. "It was two years ago in March when we crossed paths when I was interviewing the narco trafficker, right?"

"March twenty-first."

She nodded and grabbed the drive second from the top and plugged it into her laptop, then entered a password that was a combination of date and military alphabet words based on the month followed by the year backward. She and Leo had developed this password convention together. She'd be able to access any hard drives of his when she found his private editing studio.

The drive unlocked and she searched the menu for the applicable dates.

There were hours of raw footage from that day—Leo had always turned on the camera whenever he could. They had footage beginning long before the interview when they were miles away, waiting for the go-ahead first from her security team, then from the source who'd arranged the meeting.

Her source had been a falcon—the lowest-level member in any cartel. He'd told Signe that his boss, a kingpin known as La Jirafa Macho—the male giraffe in Spanish—had asked him to set up the meeting. This wasn't entirely unusual, but uncommon enough that Signe had agreed to the interview even though she wasn't working on any particular story about drug traffickers at the time.

La Jirafa Macho was new in town, supposedly sent north from Mexico to take over parts of the business that were in disarray after arrests by the FBI in the previous year. But Signe had a feeling La

Jirafa wasn't from Mexico at all and was instead a local who'd been a lieutenant in the cartel and had seized a leadership role in the power vacuum caused by the FBI bust.

Now he hoped to use her to establish himself as a player among traffickers in Southern California. She had no intention of being used like that, but she still wouldn't pass up the interview.

To get to the meeting, they had to wear hoods and ride in the back of a big, battered SUV. Leo got footage of her being hooded before he tucked the camera away and was hooded himself. Her security team wasn't happy, but this was par for the course and Leo was with her.

Signe remembered that an hour later, when the hoods were removed, they were parked inside a large warehouse that smelled of rotting fish. Must be on the docks, but SoCal had a lot of waterfront with multiple ports, big and small.

Signe had zero interest in trying to find the warehouse later. It wasn't her job to do the work of law enforcement.

Hoods off and cameras on, she stood waiting to meet the crime lord. Other falcons and lieutenants entered the parking bay where Leo had set up a camera on a tripod. At one point, he crossed in front of that camera and pulled Signe close and kissed her.

Watching the video now, she remembered that moment. It wasn't the kind of thing he ever did when they were working, so it had thrown her off. She pushed him back, irritated, and he'd whispered that he thought she looked worried after the long, hooded ride.

Now she watched as his hand settled on her butt and squeezed. It was clear from his face and the way he positioned her that he knew his actions were being recorded. He glanced at the camera and there was a smug expression she'd seen many times, but not in quite this way. It was a look that wasn't meant for her, it was for whoever would watch the video.

Her body flashed with cold. For the first time, she wondered if Leo had ever filmed them in bed together.

Cole made a low sound in his throat. He'd spotted Leo's grop-ing hand.

She ate her salad as they watched at double speed. She'd set the files to auto play in order. At one point, Jasper got up and popped the caps from three bottles of beer, setting one in front of her.

She sipped as they watched the monotonous video in silence.

She'd once joked that if she and Leo ever had a kid, Leo would record so much video, it would take half their child's life just to watch it.

Now she thanked the goddess of birth control that she'd never procreated with him.

It was strange, this numb feeling of acceptance she'd settled into. Her marriage hadn't been what she'd thought it was, and Leo wasn't the man she'd believed him to be.

On her laptop screen, Jasper entered the bay. He spotted Leo with a camera in his hands and tried to back out.

They rewound and changed the speed to real time, then watched again. This was footage from the tripod. Next they'd watch the record-ing from Leo's handheld.

Jasper kept his face averted from the tripod. But Leo came after him, and looking at Leo in this new light, it was clear he was trying to get everyone on video as much as possible—which was different from their usual protocol. Criminals were, by necessity, camera shy. She had developed a system over the years designed to put her subjects at ease. They had a lot of rules around filming and Leo was a pro.

It had never occurred to her that he didn't always follow those rules. They'd worked together for so long, she'd stopped paying attention.

"Why *this* interview?" she muttered under her breath. "If Leo was going to break every rule we established over years of collaboration, why did he do it on this day?"

"He was expecting La Jirafa—or someone who worked for him—to give him something," Cole said.

"You think he was working with someone in the organization? A side deal?" Signe studied the screen. Watched herself standing near the battered SUV, drinking from a bottle of store-bought water. She always brought sealed bottles to these kinds of meetings. The crack of the twist-off top was her assurance her drink hadn't been tampered with. Listening for it had been ingrained.

The irony of being vigilant at work, but not in a bar with a margarita glass that had a rim the size of a salad plate.

The camera caught a person in the corridor doorway where they'd first seen Jasper. A young woman. Pretty. Dark hair. Asian features.

The camera shifted and La Jirafa entered the room. He was covered from head to toe—gloves on his hands and a full hood like a mummy, but dark fabric with a thin layer of cheesecloth over his eyes.

On-screen, everyone was looking at La Jirafa Macho, but Signe wasn't interested in him now.

"Go back," Jasper said.

Her fingers were already on the mouse. "The woman."

Jasper nodded.

She clicked on the player and slid the bar at the bottom so it would go back thirty seconds. When the woman appeared, Signe hit "Pause" and zoomed in.

The video was crisp HD. She zoomed in on the woman's face. Not familiar. She scrolled lower, to the woman's chest.

Cole broke the silence. "Holy fuck."

There it was clear as day. She wore a retro-style T-shirt with a font that was straight out of a '70s movie. Maybe even the same font that was used on the *Saturday Night Fever* movie poster. The words DISCO FEVER were written in an arc over a shiny silver disco ball.

CHAPTER 42

"So is she DiscoFever, or did someone use the name because of the shirt?" Cole asked.

Signe leaned back in the vintage—predisco-age—chair as she studied the woman. They'd watched the rest of the day's footage and caught only two more instances of her, both from a distance. Both brief.

"I need Leo's notes from that day. He kept a record of everyone he caught on film. Maybe *he* called her DiscoFever."

"And she knew about it?" Cole asked.

Signe shrugged. "Looks like she was at the lowest level of the crime pyramid, which is where we start looking for contacts. Leo did some of that groundwork."

"But this interview was different. The request came from the top of the pyramid," Cole said.

She nodded, then turned to Jasper. "Do you remember her?"

"No."

"Still, she somehow found out you were FBI and messaged you, asking you to set up a meet with me."

"I doubt she knew she was reaching out to *me*. The contact came from a CI. Someone in La Jirafa's network had intel on human trafficking they wanted to share with Signe Gates. It had the potential to be huge, so I jumped on it. I messaged the number given to me with the number I got from you that night at the bar. I told them I would facilitate your meeting."

Having gleaned everything they could from the woman in the Disco Fever T-shirt, they switched to watching the interview rushes in real time with the sound on.

Watching La Jirafa now made Signe's skin crawl. She vividly remembered the discomfort of the moment. Even though he was covered completely and there was no contact with actual skin, she'd been deeply uncomfortable with his repeated attempts to touch her.

He'd also hit on her and in the end outright threatened her.

Now she watched the video as La Jirafa slowly ramped up.

"He's sexualizing you as a message to Leo," Cole said.

La Jirafa had a high-end voice changer—a collar at his throat held a quarter-size speaker so the sound projected slightly below his mouth as he whispered into a microphone. The resulting voice wasn't distorted like the one in her nightmares, it was just different from his natural speaking voice. A higher, breathy pitch that could be male or female.

"I'm used to these guys sexualizing me at the start, but they cut it out after I make it clear it's not welcome." She looked at Jasper. "I do *not* flirt with my interview subjects."

He nodded. "This is the only interview I ever witnessed in person, and I only saw pieces because I didn't want to get on camera. But yeah, I remember how much he came on to you. I see now you deflected as much as you could."

It was as close to an apology as she would get from him and she supposed it was enough. He hadn't been wrong about this being a sexually charged interview—it was just one-sided.

"I was never able to use anything from this interview." She stared at the paused image on the screen. "I just wanted to take a shower afterward."

"My guess is it was La Jirafa's way of putting Leo on notice that you were a target if he continued to cut into the business," Cole said.

Her stomach churned. She hadn't told them the details of her rape. They needed to know one thing. "It's possible he ordered my rape as a message to Leo. Even a . . . humiliation. To him as a husband. They used a drug cocktail to . . . *heighten* things for me. So it would look like I was participating voluntarily." Her throat was tight as she pushed the words out. She'd been drugged and had no choice and yet she still found herself feeling defensive, fearing Cole and Jasper wouldn't believe her if they watched the video.

"What can you tell us about La Jirafa, Jas?" Cole asked.

"Not much. Pretty sure he's Caucasian. From LA and was a lieutenant in the cartel. Took over the drug side of the operation in a power vacuum. My guess is Leo was also making inroads during the same period and managed to scoop up the human-trafficking side of the business."

"How did it start?" Signe asked. "With Leo, I mean."

"Near as I can tell, about three, four years ago, the cartel had a '*shipment*'"—Jasper used air quotes around the word—"of farm workers from Mexico who he managed to get over the border in a truck. Leo's job was to receive the shipment and fold the workers into existing farms. Beef up security so they couldn't escape. Problem was, with everyone speaking Spanish and the holes in security after the recent spate of arrests, the men were escaping. They had an underground railroad of sorts.

"Leo gets the bright idea to look elsewhere for laborers who don't speak English or Spanish or Chinese or Korean. He settled on the Philippines because it's an easy target for human trafficking. Problem is, English is an official language of the Philippines. Solution: when you get to the remote areas, you can find people who only speak Tagalog or another local language, and you find much fewer Tagalog speakers in California."

Signe cleared her throat. "This would be when Leo went to the Philippines without me to film a nature documentary. He was gone for six weeks, came home with days and days of footage, but then sidelined the project when he got a job filming a World War II in Alaska history piece for PBS." She rubbed her temples. "He'd been financing the Philippines piece himself, and I nagged him about it for months. I'd seen a lot of the footage and it was good stuff. I wanted him to finish the project so people could really see him shine. He always called the nature stuff the work of his heart. He said he did the crime stuff for me."

Goddamn, her ex had been a manipulative bastard. Blaming her for not working on the projects of his heart, all while using her to ingratiate himself in the criminal underworld.

"That sounds about right," Jasper said. "It was some time after that we saw an uptick in trafficking from the Philippines. I was on the fringes of the organization, searching for the port of entry for the *'shipments,'* as everyone insisted on calling them. They were bringing in kids for sex trafficking, but males over sixteen were generally sent to work manual labor. Once Leo had his system set up and running smoothly, La Jirafa wanted to cut him out. He had everyone searching for the port of entry for the *'shipments'* so he could seize them out from under Leo." He paused, then added, "Mind you, I didn't know it was *Leo* all this time. I just knew there was someone out there who was the human-trafficking kingpin and it wasn't La Jirafa Macho, which pissed the male giraffe off greatly."

"Do you have any clue who La Jirafa is?" she asked.

"I was sort of hoping you knew."

She shook her head. "Were you able to find the port of entry?"

"Yeah. Just a few blocks from where you interviewed La Jirafa." He nodded to the screen. "It's where they dumped my body."

She flinched. "How—how did you survive?"

"I found him," Cole said. "He'd told me about the warehouse just days before he disappeared. I found him in a dumpster."

Jesus. Jasper was thrown away.

"Did you tell the FBI about the warehouse after you found Jasper?"

Cole shook his head. "They stopped using it."

"But why didn't you tell them?"

"We didn't know if someone in the bureau or customs was tipping off the cartel in advance of surprise customs inspections, because the warehouse was always magically clean. If I told the FBI to check out the warehouse—a case that was *not* mine—it could have tipped them off that Jasper was alive. Plus, the cartel knew they had a mole in the organization—they just didn't know it was Jasper until Leo identified him."

And that was my fault.

The words weren't said aloud, but she knew they were all thinking it.

She cleared her throat. "So. You're investigating the FBI or customs as well as your own murder—or rather, attempted murder."

Jasper nodded.

"So what is our next step? Do we report that Jasper is alive and Leo is dead to the FBI?"

Both men shook their heads.

"We need to find Leo's studio first."

"As much as I want to get there first so I can protect my sources, the FBI could probably find it faster. Don't you have databases you can search?"

"Every search on Leo Starr has been a dead end," Cole said. "But also that's not what I meant about *first*. We need to find Leo's studio before whoever killed him does. His studio will have the mother lode of evidence, including everything the FBI could want to put human traffickers in prison for the rest of their lives. *That* is what whoever killed Leo is after.

"Leo has hours and hours of footage of people committing crimes. It's his security against being harmed or pushed out of the business. He could bring the entire cartel down. They want to find his studio to protect their business. We want it for justice for Jasper, Manny, and every person who has been trafficked by your ex-husband and his cronies."

CHAPTER 43

Cole knew Signe had crossed the line into full acceptance when she simply nodded. "Leo never deletes videos. He'll have everything saved and backed up."

She'd agreed to the search earlier, but that was before she was convinced. Now it was time for her to fully commit. Cole leaned forward and held her gaze. "If anyone can find his hidey-hole, it's you."

"I'll call Steven in the morning and ask about the Tahoe cabin."

"You'll call Steven right now," Jasper said.

She glanced at the clock. It was almost one a.m., but again, she nodded.

She picked up her phone, then frowned. "Shit. I had Roman delete Leo and Steven from my contacts list a few months ago after I drunk dialed Leo one night when we were in Panama."

"Roman? *He* deleted Leo's and Steven's phone numbers?" Cole asked.

Jasper sat ramrod straight. "Shit. If Roman—"

Cole frowned. "If Steven knows anything, he is in danger."

She rubbed her temples. "With Leo's murder, I forgot about Roman. But I'm not sure how he could be involved. Leo and Roman never worked together. I introduced them." Her face went pasty white. "I needed Leo to let his informants know they'd be dealing with Roman moving forward."

"And in doing that, Leo gave Roman the keys to the castle," Jasper muttered.

"No." She bolted to her feet. "Goddammit! No."

"Yes," Cole said softly. "Yes. Leo was probably keeping tabs on you using Roman. Steven could be in danger. How do we find him?"

"I haven't talked to him since the separation. He was in grad school, studying forestry. Leo and I paid his tuition, so I should have an address for him in the papers somewhere."

"Where does he go to school?"

"Cal. The Rausser College of Natural Resources."

"So he's living in Berkeley?"

"Last I heard, yes."

"See if you can find his number in your papers."

She huffed out a breath. "Steven always used our address to maintain California residency. He took a gap year after high school and again after undergrad. The second one was more like two years, and he was living with a girlfriend in Texas, so it was important he keep residency. But I'm afraid that means most of the places he's lived haven't been in his name. He might be hard to trace."

She must've read the look on Cole's face because she said, "He's *not* a little crime lord in the making."

Cole shrugged. "He's either innocent or complicit. Just like you."

"The difference is, I am neither innocent nor complicit. Not in Leo's trafficking crimes anyway."

"If it makes you feel better, we don't think he was a crime lord when you married him," Jasper said. "Your timeline of when he had the safe installed and his filming in the Philippines fits with what I've been able to piece together since I died."

She stared at Jasper, her face expressionless, which, given everything she'd taken in today, was something in itself.

Signe slid the computer over to Jasper. "You keep going through the videos. I'm going to search for Steven's address."

Cole watched videos over Jasper's shoulder even as he used his own computer to search for information on the dead man's baby brother. Every path led right back to Signe's or Leo's current addresses. If Cole didn't know better, he'd believe Steven Higgins was a figment of her imagination.

If he had access to FBI databases this would go much faster, but remote login wasn't possible.

Signe let out a groan, rose to her feet, and started pacing. It was clear she was agitated as she made a circuit from the entryway to the couch, hallway, and back to the kitchen.

"What's wrong, Sig?"

"Oh, I don't know. Just *everything*. It's creepy as hell that there is no indication of where the editing studio is. How does one make an office disappear? There's got to be some paperwork."

"Leo destroyed any paperwork regarding the purchasing of equipment. We can only assume that papers that can't be destroyed—like a deed or title—are in a safety deposit box somewhere."

She shook her head. "We cleaned it out when he had the safe installed."

"But you did have one at one point."

"Safety deposit box, PO box, storage units, gym lockers in multiple cities—we had all that as avenues for communication with informants."

"Gym memberships?"

"Bus and train stations don't have lockers anymore. But some gyms—especially older ones in poorer neighborhoods—still do. Leo would pay a fee to the gym owner, asking them to keep it off the books. The owner had the lock combination—a way to ensure drugs and guns weren't being exchanged. It was always just coded notes between Leo and informants. Lockers are perfect because you can slip a paper inside without having a key. Only Leo retrieved the notes. It was a way for informants who needed absolute anonymity to get in touch with Leo."

"How did he get in touch back?"

"It depended on what the message said. Sometimes it was a meet point—date and time, like with DiscoFever—and sometimes it would be a phone number."

"And Leo continued to use this system after you split?"

She shrugged. "I wouldn't begin to know where the lockers are." After a beat, her eyes widened. "I need a computer with internet."

"Why?"

"Not long before we separated, I . . . I was searching Leo's computer because I'd gotten a cryptic call. It could have been an informant or a woman he was having an affair with, and so I logged in to his computer to figure out which it was. If it was an informant, I needed to respond."

"And if it was a woman he was having an affair with?"

"I hadn't decided. On the one hand, we hadn't had sex in months . . ."

"Doesn't make it okay," Cole said. He clenched his jaw, imagining the gaslighting going on as Leo tried to make her feel guilty all while the bastard *knew* she'd been raped and brutalized.

"What did you find on his computer?" Jasper asked.

"There was an app called something like 'locker talk' or 'vault room' and it wasn't social media or a dating site or anything like that. It was a secure server for sending anonymous messages. Dark-web-level encryption but accessible to laypeople who were willing to pay a five grand setup fee. Bank transfer only—no crypto allowed."

"Steep price," Cole said.

"Yeah. Honestly, it looked like a scam. Huge setup cost, paid up front with no guarantee it would work. I asked Leo about it and he said he got conned. I pressed and he said he'd decided to try it because once he had the setup, he could give informants a five-digit code and they'd be able to message him in the vault. Easier than gym lockers.

"He could also send messages from the vault—unlimited, anytime, anywhere, and all would be tagged with an untraceable five-digit code. The messages would disappear when read, like a lot of apps out there, but the recipient didn't have to be logged in to the locker for their messages to disappear."

"Leo lied about being conned."

"Probably. He was angry I searched his computer—even though in all our years of collaboration, we always made a point of sharing passwords. Given the stories we were working on, it was vital we could access each other's systems. We set up a system for passwords, so I would be able to guess his password within three tries without getting locked out."

"Would Leo continue using a password system you could crack?" Cole asked.

She shrugged. "Why not? I never had access to his computer again. It was a few days later that he found out about my STD and left me." She raised her chin defiantly. "At the time, he said searching my medical records was tit for tat because I'd searched his computer."

The truth hit Cole the same moment it did her. "He was looking for a reason to divorce you. Because you were on his computer and it was getting harder and harder to hide from you what he was doing."

She nodded.

He rose from his chair and waved to the computer. "Find the app. See if you can log in as Leo."

◆ ◆ ◆

It took several searches before Signe hit on the right key-word combo and found the developer of Xvault. The website was as secretive as ever—it was clear the business thrived on word of mouth because they weren't trying to show up at the top of any search engine and their rates and methods were hard to suss out, but she finally found a forum of users who offered troubleshooting tips if an account was locked—part of being a vault meant that the usual password recovery tools weren't available.

The workaround some users had discovered was reinstalling the app, but you had to know your password to be able to access the app download files. A chicken-and-egg scenario except one kindly soul made a spoof of the .exe file that tricked the app into thinking it was loaded so multiple password attempts could be made. Then, once the user was logged in, they could download and reinstall the app and access their conversations.

Before she made her first attempt, she closed her eyes and pictured Leo's computer screen that day a year and a half ago. Which of his favorite usernames had he employed? She was pretty sure he'd used a variation on his last name. With five letters, he needed only three more for most logins, but he would never use his own full name for something like this.

She typed *Starr0826x*—his birth month and date—which he used for a lot of businesses, plus the letter *X*, which was the first letter of the app name.

She wasn't kicked out for not being the right format or having too few characters, so she studied the password box. From the forum, she knew it was a twenty-digit password. Not surprising that an app called Xvault would require a long password with special characters, numbers, and lower and uppercase.

Her first attempt was the app name forward and Leo's name backward after every letter followed by the pound sign after each name and his age followed by Signe's age: *xrvraautlSt#o4e5L#37*.

When that failed, she remembered that he wouldn't have updated his age and her age to the current year. She changed 45 to 43 and 37 to 35 and hit "Enter."

And she was in.

"Wow," Cole said. "That's a complex system."

"It varies based on how many characters are needed and other requirements, but it generates a memorable unique password for every login."

She couldn't view Leo's existing conversations without downloading the full app, which she would have sent to her phone but Cole gave her a directory on his laptop that was configured to mimic a phone operating system.

In minutes, the app was installed and both men watched over her shoulder as she logged in for real this time.

It was a no-frills system. There weren't pretty buttons or graphics. Just a list of conversations and a plus sign to start a new one.

She spotted her cell phone number on the list of conversations and opened it.

Her stomach dropped as she read the last texts sent:

28907: You going to fuck him tonight?

28907: He won't give it to you like I did.

Beneath was an audio file attachment. And once again, she heard herself scream.

CHAPTER 44

Cole could hear the sound of Signe retching through the thin bathroom door. He crossed back to the table and looked at the list of messages, then opened a different conversation that was also sent to Signe's number.

"He was taunting her about being raped," Jasper said.

"I wish he wasn't dead so he could be killed more slowly with lots more suffering."

"The one thing I've believed through all this is that he loved her." Jasper's voice was a low whisper.

"Same. I figured he did what he did to separate from her because he was ordered to or she'd be killed—because if she wasn't complicit, she could uncover the whole organization at any time."

"Yeah. But these messages, they're just cruel. Did you know she received these?"

"No. I knew *something* had frightened her at Glacier and again when I was meeting you in the store to get the GPS, but I had no idea it was anything like this."

Jasper dropped his head into his hands. "She received these, then I went after her with chains and the distorted voice. It's a wonder she didn't kill you in your sleep that night."

"It's a wonder she made it out of the park on her feet like she did." Cole dropped back into the chair. "We need to see who else Leo was talking to. Take down these numbers. One of them will be Leo's killer. Others might be accomplices."

There were two dozen conversations on the list, dating back to when Leo bought the app a few months before he left Signe.

She might be able to offer context for some of the messages, but Cole didn't want to wait for her to return. If there were more nasty messages waiting, maybe he could soften the blow by warning her at least.

Jasper compared the list of numbers with what they'd compiled so far. "Third one down is Roman Wiley."

Cole clicked on the directory. This was a long conversation with replies. Presumably, Wiley had no record of this on his phone, unless he also had an Xvault account.

Leo: She's at Glacier. Get the fuck out of there before she sees you.

Leo: Are you still there?

Leo: Where are you?

Roman: I'm gone. Don't worry, she didn't see me. Too busy sucking face with the new guy.

Roman was baiting Leo. Interesting.

"Roman didn't know Connie got video of him at Glacier," Cole said.

Connie—the woman who'd been in the car when Jasper picked Cole up—was a prostitute who worked in the neighborhood where Jasper had lived for the last two years. Unbeknownst to Cole, Jasper had hired her to accompany him into Yosemite. He'd kept it a secret because he'd wanted Cole's reactions to be genuine if Connie interacted with him and Signe.

When Jasper had explained his reasoning on the long drive back to LA, Cole had complained. *"I've been undercover for five years and hiding that you're alive for two of them and you think I can't act?"*

"Fine, so it was more fun for me *that you were baffled once you realized Connie wasn't a fan."*

Signe hadn't been the only target for Jasper's manipulation and anger.

For her part, Connie had enjoyed her role in the drama and did better than Jasper expected when he tasked her with making sure Signe and Cole caught sight of Roman. Jasper had been stunned to see Signe's new cameraman—a guy who'd never been on his radar as potentially involved with Leo's business—and wanted to make sure Cole knew the man was in play.

After her stint as a superfan, Connie had made friends with tourists at Camp 4 and spent two nights there while Jasper tracked Cole and Signe through the forest. The final morning, he'd used his satellite phone to call the woman, instructing her to pick him up at the Lukens Lake Trailhead so he'd be in position to pick up Cole on Tioga Road.

"Roman is up to his eyeballs in this, but he thinks we don't know," Cole said. "Thinks he wasn't seen."

"We can use that to our advantage."

Jasper then pointed to a text from Leo to Roman, sent when Roman was in Singapore with Signe.

Leo: One of the runaways was spotted talking to a climber who speaks Tagalog. If we can find the climber, we'll find the runners.

Before that, there were messages stating that five of the fifteen workers on custodial duty in the park had escaped in the high country.

"If we can trace the park's concessionaire contracts to the subcontract with custodians, we'd have the money trail to nail the organization with human trafficking and enslavement," Cole said. "The park is paying someone and NPS doesn't pay with crypto."

"We can do it that way, but we'll find the paper trail faster in Leo's phantom studio."

Cole continued opening message threads. Most were one-sided. Leo anonymously informing someone of where to leave payment.

"How was he laundering all this cash?" Jasper asked.

Signe reentered the room. Cole glanced over and took in her wet hair. She must've dunked her head under the faucet again, because he hadn't heard the shower.

Without a word, he rose from the seat to let her take over. She studied the open thread on the screen. "He probably claimed some of this as crypto earnings cashed out. He said he did that to pay for Steven's tuition and other expenses a few times. Grad school is about fifty grand a year. I'm sure he shuffled things around to make the deposit into Steven's account look legal. We had accounts in the US and Mexico because we filmed there a lot and it was easier. I wouldn't be surprised if Leo has money in the Caymans. Until we divorced, I stupidly left him in charge of the money."

"Don't call yourself stupid," Cole said.

She faced him and he could see her eyes were red and a bit puffy. "Aren't I, though? I've made a career of studying criminals and until about eight hours ago, I didn't know I was married to one. For *years*."

She clicked on the list of conversations and opened her phone number again. "He did *this*. To *me*."

"I'm sorry."

"Don't apologize for what he did," she snapped.

He held up his hands. "I'm not. I'm sorry you are in pain. I'm sorry I was the bearer of this news. I'm sorry he didn't deserve you."

She turned back to the computer. "Yeah, well, I'm sorry he was a monster too." She clicked on a random conversation and said, "What did you learn while I was wallowing?"

He wanted to tell her that vomiting because her ex had taunted her about being raped was hardly wallowing, but they needed to get back on track. He brought her up to date, including the texts showing Roman's involvement, then they continued reading the conversations, trying to guess who the recipients were.

Signe opened another conversation and this one included an email address with the order to contact that account.

"Wait. I've seen that email address before."

Signe grabbed her phone and scrolled through it. Then reached for her laptop, which Jasper had been using to view videos but now ignored in favor of Cole's with the open Xvault threads. "Any email I received from that address should be on my computer." She opened the email application and typed the address in the search bar. "Got it."

Cole noticed her hands shook as she opened the email and he understood why after reading Leo's other anonymous communications with her.

"Leo was pretending to be an informant. One of his, who reached out to me after we split. He contacted me a half dozen times in the eighteen months since we separated, offering tidbits on a story I back-burnered because I didn't trust that I wasn't being lured into a trap."

"See? Not stupid. Your instincts were spot-on."

She drummed her fingers on the table. "Was this Leo luring me or just keeping tabs?"

"Both would be my guess," Jasper said.

Cole studied the email address. It was a basic free online mailbox. As anonymous as it was ubiquitous. "Could you log in to this account?"

She went to the online portal and typed in the email address in the login box. "I bet I can guess his password in one try."

She won her own bet.

"Leo was careful in many things, but he was also a creature of habit and given that he would never expect me to discover this email address was his, he had no reason to worry I'd hack it."

She skipped the inbox and went straight to the flagged messages. "Any information Leo needed to access quickly would be flagged."

She opened an email Leo had sent himself and laughed.

"What's that?" Cole asked.

It was Jasper who answered. "Looks like a Bitcoin key to me."

After taking screenshots of the sixteen-digit password, Signe moved to the inbox and found emails related to yet another secret email account.

Leo had set up this account to authenticate another account, because he didn't dare connect a cell phone to any of these email addresses.

She opened a different browser that wasn't already logged in to email and typed in the new address and his basic password. The authentication box popped up and she had the code sent to the other email address. The email arrived with a ping and she copied the code.

She was in. Even better, this was Leo's *real* email account. The one he used to access information from his secret lair. She turned to Cole. "I presume the FBI can trace the IP address on these emails?"

"Wouldn't Leo use a virtual private network?"

She frowned. "Maybe. He's savvy enough to know he needs secret email accounts, and he knows film editing like nobody's business, but I'm not sure if he knows how to access a VPN that would hold up over time, and I'm certain he configured his secret office all by himself—otherwise it wouldn't still be a secret."

"In the morning, I'll reach out to a friend at the bureau. It would raise too many alarm bells to get a request to do an IP address search in the middle of the night when I'm supposedly on vacation."

Signe continued scrolling through emails, looking for something that might contain an actual address.

She clicked on the date stamp to sort messages from oldest to youngest, and there it was at the top of the screen. Confirmation from the internet service provider that the service would be hooked up to K. L. Burns's residence the following day.

"You always had dreams of being Ken Burns, didn't you, Leo?" Signe murmured.

The date for the installation matched the time period when he'd been building a studio in the cabin he and Steven had inherited.

Even better, the cable company included the address.

But the cabin wasn't in Tahoe. It was in the San Jacinto Mountains.

CHAPTER 45

Signe stared at the computer, almost in a daze. They'd found a longer email chain between Leo and Roman about the escaped "workers," including Leo's plan to enter the park and join the search. He would use his press credentials to give his questions legitimacy. His focus would be Camp 4 and finding the Filipino climber.

She stared blankly ahead, breathing deeply as she considered Roman Wiley. She'd known him for only eighteen months. How long had he been working for Leo?

"So Leo and Roman were in the woods with us last week. Their plan was to follow us to the rendezvous area." She paused and turned to Cole. "Wait, they didn't need to follow us. You sent the coordinates before we set out Wednesday morning."

His nostrils flared as he gave a sharp nod. "It would have taken them a lot longer to find the camp even if they had a car and parked at one of the trailheads along Tioga Road."

She gave him a faint smile. "Neither had your mad archaeology skills. Or a quad map with known sites in the area."

"They needed every minute they could get to find the camp before you got there. Leo even ordered me to delay you."

Her heart ached as she remembered the empty camp. "So Leo and Roman found the missing workers." She cleared her throat and added, "They'd have killed them and hidden their bodies, because there is no way the two of them could haul four men five or so miles across the wilderness to the road."

Cole nodded. "It's possible they're still alive and hiding, but they were emaciated and weak after more than three weeks in hiding, and the blood on Manny's shirt doesn't give me much hope."

"Same." She took a short breath, then continued. "We know Leo is dead, and we presume Roman is not," she said. "But why did Roman and Leo hang around and go to the meet point? Wasn't their goal to find the workers?"

"I'm sure they wanted to identify DiscoFever," Jasper said. "If they thought the informant would be there in person, they would have gone to the rendezvous point at the appointed time."

Her head jerked up. "What do you mean? Leo had been dead for *hours* when we got there. His skin was cold to the touch. And we were early for the meeting."

Cole's nostrils flared. "There's something I haven't told you."

Cold dread slid down her spine. But at the same time, her heart cracked. She was so tired of betrayal. "What?" All she could manage was a low whisper as she braced herself.

"I told Leo the meeting was at five a.m."

Five a.m. Around the time she'd woken up to find Cole gone. He'd had his gun with him.

"The plan was to have Jasper and me there, waiting for him."

Her throat closed, making her words come out as a dry rasp. "Why kill him? There were two of you." She managed a deeper breath and her voice grew louder. "You're fucking FBI agents. He's a documentary producer. You could have taken him easily."

"That's not how it went. We heard a shot before Jasper and I met up. We tried to track the shooter, but I never spotted him and had to get back to you. You were suspicious enough as it was. I never climbed the hill. I didn't know what we'd find that morning."

◆ ◆ ◆

Signe's exhaustion went bone-deep. Her mind reeled as it occurred to her that she had nothing left to hope for beyond justice for Manny and the others.

There was no way her career could be salvaged after the depth of Leo's corruption came out. She would maybe, just maybe, avoid charges of her own. But her days of interviewing crime lords were over.

Not that it mattered.

She'd always had a hunger for knowledge, to understand how the world worked, especially the more unsavory elements. She no longer wished to know more about crime. Didn't want a deeper understanding.

Her firsthand experience was more knowledge than she'd been seeking.

And yet she knew less now than she did last week. She didn't even know if she could believe Cole and Jasper, but recognized that at this point, she was out of options.

She went back to Leo's email and read a message her crime-lord husband had received from La Jirafa, in which Signe herself was demanded as payment for Leo's transgression of moving into his business.

La Jirafa had managed to confirm Leo's identity. He couldn't kill Leo, so instead he would exact revenge.

Leo replied to his new overlord stating that Signe would be in Oakhurst on July 14 and included the name of her hotel. This message was dated July 11—the day after Jasper had been taken, beaten, and left for dead in a dumpster.

Several days after Bastille Day, La Jirafa sent Leo a link. As always in her line of work, Signe clicked. She was automatically logged in to an encrypted cloud server. There was only one file on the server. A two-hour-long video. Viewable, but not delete-able, by Leo.

Cole put a hand over hers before she could click the "Play" button. "Don't do it, Signe."

"I've already seen it. Maybe this one isn't blurred and I'll see their faces."

"Let me see it first. I'll tell you if the faces are visible."

"So you can get off on watching me be raped just like La Jirafa? He said he wanted the sex tape for his spank bank."

Cole turned pasty white. "Hell no. I don't *want* to watch it. I don't want you to watch it either. I'm trying to take the hit for you. Maybe you can avoid it."

"No. I can't hide from this."

She hit "Play." It started with her on a bed, still dressed. The video she'd been sent eighteen months ago had a blurred background along with blurred faces. This was the first time she was seeing the room where she had been assaulted.

She hit "Pause." "This isn't the hotel in Modesto where I woke up. It doesn't look like a hotel room at all."

It made sense. The video of her taking the bribe for Jasper's name hadn't been in a hotel room either. Plus, she must've screamed horribly. No way other guests wouldn't have heard.

"Looks like the primary bedroom of a house," Jasper said.

She braced herself for what she was about to see and hit "Play" again.

She could do this. Face the truth that was buried in her mind.

In the end, she wished she'd let Cole view it first, because the truth was too much. An irreparable blow. In spite of the drugs, she hadn't been responsive at first, and that would never do. Not for what La Jirafa had demanded.

To fix it—to fix *her*—Leo had entered the room and coaxed her into arousal. Then he stepped off camera and let three strangers have her.

CHAPTER 46

The bedroom door slammed, leaving Cole alone with Jasper.

"She must not have had anything left to vomit," Jasper said.

Cole stared at the frozen image on the screen. It was a testament to Signe's control that she hadn't smashed her computer. She'd broken the mouse, sure. But the computer could be used with the trackpad.

He hit the playback-speed button and dialed it up to three times normal. At two hours long, there was no way he could stomach it in real time, but they needed to know if there was another cameo by Leo or other information.

As they watched, he increased the speed. Only the earliest shots showed Signe as any kind of potentially willing participant. It got violent after that. She must've had bruises and lacerations for days.

And now he understood how she got the scars between her thighs.

Just before the video ended, a woman entered the room. DiscoFever. She wasn't wearing the shirt, but Cole recognized her. He slowed the playback to real time and rewound to the moment the woman entered carrying a mug with a spoon.

Her face was expressionless as she sat on the edge of the bed next to Signe, who stared glassy-eyed into the distance, her body battered and bloody.

DiscoFever used coaxing words to get Signe to open her mouth so she could feed her broth one spoonful at a time. The liquid dribbled down Signe's chin and neck, but DiscoFever continued feeding, her voice flat, clearly aware of the camera.

The recording ended. For the moment, Signe's torture was over.

Cole stared at the blank screen in horrified silence. Jasper appeared equally dazed.

The refrigerator cycled on, a loud rumble in the still room.

Finally, Jasper said, "My guess is the house is near Oakhurst. DiscoFever was there. It's probably where they hold the workers. There are lots of farms in the area."

He understood why Jasper went straight to the information they could glean. It was why they'd watched the recording, after all. But Cole wasn't ready to wrap his brain around the meaning of it all beyond the horror they'd just witnessed, so he simply nodded.

"This also explains how DiscoFever knew about the rape and connected it to the murders in the park."

Again, Cole nodded.

Finally, Jasper said, "You need to go to her."

He took a deep breath. "She won't like that." Hell, she'd rejected him for just asking about the scars. Now he'd watched her nightmare in Technicolor.

"Don't be a chickenshit. She *needs* you. Jesus, I'm traumatized and it's not even *me* in that video."

Truth.

Cole felt the same way. "She really loved him, you know."

"Not anymore."

No. Not anymore.

Cole closed all the tabs and shut the laptop, then rose to his feet. "We'll figure out what's next after we get a few hours of sleep."

He walked the short distance down the hall and raised his hand to knock but then thought better of it. He could hardly be considerate of her need to have her boundaries respected if he sent him away. And Jasper was right. She needed him.

He turned the knob and stepped into the darkened room. He expected to see her on the bed, curled in a ball, but instead she stood by the window, looking out into the dark night.

He approached her, his shoes making only the slightest of sounds on the worn wood floor, just enough that he wasn't sneaking up on her.

He wrapped his arms around her and felt a surge of relief when she leaned into him.

He searched for words, but had none that would offer actual comfort. He could hardly apologize for Leo's actions. All he could do was hold her.

She turned in his arms and pressed her face to his chest. Her body trembled against his but she wasn't crying.

She raised her head and the look in her eyes told him that she was shaking with rage. He felt a fierce smile tug at him. She was sinking into the one emotion that would keep her going.

Rage had motivated Jasper for two years. Cole would bet she had a rage on that would power her for a decade or longer.

"We're going to bring them all down, Signe. Everyone who did this to you."

She nodded. "I know. It's just a shame Leo is dead, because I'd really like to kill him myself."

He cupped her cheek. "Same."

"Was there anything I need to know in the rest of the video?"

"DiscoFever was there. You were in a daze, but she managed to feed you something. Looked like broth." He closed his eyes and added, "The rest you could probably guess from your injuries. It got very violent."

She nodded. "Was Leo in the room for that part? When they cut me?"

"I don't think so. He wasn't on camera again."

"Might need to watch with the sound on to be certain."

"There's no need to be certain, and no way in hell am I watching that with the sound on. We already heard the one clip of you screaming."

"The video will go a long way toward clearing me with the FBI."

He nodded.

The faces of the men who raped and beat her had been clearly visible from the first frame. Leo's involvement even proved she'd never been willing. He'd thoroughly betrayed her.

"Between Jasper's near-murder and the human trafficking, this is a federal case. Jasper's case will go to the Central District of California US Attorney for prosecution, because Jasper was in LA when they tried to kill him, but your assault happened in the Eastern District, and that's where the trafficking victims were held and where John Doe was murdered. The two offices will probably come to an agreement and combine the cases, but there'll be a lot of coordinating—and duplicating of files. I'm just warning you, not discouraging you. They'll be careful with sensitive material like the video, but you know if it goes to trial for one of your rapists, a jury would see it."

She nodded. "They might be counting on me not wanting it to be seen and push for a jury trial for that reason. But I won't let them victim shame me. I didn't have a choice in what was done to me."

He tightened his arms around her. "You're amazing, Signe."

"No. I'm angry."

"That too."

She pulled his head down for a kiss. Like everything else about her in the moment, the kiss was fierce.

He kissed her deeply, giving her back the same energy and anger before raising his head to slow her down. Slow himself down, too, to be honest.

She rose on her toes and raked his chin with her teeth, then captured his bottom lip. It was just shy of a bite as she rode the edge of her anger.

He cupped her face as he pulled back again. "I get that you're angry, I'm angry too. But I won't be your angry fuck. Not like this. I won't have sex with you when your emotions are in turmoil and you're angry at the world and want to lash out. I'm not a punching bag."

"I wasn't planning on *punching* you."

"But if you use my body in anger while thinking about *Leo*, then that's what it would be. When I'm inside you, I'm the only man who should be in your head. The only exception I'll allow is Channing Tatum."

That drew a laugh from her, but then she seemed to deflate.

She pressed her head to his chest. "I'm so fucking angry right now. And I want sex to prove to myself it's something I can have again, for me."

"You don't need to prove it right now. We already proved it once, and I'll be here for you next week."

"Will you, though? How do I know you aren't repulsed by what was done to me?"

"I am repulsed, but *you* do not repulse me." He tucked her hair behind her ear. "Neither of us is thinking clearly."

"Why do we need to think clearly? It's just sex."

He asked himself the same thing. Why was he arguing with her? He could give her what they both wanted. It wasn't like they hadn't crossed this line already.

But he knew why.

He released her and stepped back. "That's the problem. It's just sex for *you*. But not, in this instance, for me."

CHAPTER 47

They slept for five hours. Signe in the bed, Cole on the couch. It was good that she'd slept alone, as she'd been violent even in her sleep, fighting the dream memories that now came to her in crystal clear HD.

She knew their faces. She knew their bodies. But the biggest monster of them all was Leo.

The smell of coffee pulled her from the bed in the late morning. At least she was back in the land of coffee makers and this morning someone else had even made it before she was awake. That hadn't happened since she was married. Well, except when Cole got her a cup from Curry Village on Wednesday. Of course, now she realized he'd probably gone to meet with Jasper one more time before their hike.

Neither the first nor last deception he'd painted as kindness.

She wandered into the kitchen to find Cole and Jasper both shirtless and sitting at the table. It was clear Jasper had spent much of his free time these last two years at the gym. His lightly tanned arms and torso sported bigger muscles than he had back when she first met him. His hard body was a good match for his scarred face. Not the sort of man one would dare fuck around with. If he returned to undercover work, he'd be perfect in the role of hitman—just above falcon but below lieutenant in cartel hierarchy.

He'd have to move to a different region, but there wasn't a shortage of big cities with criminal underworlds for him to infiltrate. She could give him tips on who to contact in Chicago and Miami.

Of course, the FBI was likely to be a tad angry he'd played dead for the last two years. So perhaps he shouldn't respond to hitman job postings just yet.

She poured herself a mug of coffee and sat at the table.

"Nope," Jasper said. "This place has a dress code for breakfast. No shirts allowed."

Curious to see how Cole would react, she reached for the hem of her T-shirt and said, "Whatever."

He grabbed her hand. "Nope. We also have a *no topless women in front of Jasper* policy."

"You guys have really specific and conflicting rules."

Jasper shrugged. "That happens with roommates."

She sipped her coffee, wondering what their apartment had been like before Jasper's murder. Maybe she'd get a roommate after this. Make friends. For the first time, she could imagine . . . *something*.

The oppressive weight on her chest just might be lifted.

She picked up her phone from the center of the table where she'd left it last night and powered it on. "Maybe DiscoFever tried to reach out in the last few hours."

Cellular was still turned off, but with Wi-Fi, she could see if she had voice mail messages or texts.

A half dozen text message pings sounded and she opened the app. "Not DiscoFever. Shit. *Steven*." She read the messages and dread filled her. "He's looking for Leo. Some guys came by his apartment last night, asking questions about the cabin he inherited with Leo."

She glanced up from the phone. "He says he doesn't know anything about an inherited cabin."

"So Leo lied to you about that too," Cole said.

"It appears so."

"Unless Steven is lying," Jasper said.

"I hope he's not. If the guys who questioned him think he's holding out on them, they'll be back. I should warn him."

Cole shook his head. "You can't. No calls. No texts. You can't even let him know you *read* his texts. He's being watched and is safer if you stay away. Your phone doesn't send read receipts, does it?"

"Of course not."

"Good. Ignore Steven, then. At least we no longer need to track him down," Jasper said.

"Shouldn't we tell the FBI to watch over him? Put a guard on his apartment?"

"That'll just put a target on him," Cole said. "And we can't involve the FBI until we have Leo's files from the cabin. The FBI would detain you and take the files. And if anyone from La Jirafa gets to the cabin first . . ."

"The fact that they questioned Steven means they're still looking," Jasper said. "They're no closer to finding the cabin, while we have the actual address."

She sighed. "Okay, so breakfast, then we hit the road for the San Jacinto Mountains." The cabin was about 110 miles away from the rental house. Traffic and winding roads would likely make it a two-and-a-half-hour drive.

"I'm not going with you to the cabin," Jasper said. "I'm going to tap some of my old contacts in the cartel and see if I can find DiscoFever."

She jolted. She wanted to find the woman—especially knowing she'd cared for Signe during her missing hours—but still her heart squeezed with fear. "Isn't that . . . a completely and horrifically danger-ous thing for you to do?"

"If they don't know who DiscoFever is yet, it's only a matter of time. This is our chance to save her and the ten workers who didn't escape in Yosemite that day. They're probably all working on a farm near

Oakhurst. I'd like it if we could walk away from this case with at least one win for the good guys."

She let out a small gasp. It hadn't crossed her mind they could still save people. She'd been too focused on what had happened to her. And really, what had happened to her was nothing compared to years of enslavement. She reached out and squeezed Jasper's hand. "How can I help?"

"You can start by giving me your car."

◆ ◆ ◆

Twenty minutes later, they were on the road, heading back to Signe's so Jasper could claim her hatchback. They agreed to check in throughout the day, although they all knew Signe and Cole wouldn't have cell coverage at Leo's cabin.

After parting ways with Jasper—a hug for Signe and a manly fist bump between the two undercover agents—she and Cole were in his vehicle, heading for the mountain range that was almost due east of her Redondo Beach home.

As he drove, she realized it had been exactly one week since she and Cole entered the park.

One week.

She'd been unsure if DiscoFever was an ally or leading her into a trap. She'd brought a gun in case it was a trap and hired a guide in case it was not.

It was strange to think about how many times her opinion of her guide had flipped since he stepped into her hotel room.

She'd been certain he'd killed Leo. Been certain he'd sent her the horrific texts. She'd believed he'd haunted her sleep with chains and a distorted voice.

But no. If she were to guess, it was Roman—or another employee of La Jirafa—who killed Leo. She knew Leo had sent the texts, and Jasper was the specter with the chains.

Cole had been her guide. He'd found the camp using his knowledge of archaeology.

She could trust him.

Couldn't she?

◆ ◆ ◆

Signe turned on her phone's GPS before they reached the mountain road that led to Leo's hideaway. Within a few miles of the first turnoff, cell coverage stopped but the satellite connection remained to aid their navigation. Miles after that, the road became a gravel track that was pitted with potholes. They wound up the hillside, the road shaded by tall trees.

She understood why Leo had chosen this spot. It was remote and hidden and without cellular coverage, so no one could track his phone pings on cell towers.

She guessed Leo had buried the purchase of the cabin with shell companies. He'd had up-close instruction on how to commit real-estate fraud thanks to one of her stories, and she'd also researched how assets were hidden from the IRS.

Tax crime didn't interest her unless it intersected with organized crime—*hello, Al Capone*—so she'd never done much with the buried assets data she'd gathered.

But Leo had.

As they went deeper and deeper into the woods and higher up the remote hillside, she could see how this would be the perfect place for a crime lord to set up shop, especially if he didn't want his investigative reporter of a wife to catch on to what he was doing.

What would he have done if she'd asked to join him at the cabin sometime?

Exactly what he'd done when she searched his computer: divorced her.

Even then, Leo's secrets had been unraveling, but she was too fogged by the shock of her rape to see it. Now she realized that, too, had been part of the plan.

◆ ◆ ◆

After two years of investigating and last night's deep dive into Leo's files, Jasper was certain he had it figured out. DiscoFever had worked for La Jirafa back around the time when the kingpin suspected it was Leo who'd stolen a chunk of his business while he was still consolidating power.

That was why La Jirafa had requested the interview with Signe. Once the male giraffe was certain it was Leo, he'd demanded payment in the form of Signe. DiscoFever had witnessed what La Jirafa did to bring Leo to heel.

The minute Leo agreed to hand over his wife to the organization was the moment he proved there was no limit to how low he'd go. That he'd participated in his wife's rape had ceased to be shocking. It was Leo, through and through. He would do anything to save himself above all others. So he let himself be recorded, knowing La Jirafa could use that recording against him at any time.

But La Jirafa didn't need that last piece. He already owned Leo, but knowing how La Jirafa's mind worked—and Jasper had gained insight into the monster in his days undercover—he guessed the man got a sick thrill out of capturing Leo's utter depravity and making sure he knew he had the ultimate weapon to destroy him at any time.

After that, Leo was just a tool in his crime kit.

Except, Jasper figured Leo proved smarter than La Jirafa had expected. There were hints and threats in the emails they'd read last night. Leo had his own records of La Jirafa's business. His own blackmail.

Mutual assured destruction.

La Jirafa didn't dare kill Leo, not when Leo could ensure his identity would be exposed. So what had made it safe to kill Leo now? La Jirafa wasn't the type to take such a risk, not when Leo's video files could fall into the wrong hands—specifically, FBI hands.

Which is exactly what would happen when Signe recovered the files.

Jasper itched to be with Signe and Cole. He wanted to see the evidence Leo had collected for himself. But he was the only one who could find DiscoFever, and she, in turn, could point them to the rest of the trafficking victims. He needed to do it before everyone met the same fate as John Doe.

And so he would tap his sources in La Jirafa's organization. It was time to become one of the undead.

He parked in front of Pietro's apartment. Pietro was a hitman for the cartel. Midlevel. A fighter who did the bare minimum and tried to fly under the radar. He was smart. A watcher. Always looking for an angle he could work, but never quite drawing attention to himself. If Jasper didn't know better, he'd think the guy was an undercover cop.

But no. Pietro was just cold and savvy and a survivor, much like Jasper had presented himself as to the various groups he'd infiltrated in his years undercover.

Pietro would never make lieutenant because he was everyone's buddy. Today he would be Jasper's.

Pietro's unit was on the second floor. There was a long walkway with doors to each apartment, like a run-down motel from the seventies, but these were one-bedroom units, not motel rooms.

Jasper went old-school and knocked on the door, not expecting a response. Pietro wasn't the type to bother answering a knock, especially not before noon.

Jasper pulled out his lock-picking tools, appreciating the cheap, old mechanism. The hitman didn't need an upgrade. None of his neighbors would dare mess with him and his ability to be everyone's buddy but no one's friend kept him off the target list when shit went down.

It took less than twenty seconds to spring the lock. Jasper pulled his gun and stepped inside.

The main room was a dark rectangle. The only window being the one next to the door. The apartment backed up to another unit on the back side of the building, which meant each unit had only two windows on the same face: living room and bedroom.

Beyond the living room was a small kitchen. A doorway in the middle of the right wall led to the bedroom with attached bathroom. Compact, efficient, and dark.

Living room and kitchen were empty, so he entered the bedroom.

He nodded in greeting to Connie, who lay in the bed, wrapped in a sheet. "'Bout time you got here. I've got places to go."

He smiled and gave her two hundred-dollar bills. "Thanks for keeping him busy. He in the john?"

She nodded as she rose from the bed and picked up her clothes from the floor. "Make my excuses for me, will ya?"

From the doorway to the bathroom, a male voice said, "Shit. I shoulda known there was a reason you gave me a freebie."

Jasper turned to see a fully nude Pietro leaning against the doorsill holding a pistol, which, like Jasper's, was pointed to the floor. Relaxed, unconcerned, but armed even while naked.

That was Pietro.

Connie winked at him. "Still free to *you*, though." Dressed, she slipped on her heels and exited the room.

Jasper waited for Pietro to recognize him. How he reacted would tell him a lot about the lay of the land.

It didn't take the man long. "Shit. Bobby Jenkins. Thought you were dead."

"Good. That was the point. Got the crap beat outta me and figured I'd take a sabbatical."

Pietro laughed. "Sabbatical. I like that. Gonna tell the boss I'm due." He raised his gun, pointing it at the ceiling. "Am I gonna need this?"

"Up to you. Did you enjoy my present?"

"Connie? Well, I liked it more when she found me so irresistible she didn't charge me. But yeah."

"She told me she wanted to give it to you for free, but I insisted on paying her."

Pietro set his gun on the bed and laughed as he reached for jeans discarded on the floor. "So what brings you back from the dead?"

"Score to settle with the guy who did this to me." He pointed to his face.

"You know I don't get involved in internal problems, Jenkins. I'm a lover, not a fighter."

Right. Jasper had seen him slice a man's stomach open. You didn't survive as long as Pietro had in this world without proving yourself willing to get dirty and defend yourself.

"Not asking you to choose sides. I just want information."

"Information doesn't come cheap."

"I bought you Connie for a whole night."

"That was a gift."

Jasper pulled out his wallet and extracted two hundreds.

He took the money. "What do you want to know?"

Jasper pulled a printout of DiscoFever's face from another pocket. "I'm looking for this woman. She used to work for La Jirafa."

Pietro held up a hand before looking at the photo. "Two hundred was the fee for listening to your question. It's gonna cost extra if you want an answer."

"How much?"

"Depends on who's in the photo."

Jasper handed it to him.

Pietro let out a low whistle. "Damn. Okay, that'll cost a grand."

"I don't have that much on me after paying Connie."

"Bullshit. You're here on revenge. You'll pay me anything. In fact, one K is probably too low."

Jasper made a show of cursing and counted out eight hundreds. "The first two hundred was a deposit."

Pietro pocketed the money with a shrug.

"So who is she?"

"She's a translator. Well, reluctant translator. She was brought here three, four years ago? Shipment from the Philippines. Was going to be sent off to work on one of the farms, but Boss Man took a shine to her."

Jasper's stomach twisted. DiscoFever had been put through hell.

Some would probably call him a hypocrite for paying Connie to have sex with Pietro, but Connie had chosen her profession for herself. She was a willing sex worker and while Jasper had never purchased her services for himself, this wasn't the first time he'd paid her for her assistance. She liked the arrangement because he paid triple her usual rate, giving her cash up front. The two hundred he'd given her this morning had been a bonus because she didn't do sleepovers and he was thankful.

Unlike Connie, DiscoFever wasn't and had never been willing, and likely found herself in an untenable position when the boss chose her from a "shipment."

"There was trouble with some of the workers and the boss realized she could translate. Convince the men that if they played by the rules, in two years they'd have earned their way free and they'd have a green card."

That was how human trafficking always went. Men and women were convinced back in their home country that there were jobs in the US waiting for them. They signed a contract to pay a certain amount for the passage across the ocean, not knowing they were signing themselves up for enslavement. There was no legitimate job. No green card. No future beyond working as laborers on farms or in some cases factories. Living in dormitories that were actually prisons.

"So it was her job to convince them so they didn't fight or try to escape."

Pietro nodded. "Haven't seen her in a while, though. I heard she was shipped north to one of the Sacramento Valley farms about two years ago."

The timing fit. After Jasper was beaten and left for dead, and Signe drugged and raped, there had likely been some chaos within Leo's corner of the organization, and Jasper had no doubt now that Leo was the boss Pietro was referring to.

Jasper wouldn't be surprised if everyone who'd been in Oakhurst—in the very house while Signe was raped—had been dispersed to other farms and factories. Some had probably died in the intervening years due to the working conditions.

But at some point, the Oakhurst operation had started up again. Subcontracts with Yosemite had to be fulfilled. And perhaps she'd been returned to Oakhurst to act as translator again. The men sent into the park were in a unique position in that they could have opportunities to speak with tourists. With the number of people who moved through the park, it was only a matter of time before they came across someone who spoke Tagalog who could help them escape.

Escape wasn't possible for DiscoFever—who likely never rode the van into Yosemite—but she could give others hope. Tell them what they needed to do to be free.

CHAPTER 48

Signe stared at the small wooden structure. There was a keypad on the front door. She wondered how many digits were required or if Leo would use a new PIN here.

She went with tried-and-true and punched in his favorite four-digit passcode. The lock clicked and she twisted the dead bolt keyhole.

The door swung open.

Inside there was an alarm system, but not the kind that would alert police and fire. It would alert Leo.

Her gaze swung to Cole. "His phone. Whoever has it knows we're in the cabin."

"You can't shut off the system?"

"I can try, but I bet it alerts his phone that the system has been turned on or off no matter what."

She punched at the keypad—this time using the six-digit code Leo had set up at their cliffside house. The system reset. "It's armed again." She gave Cole the code. "We'll need it to exit."

They didn't waste time exploring. Leo had told her just enough about the place—including what she realized now were fake childhood memories—that she knew the editing studio was in the basement, which had been unfinished until he installed the home office.

She found the stairs, but Cole stopped her from leading the way. "I go first. We don't know what we're going to find." He unholstered his gun and took a stance that reminded her he was an FBI agent even if he'd spent the last several years pretending he wasn't. For the first time, she saw the G-man.

He was kinda hot.

He descended the stairs with the gun out. She waited at the top until he shouted, "Clear."

The main room had the promised pool table, dart board, and man-cave bar. "Who the hell was he planning to play pool with?" Signe asked.

"He probably played solitaire." Cole nodded to the door with the big dead bolt. "Not a combination lock."

"No. Which means the key is hidden somewhere. Leo wouldn't rely on carrying keys."

"Hence all the locks with keypads."

She nodded. "He lived in fear of keys being taken and getting stranded."

"Not an unreasonable fear when interviewing criminals and becoming one yourself."

She nodded.

They made a circuit of the room, looking for hiding places. Cole pointed out one pool cue wasn't dusty like the others. He pulled it down and studied the heavy handle, then smiled and twisted the black end piece.

To her amazement, the butt of the cue separated. Cole tilted the shaft into his palm and a metal cylinder slid out. He popped off the top and extracted a thin metal key. He studied the cue stick, which now was in three parts. "Nice design. No rattle or sound. No hint there's a hiding place."

"I *never* would have looked there."

"Well, this kind of search is part of my training. The lack of dust when the rest of the sticks are coated is a big giveaway."

He set the cue pieces on the pool table and went to the door. The key turned and they were in.

The editing room was similar to the one in her home. Five monitors stacked in a pyramid. Professional editing console. A hub for plugging in hard drives. Speakers at either end of the wide V-shaped desktop.

She sat down and flicked on the main power switch, and all across the console, LED lights came on, while five monitors lit with color tests.

Boot-up finished, the login screen appeared. She typed Leo's standard password and was in.

"I don't even know where to begin. He'll have thousands of hours of recordings."

"Start with the day before Jasper was abducted."

She sorted the directories by date and, as expected, found dozens of video files from that week.

One had a name that wasn't part of Leo's sequence, so she opened that one first. As expected, this was a recording taken of Leo, sent by La Jirafa.

The video showed Leo sitting in a chair, much like the ones they used when Signe conducted interviews in run-down factories or warehouses.

Leo was tied down and blood dripped from his lip. His cheek was red. Was this video taken when La Jirafa confirmed Leo was the one who'd siphoned off his business with the cartel?

Probably. She'd never seen the bruises or cuts because by the end of the week, she had bruises of her own she didn't want him to see. And last night, when she'd seen him on the rape recording, she'd been too consumed with rage and horror to notice bruises.

"Why should I keep you alive?" the distorted voice said.

"You kill me and everyone will know your real name. I have recordings that will be made public. Plus, I have contracts. Legitimate business deals. Without me, you won't get paid for labor. But I'll cut you in. We both win."

"I will kill your wife. She won't be able to go to the FBI when you die."

Leo sat up straight. "No. She's not my fail-safe. She's clueless."

"A smart woman like that and you expect me to believe she has no idea what you're doing."

All the statements in the distorted voice came out flat. No inflection. Cold and mechanical.

"*You* didn't know about me until two hours ago. I'm careful."

"I've known about you for months. Two hours ago you fucked up and confirmed it."

"And you fucked up before that when you let a fed into your business. That's who you should be worried about."

"I know about the fed."

"But you don't know who."

Silence.

"Give me a reason to keep you alive. The fed or your wife."

"Bobby Jenkins."

Silence.

The video continued but Leo didn't move. For a moment, she thought it was a glitch, but then she saw the rise of Leo's chest. Finally the voice said, "You will be released. But remember, you work for me now, or your wife will receive this recording."

They continued through the files. Signe avoided the ones recorded during the days of her abduction. She knew everything she needed to about that.

Her cell phone vibrated and she jolted. "My phone shouldn't have service here."

She checked the screen and saw the Wi-Fi icon was fully lit, and it hit her. Leo had the same network name and password as the one they'd used in Redondo Beach. As soon as she'd powered on the system, the modem had booted, and her phone had synced.

And she'd had location data on during the drive, to use the GPS.

She met Cole's gaze. She knew as well as he did that her phone, while secure from having the camera or mic hacked, would still give up locational data if it wasn't turned off. If someone knew how to search, they could find her. And she had no doubt the men on La Jirafa's payroll knew how to get what they needed.

"How much time do you think we have?"

"Depends on if they know the general area where Leo's cabin is or not. If they believe it was Tahoe, then they might be nowhere near us."

"My phone would have pinged when I first set up the GPS. We were out of range quickly, so I didn't worry about it. But that could have given them a starting point and I doubt they believed the Tahoe lie."

"Then we have an hour at most."

Signe grabbed a half dozen hard drives. The ones that were most likely to incriminate Leo and the others while exonerating her. But they also needed the location of the property where the workers were being held in Oakhurst. Her bag was bursting with hard drives.

It would be enough. It had to be. Whoever was on their way here might try to burn the place and destroy all evidence. She'd salvage what she could. Just in case.

They locked the room and replaced the key, but Cole cursed and said, "We don't have time to dust the entire room."

Signe pulled her shirt over her head and quickly swiped down the other cues and then did the same for a few liquor bottles on the bar. "Maybe that will slow them down." She yanked her top back over her head.

"If they're even going to bother to try. My guess is they're going to torch the place."

"This might be a good time to call the FBI."

There was a long silence, then Cole said, "It would be, sure. If I were an agent."

She went rigid as she felt her face go white. Blood raced from her extremities and toward her belly.

"What?" Her question was a cold, scared rasp. "You aren't an agent?" The bag of hard drives slipped from her fingertips and hit the floor with a clatter.

"Still, I mean. I was. But they fired me eight months ago."

Her heart pounded. Nothing made sense anymore. In the last day, she'd erred on the side of trusting him after believing he was the worst sort of monster. But he'd been lying to her. Again.

Again.

She'd led him right here. Given him Leo's passwords. Even the code to enter the cabin.

"They thought I was on the take," he said. "The work I was doing to hide Jasper—it raised questions. No proof, so they quietly let me go. I had open cases they didn't want to screw up."

Was he lying even now? Had he *ever* been an agent? "You had a badge."

"Jasper's."

"You could have told me yesterday."

"Would you have believed a disgraced, fired agent? You were in danger. We couldn't risk you kicking us to the curb."

It was just a little too tidy.

She picked up the satchel and backed slowly toward the staircase. No wonder he and Jasper had been so eager to keep everything on the down-low. They'd been desperate to keep the FBI in the dark.

Keep Leo's murder a secret.

We can't access FBI databases.

We think there's a mole in the bureau.

But that hadn't been the issue at all. No. Either he was never an agent, or he'd been on the take. An undercover agent who flew too close to the sun.

And what about Jasper? Was he dirty too?

The beating had changed him. Maybe he'd turned to the dark side to survive. After all, today he said he was resurrecting himself, and he hadn't seemed worried. Perhaps he had a new alias. He could be in deep with the cartels with a new name. No longer a fed. A falcon or a hitman.

Locating Leo's headquarters with all his recordings was sure to promote him to lieutenant. Hell, with what was in the editing studio, they could take over his part of the business. The only person they'd answer to would be La Jirafa himself.

You're the key, Signe.

We need to be the first to get to Leo's secret crime headquarters.

You know all his passwords? Show us.

She would shake her head at her gullibility, except she'd been hit by blow after blow until her instincts were shattered. She'd stopped being a reporter and asking the key questions when the story became about her.

She hadn't checked with sources in the FBI because she didn't want to tip them off that Leo was dead before she could get the tapes to protect what remained of her sources.

She'd played right into Cole's and Jasper's hands. Given them everything.

"Signe, you know you can trust me. We have what we need now to get me reinstated in the bureau."

She continued climbing the stairs backward, eyes on Cole. Her heart pounded as she waited for him to give up trying to coax her and just pull his gun.

But he couldn't do that. She hadn't told him *all* the passwords. Just some of them.

She reached the upper landing and turned in a circle, trying to figure out what to do. The SUV out front was Cole's vehicle. The keys were in his pocket.

Christ. She'd given Jasper her car so he could pretend to go off to find DiscoFever. Or maybe really find her so they could stop the trafficking victims from escaping ever again.

She glanced at the key rack on the wall by the door that connected the kitchen to the garage. A car key hung on a peg. Maybe she'd get lucky.

She swiped the key and shoved it in her pocket as Cole reached the top of the stairs.

She took a step backward. His linebacker build intimidating her once again.

He held up his hands. "Signe, I don't know what you're thinking, but whatever it is, you're wrong."

He circled her, cutting off her escape to the garage.

She lunged and grabbed a knife from the butcher block on the counter. "Don't come near me."

He reared back in surprise. Of course he didn't expect her to defend herself now. He'd only seen her as a victim.

And that was how he'd managed to play her.

Using Jasper to torment her one moment, then being there with comfort the next.

"Do. Not. Come. Near. Me."

"Put the knife down. I won't hurt you."

"You already have."

"Physically."

"You forgot how you tackled me in my bedroom? Nearly suffocated me."

"Today."

"Cute."

Her phone rang.

"You should see who that is."

"Why, you expecting a call from your accomplice?"

"If you're referring to Jasper, then you mean *partner* and yes, I do expect to hear from Jasper."

She pulled out her phone and flicked her gaze to the screen. She didn't think she had it in her to be surprised yet again, but she was. She turned the phone so Cole could see the name of her contact in the FBI.

"Still want me to answer it?"

His eyes widened. "No."

He lunged for the knife. She swung the blade, striking his side and creating an instant ribbon of red. He stumbled backward.

Seeing a clear path, she pushed past him and bolted out the side door and into the dark garage.

CHAPTER 49

Signe hit the button to raise the garage door, which moved achingly slow as she yanked open the door of the only vehicle.

She didn't think the blade had gone deep. Cole could be right on her heels.

He appeared in the doorway as she rammed the key in the ignition. The engine turned over and she hit reverse. She didn't care if the garage door wasn't all the way open.

It registered as she scraped the roof of the vehicle on the ascending door that this wasn't a car that belonged to Leo. It was Manny Lontoc's missing Plymouth Breeze.

Goddammit, Leo.

She wasn't fully into the driveway when she realized her escape had run into a major snag. Cole's car blocked the driveway and there were far too many trees to be able to drive around it. She'd need a motorcycle or dirt bike to get through this forest.

He stood in front of his large SUV, arms crossed as he waited to see what she would do.

She pulled her gun from her bag and racked the slide, then pointed it at him one-handed while she opened the door. She scooped the bag with storage drives from the passenger seat and slowly climbed from the vehicle. "I'm leaving on foot. I suggest you don't try to follow me."

"You don't have food. Or camping gear. We're miles from nowhere."

There were other cabins on this mountain. She'd seen the driveways as they drove in, but she refrained from saying it. No point in endangering the neighbors or tipping him off to her rather obvious plan.

"Signe, we need to leave before La Jirafa's henchmen get here."

"Right. I've got to hand it to you, you're far more cunning than his other falcons. After all, you didn't need to drug me first." She walked backward into the forest. "Goodbye, Cole. Don't follow me unless you want to get shot."

◆ ◆ ◆

Cole let her have a head start. His senses were on fire, telling him La Jirafa's henchmen would be here sooner rather than later. He needed to throw them off Signe's trail.

If they knew she was alone in the woods without supplies, it was all over.

He returned Manny's car to the garage and closed the door, then put the bloody knife back in the butcher's block.

His side stung like a bitch but the cut wasn't deep. He'd bandage it later. He grabbed a half dozen protein bars and a bag of granola cereal from the pantry. It wasn't much but it was better than nothing.

He reset the alarm and tucked a cordless microphone in a shrub next to the driveway. A camera would be better but he didn't have time to set one up. At least this way he'd be able to monitor activity at the cabin.

He climbed into his vehicle, hoping he'd have time to move it down the road before anyone showed up. He drove the opposite direction from the way Signe had run. Anything to buy her time. He'd driven about a mile when he spotted an overgrown driveway with a chain across it.

He said a small prayer and pulled over. His prayers were answered when he discovered the simple barrier wasn't locked.

A few minutes later, his SUV was safely hidden. He threw the food he'd grabbed into his pack, then locked his vehicle and set out to find Signe.

He found himself praying again that he hadn't taken too long, and feared that for a godless man, he'd used his quota of free prayers.

◆ ◆ ◆

Signe climbed the hill behind the cabin at a run, but it was steep and there weren't any convenient switchbacks, so she quickly ran out of breath and had to stop. She braced herself against a tree trunk to keep from sliding down the elevation she'd managed to gain.

She wished she had her binoculars. Or a real backpack and not a damn satchel. It was a big bag for hauling around her camera and other gear, but still, the weight was unbalanced and carried on one shoulder.

She pulled out the camera and looped the strap around her neck, then used the zoom to see if she could get a line of sight on Leo's cabin. Small glimpses were visible between the trees.

She scanned the long driveway and caught movement. A gray vehicle heading up the drive. Cole's SUV was blue and would be going the other way. She searched for any sign Cole's vehicle was still parked in the front, blocking the drive. It wasn't there.

She relived the last minutes in the cabin in her mind.

Was there any chance she'd misread the situation? If it was true he'd been fired but also wasn't in league with La Jirafa, he could have told her. Instead he'd lied repeatedly, giving one excuse after another for why they couldn't go to the FBI.

If he *had* told the truth, it was yet another bitter pill that after everything they'd gone through, he was just trying to clear his own name.

And that was the best-case scenario. It was more likely he'd been trying to find Leo's lair for his true boss.

That Cole hadn't wanted her to answer the phone was damning.

She pulled out her cell. She was beyond the range of the house Wi-Fi and couldn't get a signal, but voice mail recorded to the device, and Agent Paula Riggs had left a message.

She hit the "Play" button and held the phone to her ear as she watched the gray SUV park between the trees in front of Leo's cabin.

"Signe, it's Agent Riggs. I just got a call from a . . . source within an organization you are familiar with. He said a hit has been ordered on you and your associates. You're in serious danger if you try to meet any informants. There's also chatter that an informant by the name of Jenkins is alive but won't be for long if he shows his face again."

No mention of Cole. What did that mean?

And was Jasper—a.k.a. Jenkins—working for La Jirafa or not?

"Please call me ASAP. I'm going to talk to my boss and see what our embedded agents know. I don't need to tell you a direct call for a hit is bad, Signe. We need to get you to a safe house."

The message ended.

Huh.

A safe house.

More than once over the years, her relationship with the FBI had been antagonistic when she refused to give up a source. But she knew their policy of protecting anyone who could help them, and in this instance, boy could she help them. The heavy satchel shifted as she adjusted the weight on her shoulder. She needed to get these hard drives to the FBI before she finally got a personal interview with an assassin.

A car door slammed and she returned her focus to the camera and the men who'd exited the vehicle. She stared at the screen.

Disbelief filtered through her. She felt dizzy.

It was no surprise to see Roman.

No. It was the three men with him who triggered panic.

She slapped a hand over her mouth to squelch her reaction.

They were here. Her rapists. The wiry tattooed man with light brown skin and the two large white men who'd brutalized her and carved letters or numbers into the tender skin between her thighs.

Chapter 50

From his vantage point on the hillside above Leo's cabin, Cole watched with dread as Roman and three henchmen stepped out of the cabin and scanned the woods in the direction Signe had fled. That these four men had been selected to go after Signe didn't surprise him, but he feared seeing them would petrify her.

This was endgame now. They had the location of the cabin and didn't need her anymore. They'd been sent to kill Signe.

He listened in on their conversation with earbuds set to the frequency of the wireless mic he'd planted in the bush. The system worked on radio signals and wasn't dependent on cellular or satellite connections.

"We're supposed to burn the place down," Henchman One said.

"No," Roman said. "You saw the blood. Gates and Banner fought. With a kitchen knife. No way is she with that prick now. She probably took off on foot. We can hardly set fire to the house now, not while Gates is out here. Last thing we need are firefighters in these woods while she's on the run."

Cole wanted to curse. He'd hoped Roman would believe Signe had left with him in the SUV.

"The boss said burn. We should burn." This from Henchman Two, the other white man.

"We'll burn. After we find the woman, get her to give up the passwords. Then we'll burn."

The smaller, tattooed man gave Roman a cold look, and Cole was certain he was onto Roman. Roman didn't want to burn Leo's cabin because he wanted to access the drives that held proof of La Jirafa's identity.

The primary reason Leo hadn't been killed after the events of Bastille Day was because he could expose La Jirafa. Roman wanted that insurance too. Hell, he probably wanted Leo's chunk of the business and made the decision to kill Leo when they were alone in Yosemite with that goal in mind.

Odds were Roman was the one to tell La Jirafa that following Signe to Leo's secret hideaway was the key. Just as he'd bet it was Roman who realized going to the rendezvous point would lead them to the escaped men. Had that been when Roman presented his application to La Jirafa, or had he been working for the kingpin, and not Leo, all along?

Right now, the only thing that mattered was finding Signe and getting her away before Roman got his hands on her.

Because Cole knew exactly what Roman would do to extract Leo's passwords from her.

◆ ◆ ◆

Away. Away. Away.

She had to get away.

La Jirafa had any number of henchmen who could be with Roman. That he sent these three was a message. One he'd begun eighteen months ago, when he sent her the video so she would recognize her rapists, at least from the neck down. She saw their faces yesterday when she viewed the unedited video, but she realized now she didn't really need their faces to know who they were. The combination of the three of them together. Their size and skin coloring. It was obvious.

It was ridiculous that she'd ever suspected Cole. He wasn't beefed up from steroids. His size was due to natural build and fitness.

Cole was strong, but these men could crush her like a fly. And the dead look in their eyes in the video said they'd do it in a heartbeat.

She scrambled up the slope, moving as quietly as she could.

Away. Away. Away.

She reached a flat and headed across. Away from Leo's cabin. All she cared about now was distance.

She lost track of time as she burrowed through undergrowth and climbed over roots. Sticks cracked under her feet but she couldn't worry about stealth. She was in full flight mode.

The hillside was steep going up, so she took the easier path downward. There had to be another house this way. It would be at the base of the hill, like Leo's.

She wished she had her trusty GPS.

Or a water bottle. Even a compass. She pulled out her phone. Surely the compass worked even without cellular service?

It did . . . and she wasn't facing the direction she'd thought she was.

Had she gotten turned around?

She flopped on the ground and tried to open the GPS app but couldn't connect. She must have somehow managed a switch back, when the hillside curved around. She was lower, but was the road to the south or to the east?

She stared at the trees. How ironic to be utterly lost now, after learning to navigate her way through Yosemite.

But of course, then she'd had Cole's paper map in addition to her digital one.

She considered burying the drives so she could hike faster, then retrieve them later, but being lost as she was, odds were she'd never find them again.

She needed to head downslope, in one direction, without shifting. If she kept going west, in a hundred-plus miles she'd hit the ocean.

More important, long before she reached the Pacific, she'd find a road. A town.

A metropolis.

She was less than a hundred miles from Los Angeles.

But the slope was south-facing, not west, so that's the direction she went. Hours passed and now darkness was settling in, but the air remained hot on the mid-July night.

Who was Cole Banner? Disgraced undercover FBI agent or something worse?

Was it possible he was something better? A loyal friend who risked—and even eventually gave up—his career to protect Jasper?

Had she been rash in the cabin?

Of course she had—she hadn't exactly had time to make a considered decision. Not with Roman and the monsters en route.

But now, with more time to think and less panic to cloud her brain, she wondered.

She'd cut him with a sharp chef's knife. Leo liked to cook and he had a thing for sharp knives.

It was a wonder she hadn't seriously wounded him. But then, maybe she had. He hadn't looked fazed as he stood in front of his vehicle. Of course, it probably took a lot to faze a man who'd worked undercover as long as he had.

If he'd worked undercover.

She heard a trickle of water and felt a surge of hope. Her throat was achingly dry.

Please let this be a stream.

She carefully followed the sound and there it was, a small creek tumbling down the hillside.

She set the bag of hard drives at the base of a tree and paused, her gaze scanning the narrow break in the trees where water flowed south.

She'd be exposed while she drank, but did she have any choice? She needed water. Desperately.

She crawled forward. When she reached the rock-strewn creek, she placed her hands on the shallow bank, dipped her head down, and drank like a game animal.

It wasn't a comforting comparison.

Still, she wanted to weep for the relief of the cold water on her throat. She drank and drank until her stomach protested and threatened to revolt.

Then she crawled backward into the trees, grabbed the bag of drives, and retreated farther until she found a tree to lean against while she took a short break, just like she had in Yosemite only a few eternally long days ago.

CHAPTER 51

The moon was high when Signe set out again. She would follow the stream as best she could from the shelter of the forest.

Her belly sloshed with the abundance of water. Or at least it felt like it did.

With each step, she made her plan. Find the road. Parallel it from the forest until she found a house. Break in if she had to and hope they had a landline.

It was a good plan. A solid plan. The only plan.

But in the end, it was useless, because Roman and the three monsters caught up with her before she even reached the road.

◆　◆　◆

She heard them before she saw them and swept the woods with her gun as if she were panning with a camera. Her hands shook as she searched the shadows. "Don't come near me. I will shoot anything that moves."

"You forget I know you're a lousy shot, Signe."

Roman. Taunting her. How had she ever worked with him?

But then, she could ask the same thing about Leo but also add *married* to the question.

"Why are you doing this, Roman?"

"I figured out what Leo was looooong before you." He said this proudly. So smart. But then, he did have that over her. She'd been in denial longer than was reasonable.

"Good for you. Why kill him? Orders, or so you can take over his business?"

There was a pause and she knew he wanted to brag, but he couldn't in front of minions.

Falcons, or more likely hitmen. Not a lieutenant like Roman.

He ignored her question and said, "Did you know Leo told my uncle to recommend me? Leo handpicked me to work with you so I could keep him in the loop. He worried you'd start working your own crime story."

"And then I did."

"And then you did. But silly thing. You called me and asked if I could take you into the park."

"Yet you declined. How is the ankle?" The sarcasm in her voice was impossible to miss.

"I knew the minute you said Yosemite what this was about. I called the boss and told him I knew how we could find the missing workers."

"They weren't 'missing' and they weren't 'workers.' They were enslaved men who'd escaped."

"Men *Leo* enslaved, but whatever. I knew you'd been contacted. I told the boss I could find them. All he had to do was let your contact give you the coordinates. Your informant is dead, by the way. No longer useful after he sent the coordinates."

Her heart dropped until he used the male pronoun. She was almost certain DiscoFever was a woman.

But not 100 percent.

She reminded herself that he would easily lie to demoralize her. She hated that it worked.

Roman spoke again. "Where is your lover boy?"

"Probably bleeding out somewhere. That's what I do to men who touch me when I don't want to be touched. I cut them."

"Not true. I've seen the video. In fact, they cut *you*."

The scars on the insides of her thighs pulsed with phantom pain. She breathed deeply through her nose.

Don't let them feed on your reaction.

"I brought some old friends to see you, Sig."

"Fuck you, Roman. Also, you're fired."

"I'm going to make a documentary about you when you go missing. It'll be a sad one. All the questions. The spiral. We'll keep Leo out of it, naturally, so I can run his business. It'll be about where you went wrong. How your lust for fame and getting the big story led to you committing crimes so you could get the scoop. And then you just . . . disappeared. Poof. I'll probably get a Peabody."

"Without me, you couldn't even get a participation trophy." She shook her head. "You really want to be Leo, don't you? You want the respect he had as a producer and filmmaker, and you want his cut in a grotesque business. Why are you so obsessed with my ex-husband?"

Roman didn't answer and she wished she could see his face. She knew his petulant look. He *hated* it when she corrected him on how a shot should be done, but she was the producer, he was the cameraman. She had final say in everything.

"You think your uncle will finally respect you like he did Leo?"

"Leo didn't deserve his respect."

"On that, we agree." She took a step forward. "Now, if you don't mind, I have places I need to be."

"You've got balls, Gates."

"Actually, I don't. And I'm good with that. Now. Go back to your boss and tell him you had to let me go because if I end up dead, Bobby Jenkins is going to deliver all of Leo's files to the FBI."

"That'll be hard for Bobby to do, considering he's dead."

"Oh? Haven't you heard? He's very much alive."

"No. He isn't. I got the call an hour ago. DOA at the hospital. His resurrection was short-lived."

He was lying. Just like with DiscoFever. Lying.

From nowhere, an arm reached out to grab her and she swung around and fired the gun. The man was huge. Built like a linebacker. For a heartbeat, she feared it was Cole. The horror that thought triggered told her she trusted Cole Banner beyond a reasonable doubt.

Then her heart surged with pride at another realization. She'd just shot one of her rapists in the belly.

CHAPTER 52

Cole couldn't breathe. From the moment Signe engaged with Roman, his throat had seized with a level of fear he hadn't felt since he'd searched for Jasper, expecting to find a lifeless body.

She held her own, but she was in the dark and had no clue where to direct her gun. She also wasn't trained in weapons. Not like the men she was up against.

Cole didn't see the shadow move behind her until it was too late. He'd have given up his position and shouted a warning if he had.

Then he watched the impossible. The man stumbled back. She'd shot him in the gut.

Rage took over the man's face and he lunged for her. She fired again, hitting him in the chest. When he kept coming, she spent a third bullet and this one hit him in the face.

The man dropped.

Signe's hands shook as she twisted in a circle, making it clear she could and would shoot again.

Cole had been an agent for seven years, undercover for five. In that time, he'd never once fired his gun in the line of duty.

Signe Gates was a force to be reckoned with.

But even in her moment of triumph came a mistake. A hole in her defenses. Henchman Three was in position to grab her as she turned in a circle. There was only one move Cole could make to help her.

He had to draw their fire.

◆ ◆ ◆

"Behind you, Signe!"

Cole's voice.

She pivoted and fired into the darkness that had been at her back. There. One of the monsters. He'd been within arm's reach, making a grab for her. Her bullet and Cole's warning had him turning as well.

And there was Cole, rising from the darkness like a specter.

All at once, shots rang out, coming from all directions, and she realized what Cole had done by revealing his position.

He'd sacrificed himself.

For her.

He fired again, this time in the direction where she believed Roman was. That left her to shoot Monster Three in the back. She didn't hesitate.

It wasn't until Cole fell to his knees that she realized he'd been hit.

There was one henchman left standing, and he turned to her.

She pulled the trigger and discovered her gun was empty. She didn't remember firing ten shots.

The man approached her. The moonlight made his features grotesque as he gave her a malicious smile. He grabbed her shoulder and yanked her toward him. "Remember me? We're gonna have us a good time again."

She felt dizzy. She hadn't come this far only to end up here. Her knees gave out.

The bark of another bullet echoed down the hillside, and the monster pitched backward.

A spot of blood sprouted on his forehead.

She turned to see Cole on the ground holding his gun in both hands. "Good. I needed you to drop. To get a clear shot."

The gun slipped from his hands as he passed out.

CHAPTER 53

Cole had been shot in the side. She yanked off her shirt and pressed it to the wound, praying his lung wouldn't collapse. That he wouldn't die here. Now.

Because of her.

It wasn't lost on her that he'd done the thing Leo had never once considered.

Protect her. Draw fire to him.

"Don't you dare die on me."

"Hey. Aren't you the one who stabbed me earlier?"

Tears spilled down her cheeks. She was relieved he was still conscious after all. "Cut you. Stabbing is different."

Cole's hand was covered with blood. He must've pressed it to his own wound right after he was hit. Now he touched her face and she felt the wetness of the fluid on her cheek. Could smell the metallic odor.

"I'm not gonna die on you."

"I don't know what to do. We're in the middle of nowhere."

"Take my gun, I still have a bullet left. Approach Roman. Shoot him if he so much as twitches. Grab his satellite phone and call 911. Then the FBI. I'll tell you the number. Also grab Roman's car keys. His SUV is only about a quarter of a mile away."

"I can't carry you ten feet, let alone a quarter mile."

"You get the car keys, I'll find a way to walk. Promise."

She did as instructed. Roman was as dead as the others. He'd taken a bullet to the neck and died instantly. Just like Leo, his eyes were open as he faced the night sky. But unlike when she'd seen Leo's corpse, she didn't have an iota of remorse.

She returned to Cole's side with keys and phone. Her call to 911 was brief. She handed him the phone after she dialed the FBI.

He told the person on the line which hospital to meet them at, then asked about Jasper.

Relief flooded Signe's system when he relayed that there was no DOA involving Jasper Evans that anyone knew about.

Calls done, the hard part was next. Signe had to get the two-hundred-dred-plus-pound linebacker to his feet.

She was all of five foot three.

"I might find the energy if you kiss me," he said, sounding alarmingly delirious.

Once he was on his feet, he still had to walk.

"You've got to be kidding."

He gave her a weary smile. "Do I look like I'm joking?"

With blood everywhere, definitely not. She pressed her mouth to his, then slipped her tongue between his lips. A fast, deep kiss. "There. Now stand."

"Crap. Guess I gotta now."

"Yes. Or I will kick your ass for lying to me again."

After pulling the satchel with the hard drives over her shoulder so the strap crossed her body but the bulky bag was on her outside hip, she tucked herself under his arm and rose. He pushed off the ground with his other hand. They wobbled a bit, but they made it upright.

Walking would be a different story, but dammit, they would make this final trek together.

One slow, teetering step at a time, they picked their way through the forest. Cole almost tripped several times, but somehow they managed to stay on their feet. Which was a good thing because she doubted he'd be able to stand again if he fell.

At last, they reached the road and the SUV parked on the shoulder. Signe hit the button on the key chain twice to unlock the passenger door, then leaned Cole against the rear panel as she opened it.

"This is all on you now. I can't lift you."

"Kiss me again."

She didn't argue this time and planted her lips on his. She kissed him as if her mouth had the power of an energy bar and healing power of a shot of antibiotics and blood transfusion.

"I like you, Signe Gates," he whispered against her mouth.

"I like you too. Now get up and in."

"That's what she said."

She let out a pained laugh and shoved at his butt as he boosted himself using the open doorframe.

Magically, he landed in the front seat. She didn't even bother with the seat belt lest he fall out the open door while she fussed. Instead, she slammed it closed, then ran around to the driver's side.

Minutes later, they both were buckled in and she was driving down the winding mountain road toward a hospital.

CHAPTER 54

Cole was taken directly to surgery. Signe spent the last thirty minutes of the drive on the phone with the hospital and FBI so they were prepared for their arrival.

He disappeared behind double doors and she faced an FBI agent who'd made it there in record time. It wasn't long before more agents from the LA Field Office arrived, including a Special Agent in Charge and two Assistant Special Agents in Charge. A crime scene unit had been dispatched to the woods and Signe did her best to describe where the bodies would be found. Another group was sent to Leo's cabin.

She handed over her sack of hard drives. No time to scrub her informants' names and faces from Leo's files, nor would she taint the evidence in that way. All she could do was hope investigators would respect the danger everyone would be in if they used that information to make arrests of informants not directly related to Leo's crimes.

In the moment, she didn't care about any of that. All that mattered was Cole's survival. He'd taken a bullet to the same side she'd sliced hours before.

She had regrets. Deep regrets.

Her heart surged when Jasper entered the waiting room, and without hesitating, she ran to him and he hugged her tight.

Finally, he leaned back and studied her face, which she'd splashed with water but knew still had streaks of blood.

"You look like shit." He gave her his crooked, scarred smile, and said, "But then, I'm not one to judge."

She shook her head. "Hush. I like your face, even if it's lopsided."

"Yeah. It's growing on me. I hear chicks dig scars."

"What's the word on DiscoFever?"

"We found her. We found them all. Farm outside Oakhurst like we thought. There were ten who didn't escape with the others. Maria—DiscoFever's real name—returned the cell phone to the guard she'd stolen it from after sending the coordinates. He was getting suspicious, so she didn't dare try to access it again. She told the person who interviewed her that she knew—from overhearing Leo talking to the hitmen on the search—that you were in Singapore. That's why she waited to send the first message. She figured if anyone would believe the cry for help, it would be you, and she couldn't risk local law enforcement who might be on the take—as had been the case when an escape was attempted last year in the Sacramento Valley."

Signe took in Maria's faith in her.

She'd failed. She had little hope the men who'd escaped in Yosemite were still alive, but at least now a real search for them would begin.

"We found Manny's car."

"I heard."

"Leo killed Manny." She shuddered again at the horrors her ex had been capable of.

"And it appears Roman killed Leo after they found the men who escaped. Search and rescue—or more likely, recovery—will begin at first light."

She nodded, her thoughts bleak when it came to what she expected the searchers would find. "But ten were saved, right? Plus Maria. That's what Manny wanted."

Jasper said nothing, just cupped her cheek. She understood. There were no words. She wasn't in law enforcement but she knew crime as much as anyone and sometimes all you got were small victories. She should be grateful there'd been any victory at all.

However, in this instance, there were some big wins yet to come. She managed a weak smile. "La Jirafa is going down for good."

"You got the tapes?"

She nodded. "There was no time to watch more than a few videos, but I have no doubt Leo got La Jirafa Macho's face at least once."

"If he did, it's all over for the crime lord."

That would be satisfying. But first she had to wrap her brain around the fact that she'd been married to a trafficker just as bad. "Someday I might try to understand Leo, but right now I think I just want to hate him."

"Sounds reasonable to me. I'm not a fan either."

She touched his scarred cheek. "I can't imagine why."

He brushed his lips over her forehead. How far they'd traveled in such a small amount of time. "So tell me how Cole got shot."

She shared the story once again. When she got to the part where he'd sacrificed himself, Jasper appeared to be holding back emotions. "That's Cole for you. You know I told him to protect his career and just accept I was dead? But no. He knew it would get to the point where he'd lose his job, but he never wavered."

"I—I had a moment there where I thought he was working for Leo when he told me he'd been fired. I might have accidentally cut him with a chef's knife."

"Blame me for that, Sig. He wanted to tell you everything. I insisted there was no way we'd get your cooperation. I gave him my badge so you'd believe him. Convenient thing about being missing and presumed dead, when my badge was never found, no one asked questions."

"But we will now, Agent Evans."

Signe looked up to see the SAC looming. Reunion with Jasper time was over.

Jasper released her and faced the SAC. "Guess it's time to rejoin the land of the living."

Good luck, she mouthed.

There were more questions for both of them, but finally she was granted another reprieve and sat in the corner, staring at the door where eventually a doctor would emerge and tell her if Cole was dead or alive.

Six hours after Cole Banner had been rushed into surgery, a doctor stepped out with a grim look on his face.

As there were no family members present, he pulled the SAC aside and gave him whatever news there was to share.

Jasper stepped up beside Signe and took her hand and squeezed.

After the doctor left the room, the SAC turned and scanned the room until his gaze landed on her and Jasper. He approached, his face solemn, and she tried to keep from collapsing before he could say the words.

"He's alive. But barely. He flatlined once during surgery. He'll be in ICU until he stabilizes."

CHAPTER 55

The following forty-eight hours ranked as the second-worst two-day period in Signe's life. Cole's prognosis was bleak before he began to stabilize. When he was finally strong enough to move out of ICU, several days had passed.

The assistant US attorney charged with building a case against La Jirafa requested a meeting in her office. Leo had video of an unmasked La Jirafa, and dominoes were falling. The warrant for the kingpin would be served within days. Testifying against the kingpin would mean witness protection for most people, but Signe didn't see a way that would work in her situation. Once the warrant was served, her face would be all over the news.

With Cole out of the woods, she knew it was time to put her energy where it would have the most impact: bringing down La Jirafa and the entire cartel. To that end, she left Cole's side, not knowing if or when she'd return to the hospital.

As Cole had suggested the night they viewed the videos, the Central and Eastern District US Attorney's Offices both had jurisdiction, but they'd settled on the Central District taking the lead, as that was not just the location of Jasper's attempted murder but also where the trafficking victims entered the country and was where La Jirafa conducted the bulk of his operations.

AUSA Alicia Beckett was in her early fifties and had an impressive conviction record. She was no-nonsense but not cold, and Signe's research as she sat by Cole's hospital bed indicated Beckett was good at prepping victims of sex crimes to face the additional trauma of a jury trial.

"Before we get started," Beckett said, "I wanted to let you know we located Manny Lontoc's family after we traced his car back to an uncle." She paused. "Their situation explained why Manny chose not to go to law enforcement when he learned about the escaped trafficking victims. Lontoc and his parents overstayed their visas when he was a child. Their presence in the US remains unlawful."

Signe placed her hand to her heart as she imagined the situation Manny had been in. He was a dirtbagger squatting in a house with friends who ran an illegal weed-grow operation, and he and his parents were without legal residency status. "No wonder his parents never came forward to claim his remains." She looked sharply at the prosecutor. "You aren't deporting them, are you?"

"We're doing what we can to get them a change of status, citing the need for them to testify. But it would help if someone with means hired them a good immigration attorney."

The words hung in the air and Signe understood. The US Attorney's Office couldn't provide the family with legal counsel for anything beyond keeping them in LA through the trial. And given that Manny's murderer was dead, their testimony might not be needed at all. "I would appreciate an opportunity to meet with the Lontocs so I can tell them how incredibly brave and generous their son was."

"My office can facilitate that."

Signe would bring the best immigration lawyer she could find with her to the meeting and let the parents know she would cover the fees. She had money. Most of it was tainted. If she could use it to help people who'd been Leo's victims, it would be put to good use.

Beckett gave a sharp nod. "Now, about your testimony, witness protection is still on the table."

"You won't need my testimony if you use the video. No one can hold me responsible when I'm clearly a victim. My husband set me up. If I don't take the stand, I won't be a target for vengeance. They can't make an example of me when it is their damn video of my assault that was used in court."

The AUSA hesitated. "If the video is entered into evidence, we could lose control over it."

"And if that happens, I expect you will go after opposing counsel to the full extent of the law."

"Of course."

"Then use the video."

"Some will claim it's deep fake. Your husband had the skills to deep fake that and so much more. Roman Wiley too."

"No, Roman didn't have those skills. But yes, Leo did. You'll have to bring in your experts to show it's not. I have the scars to prove it's real."

"About that," Beckett said. "We believe your scars are La Jirafa Macho's initials, directly tying him to the assault even though he wasn't in the video."

"O-G? Who is he?"

The woman shook her head. "Not O-G. G-O. Grayson Odem. He was in talks with Leo for a stand-alone documentary."

Signe felt dizzy. Grayson Odem. The man Cole had argued with at the museum. The man Leo had warned her away from. *"Don't even make eye contact."*

Leo had been in so deep, he'd invited his kingpin boss to the fundraiser and was in talks to put the man in a documentary.

She remembered Odem's smug smile that night. That same man had demanded she be raped so he could add the video to his spank bank.

"He's a white supremacist. A pseudoarchaeologist who uses made-up history as a recruitment tool."

"Yes. On the cartel side, we believe that in addition to making money, his goal is to use drug wars and human trafficking to destroy people of color and their communities."

"Will my scars help convict him?"

"We think so."

"Use them. Use me. I want him to rot in prison until the end of time."

"You're a brave woman," the AUSA said.

"No, I'm just done. I'll never get my old life back, but I'd like a chance at a new one." She leaned on the desk and looked into the woman's eyes. "Make him—make them all—pay. For me. For Maria and all the people they enslaved. For Manny and all the people they killed. I've always looked at crime in the abstract. My stories couldn't get anyone justice. My work explained the hows and whys. I even said I was never looking to unmask a killer because usually the men I interviewed didn't bother with masks. It wasn't about *who* did it for me. This time I know the how. I know the why. And I want justice served on the who."

"With all the videos we got from Leo's studio, you'll get it. And with your rape video entered into evidence, we might be able to avoid trial, at least for the players below La Jirafa in the food chain. And if we can get them to turn, we'll have La Jirafa dead to rights."

Signe nodded. "I'll testify if you need me. I won't sit on the sidelines anymore."

CHAPTER 56

Weeks later, Signe watched with satisfaction when news broke that an arrest warrant for La Jirafa—a.k.a. Grayson Odem—had been served. She was amazed the man hadn't fled the country when Roman and his henchmen didn't return from the forest, but he must not have imagined Signe would insist the rape video be entered into evidence—after all, it appeared she was an enthusiastic participant for the first few minutes of the heavily edited version.

The full video told an entirely different story.

She shut off the TV as her cell phone buzzed. Jasper calling to tell her Cole was settled in the convalescent facility and was asking for her again.

Healing went fast once they got rid of the secondary infections. It wasn't the bullet wound that had caused so many problems. It was the infection that he'd probably picked up in the forest, and another one he'd gotten in the hospital.

A glance out the window showed news vans arriving. Leo's role in La Jirafa's organization had also been revealed—another item Odem had expected Signe to hide. He probably thought she'd destroy those recordings herself.

She told Jasper she would be hiding out for the time being. Once again, she was grateful for food delivery services.

It was a relief the warrant had finally been served. In the videos recovered from Leo's studio, the FBI had found the recording in which she'd given Muriel's name along with a half dozen other informants. The remaining informants had been placed in protective custody until the arrest warrant on La Jirafa was served. Now she could be certain they were safe.

Evidence provided by DiscoFever and others, however, indicated protective custody might not have been necessary. Her informants might have been safe from the moment Leo was killed. At this point, it appeared Leo was the crime lord who'd both threatened and ordered the murder of Muriel, not the kingpin.

Leo had been desperate to keep Signe quiet about what had happened to her because any investigation into her would inevitably lead to him.

He'd likely chosen Muriel because she was an informant who had no association with either La Jirafa Macho or Leo. As Signe's informant, Muriel had never crossed paths with Leo. The woman's remains had been found within days of her death, but her fingerprints and DNA weren't in the system and her face had been unrecognizable. She matched no missing person reports, because no one—including Signe—had reported her missing.

It wasn't until after Signe gave the package containing Muriel's necklace and the links of chain spattered with her informant's blood that a positive ID had been made.

Now that she'd been identified, she would be buried alongside the remains of the escaped trafficking victims. Their bodies had been found more than a mile from their squatters' camp after two days of searching.

Leo was responsible for so many deaths. And these were only the ones they knew about.

By the time the media gave up on Signe, two more weeks had passed. There were more meetings with the AUSA as they dug ever deeper into Leo's crimes. On the personal side, Jasper kept her informed on Cole's progress, and she was satisfied with that.

She figured in the long run, it was better that she not see or speak to him. Now that the danger was over, they wouldn't have much common ground. He wanted to return to being an undercover FBI agent tracking down art and artifact thieves and drug smugglers, and she . . . hadn't the slightest clue what was next for her.

Could she even be a journalist again? The crime beat was out.

She'd put her research skills to the test to look into Leo's slide into depravity and had given the FBI and AUSA everything she'd learned about Leo's losses in Bitcoin that led to him buying and selling humans.

He'd done a good job covering his tracks, but once Signe had a thread to follow, Leo's financial situation unraveled.

She itched to do more investigations like this, nitty-gritty financial crimes that blew up into something much more sinister. Maybe after this, she'd use her investigative skills to help law enforcement. Start with the financial picture and see where the stories led. She could write books. Or host a true-crime podcast.

Or . . . she didn't know.

Much to Steven's relief, Leo had left his entire estate to Signe, and he'd been worth millions due to his illicit activities. Being forced to deal with his half brother's estate would have been an undue burden for the grad student, who had nothing to do with Leo's crimes, but for Signe it was an opportunity to make reparations.

She intended to donate every penny that wasn't seized to organizations to support victims of human trafficking. She was paying Manny Lontoc's parents' legal fees and doing everything she could to ensure they could stay in the country where they'd raised and lost their only son.

There was much to sort out, but the only immediate action she could take was to put her house on the market. To that end, she'd begun packing and sorting her belongings one room at a time and was busy packing books when the doorbell rang.

The media vans had been gone for days, and other reporters knew she wouldn't answer the door. But still, they tried because she also refused to answer the phone or emails.

She checked the doorbell camera and her heart stuttered.

When had he been released from the rehab hospital? Jasper had promised to keep her updated.

Deceitful bastard.

She stared at the image on her phone. Cole looked far better than Jasper had led her to believe, but still tired. He leaned on a cane like he'd collapse without it. He shouldn't be standing on her doorstep. Shouldn't be standing at all.

She ran for the door and yanked it open. He straightened. Tall. Strong. Robust color in his cheeks. All at once she knew she'd been had.

Two deceitful bastards.

Cole grinned. "What took you so long?" He brushed her aside and stepped into the foyer, then turned to face her.

She closed the door and leaned against it. "So. They sprang you."

"A few days ago."

"How do you feel?"

"Like I was shot in the gut."

"That sounds unpleasant."

"It is. But I'm told I'll live."

"Glad to hear it."

"Huh. Wouldn't think so with the fact that you didn't come visit."

"I spent five days by your side. Not my fault you slept through it."

He dropped the cane he clearly didn't need and took a step toward her. "I've had a little extra time to think lately."

"Really? How so?"

"Smart-ass."

Only inches separated them. She'd longed for this moment, but she'd feared it too. She didn't know what she wanted or where to begin. She'd even gone to the hospital twice to see him after he was awake, but never got farther than the parking lot.

Parking lots were her kryptonite.

Finally, she said, "You sacrificed yourself. For me. I'm—I'm afraid I don't deserve it."

"Shouldn't I be the judge of that?" His lips brushed hers, ever so softly. He raised his head and held her gaze. "I would like to date you. We should go out to dinner. Catch up on the last few weeks. Although I'm afraid I don't have much to tell. Slept. Ate. Argued with my physical therapist."

She breathed in his scent. He no longer smelled like hospital or forest. He smelled like the man who'd held her after she watched the video that showed Leo's role in her assault.

And once again, Cole had kissed her but she was thinking of Leo. Enough of that.

Cole deserved better. She deserved better.

She *wanted* better. She wanted Cole.

The least she could do was give them both a chance.

Her heart hammered. "I'm not much for eating in restaurants these days. Reporters really are the worst, you know?"

He smiled at that. "Don't I ever."

"Maybe we can skip dinner?"

He shook his head. "If you think I'll put out without you buying me dinner first, woman, you've got another think coming."

She raised a tentative brow. "We could get takeout?"

"That's more like it."

She stepped back. Teasing was fun, but she had real questions. "I don't understand. Why are you here? After everything I said and did?"

He moved forward and wrapped an arm around her waist so they were chest to chest.

"Oh, Signe, don't you get it? Your fierceness. Your loyalty. Your fire and thirst to understand the impossible. We're a good match. You understand the world I immersed myself in for the job."

Unsaid was the fact that he wouldn't use her knowledge to commit crimes. He worked to stop them.

"I'm a mess, though."

"Aren't we all?"

"I cut you."

"And you got me to the car. To the road. To the hospital. You're so damn strong, Signe. I want you to see that. See what I see."

He brushed his lips over hers again. "You are *it* for me, Signe Gates. And I hope you'll come around to thinking I'm it for you too."

He didn't see her as complicit—unwitting or otherwise. She wished she could believe that of herself, but she didn't know the path to self-forgiveness. Not even the best GPS would help her wayfind that particular route.

Still, he wanted her with all her baggage and flaws. Which said a lot about this man, who loved rock climbing even though he'd never excel at it.

"Okay. I'll buy you dinner."

He grinned. "Just know that I rarely put out on the first date."

She glanced at her watch. "It's early yet, maybe we can get in two dates before nightfall."

"That works."

She gazed into his warm brown eyes, heart pounding as possibilities she'd refused to hope for opened up. "One thing I feel like I need to get out in the open. Lest you've gotten the wrong idea about me."

"What's that?" he asked.

"Is it a deal breaker for an ex-dirtbag and ex–dig bum if I admit I'm not much into hiking?"

He smiled and shook his head. "You're still it for me."

EPILOGUE

Los Angeles, California
September

Signe sat in her car with the engine idling in the parking lot outside the LA federal building, wishing Cole were here to bolster her. In the three weeks since he'd reentered her life, they'd gone on more than a dozen official dates—at his insistence. He was determined to give her a mental break.

To that end, they went to movies, the zoo, museums, a Dodgers game—anything to get her out of the house and out of her head. Sometimes, like at the baseball game, Jasper joined them and made jokes about how emerging from the dead should warrant better seats. Or at least a win for the home team.

Once, Cole took her to the library, claiming he'd always wanted to make out in the stacks, but he'd checked out a lot of books and only kissed her a little.

The end result was he was loading her up with good memories to draw upon, all while giving her room to vent and cry and process. And late at night, when the nightmares had her waking up screaming, he was always there.

He made her laugh, held her when she cried, and showed her what love looked like.

Someday she hoped she'd believe she was worthy of him, because he really was it for her.

Today, however, he had a meeting with AUSA Alicia Beckett and was right now miles away at the US courthouse, while she sat in her car and braced herself to enter the FBI's LA Field Office. Two years and one month ago, she'd sat in nearly this exact same spot and debated her options until she received a message telling her that Muriel Klein was about to be murdered.

While Muriel wasn't the reason Signe had driven here today, she was the reason Signe sat in the parking lot with the air conditioner on high. Once again, guilt pressed in on her and her head throbbed. So much like the headaches she'd suffered two years ago.

So many people had been victimized by Leo, but Muriel and Jasper had been targeted specifically because of Signe. But then, Leo had learned the tricks of the trade from working with her, so really, all his victims were at her feet.

Could she even do this?

She gripped the steering wheel and considered skipping the meeting and driving away. It would be cowardly, but she was tired of being strong. Tired of facing her demons.

But mostly, she was scared. Scared of what she would see at this meeting. Scared of the blame she would have to bear.

Her gaze shifted to the dog park. She could go there instead. Beg an owner to let her pet their dog. Maybe she should go to a shelter and find an animal to adopt so she wouldn't inflict her erratic moods on the pets of strangers.

She needed to work through the ball of fear in her belly. Deal with the weight of guilt. She doubted a dog would fix those things, but at least she'd have a dog.

Her phone pinged with a text.

Cole: You can do it.

She closed her eyes and gripped the phone. He was here to bolster her after all.

She didn't wonder how he knew she needed his timely text. Jasper was part of this meeting, and he was probably waiting impatiently on the front steps. She'd bet he had messaged Cole and asked him to nudge her.

She shut off the engine and wrenched open the door.

She could do it. And not just because Cole believed in her, but his faith in her helped. It helped even more to know he'd be there for her when she got home tonight.

She approached the front of the building, and there was Jasper as expected. He opened the door without a word and she stepped inside.

They went through the metal detector and signed in, then he led Signe to the conference room to meet with the ASAC who'd arranged the meeting.

Outside the door, Jasper paused. "You go in first. I'll join you later."

She started to protest, but he nudged her forward, then reached in and pulled the door shut.

Signe turned to face the room, expecting to see the ASAC and maybe an admin or two in addition to the woman in protective custody she was here to meet, but there was only one person in the room, sitting just a few feet from the door.

The woman slowly rose. She was small, like Signe. Maybe even an inch shorter. Her glossy, dark hair was pulled back in a ponytail, and Signe startled at seeing the decoration on the ponytail holder was a shiny mirrored ball.

Maria Ngu—a.k.a. DiscoFever—gave her a tentative smile.

Signe had tried to prepare for this meeting, but Maria wasn't a source, nor was she an interview subject. Not this time. Professional distance was impossible as emotions flooded her. All of them messy.

Maria opened her arms and Signe burst into tears as she fell into them. The young woman who had suffered so much more than Signe, yet had cared for her during her lost hours, held her tight.

"I'm so sorry for what Leo did to you," Signe said.

"Shh," Maria said in a soft, accented voice. "The only person who can apologize for Leo is Leo. And he wasn't sorry."

Signe stepped back from Maria's embrace and swiped at her eyes. "Then I'm sorry for my part. For introducing him to criminals and for what he learned because he worked with me."

Maria gave her a sad smile and shook her head. "I think—no, I *know*—I knew your husband better than you. And he . . . enjoyed the game. Fooling you. Fooling everyone. Even without you, he'd have ended up in the same place. It's not your fault."

If anyone else had uttered those words, Signe would have brushed them off as someone who didn't understand and only wanted to make her feel better.

But Maria Ngu wasn't just anyone, and for the first time since the entirety of Leo's sins were laid bare, Signe felt a slight shift in the weight on her chest.

The journey to healing and forgiveness would be long and painful, but Cole had promised she wouldn't make the trek alone. Now, with Maria's words, she could see a path and knew she'd just taken the first step.

NATIONAL HUMAN TRAFFICKING HOTLINE

Information provided in this section comes from the National Human Trafficking Hotline website at https://humantraffickinghotline.org/. All phone numbers are for use in the United States.

If you or someone you know is in immediate danger, please call 911.

Human trafficking occurs when a trafficker uses force, fraud, or coercion to control another person for the purpose of engaging in commercial sex acts or soliciting labor or services against his/her will. (Force, fraud, or coercion need not be present if the individual engaging in commercial sex is under eighteen years of age.)

Contact the hotline if you or someone you know:

- Is being forced to have sex for money or something of value against his or her will
- Is under eighteen and engaging in commercial sex
- Is being forced to work or perform services against his or her will

If you believe you may have information about a trafficking situation:

- Call the National Human Trafficking Hotline toll-free at 1-888-373-7888.
- Text the National Human Trafficking Hotline at 233733. Message and data rates may apply.
- Chat the National Human Trafficking Hotline via humantraffickinghotline.org/chat.

Anti-Trafficking Hotline advocates are available 24-7 to take reports of potential human trafficking.

ACKNOWLEDGMENTS

Launching a new pen name is daunting, and I never would have had the courage to embark on this adventure without the support and encouragement of my editor, Lauren Plude at Thomas & Mercer. Thank you, Lauren, for your vision and feedback that brought Signe (and R.S. Grant) to life.

Also responsible for the birth of R.S. Grant is my agent, Elizabeth Winick Rubinstein of McIntosh & Otis. Thank you so much, Liz, for your support and belief that I could make this genre shift.

Thank you to my developmental editor, Charlotte Herscher, for your brilliant feedback that helped me find the direction and core of the story. Thank you also to author Manda Collins for your beta read and excellent suggestion for ramping up the suspense. Thank you to Gwen Hernandez for your early plotting help when this story was just an amoeba. Thank you to Toni Anderson for all the last-minute feedback.

To my group-chat author friends and the 1k1hr crew: Darcy Burke, Toni Anderson, Annika Martin, J. Kenner, Jenn Stark, Erica Ridley, and Elisabeth Naughton, thank you for your daily support, encouragement, and advice.

Kate Davies, Serena Bell, and Kris Kennedy, thank you for the years of friendship and giving me a reason to put on pants and leave the house occasionally.

To my husband, David, and children, Jocelyn and Cael: thank you for your support and love and for just being you. Lastly, to our cat, Malala: I'd get more work done if you didn't insist on sitting on the keyboard, but I think you know this. Still, thank you for the company while I write.

ABOUT THE AUTHOR

R.S. Grant also writes as Rachel Grant, the *USA Today* bestselling author of the Flashpoint series, the Evidence novels, and *Dangerous Ground* and *Crash Site* in the Fiona Carver series. She worked for more than a decade as a professional archaeologist and mines her experiences for story lines and settings as diverse as excavating a cemetery underneath a historic art museum in San Francisco, surveying an economically depressed coal mining town in Kentucky, and mapping a seventeenth-century Spanish and Dutch fort on the island of Sint Maarten in the Netherlands Antilles. In all her travels and adventures, Rachel has found many sites and artifacts, but she's unearthed only one true treasure: her husband, David. Rachel lives on an island in the Pacific

Northwest with her husband and children. For more information visit www.rachel-grant.net.

Find R.S. Grant online

Website: https://rachel-grant.net
Facebook: https://www.facebook.com/RachelGrantAuthor/
Twitter: https://twitter.com/rachelsgrant
Instagram: https://www.instagram.com/rachelsgrant/